Also by William Wharton

BIRDY

THIS IS A BORZOI BOOK
PUBLISHED IN NEW YORK
BY ALFRED A. KNOPF

DAD

DAD

a novel by WILLIAM WHARTON

ALFRED A. KNOPF NEW YORK 1981

THIS IS A BORZOI BOOK
PUBLISHED BY ALFRED A. KNOPF, INC.

Grateful acknowledgment is made to the following for permission to reprint from previously published material:

Shapiro, Bernstein & Co., Inc., and ATV Music Ltd.: Excerpt from "The Prisoner's Song" by Guy Massey. Copyright 1924. Renewed by Shapiro, Bernstein & Co., Inc., New York, N.Y. 10022. For the British Commonwealth, Great Britain and Colonies, and Ireland, Copyright 1924 Lawrence Wright Music Co., Ltd. Used by permission.

TRO and Leo Feist, Inc.: Excerpt from "I Don't Know Why (I Just Do)," words by Roy Turk, music by Fred E. Ahlert. Copyright © 1931 and renewed 1959 Cromwell Music, Inc., New York, N.Y., Fred Ahlert Music Corp., Los Angeles, Ca., and Pencil Mark Music, Inc., Scarsdale, N.Y. Rights outside the U.S. administered by Leo Feist, Inc. Used by permission.

Library of Congress Cataloging in Publication Data
Wharton, William. Dad.
I. Title.
'PS3573.H32D3   1981   813'.54   80-2725
ISBN 0-394-51097-6

Manufactured in the United States of America
First Edition

That man's father
is my father's son.

—SECOND HALF OF A RIDDLE

DAD

1

AAA CON is the first name in the phone book of most large American cities. This outfit arranges drive-aways; searches out people to drive cars for delivery from one place to another.

My son Billy and I are waiting in the L.A. AAA CON office. I've had my medical exam, deposited a fifty-dollar bond, filled out forms and given references. Billy's too young to take a drive-away; the minimum age is twenty-one. A car's already been assigned to us and we're waiting now for them to drive it up.

Billy's excited because it's a Lincoln Continental. I dread telling him he isn't going to drive. I'm not a super-responsible person, but I'm *that* responsible, especially with someone else's fifteen-thousand-dollar automobile.

So I'll be driving all the way across this huge country and I'm not looking forward to it.

The office here is grim. These places are only processing centers; nothing's spent on carpets or fancy furnishings. I figure they make a hundred bucks or so on each car they move cross-country.

Finally, the beefy fellow at the desk calls us over. He asks what route we want and agrees to 15–70–76. It's the least trafficked by trucks because of the high, unfinished pass at Loveland. After that, it's double-four most of the way.

We'll be delivering this car to Philadelphia, my old hometown, then we'll take a plane to Paris. Paris is our real home now, has been for fifteen years.

Half an hour later we get the car. It isn't new, maybe two years old, deep maroon with a black vinyl top; flashy-looking affair; looks like a gangster's car. We're delivering to somebody named Scarlietti, so who knows, maybe we're driving a bump-off car.

This must be the twentieth time I've driven cross-country; more than half those trips Drive-Away.

One time we moved a pale yellow Chevy Impala convertible. That was in the days of convertibles, before air conditioning and stereo. We tied our kids in that car with jump ropes so they couldn't fall out, then zoomed west to east mostly on 66, top down, wind, sun in our faces. The kids could fight, scream, play, holler, make all the noise they wanted; we couldn't hear a thing. It was almost like a honeymoon for Vron and me.

We got good mileage on that Chevy, too. But this Lincoln's going to put me down an extra thirty bucks in gas. At least we'll be comfortable; it's no joke beating a car three thousand miles across the whole damned country in eight days, and I'm getting too old for this kind of thing.

The part I've been dreading comes after we pull out with the Lincoln. We need to pick up our bags and say goodbye to Mom. Billy's jumpy, too. We know it won't be easy; nothing's easy with Mom; but considering all that's happened this is going to be especially hard.

We ease our giant floating dark red boat up Colby Lane. A car like this isn't designed to move around narrow, old-fashioned residential streets. Dad bought the lot here for twenty-six hundred dollars about twenty-five years ago. He built the house himself at a total cost under six thousand bucks; it must be worth over eighty thousand today.

We park on the driveway and go inside. Mom's dressed to kill, looking damned good for someone who's had two heart attacks in the past five months. Still, she's weepy around the eyes, pale; walking with her new peculiar shuffle. It's as if she has a load in her pants and is balancing a book on her head.

She starts straight off crying, asking what she's going to do when I leave; insisting she'll be all alone, because, according to her, Joan, my sister, doesn't care if she lives or dies.

I've been listening to Mom complaining all my life, especially during the last months. I keep thinking I'll get immune to it; I should be thoroughly inoculated after fifty years, but sometimes it still hurts. Sometimes I really listen and sometimes I can't take it anymore. This time I'm only numb.

I wait until she slows down. I tell her again how some things must be. I need to go home. It's been too long since I've seen Vron and Jacky. I can't spend the rest of my life taking care of her and Dad. She knows all this, we've been over it enough.

Billy stands in the background listening. He starts turning television channels, looking for something, anything. I can't blame him. Mom keeps at it. I'm nodding my head as I work our bags to the car. She's also pushing a child's lunch box filled with pills on us. It's her way of showing love, taking care, making us feel dependent.

But we do finally get away.

The next part's even tougher. We cruise up Colby to the convalescent home where Dad is. The home is only a block from my parents' house. We chose it so Mom could be near. We experimented with another place but settled on this one. It has its limitations but Mom can walk here when she wants. It probably isn't good for Dad but nobody can deny her this.

We park around the corner and go in. The smell is something I'll never get used to. It's a combination of the smells in a men's room and an animal shelter. When I was sixteen, I worked for a small-animal vet. I'd come in mornings and hose down the cages, wash out all the dog and cat crap from the night before. This is a combination of those smells, plus the smell of general decrepitude.

I never knew what the word decrepitude or corruption really meant. As kids, we used to say piss, shit and corruption. Now I know. Corruption is when something is being corrupted; rotted by bacteria. These poor, old people here are being corrupted, rotted, decayed. The result is decrepitude, being wasted, worn out, used up.

Smells like this are hard to cover. All the carbolic acid, strong soap and aerosol in the world won't do it. This is the smell of death, the going back to earth none of us can avoid.

A German-born brother and sister run the home. People couldn't be kinder. Of course, they're doing it for money, lots of money. The cheapest you can have a shared double is twenty-five bucks a day. But I wouldn't do it, night and day, day in and day out. I couldn't.

They tell me Dad's still in the same room but they don't think he'll know us; he's under sedation. I've accepted this; sedation is the best thing for him now, anything to make it easy. There don't seem to be any real, practical, permanent answers. There's no room for him in this world anymore. I know something about old age now. You're old when most people would rather have you dead.

We walk along the hallway looking into rooms. We peek in at thin, worn shells of human beings; people with oxygen tubes on their noses and catheters coming out from under bathrobes. They're propped up in bed or sitting in wheelchairs. It's only afternoon, but they're all dressed in bed clothes. Some are hunched over, listening to radios or staring at television sets; mouths open, mostly toothless. As we go by, some look out, latch on to us with their eyes, like prisoners peering from cells. I feel guiltily healthy, young, with an unending future. How must Billy, beside me, feel at nineteen?

Dad's on the men's side; so stupid to carry that farce to this point in life. He's in a gigantesque kind of crib. He's lying in the darkened room with the drapes drawn. His eyes are open, fixed on the ceiling.

There's a roommate. The man is deaf and smiles at us. They chose him on purpose because sometimes Dad screams out in the night.

All together, Dad's been in this place two weeks. He came out of the hospital again a week ago. He'd begun dehydrating.

I look down. He's somehow dead already; yellowish skin but not a wrinkle. He'd lost so much weight, then gained some of it back; now he's skeleton thin again.

We lean close over him. I say hello. He hears and turns his eyes but there's no recognition. He stares at our eyes just as a baby or a dog does, not expecting anything, only seeming fascinated in a passive sense by the eye itself. He's gripping and ungripping, twisting the blankets and sheets the way he does most times now. It's a constant tight turning; nervous movements. Sometimes he'll grit his teeth and bear down, pushing one side against the other, trying to make it all hold together. But right now he isn't too active, only twittering with his fingers, maybe proving to himself there are still things; that he's still here and alive. He looks past me and speaks through quivering lips.

"I have to take a piss."

This is so unlike Dad. He never used those words. It's hard seeing Dad in this condition, saying "piss" in front of Billy. If he knew what he was doing, it'd never happen; he wouldn't even say that to me.

We pull a catch lowering the side rail to the bed, help Dad swing his legs out. I slip his robe over his shoulders; his slippers onto his feet. He's wearing socks. He has no catheter yet. I'm hoping he can stay off one long as possible. He's so privacy-conscious, a catheter makes him go downhill fast. Having nurses check and change it is degrading to him. When they do use one, it won't be indwelling, only a condom you slip over the penis with a tube into a bag; at least it won't hurt.

Billy and I lift Dad up and he grabs hold of us. His fingers, hands and arms, though shaking violently, are still strong. We help him slide across the gray asphalt-tile floor to the small bathroom. He's moving one foot in front of the other, but only with enormous concentration. In the bathroom, he leans over the toilet with his hands against the wall. He's not looking at us, only into the toilet. He spits into the bowl; but he can't piss.

We stand there and nothing comes. Billy looks across at me. I flush the toilet thinking it might help but Dad only spits again. He never spit, I know of, or maybe he's always spit in the toilet, a closet spitter. Actually, I never saw him even go to the toilet till these last months.

I figure we'd better maneuver him back to bed. But, when we try taking him away, he has a tight hold on the pipes over the toilet. He has such a tight grip his knuckles are white. I try unlocking them.

"Come on, Dad. Let go of the pipe."

He won't. He won't look at me either; he only bears down and grits his teeth. I try undoing his hand, opening one finger at a time, the way you do with a baby when it grabs your beard. Then, suddenly, he lets go and latches on to another pipe. This pipe's the hot-water line; his hand must be burning but he holds on tight with manic fury. Billy's pulling at his other hand.

"Come on, Gramps; let go! Come on, let go now."

I'm almost ready to give up, call for help, when we finally pry him loose. We turn him around. As soon as he's turned away he seems to forget the pipes. We try working him through the doorway but he goes into his usual hang-up, checking molding, running his hand up and down as if it's some new thing he's never seen before. This is a man who built his own house from the ground up and has done carpentry work since childhood. These days, it's almost impossible to move him past any doorjamb; but we manage.

We slide him to the bed, sit him down, take off his robe and slippers, then help him lie back. As usual, he's afraid to put his head down. I cradle his head in my hand and lower him slowly onto the pillow. He's deeply tense. He stares at the ceiling and his mouth starts moving, chattering, his lips opening and closing over his teeth, up and down with a quivering, uncontrolled movement.

Strangely, Dad still has all his teeth. Here he is, a seventy-three-year-old man and he has all his perfectly beautiful teeth, somewhat yellowed, long in the gum but not a filling. I'm already missing six, and Billy beside me has several teeth missing, three root canals, filled with gold and porcelain-covered. If anyone ever X-rayed Dad's head and Billy's, not seeing anything else, they'd think Dad was the young man.

He continues staring at the ceiling. I stroke his head, try to calm him. He holds my hand and squeezes it hard. He gives me a good squeeze as if he knows, and then squeezes again. I like to think of those squeezes as the last real message Dad gave me.

We go outside. I'm barely making it. For some stupid reason, I don't want Billy to see me crying.

When we come out the door, who's standing there leaning against a tree but Mom. She's pale and breathing hard. We run over to her. She's got that damned lunch box in her hand. We'd forgotten it.

She puts one of her digoxin pills under her tongue. She's in a bad state, gray-white. She gasps out her story of how she's worked her way up the street, stopping and popping pills so she can fight her way to us.

I can't hold myself back.

"Mother, it couldn't be that important. It's insane for you to run up here with a box of pills. You'll kill yourself for nothing."

But she had to come. She knew we were only up the street, here with Dad, and she wasn't. She couldn't stay away.

We help her into the car and drive home. I put her to bed, make her take a ten-milligram Valium. We go through the entire goodbye scene again.

I signal Billy to get in the car. I tell Mother, firmly as I can, I must go. I say goodbye, kiss her, turn around and leave. Joan has finally found somebody to come twice a week, and she herself will come twice more; still, I feel guilty into my very soul.

Our plan is to head straight toward Vegas, packing as

much desert as possible behind us during the night. Summers, it's damned hot out there even in an air-conditioned car.

We begin having trouble before we get *near* the desert. We're twenty miles from San Bernardino when the voltage indicator starts flashing. The only thing is to turn back; we might make it to L.A. but that's about all.

We pull into a garage I know on Pico Boulevard. The voltage regulator is shot, has to be replaced, a minimum hundred bucks, parts and labor. Damn!

I call AAA CON and tell them what's happened. They tell me to call the owner, collect. I do that. After considerable shuffling around I get an OK. This means money out of pocket but we'll get it back when we deliver. The garage says the car will be ready by morning. I get a few extra days travel time from Scarlietti, too.

We can't go back to Mother's. I don't think I could sleep again in that back room, too many bad memories, bad nights. Marty, my daughter, lives near the garage so Billy and I hoof it over there.

Marty gives me two aspirins and puts me down in their bedroom. I can hear them, Marty, her husband Gary and Billy in the front room watching TV, a rerun of *Mission Impossible*.

I have a tremendous yen to cry. Twice I go into the bathroom, sit on the toilet, but the way Dad couldn't piss, I can't cry. I spread-eagle on the bed and it catches up with me; I'm gone.

Marty and Gary sleep on the floor and Billy sleeps on the couch. I have the only bed in the house all to myself. We sure have nice kids.

We're all up at seven for breakfast. Both Gary and Marty need to be at work by eight.

When I call, the car's ready; but the bill's twenty-five dollars over estimate. We walk down and pick it up.

We cruise out Wilshire Boulevard. I bid a silent farewell to L.A.: all its artificiality, the sugar-coated hardness. I can't say I'm sorry to go; it's been a rough stay. I know I'll miss Joan but I've learned to live with that.

We drive into the sun, due east. Then out through San Bernardino and up over the pass.

Coming down the other side, heading toward Vegas, maybe a hundred twenty miles outside L.A., an enormous dog dashes in front of our car. I jam the brakes but they don't grab straight and we almost flip. Lucky there isn't much traffic because we rear-spin and I hit the dog anyway. He thumps front left and bounces off right. I pull up on the shoulder and we run back.

The dog's spinning around; his hindquarters are smashed. He should be dead but he's twisting and howling. It's hard to look or listen; he's snapping and we can't get near. It takes almost five awful minutes for him to slow down and die. There's no collar or identification so we drag him off to the side of the road, into the bushes. It's some kind of German shepherd, big as a wolf. We take out the tire iron and use it as a shovel to dig a shallow grave in the sand. We cover it with dry grasses and pieces of brushwood.

There's not a mark on the front of our car. It's incredible the difference between machines and animals. We must've hit him with either the tire or the bumper. Back in the car, we don't talk much for the next hundred miles.

Then, about forty miles this side of Vegas, there's some kind of motor-cross race up on the hills beside the road. Billy's excited by this so we stop. I stay in the car. To me, it looks baked, barren, violent, but this is terrific for Billy. Everything that's attractive to him—the unfinished, random quality, the rough-and-ready atmosphere, the noise, the smells—only reminds me of things I don't want to remember. At Billy's age I had too much of it, enough to last more than a lifetime. Comfort gets bigger as I grow older, comfort and the illusion of predictability.

After ten minutes, Bill's back, eyes flashing in vicarious thrill; he's seen some new four-stroke he's never seen before.

An hour later, we roll into Vegas. The town's just had a flash flood. Caesar's Palace is thick packed clay up to the terraces. The parking lots are caking mudflats. It makes even more obvious how Vegas, plumb smack in the middle of a desert, is an insult to nature.

It's weird seeing this counterfeit world inundated with thick, caking, beige mud, cracking in the sun like a Christmas tree in a trash can, tinsel still sparkling.

We park close as possible and hurry in from under the heat. It's well past noon. Lead-heavy sun is forcing itself hard into the tops of our heads. It must be a hundred or more in the shade.

We walk into a sudden shock of cold. We tromp mud onto pus-yellow and blood-red carpets, on into the dimness. There's the whir and tinkle of slot machines. There's a refrigerated-air smell mixed with the heavy smell of perfume, money and fear. We're wrapped in the cloying atmosphere of this warped, hopeful, hopeless world.

We're going to spend a buck in nickels each. Billy loses his in five minutes. He says the percentages against throwing in twenty nickels without a single payoff are astronomic, but that's what he does. I only want to get through mine but I'm having the opposite problem. I'm soon to where I have over twenty bucks in nickels; my hands are full, my pockets bulging. I keep giving handfuls to Billy so he can lose them. I want to get the hell out. Something in me doesn't want to win; I don't want to take any of those nickels with me.

But it takes an hour of hard work before we finally do it. We'd be down to ten nickels and I'd hit another jackpot. Bells would ring and girls dressed like twirlers would come over to help me! Thank God, Billy's having such awful luck or we'd still be there, pumping machines with bloody hands while slots spat nickels.

We go out in the heat and drive on, looking for something to eat. We both want a Mexican restaurant for our last Western tacos, but settle on a place called Pizza Hut. We go in; more air conditioning; checkered tablecloths. We split a pitcher of beer and have a pizza each. I'm beginning to feel I just might, at last, be getting away; going home.

It's past three in the afternoon when we roll again. We're pushing to make Zion. I know a good motel there, right at the opening to the park. But I make a mistake between Zion and

Bryce. We drive through my place and it's eleven o'clock before we get to Bryce. There are no restaurants open and we
can't find a motel. I've really screwed us up royally but Billy
isn't complaining; not out loud, anyway.

Finally, we find a small bar, just closing up. The counter-
man makes us pork sandwiches with mayonnaise. He serves
us a beer each. This guy also phones some cabins in Bryce
and there's room. One of the great things about traveling is you
find out how many good, kind people there are.

We drive up into a wooded area, right in the park; the
cabins cost fourteen dollars a night. I take a shower, hoping
it will calm me. I'm jittery, nervous. I have some Seconal but
I won't use it if I don't need to. I have Valium, too. I've gotten
to be quite the pill freak from this whole experience. I'd never
taken a tranquilizer or sleeping pill in my life before.

I lie back and decide to give myself an hour. If I'm not
asleep by then, I'll do something. That's the last thought I
have.

2

It was just after New Year's Day and we were down at the moulin for Christmas vacation.

The moulin is an old water mill we bought ten years ago and fixed up. It's in an area of France called the Morvan. We spend most summers and other school holidays there.

We were having unusually warm weather for winter in that part of the country, so I'm out painting. I'm wearing three pairs of socks and gloves but it's good painting light. There's something special about painting landscape in the cold when it isn't snowing. The colors are toned down, muted, and the forms are much more visible.

I'm on the road out to the woods where Billy built his cabin. There are beautiful views from there toward our village, with rolling hills behind. There's a pair of tall poplars closing the left side and a spreading linden leaning over a road twisting under on the right. I'm doing a horizontal composition on a size 25 Figure, about two feet by three feet.

The weather's warm enough so the paint doesn't thicken but I've turned cold, so I'm packing my way in for some *vin chaud*. I have the box on my back with the canvas strapped to it. I'm lazing along, pretending I'm walking into my own painting, when I see Jacky, our youngest, running up the road toward me. He has a blue paper in his hand.

I recognize it, even at a distance, as a French telegram. They write them in longhand so they're almost impossible to understand. I'm old-fashioned enough so a telegram starts my adrenaline going, especially in this deep country. I'm feeling open, vulnerable, there's nothing to prepare me.

I put down my box. Jacky's wearing boots and a jacket with a hood. He ran out without buttoning his jacket.

"Daddy! Mommy said, 'Give this to Daddy.' "

He hands me the telegram. I hug him and button his jacket. I really don't want to open the damned thing.

Jacky doesn't ask to look at the painting. None of our kids are interested in my work. It's as if I work for IBM. It's what Daddy does. He puts a wooden box on his back, goes out and paints pictures for money.

I pick up my box and we begin moving toward home. The ground's hard but there's no ice. I open up the telegram; it's from my sister.

*Mother had a serious heart attack
stop can you come stop love Joan*

Well, that shakes me. In her special way, my mother has always seemed so indestructible.

When we get back to the mill, I show the telegram to Vron. I sit down but I'm not hungry. It's obvious I must go back. Joan is not a panic type. If she says it's serious, it is.

With Vron's help, I start packing. She's so calm, so reassuring; definitely the cool head in our ménage. I'm still not believing what I'm doing. I'm going to be leaving all this quiet beauty. Within a day I'll be in Los Angeles, in Palms, on the dead-end street where my parents live. I try to be calm, try not to frighten Jacky. I tell him his grandmother's sick and I must go see her. It's hard for an eight-year-old to comprehend what it means. He has no idea how long I'll be gone; neither do I, for that matter.

Vron drives me to the train for Paris and I catch an Air France flight direct to L.A. Eight hundred and fifty dollars for a twenty-one-to-forty-five-day excursion ticket. Excursion, hell! But it's significantly cheaper than a regular ticket.

I've telegraphed from Paris, giving my flight number, so when I step out of the plane, Joan and her husband, Mario, are there.

We pile my things into their VW camper. Joan and Mario always drive either a camper or a station wagon; they have five kids. We're pulling up onto Sepulveda when Joan starts telling me what's happened.

She came over to see Dad and Mom but they weren't home. She took the opportunity to vacuum and wash some windows. Then she began to worry. They're probably shopping, they don't go much of anywhere these days; but it shouldn't be taking so long.

She drives over and finds them in the shopping mall. Mother is sitting on a bench next to the Lucky Market, white-faced. Dad, not knowing what to do, not believing what's happening, is packing and unpacking groceries in the trunk of the car.

Joan's frightened by the way Mom looks. She drives them home in their car, leaving hers in the parking lot. At the house, she tells Dad to put the groceries away and rushes Mom off to the Perpetual Hospital. Mother doesn't want to go. She's a hypochondriac who likes doctors but doesn't like hospitals.

At the hospital they spot immediately she's having a coronary crisis. They rush her into an intensive care unit and plug her onto monitoring systems, IV, oxygen; give her tranquilizers, blood thinners.

On that first night in the hospital, she'd had the big

coronary. If you must have a coronary, an intensive care unit is a good place for it. They tell Joan it was massive and if she'd had it outside the hospital, she'd never have survived. The final tests aren't all in, but they're sure she's lost a significant part of her lower left ventricle.

Well, she isn't dead, but it doesn't sound good.

We go directly to my parents' house. One reason Joan wants me here is to look after Dad. She seems more worried about him than Mom. I'm the same. I don't know why we both have this feeling Mom can always take care of herself, but we do; it doesn't make sense. It's probably only a defense.

Dad's standing at the screen door waiting. I'm sure he's been getting up and looking, every time a car's come near. We shake hands; men don't hug in our family. He isn't crying but his eyes are filled with tears and his face is yellow. He's nervous and his hands are shaking.

He sits down in his platform rocker just inside the door while I carry my bag into the middle room down the hall. He seems much frailer than the last time I saw him. It's been almost two years. He doesn't look particularly older, or even thinner, only less vital.

On the way, Joan said I should make as little of Mom's attack as possible because Dad's scared out of his wits. So we have a glass of that crummy muscatel my folks drink for wine. They buy it in gallon jugs, then pour it into a fake crystal bottle. It's part of Mother's effort toward elegance. It's not bad if you're munching on a toasted cheese sandwich, but God, it's sweet as candy. If you don't like wine it's fine, somewhere between cream soda and a Manhattan.

We sit there. Dad still hasn't been to the hospital; Joan told him there were no visitors allowed. So when I leave, I sneak out the side door and ease my parents' car out of the patio. It's a 1966 Rambler, and has all of twenty-five thousand miles on it. Here's an eleven-year-old automobile in showroom condition. They keep it covered with plastic; even the seat covers are plasticized. It has air conditioning, a radio, power brakes, power steering, the works. It's like stepping into the past when you drive this car. It drives smooth as hell with

automatic drive and is heavily horsepowered for a small car.
Dad bought it, when he was still interested in cars, as his
final, retirement automobile. He made a gamble on this one,
and it's been a real winner, simple classic lines, square back.

At the hospital, in the lobby, a nice woman tells me how
to find intensive care.

Most likely, nobody ever gets used to hospitals, or is comfortable in them, except perhaps doctors or nurses. The vibes
are all trouble: pain and death.

But this hospital is somehow different, modern. There's
carpeting, and Muzak playing everywhere. There's no hospital-
white-tile-and-shiny-waxed-floor feeling. It doesn't even smell
like a hospital; more like a Holiday Inn. Even the elevator:
little ding when you get in, self-operated; Muzak. Muzak on
every floor, same soothing music playing all the time everywhere.

Following signs, I work my way to the intensive care
unit. At the desk I identify myself, ask if I can see my mother.
They tell me she's very sick and can't take excitement. I tell
them I've come all the way from Paris. There's a brief conference; it's decided I can go in but must be very quiet.

I move softly past rows of cubicles. Everybody's plugged
in and taped up, most of them unconscious. This is truly the
final stop before the grave, the modern version of an Indian
dying house.

I don't know what to expect; even without heart attacks
people change tremendously in two years. It's always a shock
to see somebody this age after some time has past. I know
we're all changing, the kids, Vron, me; but we see each other
so often we don't notice.

I look in and there she is. Probably, since I was a kid, I
haven't seen Mom in bed. I left home for the army at eighteen,
and before that I don't think I ever went into their bedroom,
at least not after I was ten. Now I see her there, bed tilted,
oxygen tube up her nose, all the monitors, IV, catheters.
There's a computer readout screen over her head showing an
ongoing cardiograph, there's also a little red dot indicating
her pulse with a digital readout. She looks like a failed as-
tronaut.

She's a greenish-white color and her eyes are closed. Her face is a mask.

It's a strange thing about Mom's face. It has all the lines and marks of her past expressions, most of these negative. There are hard traces of suspicion, strong lines of dissatisfaction and complaint. They're deeply incised, even in repose. At the same time, there's something young about her. She keeps her hair tinted toward black and her hair is husky, hard, thick. So different from Dad. His face is smooth, satin smooth, his hair only white tufts over his ears.

Mother uses a medium amount of makeup, not exaggerated for a woman seventy. She's never looked her age. I look at her, even here sick, maybe dying, and she doesn't look much over fifty-five.

I sit down in a chair beside the bed and watch the machines trying to tell me what's happening. I know they have monitors out there in the central nursing station. I wonder what would bring them rushing in.

I watch the pulse rate and it's up to 87 down to 83, up to 92. I never knew the pulse varied so much. Could it be because of her heart?

I'm staring at the screen and more or less inside myself, when I hear her voice.

"You did come, after all. I must really be sick."

This's classic Mom. First, recrimination, doubt I'd come; second, self-pity. I lean down and kiss her on the turned cheek.

"Oh, you're not so sick, Mom. I came for something else anyway."

What a stupid thing to say! She might be half dead, but nobody could fool my mother that easily. A person who's suspicious even about truth is hard to fool.

"Don't kid me, Jacky."

She closes her eyes, then slowly begins her dramatized version of the heart attack. She ought to write soap operas. She can make almost anything interesting and gives herself terrific starring roles.

"Daddy didn't know what to do. . . . I'm staying alive by willpower, telling Daddy it's only indigestion. I'm praying to

Saint Jude, patron saint of hopeless cases, when Joan comes in the nick of time and saves my life."

She grudgingly gives this to Joan, then takes it back by saving the McCarthys, her side of the family, are always good in emergencies, while the Tremonts crack up. Thank God, Joan has good McCarthy blood.

Now there's the scenario about what the doctors have told her. If they talked to Mother as much as she says, she couldn't find time to sleep and nothing else in the hospital would get done.

And they're all so impressed with her strength; she has the willpower of somebody half her age. Mother probably considers this an insult; nobody half her age has her willpower.

But she does admit she's scared.

Next we start the planning, stage-managing.

"Don't say anything to Daddy about a heart attack! Just tell him it's something with my 'insides.'

"He'll understand that, Jacky, because I had the hysterectomy. You tell him it's only something went wrong with my 'insides.' "

She likes that idea.

"And whatever you do, Jacky, don't mention cancer, you know he's scared to death of cancer."

I don't know what cancer has to do with the whole thing but I nod. I'll talk to Joan and we'll figure how we can handle Dad. There's no way to keep it from him that Mother's had a heart attack. Having a heart attack is not like having a hysterectomy. When you've had a heart attack, even if you survive you're a coronary patient for life.

But there's no sense saying these things to Mom now. I stay on for a while and watch. She drifts in and out, sometimes thrashing in her sleep. Once, she pulls off the monitor and three nurses come dashing in. Boy, are they ready for action!

Mother is an extremely active person, even in her sleep; she's nervous and moves quickly. The nurse tells me it's the fourth time she's torn off the monitor. This time they do everything but nail it to her arm; gluing and taping from elbow to wrist. The IV tube is another whole problem.

When I leave, I'm surprised I don't feel any tendency to cry. Mostly, I feel discouraged and peculiarly restless. Seeing her down that way is like looking at an old, familiar tree that's been struck by lightning and is stretched across the path.

I go back determined to put on the brightest face possible. In our family my role is the joker, the comedian, the clown.

I *know* what's expected; you get a feeling for a role like this. I park Dad's car up the street, then walk to the house. Usually we park this car on the driveway or in the patio. Dad meets me at the door.

"Where's the car, Johnny?"

"Well, Dad, I visited the hospital. When I got there, Mother was all packed, ready to go. The doctor said she ought to take a vacation and rest up, so she's on her way to Palm Springs. I gave her the car and took a bus back."

Now, this is cruel. Dad's believing me. He's glad Mother's well, but he's crushed she's going to Palm Springs without him. Joan pushes past me and looks down the street.

"Jack, you're impossible! The car's right down there, Dad. You have a real screwball for a son."

It gets us past the hard point anyway. I have some time to pull myself together.

The TV's on and I settle onto the gold chair, Mom's chair. They're watching a game between the Angels and Oakland. Oakland's winning, of course. Dad realizes I've been to the hospital and he's trying not to make a big thing of it.

"How's she look to you, Johnny? Does she seem all right?"

Then, with hardly a pause.

"When's she coming home?"

"She's fine, Dad, but she'll be in the hospital for a while. She said to say hello and sends you a big kiss."

He doesn't ask what's the matter with her. I don't think he wants to know. I look over at Joan on the couch and she puts her finger to her lips.

We watch silently. Oakland's ahead by five.

Joan stands quietly, points to the first back bedroom and leaves. I think it's called a back bedroom because it's behind

the living room, kitchen and bath; she means the side bedroom.

There's another bedroom further back; the *real* back bedroom. This house is built in an L, the bottom part facing the
street. This is the living-and-dining room. The long part of the
L extends on the left toward the rear, with a patio on the
right. Along this are the kitchen and bathroom, back to back;
the middle, or first "back" bedroom, then the real back bedroom at the end of the hall. Actually, there's another bedroom
in the garden; this is sometimes called the back bedroom, too.
My folks' house has three back bedrooms, no other kind.

Joan's waiting for me. With men on first and third, one
out for the Angels, I leave as if I'm going to the bathroom; Dad
and Mario don't look up. I go in and close the bedroom door
quietly. Joan's stretched out on the bed, I sit on the floor.

As children, Joan and I developed our own world, fighting
what I now call the poverty mind. This poverty mind constantly suspects anything out of the ordinary, anything not
known or accepted; also if it isn't practical, it isn't good.

Now Joan has five children. She's a natural mother, one
of the incredible women who truly play with their children.
And I don't mean only when they're babies; she plays with
them all the time. She has a twenty-four-year-old son, Yale
graduate cum laude, and she still plays with him. You might
find them out in the yard playing marbles or shooting a BB
gun.

Mother calls Joan the "simp" when she does this. "Look
at the simp playing on the floor with her grown kids."

"Simp" in Mom's lexicon is short for simpleton, I think.
I've never asked her. Whenever anyone does anything she
doesn't agree with, they're automatically classified as "simp."
She snorts through her nose when she says it. Joan is a "simp"
(snort) because she plays with her children; "They'll never
have any respect for her. Honest to God, they think she's only
another kid."

Joan and I *still* play together. Here I'm fifty-two and she's
in her late forties, but when we get together, it's playtime.
Our play is based on deep confidence. What's hide-and-seek

if you peek? Can you relax and have fun on a seesaw with someone you don't trust?

"How'd Mom look to you, Jack?"

She laughs when I tell her Mother's first line. I admit she didn't look so hot.

"The doctor says we just have to wait and see what damage was done."

She pauses.

"I'm worried about Dad. I could move him out to our place but he's better off here where he can putter around his garden and greenhouse."

I nod.

"How long can you stay?"

"The ticket's for twenty-one to forty-five days."

"That should be enough, I hope."

She rolls onto her side, slips off her shoes.

"Don't worry, Joan. I'll stay with Dad. It'll work out. At home, I'm a newfangled house husband."

She shoots me one of her "straight on" looks.

"Are you sure? You know he's practically a baby."

"Don't worry. He's my father too, you know."

"That'd be great."

Joan gives me a rundown on a typical day here. She says the main thing is keeping everything on an even keel. She explains how Mother has a schedule and their whole life is essentially one long routine.

"First, Mom gets up early and does her exercises. For her, it's the best time of day; she has the whole house to herself. At about ten she takes a cup of coffee in to Dad, gives him his blood-pressure pills, vitamin pills and any other pills she's into. The morning coffee is real coffee, not decaffeinated.

"You know, Jack, Dad has somehow managed over the past eight years to keep alive the feeling he's on an extended vacation; that sooner or later he must go back to work. He lives each day as if it might be his last."

She tells me the pills Dad takes. I recognize some and he's heavily medicated. I think maybe I'll try getting him into meditation or even Yoga. I hold my own pressure down that way. I've brought my cuff with me, so I'll check him when I do myself. That reserpine he's on is deadly stuff; it's basically poison.

Joan reels off the rest of this daily routine, including mandatory soap operas. I tell her I'll try sticking it out; but my mind is spinning, figuring ways to sharpen life up. I can't leave other people's lives alone. I especially want to wean him from those three hours of "soaps" in the middle of the day. What a waste, to be living in California with all the sunshine out there, sitting inside staring at moving colored lines. My God, the ocean's less than ten minutes away.

"Another thing, Jack, Dad works a bit in his shop but he doesn't have his old coordination; this drives him crazy. You know how he could fix almost anything? Now he has trouble keeping his own electric razor running."

Her eyes fill and she looks down.

"He's beginning to think I'm a mechanical genius because I can fix his razor; clean it, replace the blade, things like that."

"But you *are* a mechanical genius!"

When we were kids, she was roller-skating at four when I was seven and I couldn't even stand up on the damned things. She rode a two-wheeler before I did. I got the Erector set for Christmas and she played with it. That's the way it was.

"Try going along with him, Jack; help without making him feel inept. He's fine as long as he doesn't get flustered."

She gets up from the bed, slips on her shoes.

"We'd better get out there before they think we've flown the coop."

The game's still on. Oakland's running away with it. We come in just after Rollie Fingers hits a bases-loaded homer. We watch the replay.

Joan and Mario leave after the home run. I'm alone with Dad. I can't remember when I was last alone with him. As we watch the end of the game, I go over in my mind the things Joan told me. I'm a fair-to-middling cook and housekeeper but it scares me trying to fill in for Mother.

Before she left, Joan fixed dinner, so, at about six-thirty, I go in the kitchen and heat it up. I set the table for two. Dad's in his regular place at the end of the table and I take my usual place to his left. I don't take Mom's place on the kitchen side, even though it'd be more convenient.

Dad's watching me. I bring out the butter, salt, pepper, dishes, knives, forks, spoons. I carry the meal hot from the stove and put it on a plate in the middle of the table.

"Where did you learn to cook, Johnny?"

Dad usually calls me Johnny; once in a rare while, John. I don't know how he decides which. Mom always calls me Jacky. I changed my name from Johnny or Jacky to Jack when I went to high school. But at home it never took. I don't know why Mom and Dad call me by different names but that's the way it is. It's almost as if I'm a different person to each of them.

"I didn't cook this, Dad; Joan did. I'm only putting it out. Come on, let's eat."

I know he doesn't believe me. I'm bringing food out of the kitchen so I must be cooking it. People cook food in kitchens. He designed this kitchen, put in the stove, sink, refrigerator; built the cabinets; maintains it when anything goes wrong. But using it is an absolute mystery to him. He can no more use a kitchen than he can use one of those jet airplanes he helped build at Douglas for twenty years.

It's a fine meal and afterward we watch more TV. During the station breaks and ads, I scoot in the kitchen and clean up. Then I begin hauling my things to the back bedroom out in the garden. I carry some blankets along with my bags. Dad's watching me.

"I wouldn't sleep out there, Johnny, it's awfully cold and damp; you'd be better off sleeping in here. I leave the heat on low at night so it's warm."

Frankly, I like sleeping in the cold. My parents keep their house too hot for me and besides, they're electric-blanket people. I'm not. I don't feel comfortable, even in California, unless I have weight on top of me; a light electric blanket with only a sheet leaves me feeling vulnerable. I know I'm warm but I don't feel I should be. But I can't tell Dad these things; he'd take it as an insult.

Still, I'm getting the message. He's scared. He'd probably like me to climb in bed with him back there but he could never ask; even if I volunteered he couldn't. He probably hasn't slept alone since the last time Mother was hospitalized, over thirty-five years ago. He's dreading it. So what do I do? I can't take him by the hand, lead him to the bedroom and dress him in his pajamas.

"Well, Dad, we'd better hit the sack."

Reluctantly he gets up and turns off the television. Then he sets the thermostat down a fraction. He checks all the doors and windows to see if they're locked. These are his routines I know about. He puts out the lights except for a night-light on the baseboard in the hall. He goes back to his bedroom.

I decide I'll sleep in the side bedroom; I can't leave him alone feeling the way he does. I'll shut the vanes on the heater vent. I'll close the door and open the window.

I've just climbed into bed when he knocks on the door and opens it.

"Johnny, I can't find my pajamas; I don't know where she keeps them."

I paddle barefoot into his bedroom with him. There's a closet and a chest with three drawers. I look through the drawers and find them right away. Mother's organized herself into the top drawer; the middle drawer is for Dad and the bottom drawer is filled with sweaters. I hand him the pajamas. He looks at me as if I'm a wonder man.

We say good night again and he asks me to leave on his baseboard night-light in the hall. He's holding on; he doesn't want to be left in that bedroom alone. If I were a really sensitive, loving, thoughtful son, I'd've offered to have him sleep in the side room and I could've slept back there. That big, empty bed without Mother is scaring him. It's hard to know the right thing.

3

"Hey, Dad; wake up! Come on, Dad!"

Christ, maybe he's dead. He's breathing; man, is he ever breathing; sounds like the death rattle.

"Come on, Dad, let's go. It's eight o'clock already."

That's real time, Pacific time. We still haven't crossed into Mountain time. He moans and rolls over. Maybe he isn't dead. With all the crap he's been through, he could easily have a heart attack or stroke. I look at him close; he *seems* OK.

I take a shower, bumping around and rattling things, making's much noise as I can. This isn't like him at all; he's usually up hassling the whole family every morning. I come out drying myself.

"Hey, Dad; let's go. Time to get up."

It's like he's stoned. Now I'm beginning to really get worried. What would I do if he dies out here in the middle of nowhere? I sit down on the edge of the bed and shake him.

"Hey, Dad. You OK?"

He moans, and opens his eyes. They don't focus and he rolls away from me.

"Come on, Dad! Let's go, huh? It's almost eight-thirty!"

Finally, he swings his legs and sits on the side of the bed. He hangs there completely drag-assed. But he's awake, he's alive.

After a shower he's fine. We'll take right off and have breakfast on the road. That way, we get in some cool morning driving time. God, I wish he'd let me drive; we're wasting this bomb crawling at fifty-five. He drives as if he's being punished. He sits hunched over the wheel, sulking, surrounded by open roads, trees and high empty skies; not even looking; just tensed up, expecting the worst.

With a power tool like this, you can lean back and let the damned thing drive itself. The great drivers all say you should relax, get a feel for the road. It's criminal running a supercharged motor at these speeds.

Before we get in again, I ask once more.

"I'm sorry, Bill."

"Why not? I've got my license."

"Don't, Bill. We can't afford to take those kinds of risks; it's not worth it."

So we start rolling. I look out the side window at the scenery going by. If I watch his driving, I'll go crazy. He has fast reactions, and they're not too fast, but there's something about it makes me nervous. He's so dead *serious;* if you get involved with his driving, you tense up yourself. It's no fun.

My dad's good at the small things. People usually think artists are easygoing, loose people. Well, that's not him. He's tight as a witch's cunt. Like getting Bryce and Zion confused. He was *so* convinced. We went past a great spot I *knew* was the place he wanted all the time, but he had his mind set and there's nothing to do; he has some kind of tunnel vision.

Maybe he's getting senile. That seems to be what getting old is; you aim yourself more.

Both Mom and Dad act old lately.

Mom's so quiet and doesn't want anything exciting or new. Even if I fart or burp at the table she makes a whole scene. They don't roll with the punch, adapt to the new life.

And, Christ, it was grim saying goodbye to Gramps. Dad was his usual self then, too; bearing down, eating it. And Grandma's such a pain. I don't think she's ever done anything for anybody without expecting something back. Life's one king-size Monopoly game to her.

Dad's got the radio on again. All we get is cowboy music and static. There's nothing good between towns and we're mostly in the middle of nowhere. We should stop and buy a cassette of *real* music, the Stones or Dylan or the Doors, something reasonable.

I've still got a hundred and fifty bucks on the money belt, but I'd hate spending any on a stupid cassette. I'll need every cent and I don't want to beg for money. He still hasn't said anything. He knows I'm not going back to school but he hasn't mentioned it, yet.

Oh, God! Now we're going to pass a truck. This is the wildest, watching him pass a truck. He won't budge till the view's clear to the horizon. Hell, there's nothing behind us for at least a mile.

He's checking the side mirror for the tenth time. Here we go! We're out there, cruising slowly along the side of a big semi. This guy's totally freaked, looking down at us as we go past two miles an hour faster than he's going. He must think we only have three cylinders firing. If Dad'd floor this thing, we'd be around clear in three seconds. No, we're taking the leisure trip, maybe saving on gas. I've got to relax.

4

Next morning I wake at eight-thirty, feeling more with it. That nine-hour time difference knocks me for a loop.

I make breakfast. At home we're not coffee drinkers but my folks are. Thank God they're not serious coffee drinkers; they don't grind or perk or filter, just instant.

It's an electric stove, flat coils; I'm not sure if the hottest is 1 or 6. I try 6. I look in the cabinet drawer near the dining room and there's the card with Dad's medication written out, just as Joan said. I sort pills and work from lists, how much in the morning, at lunch and before bed. I'll go along for now but Dad's got to take over this part himself.

I'm prepared, after breakfast, to talk about Mother's condition. Joan and I agree he'll take it best from me.

Now, this is weird, but Dad's convinced I'm working for the government in some kind of secret intelligence. He's had this idea for more than ten years. He won't refer to it directly.

He'll look at me slyly, bashfully, and say, "How's the job going, John?"

He apparently could never accept that a grown man would paint pictures for a living; it isn't within his parameter of sensible behavior.

Mother has no trouble; she has me pegged for an old hippy. I have a beard, I live in Paris and I'm most likely a drug addict. She dismisses my life as a total waste. But Dad needs some excuse and he's come up with this one.

Joan thinks it's the world's greatest joke. One Christmas she mailed me a man-sized Zorro costume she'd sewed up herself. With it was a toy detective kit for taking fingerprints and a magnifying glass.

At first, I tried disclaiming my spook status but then decide to go along. What the hell; he's doing it for me. Now I only say, "Things are fine, Dad." That's usually enough; we never go further.

I gather the pills, pour coffee in his cup and knock on the bedroom door. I'm determined not to give him coffee in bed. I call through the door.

"Time to get up, Dad; coffee's ready."

"OK, Johnny, OK, I'll be right out."

I realize, as I'm standing there, we're playing another game.

Dad was born in 1904. For men born in that year, World War I ended when they were fourteen and World War II started, at least for the U.S., when they were thirty-seven. Dad missed war.

This is lodged somehow in the back of his mind. I'm sure he knows he's lucky to have escaped, but he never lived that phony "man's man" life in the field. It bothers him.

Dad stayed at home until he was married, and then Mom took over. He's always lived in a woman-dominated environment; never lived as a single man or with other men.

All his brothers have had brief bachelorhoods; one was in W.W.I. They're also much involved with hunting. For years, Dad wanted to take me hunting with his father and brothers, but Mom wouldn't have it.

"Oh, no! If you two go, you wash all your own clothes and

stinking underwear. And I won't have any of those smelly deer-skin gloves or wild-Indian moccasins around this house either. I'll tell you that!"

Each fall, the whole bunch, including all my male cousins on the Tremont side, would go up to Maine. They'd usually get deer and sometimes bear. They'd butcher and tan the hides at Grandpa's. My cousins would tell me stories of waiting in deep, cold woods, playing cards and drinking beer. I felt it separated me from them; I'd never grow up to be a real man.

And now, my coming down the hall, knocking on the door is playing army. My saying "Time to get up, let's go" does it. I don't say "Drop your cocks and grab your socks," but it's the domestic equivalent. Dad comes plowing out in his pajamas with his slippers on, dragging his feet down the hall on his way to the bathroom.

This foot-dragging is a new thing with him and I'm not sure if it mightn't be related to minor stroking.

On the other hand, it's more likely he feels he's getting old and old people drag their feet, so he's dragging his. There's something about sliding slippers along a rug in the morning which appeals to his sense of "rightness."

He comes out of the bathroom and starts toward the dining room.

"Dad, why don't you get dressed first? It'll be a while yet before the eggs are ready."

He looks at me bare-eyed.

"Where are your glasses, Dad?"

"I couldn't find them, Johnny."

I go back to the bedroom with him and they're where he'd put them, on the bedside table, before he went to sleep. I should be glad he took them off, I guess. There's a creamy haze on them, rim to rim. I take them to the bathroom and wash the lenses in warm water. I'm careless with glasses myself, but when things start to blur, I usually wipe the damned things off anyway.

He stands beside the bed and fits them carefully several times over his ears. He's always claimed glasses hurt his nose and ears, so he's continually changing frames, from rimless to metal to plastic and back. He didn't start wearing glasses until he was over fifty and has never adapted.

The coffee's getting cold. I know he's waiting for me to find his clothes. I see yesterday's clothes on the floor beside the bed where he dropped them. I pick these up and spread them on the bed.

"Here, Dad. You can wear the clothes you wore yesterday. They're not dirty."

He looks at me closely, tilts his head.

"I never wear the same clothes two days in a row, Johnny. Your mother would kill me."

He's not complaining, only stating a fact. To be honest, I'm *not* a clean-underwear-every-day man myself.

I search around and find some underwear. Dad wears Dacron boxer shorts and the kind of undershirts they had before T-shirts were invented. These look like tops of old-fashioned bathing suits or jogger shirts; shoulder straps and big holes you stick your arms through. Pinned to the inside of his old undershirt is a scapular of The Sacred Heart. Dad slips on the new undershirt and feels around with his hand.

"Where's my scapular, John?"

It's as if he thinks he has a scapular built in on each undershirt. I unpin the old one and give it to him. He has one hell of a time pinning it on; you can tell he's never done it before. He's pinning it with concentration, bunching the underwear shirt into a ball, pinning, then smoothing out wrinkles. He pats the scapular three or four times and smiles. He's proud he didn't pin it to his skin, I guess. I give him a shirt and a pair of trousers from the closet; I put out clean socks.

"Look, Dad, you have to learn where all these things are. Mother's sick and can't do this anymore."

He smiles a wide, eager smile.

"You're right there, Johnny. I'm going to learn all these things. You'll see."

I go back to the kitchen and warm up the coffee. I cook some eggs. The pills are beside his plate. I wait and it takes forever for him to come out of the bedroom. What can be taking him so long?

.   .   .

DAD

I lean close against Milly and wash her teats clean with warm water. The udder is heavy, the milk vein swollen. The fresh water steams from the turgid pink teats into the dim, new dawn light. I push the bucket in place, squat on the stool and start the singing rhythm of milk on metal. My fingers warm with every rolling squeeze.

When Dad comes out, I serve the eggs with hash browns. Dad sits and looks at them as if they're strange outer-space food.

"Isn't there any bearclaw?"

"Sure, but let's have some eggs first, then you can finish off the bearclaw."

"Johnny, I never eat so much in the morning."

"Try it this one time, Dad. It'll give you a good start. Coffee and a roll isn't enough, even with all the vitamin pills."

Hell, he ought to have some breakfast; at least orange juice, and an egg.

He eats nimbly, not breaking the yolk till the white is eaten, then finishes by wiping his mouth with the napkin. He wipes as if he's going to wear off his lips. And this must be a cloth napkin; cloth with every meal and clean. Joan reminded me but it's something I remember.

Dad sits back and drinks his cup of cooled-off coffee.

"Right now, Johnny, Mother usually turns on the record player and we listen to music."

The player is there beside the table. It's an old-fashioned, wood-cabinet Magnavox. There's a sliding lid on top over the turntable. I find the right dials and turn it on. There's a record already in place. I close the lid. Covered, it looks like a dish cabinet; the front is a woven, metallized cloth with jig-sawed wooden curlicues.

Bing Crosby comes on singing "I Wonder What's Become of Sally." It's a deep, wooden tone, blurry but nice. All the new stereo and high-fidelity sets are very clear, very precise, but I hear that gray, smoked, transparent plastic in the music. It's so incredibly accurate, transistor-perfect. This murky, dark, wood sound of old Bing is comforting. I'm sure any serious stereo addict would curl up and die but it sounds OK to me. I sit and sip coffee with Dad.

.   .   .

When the record's finished, I clear the dishes. I start running hot water into the sink. Dad's followed me into the kitchen. He leans over my shoulder as I squeeze soap into the hot water. I scrape plates and slip them into the suds.

"You know, John, I think I could do that."

"Sure, Dad, nothing to it. You put hot water with soap on one side and rinse water on the other. You scrub the dishes on the hot, sudsy side, run them through the rinse and stack them in the dish rack."

He's watching and following through with me. He insists I leave the kitchen and he'll finish; his first housework, breakfast dishes for two.

I start sweeping. There's a vacuum cleaner but I prefer sweeping. I find a broom in the heater closet, and begin on the back bedroom. Mother's an every-day-vacuum person. The rugs are going to have a slight change in treatment.

I sweep everything into piles. When I have enough to make a pile, I concentrate it, then move on. This is a four-pile house. Our apartment in Paris is a three-pile place, the boat a two-piler. The mill's a one-piler, or I can make it two, depending on how dirty things are. Everything gets dirtier down there but it's earth dirt, not soot or grime the way it is in Paris. The dirt here is between the two, but definitely four piles.

I look for Dad, expecting to find him out in the garden or greenhouse. But he's still in the kitchen washing dishes, with intense, inner concentration. I wonder where his mind is.

Down by the well, a small bird flits its tail and takes off with a dropping upturn as I lean, lowering my pail into the water.

I sneak up and watch. He's taking each dish and examining it minutely for dirt, then washing off a spot at a time. If he had a micrometer, a centrifuge and a sterilizer he'd be happier. He's scraping away as if he's trying to rub off the flower pattern. When he's satisfied they're clean, he dips them in and out of the rinse water at least ten times.

The thing is, he's getting a kick out of it, water play.

He's enjoying washing dishes, playing with hot and cold water.

Dad can get super perfectionist over almost anything. I know I'll go crazy if I watch too long. This has always been one of Mom's laments. There's a lot of her in me, and I don't want to believe it.

Her claim is she needs to do everything herself because Dad drives her crazy making mountains out of molehills. It could be he still knows something about joy, while Mom and I are only getting through things. I back out of the kitchen.

Sometimes Mother calls Dad "Kid Kilowatt." That's one of her favorite titles. Another is "Mr. Fixit." He's also "Jack-of-all-trades."

Finally, Dad thinks the dishes are done. They're clean enough for a TV ad but it hasn't occurred to him that other things are usually classified under wash the dishes. These are the small, important jobs marking the difference between someone who's been around a kitchen and someone who hasn't. I've watched this with our children growing up and with various friends who've passed through our lives.

They say they'll "do" the dishes and that's it. They "do" the dishes. Everything else is left. They might not even wash the pots. They definitely will not wipe off the stove or clean the sink, wipe off the surfaces of tables, cabinets. They won't put things away; butter, salt, pepper, spices, cutting boards. One young woman left the dirty water in our sink. She was twenty-five years old and wanted desperately to get married. After this scene I had trouble working up much sympathy; my own old-maidness got in the way.

So I explain things to Dad. He follows everything I do, shaking his head in amazement.

"Where did you learn all this, Johnny? In the army?"

Anything I know Dad can't account for, I learned in the army.

"Yeah, maybe, Dad."

Sometimes now, I think of those poor officers and noncoms trying to keep things running with a mob of eighteen- and nineteen-year-old males. I go crazy with just one or two around the house. All the sweeping, bed-making, the KP we complained about, was only normal housekeeping.

Now, don't get me wrong, cleanliness may be next to godliness but it doesn't mean much to me, and Vron is as casual about dirt as I am.

But my *mother* is something else again. She's the cleaning maniac. Dirt *is* the devil! She used to take a toothbrush, reserved for this, and clean out the cracks in our hardwood floors. According to her, they harbored (that's the word) dirt and germs. In Philadelphia, we had a house with hardwood floors in every room except the kitchen and cellar. Once a month, Mother would scrape out the germ-harboring dirt. She'd keep it in a pile for us to admire when we came home, to see what we'd "tracked in."

Mom's also a window nut. The windows are washed once a week, whether they need it or not. When I was a kid, I wasn't allowed to come within a foot of any window. If there were some danger I might breathe on a window or touch it, she'd panic. The slightest smudge and she'd be at it with Windex, a piece of newspaper and a soft rag.

One of my great pleasures now is leaning against a window, pushing my nose close and making lip marks. I love to write on damp windows and draw pictures. All our kids are window smudgers and finger painters. Sometimes it gets hard to see out our windows.

Still, even now, when I go close to a window, there's a mother-barrier I need to crash. These little things clutter the soul.

With the kitchen done, Dad and I sit down in the living room. He gets up to turn on the television but I ask him not to. In this house, if you sit in the living room, you turn on the TV the way you lock the door when you go to the bathroom.

I'm not sure how to approach this; we've been carefully avoiding the subject all morning.

"Look, Dad, you should know that Mother's really sick."

He tenses. I watch his eyes. He's looking at me and it's pitiful; he's preparing himself for the worst.

"Is she still alive, Johnny?"

"Sure she's alive, Dad, but she's had a heart attack, not a really serious one, but bad enough. Her heart's never going to be the same. For instance, she can never work as hard as she used to."

He's nodding his head. I can tell he's not getting the message.

"I always tell her she works too hard, Johnny. She works too hard."

"You're right, Dad, and you'll need to take on a lot of the work around here. I'll teach you to do most of the light housework. Joan will come and do the heavy cleaning, washing, shopping, things like that, but the everyday stuff, cooking, picking up, simple housecleaning, you'll have to take over."

He's listening now, listening but still not comprehending.

"Then, Dad, you'll need to take care of Mother. You know how she is, she'll kill herself if we're not careful. You've got to watch over her."

He's still nodding, not looking at me, looking down at the floor.

"Yes, I can do that. You tell me what to do and how to do it, then I'll do it, all right."

"First we'll go see Mother this morning. Remember she's sick, she doesn't look so hot. The main thing is not to make her excited or worried. We need to convince her we're getting along OK ourselves."

I look at him carefully. He's hanging on to every word. I'm the captain giving orders.

"You know, Dad, Mother's convinced nobody can take care of you except her. We have to prove you can do it yourself."

Now he's shaking his head back and forth, a slow no, holding in one of his fake laughs with his hand over his mouth.

"That's right, Johnny; that's right; we'll fool her."

Oh boy!

Then I realize Dad's dressed but he hasn't washed. His pattern is broken or something, because normally he's a very fastidious person. I imagine Mom would say, "Now you go wash up, Jack," and he'd wash himself. Then probably she'd say, "Now get yourself dressed." I haven't been giving the right signals.

So I tell him to get undressed again, go in and wash. After that, we'll put on some good clothes and go to the hospital.

"We'll try to look nice because Mother likes to see you dressed up, Dad."

This means *Mother's* idea of dressed up, a cross between George Raft and John Boles. He wears a hat with a wide brim, a wide-lapel suit. This is all coming back in style now, so Mom'll need to work out a new outfit; maybe thin ties, button-down collars, narrow lapels. Or maybe that'll be *my* old-man costume.

But I know the drill. He'll wear a striped tie, with tie clasp; a gold wristwatch; clean fingernails; flat-surfaced, shined, leather-soled shoes.

I find everything and lay it out on the bed. What a crappy job I'm doing. Here I've gotten him dressed, and now, less than two hours later, I have him undressed again. It's like playing paper dolls.

Dad asks if he should take a bath.

"Usually, Johnny, I only take a bath once a week; an old man like me doesn't get very dirty."

"You just wash your face and hands, Dad; clean your fingernails and brush your teeth; that'll be enough."

I'm not going to wash and dress him. I'm not going to hold up each arm and rub soap in his armpits. Ha! Little do I know what I'll be doing.

I'm having a hard time adapting. Dad has always been a very capable person. I don't think it's senility, either. He's become lethargic, inertial, inept. It's fairly good survival technique; if someone else will do for you, let them. But he's lost the knack of doing for himself. He's debilitated.

Painfully, slowly, he washes and gets dressed. When he comes out, his necktie is crooked but I restrain myself. I roll out the car. He insists I warm it for five minutes before we take off. I have a strong respect for Dad's feelings here.

.   .   .

It's a whole story about Dad and driving. He'd driven from the time he was sixteen till he was seventy. He's never had an accident or an insurance claim. Most years he averaged over fifteen thousand miles a year, right up till he retired.

Then, when he went to get his driver's license renewed on his seventieth birthday, he panicked. He'd passed the written without any trouble, but, because of his age, they wanted him to do a road test. When he heard that, he turned in his driving license to the DMV examiner and quit.

Now, this didn't make sense because he'd driven over for the test. He was driving almost every day. He'd lost his nerve, that's all. He was overwhelmingly nervous and frightened.

In any competitive-comparative society there are hundreds of losers for every winner. Somewhere in Dad's life, deep back, he developed a dichotomy between bosses and workers. He considers himself a worker.

One of the things Dad feels about me is I'm a boss. I can't convince him how ridiculous this is. I don't have anybody working for me and abhor the idea.

"No, Johnny, bosses are bosses, workers are workers, and you're a boss. You have all the ways of a boss."

Anyway, Dad sees this guy working for the DMV, just doing his job, as a boss. He freezes, turns in his driver's license and hasn't driven since.

Also, he's convinced he couldn't've passed the test; he's sure he's not good enough anymore; there are too many things he doesn't notice, things that could cause accidents.

"John, when you're a good driver, you know when you aren't a good driver anymore."

Mother's another whole story. She didn't drive till she was in her late thirties, although Dad tried to teach her from the time they were married. He'd built his own car from discarded parts when he was seventeen. That was some automobile; it didn't even have a windshield. I've heard stories and seen one photograph of it. My Aunt Trude said her father, my grandfather, absolutely forbade any of Dad's sisters to ride in it with him.

When we were kids, the standard thing on a Sunday afternoon was taking Mom out for a driving lesson. At that time we had a 1929 Ford. Dad'd bought a wreck for fifteen dollars and fixed it up. Fifteen dollars then was a week's wages working for the WPA. As a child, I got the idea driving a car had to be one of the hardest things for a human to learn.

Dad would keep saying, "Now take it easy, Bess, relax, it'll be all right." Joan and I would be in the back seat scared, cringing, peeking, giggling. Mom's best trick was jamming the car into reverse while going forward. There would be a grinding, growling sound from the transmission and we'd be slammed against the front seat. Mother's tough on any automobile; people, too.

Mom's so hypernervous she can't put her mind and body together. She'd have wild crying fits and call Dad cruel. Several times she jumped out of the car. Dad would drive beside her, coaxing her back in, and she'd walk along ignoring him, crying.

In California, Mom finally passed her test. The guy who passed her made a big mistake. She's a menace on the roads. Is it possible to have *too* fast reactions? She's *too* imaginative, at least to be driving a car. She's constantly twisting this way and that on the steering wheel so the car weaves down the road. Under her hands, a car takes on a mind of its own, a mind totally in opposition to hers. Mom also talks to cars and conducts a running commentary on any driver within crashing distance.

Despite all this, or maybe because of it, she can't maintain concentration on the road. She's had a series of minor accidents and totaled one car. It's a working miracle she's never killed anyone or seriously hurt herself.

When Dad stopped driving, Mom became the family driver. This is nuts. Dad, at his worst, is ten times better than Mom ever was at her best. But, in a sense, it's the story of their relationship. Mother, in her determination to dominate, took over. She's become the leader. Dad, in his timidity, awareness, sensitivity, his superdeveloped sense of responsibility, gradually handed over the reins. Probably this isn't too uncommon with life in general. If you're good at something, you don't fight so hard; you don't have to.

Still, even now, Dad's the one who keeps their car in running condition. He makes sure there's water in it, has the oil changed regularly. He keeps the tire pressure right and has a full tune-up every six months.

We drive off toward the hospital. I want to see if Dad can show me the way. He had a gall-bladder operation there ten years ago and did a lot of driving back and forth.

But he can't direct me at all; he's like a child. He's stopped thinking of streets and directions; he's only watching things go by the car window. I ask what's the best route, and he shrugs.

"I don't know, Mother usually drives us."

This is such a role reversal. It's always been a joke in our family how Mom never knows where she's been. She actually got lost once four blocks from home because she'd taken a wrong turn. She went into a police station to ask her way. I have something of this myself; I get lost easily.

But I'm beginning to feel Dad is operating at less than a quarter of his capacity. I sense how this happens, how easily it could happen to me. It's frightening how a combination of resignation and lack of confidence can debilitate far beyond any physiological loss.

I determine to press Dad into naming the streets. I want to force his mind out from the back court of his hand-built house on a dead-end street nestled quietly between the arms of giant freeways. I'm pointing out streets as we go along, encouraging him to respond.

Then, in the middle of my spiel, I realize he has something else on his mind. He gives off vibrations like dead air before a storm.

"You know, John, this is a good hospital; the union recommends it."

I nod my head and turn left on De Soto.

"But there's an awful lot of niggers there; not just niggers, Japs."

He pauses, looks over at me.

"Even so, Johnny, it's a good hospital."

I try not to respond. I don't want to get into it, especially right now.

When we go in the hospital, the receptionist is a good-looking black woman and remembers me from the day before.

"Hello, Mr. Tremont, your mother seems fine today."

I'm impressed she remembers not only me but the situation. To be perfectly honest, I hadn't noticed she was black when I came by myself. I'd registered her prettiness, kindness, efficiency, but not her color. It's only because of the car conversation it hits me; that's the way it goes.

Dad's standing there smiling, but it's peculiar, as if he's looking at someone in a cage at the zoo. She *is* in a kind of cage, a glass cage; maybe that's part of it, or maybe it's all in *my* mind.

We start toward the elevator wading through Muzak.

"Do you know her, Johnny?"

"I talked with her when I came to see Mom last time."

"She certainly was nice."

"Yup, she seems like a fine person."

He shakes his head and speaks to the floor.

"The world's changed, Johnny; you wouldn't believe how the world's changed."

We enter the elevator. Dad's becoming more nervous; his face is blanched, his hands are shaking. I put my arm over his shoulder.

"Come on, Dad, it's OK. They're taking the best possible care of Mother. She's getting exactly what she needs, a good rest."

We walk down the carpeted blue corridors; wild fantasy decorative paintings are on the walls. We arrive at the intensive care unit. It's another black woman. I ask if we can see Mother. She checks her clipboard. It'll be all right but we're not to stay long. We walk around the nurse's station over to Mom's cubicle. She's awake and sees us come in.

Dad kisses her, and she cries. Dad starts crying, too. I'm feeling embarrassed. Mom and Dad have never been much for public demonstration of affection or emotion. I can't think of any time I've seen them really kiss except for a peck goodbye or hello. Joan and I talked once about this. We were also trying to remember when Mother ever held or kissed us as children. Neither of us could remember this happening.

Mother had a terrible experience as a young girl. She was one of ten children living in a three-bedroom row house in South Philadelphia. She had two sisters whose names were Rose and Anne; they slept three in a bed, Mom, the youngest, in the middle. Anne and Rose, in the course of one year, died of tuberculosis, called, in those days, galloping consumption.

Mother, all her life, has been convinced she has tuberculosis. The horror of the whole experience was that Rose, the second to die, died in Mom's arms. Mother was trying to hold her out the window on a hot summer day so she could breathe. Rose hemorrhaged suddenly and died within minutes. Mother was fourteen at the time and had what was called a "nervous breakdown." She never went back to school.

All her life, Mom's had a bizarre fear of germs. She'd never kiss us on the mouth, neither my sister nor me. If she ever did kiss anybody, she'd wipe the kiss off right away as if she were wiping off lipstick; she was wiping off germs.

Mom puts her arms out and wants me to come kiss her. She kisses me on the lips and doesn't wipe. Maybe now she's dying, germs don't count. Dad stands looking at her, tears coming down his face. Mother gives him a fast once-over.

"He looks marvelous, Jacky; you're such a wonderful son. What would we do without you?"

She pulls herself up in the bed.

"Are you all right, Jack; are you taking your blood-pressure pills?"

"Oh, yeah, Bette, I'm fine. You know, Johnny can cook and clean house, all those things; he's like a regular wife."

Mother gives me a quick look, a short almost-snort.

"You two just try keeping things going. I'll be out of here soon. Eat at McDonald's and there's food in the freezer compartment."

Now she begins a detailed description of different menus Dad likes and can digest. This involves no onions, no garlic, no seasoning except salt. It gets down to various kinds of hamburger with either noodles or those fake mashed potatoes made from powder.

I nod along. I figure I'll use up what she has in the freezer but I have no intention of eating that way. Mom might be the world's worst cook. I don't want to perpetuate the tradition. I like cooking and prefer variety in my food; if I have to, I'll cook twice, once for Dad, once for myself. But I'm sure Dad'll enjoy what I cook. The poor bastard's been living on poverty-hospital-type food for over fifty years.

Dad's staring at Mother as if he's surprised to see her in bed, staying there, not getting up and taking over. It must be worse for him than it is for me. When we're about to leave, he kisses her again; he can't keep himself from saying it.

"When are you coming home, Bette? How long do you think it will be?"

Mom turns and gives me one of her looks. Now, these looks are special. In one way, it's as if she's trying to hide an expression, usually negative, from another person, but she does it so obviously everybody must notice; a Sarah Bernhardt dramatic gesture aimed for the last row in the balcony. This time she looks at me, raises her eyebrows and turns her eyes to the ceiling. She's saying, "See, he's helpless, he has no idea."

In a sense, this is true, but he's standing right there; he *sees* it. It's either incredible cruelty or insensitivity. She does this kind of thing about my sister, about our children and about me; it's something I've never been able to take.

"You know, Mom, Dad really would like to have you home. It's perfectly natural; we all would. We'd like to get you out of here soon as possible."

I'm trying to ride over those crazy signals.

"But you just have to take your time and relax. Do what the doctor says. You'll be fine but you've got to change your way of living, Mom. You've had a heart attack and can't go back to your old wild and woolly ways."

Her eyes fill up.

"I don't know if I want to live like that, Jacky. If I can't do what I want, what's the sense?"

I hold back; it won't help getting her upset.

"OK, Mom. But do what the doctor says. He knows best and he'll let you out when he thinks you're ready."

Then she comes on with the kicker.

"You know, I'm not sure I had a heart attack, anyway. How do these doctors know for sure? It felt like gas pains to me."

This had to come but I keep my big mouth shut. What else?

I kiss her goodbye and we leave.

As soon as we get in the car, Dad begins.

"Johnny, when do you really think she'll come home?"

"She should stay in the hospital just's long as possible. The longer she stays, the better off she is."

"I guess you're right there, Johnny; I guess you're right."

But he isn't believing it.

That evening, we don't do much. We watch some TV, then I roll my old Honda 175 motorcycle out of the garden shack and into the patio. It needs some heavy cleaning and tuning; it's been sitting there almost two years. Dad comes out and works in his greenhouse. He can putter around in there by the hour, his private world.

> *The sun leans quietly up over Ira's barn.*
> *Each day a mite sooner, a bit to the right.*
> *The start for the day, an end to the night.*

5

I must've slipped off because my head jerks and the country's changed, higher, not so dry.

I only hope to hell we can keep off the subject of what I'm going to do; at least for a while. He'll never understand why I cut out of Santa Cruz. He did all the paperwork for the scholarship, establishing residence, getting high-school records in, all that crap. And now, after a year, I don't want it. Sometimes I don't even understand, myself.

But, Jesus, if he could only have seen that place. It was a giant baby-sitting operation. I mean, Santa Cruz is an old people's home for kids.

I about vomited when I arrived on my motorcycle, after ten days on the road. I'm caked with dirt from head to toe; everything I own's in my saddlebags. I couldn't believe it. There were trucks and cars pulling in with stereo sets, wall-to-wall sound systems, rugs, teddy bears, ten-speed bicycles, tennis rackets, golf clubs, fencing costumes, huge suitcases full of clothes. God, you wouldn't believe all the junk these people were dragging along. It looked like a junior-high-school garage sale.

Then, there was my crazy roommate, Flash. My *mother*, my *own* mother, picked him for me. She filled out a form with what she thought I'd like for a roommate. Would you believe it, Santa Cruz even has a form for that. Mom said how I'd like somebody with a good stereo set who's interested in electricity, motorcycles and running. I actually hunted up this form in the Registrar's Office to find out how it happened to me.

I get a guy with a terrific stereo set all right; in fact, he's an electrical genius. He's also crazy. For one thing he has a bicycle hanging on pulleys from the ceiling of our room with a monster lock on it. He designed and built the lock himself. There's a sign on this bike. It says:

IF YOU STEAL THIS BICYCLE, YOU WILL BE STEALING THE BEST BICYCLE IN THE WORLD PROTECTED BY THE BEST LOCK IN THE WORLD AND YOU ARE GOING TO HAVE THE BEST DETECTIVE IN THE WORLD CHAS-ING YOU TO THE ENDS OF THE WORLD.

Now, you know this is an out-and-out challenge. We wind up constantly locking our door. Nobody in Santa Cruz is locking doors except us, nobody even *closes* doors!

Flash wears black clothes; he wears black T-shirts, black jeans, black socks, black jockey shorts, black shoes, black pajamas. He has long black hair combed straight down on all sides, even across his face, and a brush cut on top so you can see the white skin on his skull; it's the only white you can see. He looks like something out of *Mad* magazine.

Except for examinations, I don't remember Flash ever going to class. He only left the room to ride that bike or get something to eat. That's the way it is at Santa Cruz; nobody's watching you. It's a place where nobody gives a damn what you do. At the same time, you wind up with a guilty feeling all the time that you're not doing enough. They use a pass-no-record system, meaning either you pass or else it didn't happen; you can't fail. Still, in some twisted way it's a superman nursery school; the place is like a hothouse for sequoia trees. To be honest, I actually felt more on my own at that crummy American high school in Paris; at least you could fail.

The dorms at Santa Cruz were weird. Living in a Paris apartment is like living alone in a cave on the side of a mountain compared to living in a dorm at Santa Cruz. Everybody's into everybody else's room, and after the third week it was musical-bed time. The lights were lit all the time; there wasn't one dim corner, let alone dark. I used to close my eyes sometimes, trying to remember what the dark was like. I've gone out at three in the morning and looked back. The whole building vibrated with noise and light, electricity being burned by the kiloton. And, the next day in class, these same people would talk about ecology and conservation.

Just to get away, I practically live in the library. I even work a job there; helps me hold on to a corner of my mind. Those people have no moments alone. They write their term papers surrounded with junk, noise and smells. And God, the smells would knock anybody over. The floors in all the rooms are covered with paper, food, dirty socks, clothes, books. Everybody tramps over these piles. People walk around half dressed; it's a zoo, nothing private.

Dad hasn't really gotten into why I don't want to go back. He's strange that way; he doesn't talk about things. He can talk to people; I mean, conversation; he's a great storyteller, and shit, painting's communication; but he doesn't talk where something's important. He tends to ignore anything he doesn't want to hear. Mom's the same.

But we've *got* to talk this out sooner or later, only *I'm* not going to bring it up.

What I want to do is write. Writing's something I enjoy doing. That's the way he got into painting. I know I bullshit better than most people; that should help. First, I'll try a novel or maybe a screenplay; it doesn't matter. I only want my cabin and some quiet. I'll bear down and get something done for a change. Christ, my days get by and I've nothing to show.

Maybe Debby *will* come. She'd groove on my cabin. She's shit tired of Berkeley and it'd be fine having a good woman around.

The trouble is I don't know how I can make money. I can't get a *carte de travail*. With the common market, there's no way for an American to work in France, legally. Maybe I'll hire myself out picking sugar beets. I hear you can work up a thousand bucks a month that way. I could live easy on a couple thousand a year. Debby's old man will chip in something, too.

"Hey, Dad, let's stop someplace for breakfast. I'm starved."

He nods his head. He's off spinning somewhere. We'll be crossing from Utah into Colorado soon. The Rockies are somewhere in front but out of sight.

When I pushed across on my Yamasaki, I was so much closer to things. I knew every hill, every bump. I sucked in each goddamned mile and spit it out, a mouthful at a time. I was holding down those handlebars, rattling teeth, jiggling kidneys. At nights, I was a wreck. Twice I peed blood. Also, sleeping out with gnats and mosquitoes was hell. I'd packed a tent but no mosquito net. I swear I'm allergic to mosquitoes; every morning I'd be swollen up like a balloon. Just grabbing the handle and shifting gears with thick sausage fingers was hell.

"Dad, how about if we roll down a window; OK? This canned cold air gets to me."

"Good idea. We're through the desert now."

He pushes buttons and both windows start rolling down; the bionic man. Wind blows through and around us.

"Ah, this is more like it, Bill. I get inside a box like this and lose track where I am."

Half an hour later we stop for doughnuts and coffee. Jesus, it's impossible! Just the two of us, nothing else, the bill pushes two-fifty.

The world's sure a shitload. You work your ass off just staying alive. Most any job you get only pays enough to rent a roof, feed your face and buy clothes, even secondhand junk. And there's no way to live without working; we're all locked in. Look at Gary and Marty; they've thrown the key away.

It's a bummer all right.

6

Next day, after we come back from the hospital, I begin working on my Honda. First, I spread some newspapers to catch any grease or crud. I blow out the carb jets, then pull the plugs, scrape and set them. It's been sitting so long there's *mold* on both plugs. I push the bike back and forth in gear to see if the motor's frozen but it's OK, the pistons are moving.

I clean the points and adjust the timing as best I can without proper tools. Even though I'm a crappy mechanic, I like fooling around with a small simple machine like this; it's a thing my mind can handle and I'm needing something in that category just now.

Dad comes out and watches me. He's always been such a tremendous mechanic he makes me nervous. It's the joke of our family how I'm rotten with machines. For years I was called "Hatch" because I hatcheted things requiring skill. I was away from home five years before I realized my mechanical talents were only low in comparison to Joan's and Dad's.

Dad stands over me. I point out what a fine piece of machinery a motorcycle is; nothing extra, just a motor mounted on wheels; the ideal solution for overland travel, the next best thing to wings. I know Dad thinks it's dangerous and undignified for a grown, middle-aged man to be balancing on two wheels.

I find the key where I'd hung it on the shed door. I hook up the battery, but, of course, it's run down. I pull the battery, put it in the car trunk; Dad and I drive to the nearest service station for a quick charge. They tell me there it'll take an hour.

"OK, Dad, while we wait, let's go have a beer in that bar across the street."

He looks at me.

"What?"

"There's a little bar there, let's go chug one down while we're waiting."

"Do you think that'll be all right?"

"Sure, come on, we're both over twenty-one; there's no law against having an afternoon beer in a bar. That's what they're for."

It's an ordinary bar; dim, mildly air-conditioned, an old window blower humming away. There's something I like about going into a bar daytimes, especially here in California. After a while, that high, bluish sky and the strange blankness of everything bears me down. It's a relief ducking into the dark, thick air of a bar.

We sit in a booth. This is a classic place; a few regulars are standing or sitting at the bar and there's at least one hustler working up after-lunch customers.

"What'll you have, Dad?"

"Well, a beer would be fine, but we've got plenty of cold beer in the refrigerator just around the corner."

I order two beers and ask Dad if he'd rather sit at the bar.

"Do you think that'd be OK?"

"Sure, come on."

We climb up on stools; the bartender shoves a bowl of peanuts down to us.

"Do the peanuts cost extra, John?"

"Not usually, Dad, unless inflation's really hit hard here."

I take a handful and Dad carefully picks out one.

Dad tells me he hasn't been in a bar by himself for over fifty years, not since before he got married. He's looking at the people, using the mirror behind the bar. He's peeking at the women; one of them gives him a nice smile. He looks away fast and stares into his beer.

"Do you come into bars like this often, John?"

"In Paris, it's not so much bars, Dad; we have cafés. You can sit, drink a coffee or a beer, but it isn't like this; some of them you sit outside. It's different. Not many days go by when I don't stop in one of my favorite cafés."

Dad looks as if he isn't sure this mightn't be wicked. I glance at my watch; we still have almost half an hour. I try encouraging Dad to talk about what it was like before he was married, when he was working at Hog Island carpentering with his father and brothers. I don't get anywhere. It's difficult to know if he doesn't remember or just doesn't want to talk about it. He doesn't even remember when Uncle Harry lived with us at home in Philly. That's an important part of my personal life and it's hard for me to accept he doesn't remember at all.

I know Vron has strong memories of things we did together, things I don't remember, and it's the same with me. In a terrible way, we're all alone.

We pick up the battery, drive home and mount it on the bike. I turn the key, kick it and the motor turns right over. It's a terrific feeling getting a motor moving again, bringing something back to life.

I buzz the bike up and down the street a few times. It's been sitting so long it blows off black smoke and backfires but then smoothes out. I roll in and park on the driveway. It idles, ticking over.

It's coming on to dinnertime and I consider a restaurant

but decide the business with the bar was enough excitement for one day. Dad's already missed his "soaps" and is wandering around looking at the clock, turning the TV on and off. A big part of his life didn't happen today. He's gotten to a point where that TV world is real life, and I'm responsible for a missing day.

I decide to compensate by whipping up a tasty dinner. I scrounge the freezer and find a pair of reasonable-looking Spencer steaks. I'll put together one of my quickie specials. I defrost, then fry up the steaks in a sauce made from mushroom soup. Then I pour a touch of wine over this, simmering it slowly for an hour on the back burner, set low with a cover. It comes out a savory dish somewhere between steak and stew. Using one of those toaster-oven affairs with the glass front, I unfreeze some packaged French fries, and open up a can of peas. I'm enjoying myself. Dad's out in the garden watering, then he goes into the greenhouse. I keep looking to see if he's all right but in there he's invisible to me.

Fixing a spade in the potting shed, locking its shaft in my vise; smooth hickory, shined by calluses, like time.

I set the table and call Dad. He's surprised again that I've pulled food from the kitchen; that it's hot, and on plates.

He asks if there are any onions in the meat and I assure him there aren't. I suggest we have beer with the dinner.

"We're going to get drunk drinking beer all the time, John."

"A couple bottles of beer never hurt anybody I know of, Dad. Come on, it'll help us both relax."

So we have beer with the meal and coffee after. I make a reasonably strong cup; it's instant, and only a matter of how many spoonfuls you put in boiling water, not such a big deal.

Dad pours in his usual single level spoonful of sugar, stirs it intently for almost a minute then dinks off the last drops from his spoon on the inside edge of his cup. He lifts the cup carefully, his lips sticking out the way a horse or mule goes into a bucket of water. He blows gently before he sips. My father's lips are notoriously sensitive to hot drinks.

He pulls his head back and looks into the cup, puts in two more spoonfuls of sugar, goes through the stirring and dinking routine again. This time he sips his way through the rest of the coffee as if he's drinking calvados or a good marc de Bourgogne.

"Boy, John, that's some coffee. Was that decaffeinated? Your mother and I only drink *real* coffee in the morning."

I assure him it's decaffeinated.

"Well, it certainly is strong. Is that the way they make coffee in the army?"

"No, that's French style, Dad. They drink tiny cups of very strong coffee, usually without cream or milk."

"I sure hope I sleep tonight."

After dishes, we head off to the hospital. This time Dad can point out a few street names. It's coming back. I explain how in an emergency he might need to drive Mother to the hospital.

"But I don't have a driver's license, John."

"It'd be an emergency, Dad. If it's a question of life and death, they're not going to arrest you."

I ought to have him drive me around the block a few times, for practice.

Mother's complaining. They won't let her watch TV. There's a TV hanging on the other side of the room but the nurses won't allow her a control panel. She wants to know if there isn't some way I can make them take off the monitors.

"It's driving me crazy, Jacky; those dumb green lines wiggle up and down and that red dot's blinking all the time making different numbers. It'd drive anybody insane."

I explain about the pulse and the electrocardiograph; how the nurses watch all the time.

"See, they're only using me as a guinea pig! I knew it! How's all that going to help me get better? They're experimenting on me. We pay good money and they don't care if I live or die."

Dad shakes his head.

"Now, Bette, you just do what the doctors say. They know their business. You've got to trust them."

As we're about to go, he comes out with it again. I was hoping I'd get him away in time.

"When are you coming home, Bette?"

Mom gives me another look. She has a way of not only raising her eyebrows but dropping her left eye in a slow, lewd, knowing wink. Dad sees and shrivels.

"Don't you worry, Dad; Mother's comfortable here and we'll have her home soon's the doctors say she's ready."

Mother charges in.

"Believe me, *nobody* wants to get out any faster than *I* do."

Mom insists I talk with the doctor about her indigestion theory. I tell her I'll make an appointment.

When we get home, I talk to Dad about the things he has to learn.

"I'll never remember all that, Johnny. You have to remember I forget."

I start making lists. I print these lists in capital letters with a felt-tip pen on five-by-seven cards. It's like computer programming. I reduce it all to yes-no fact, on-off thinking; binary. I try to make everything simple and clear. For example, when I say wash dishes, I list every act involved in washing dishes. There are thirty-seven distinct steps, such as: put one squeeze of soap in the water, or pull stopper from sink, wring out sponge. I hang this card over the sink. For dusting, I list all the things that need to be dusted, where the dustcloth is and finish with "put dustcloth back on hook in hall closet."

It's fun for me; and Dad enters into the spirit of things. He isn't insulted. He likes having me tell him what to do in clear terms so there's no chance he can make a mistake. It's the boss-worker syndrome again.

I put one set of cards on a clipboard with the jobs in order as they need to be done during a typical day. He carries that clipboard around. At night he puts it on his night table beside him.

Next morning he dresses himself, makes his bed and comes out, heading for the bathroom, with his aircraft-carrier cap on his head. He's reading from the clipboard as he shuffles down the hall. It's pitiful and funny, but he's happy; it's like a treasure hunt. That evening, when he isn't watching television, he goes over his board, looking at the different cards, asking me questions.

"I can do this; I'm sure I can get this all worked out."

I also begin preparing him to care for Mom. I'm worried she'll have another heart attack at home after I'm gone. So much can be done in those first minutes. Mouth-to-mouth resuscitation and external heart massage can be the difference between life and death. Dad has to learn.

I start talking to him about it, but something in him doesn't want to listen; he doesn't want to be involved with such a stressful situation. But I press on. It's somewhere in here I can't baby him.

"Look, Dad, I'll show you how. You only need to follow instructions."

He won't meet my eyes.

"This is something I learned in the army, Dad; hundreds of people's lives have been saved this way."

I hate lying to him, but I'm pulling out all stops. The only time I ever gave mouth-to-mouth or external massage was to an old lady in France and she was already dead. I learned what little I know from my personal bible, the *Merck Manual.*

When the station break and ad come on, I talk Dad into getting down on the floor in front of the TV. He lies out and crosses his hands on his chest like a corpse. He stares at the ceiling, still not looking at me. I kneel beside him, put a hand under his neck and lift.

"Now open your mouth and stick out your tongue, Dad."

He does it, I grab hold under his chin, lifting and pulling back at the same time; I pinch his nostrils shut with my fingers; he's looking at me. All the time, I'm explaining in what I hope is a calm, quiet voice.

"Now right here, Dad, is where I put my mouth over yours and breathe for you."

He begins struggling. He twists his head and turns on his side.

"Oh, no; don't do that!"

He gets to his knees.

"I wasn't going to actually *do* it, Dad, I was only explaining!"

I lie down on the rug and ask him to take hold of me the way I did him. I work his hand under my neck and stick my tongue out. I position his other hand so he can pinch my nostrils. His hands are shaking so he almost pulls my nose off. He keeps sneaking looks at the TV for the show to start again. He looks down.

"Do people do this to each other in public, John?"

"Sure, you might have to do this for Mother. If she has another heart attack, you'll need to force air into her lungs so oxygen gets to her brain. It's the only chance she'll have."

He leans back. He pushes himself up onto his feet and backs his way to the platform rocker.

"That might be right, John, but it looks sinful. Do men do that to each other? Maybe sometimes God just means for us to die."

I relax and watch TV with him. I can understand his feelings but he's got to get over it; it's too important.

At the next break, I want to show him something about external heart massage. I talk him into getting down on the floor again.

"Now look, Dad, while you're doing mouth-to-mouth, you should also give external heart massage. This is to get the heart beating again. You have to push hard, once every second, right in the center of the chest."

I lean over and begin pressing him with the heel of my hand on his sternum about half as hard as you should for effective heart stimulation, but hard enough so he gets the idea.

"Hey, that hurts! That would really hurt a woman; you'd be hitting her right on the . . . in the . . . breasts."

"She wouldn't feel anything, Dad, she'd be unconscious. It's better having a few black-and-blue marks than being dead, isn't it?"

He lifts himself up on one elbow.

"She'd never let me do that, Johnny. She'd never let me

hit her like that. I've never hit a woman in my life. I could never do that."

"You'd have to, Dad; it'd be a matter of life and death."

The program's on again; it's about some smart dolphin, if you can believe it. Dad settles with a deep sigh into his rocker. He's breathing hard and sneaks looks at me as if he's narrowly escaped from a crazed sex maniac.

While he's busy with the TV, I write out on cards, in big letters, the hospital phone numbers, the fire department, the nearest ambulance and Joan. I stick these cards on the wall over both phones, the one in the living room and the one in the bedroom. The big trouble is Dad never uses a phone. It's hard even getting him to pick up a phone and hold it when someone else has called him. To be honest, I've never seen him dial a number. We didn't have a phone when I lived at home. It's only here in California they've had one. I hate phones myself, but Christ, in this world, spread out as it is, you can't just ignore them.

So it's going to be tough preparing Dad to dial a number, then get across an emergency message. I try reducing it to simplest terms. I tape the message over each of the phones. It says:

THIS IS A HEART ATTACK EMERGENCY. THE VICTIM IS UNCONSCIOUS. COME IMMEDIATELY. ADDRESS 10432 COLBY LANE, OFF OVERLAND AT PALMS.

I have Dad repeat this till he knows it by heart. We practice dialing Joan's number with the phone on the hook till he can do it. Then I go into the bedroom and call Joan. I tell her Dad's going to phone and practice his emergency-call routine. She says she'll wait.

I put the phone down and go into the bathroom. When I come back into the living room, Dad's watching dolphins again. I crumple onto the floor in front of him and lie there with my arms spread.

"Now, Dad, I'm Mother and I've just had a heart attack. Call Joan and give her the message."

He gets up and stands over me.

"Are you all right, Johnny?"

"Yes. Now do what we practiced."

He drops to his knees and starts putting his hand behind my head, pulling away and back.

"No, Dad. Call Joan first, give her the message."

He struggles up and goes over to the phone. He dials without lifting the receiver.

"Lift the receiver, Dad."

He lifts it and holds it against his ear listening but now he isn't dialing.

"Dial, Dad."

He has the receiver wrong way around, the wire coming out of his ear.

"Turn it around, Dad."

He turns the phone around on the table.

"No, the receiver, Dad. Turn it so the wire comes out the mouth part."

He pulls it away from his head, stares at it, then slowly turns it around. He smiles. Now he concentrates on the card tacked to the wall.

"Remember, Dad. Call Joan, not the ambulance or the fire department or the hospital. Call Joan."

"Yeah, I got it, John, Joan."

He begins dialing. He dials each number with great precision, keeping his finger in the hole to and fro. From the floor I can hear the phone ringing. Thank God, it's Joan's voice. I strain to listen. Dad's holding the receiver two inches from his head.

"Hello, Dad?"

"Oh! Hi, Joan, how are you, nice to hear from you."

I loud-whisper from the floor.

"Give her the message."

"Here, Joan, Johnny wants to talk with you."

He starts trying to pass the receiver down to me on the floor but the cord isn't long enough.

"No, Dad. Give her the message, remember, the message."

"Oh, yes. I remember. Joan? Johnny's lying on the floor here, in front of me, and he says he's Mother and he's had a heart attack."

I'm not sure at this point if he's kidding. I get up and take the phone.

"Hello, Joan; guess who."

I can't get a sensible word out of her. I'd been so involved with making my invincible plan work I hadn't been seeing how funny it all is. I start laughing, too, and Dad's sitting in the chair smiling. He's glad to hear us laughing.

We practice this sociodrama till Dad has it down pat. I phone the ambulance company and ask if they'll handle a dummy call. They're cooperative and go along with it. Dad spends half an hour afterward opening the door, expecting an ambulance.

The next day he takes his usual hour making the bed. I peer in. He's carefully smoothing out every wrinkle, crawling around on his knees, checking to see if the covers are hanging evenly on all sides. I try to show how he can just pull the covers up, tuck them under the pillows, pull the spread tight and smooth it all out. It's one of those chenille bedspreads with little white bumps in a swirling diamond pattern.

Dad's worrying there are hidden folds in the sheet underneath. I'm building a Frankenstein monster. He's only got two sheets, the electric blanket and the bedspread but it's enough to occupy him for an hour.

I move along slowly with the heavy burlap sack hooked to my belt. Every foot length I push a hole in the moist earth with my staff, drop in a seed potato and stomp it down. It's like sliding eggs under a brooding hen.

I give up. It keeps him happy and gives him something to do. I have more time for myself. I begin doing my Yoga while he's fooling with the bed. I'm already fitting into Mom's routine.

Two years ago she saw me doing Yoga and went into a whole drama about it being a heathen Hindu religion and I could be excommunicated. She wanted me to confess to a priest. After that, visiting them, I carried on as a closet Yogi.

But Dad's dressing himself. With the help of his cards

he's finding his own clothes, getting washed and generally taking care. He comes out for some ham and eggs. I give him his bearclaw, too. I turn on the music. He does the breakfast dishes and kitchen, using his card, while I do the sweeping and general picking up. With only the two of us there's practically nothing to do. I scrub out the bathroom sink and tub with Ajax, then scour the toilet bowl.

I show Dad how to put his dirty underwear, shirts and socks in the bathroom hamper and where to hang his slacks. He even learns how to look in that bottom drawer for his sweaters.

The next trip to the hospital, he directs me all the way. He's beginning to enjoy his newfound capacity to participate. He even asks questions about what it's like living in Paris and how Jacky's doing in school.

Mother's groggy. I don't know whether they've medicated her or if this is the normal aftermath of a heart attack. I have an appointment with her doctor, Dr. Coe.

I leave Dad with Mom, and go downstairs to Coe's office. He's a young fellow, considerate and reasonable. He gives me a rundown on what's happened to Mother; shows me cardiograms and points out significant details. Apparently an arteriosclerotic condition has caused an occlusion and insufficient blood is reaching her heart. It's a question of how much damage was done and how well the heart can compensate. If it gets desperate, they might try a bypass, but at her age it isn't recommended. He feels bed rest with a medical approach is best.

He reiterates how it's all a dangerous and treacherous business.

I'm impressed with Coe but depressed about Mom's condition. I go back to her room and she's more awake. I tell her how I've talked to her doctor, seen all the cardiograms. She's distinctly had a heart attack, there's no way around it. I tell her she'll be fine if she only follows the doctor's advice. She just *must* relax, take it easy; she's worked too hard all her life anyway.

Her eyes moisten; she's working up her "fight back at all costs" look.

"But how can I relax, Jacky? How can I possibly take care of your father? You know how he is."

"Don't worry. We're working things out. Dad'll be able to take over when you come home. He made his own bed this morning and washed the dishes. I'm teaching him to cook. He's watering the garden and keeping the lawn up. It'll all work out fine."

Now she's crying, crying mad.

"Don't tell me. You'll go back to your beatnik life and Joan's too busy with her own family. King Kong, the big-shot wop, will never let her come over more than once a week. He won't even let her phone *me*, even though I pay so she can phone free. I know, don't kid me!"

I wait it out. Dad leans forward. He's suffering seeing Mother cry; she doesn't cry all that much.

"Honest, Bette, you'll see. I'm really trying; I'll get on top of this. Don't you worry; we'll make out OK."

Pause of three seconds.

"How long do you think it'll be before you come home, Bette?"

It's not so much the question as the plaintive note in his voice. Mother shoots me one of the looks through tears.

"*Don't worry*, Dad! It'll be a while yet. The doctor will tell us when she's ready. It costs over two hundred dollars a day keeping Mom in this intensive care unit and they don't hold people here any longer than they need to. When her heart's settled down and is working better, they'll move her to another part of the hospital, then home. We'll set up our own private little hospital for her right there in the side bedroom."

Mother's crying again.

"I'd rather be dead than live like this. You mean all my life I'm going to be a cripple, a burden to everybody? It's not fair. It's not fair this should happen to me of all people. I've always taken care of myself, exercised, eaten a balanced diet with vitamins; everything, and all for nothing. It's not fair."

This is so true. It's never been any fun eating at our house. As kids, when we sat down to eat there'd be three vegetables with each meal. Not only that, we had to drink the pot liquor from those vegetables. I dreaded meals: string-bean juice, spinach juice, pea juice, carrot juice; we'd sit down and they'd be there, each in a separate glass. No matter what you did: salt, pepper, catsup; it all tasted like dishwater. Mother'd savor these juices as if they were the elixir of life; she was a big fan of Bernarr Macfadden. Dad never touched the stuff, and when Grandpop or Uncle Harry lived with us, they got off, too; but Joan and I were stuck.

Then, every morning, we had to slug down cod-liver oil. I think if old Bernarr said cow pee was good for you, vitamin P, she'd run around behind cows with a cup. When we complained too much about the cod-liver oil, she got a brand with mint in it, like oily chewing gum. She'd hide it in orange juice, fat, minty globules of oil floating on top.

Also there was brewer's yeast. We had to take a slug of that every morning; the taste of rotted leaves and mold. This was supposed to have some other kind of vitamins in it. Mother knew about vitamins before they invented them. She ran her life, and ours, along the "live forever" line. She was years ahead of her time. Now, with all the health food stores and health freaks, she's actually more a hippy than I'll ever be.

She's right, it isn't fair. She'll never accept. I know. Right now, in her mind, she's figuring some way to lick this heart attack. And it doesn't involve lying around in bed; that's for damned sure. I can see her inventing some crazy exercise for the heart. It's wonderful she has that kind of gumption but this time it can do her in.

Dad and I get home in time for the soap operas. I go into the garden back room and collapse; the strain's catching up with me. When I wake, I make more detailed lists for Dad. I break down a few jobs like cleaning the bathroom and defrosting the refrigerator.

When the soaps are over, Dad takes me out to his greenhouse. He's a great one for starting plants from tiny cuttings, especially plants that don't flower. He has an enormous variety of fancy, many-colored leaf plants. He has Popsicle sticks stuck beside each one with the Latin name, the date and place he found it.

It's a genuine jungle. Dad's always pinching cuttings of leaves or twigs from every interesting bush or plant he gets near. In Hawaii he must've snitched a hundred bits and pieces. He packed them in his suitcase with wet towels. I'm sure Mother wasn't too enthusiastic but there's no stopping him here. Then, somehow, he manages to grow plants from these tiny snips, sometimes only a leaf or a bit of stem.

He's rigged a unique sprinkler system in the greenhouse to give a fine spray. It's tied into a humidity gauge so it turns on automatically, keeping the place jungle fresh. It even smells like a jungle; you almost expect to hear parrots or monkeys screeching in the top branches of his creeping vines. Dad spends a fair part of his free time in the greenhouse. He's more at home there than in the house.

Staking tomato plants, spindly, soft-haired, long-legged, easily bent or broken. Heavy with dark leaves, blossoms and new rounding fruit. The strong green pungent smell surrounds me. I carefully lift and catch each sprawling branch, turning it gently to the warming sun, a joining of earth to sky.

In the outside garden, Dad has avocado trees, three different varieties, so they almost always have avocados. There's a lemon tree and what he calls his fruit-salad tree. This is a peach tree but he's grafted onto it nectarine and apricot branches. The tree bears all these fruits simultaneously; it looks like something from Hieronymus Bosch.

He also runs a small vegetable garden, with Swiss chard, beets, tomatoes, lettuce, radishes, carrots; easy crops. Dad keeps this garden just for fun, says all those things are cheaper to buy than to grow but he gets a kick bringing homegrown vegetables into the kitchen.

After dinner, Marty calls. She's just come back from her gynecologist and knows she's pregnant. They've been trying for two years and she's so excited she can hardly tell me. I'm ecstatic! I'm going to be a grandfather! I put Dad on the line so she can tell him, too. He holds the phone out from his ear, listens, grins and nods his head. He doesn't say anything more than grunts of pleasure and uh-huhs but he's smiling his head off. Tears well up in his eyes, then run down the outside of his cheeks. It must be great for him being a potential great-grandfather, to know it's going on some more.

We put the phone down and look at each other. We're both smiling away and wiping tears. It's a big moment, too deep for us to even talk about.

Dad gets up and turns on the TV, but I don't feel like watching Merv Griffin *pretend* he's talking to us. I'm itching to move; I want to work off my swelling restlessness.

"Come on, Dad; let's go out and celebrate!"

"What do you mean, *out,* Johnny?"

"I know a place, Dad. It's down in Venice and it's called the Oar House. Let's go there."

"What! The *what?*"

I say it clearly and laugh.

"The *Oar* House, Dad: oar, O—A—R."

The Santa Monica chamber of commerce made such a fuss they took down the sign. There's only a giant pair of crossed oars over the door now.

This place has wall-to-wall stereo vibrating like a discotheque but with a terrific selection of music; music from the twenties to Country Western, rock and electronic moanings. They sell a pitcher of beer for a dollar and a half with all the popcorn and peanuts you can eat. There's a barrel filled with roasted peanuts in the shell and an ongoing popcorn machine. A guy could probably live on beer, popcorn and peanuts, plenty of protein, carbohydrates, and corn's a vegetable.

But the best thing is the walls and ceilings. They're covered with planned graffiti, and plastered, hung, decorated with the strangest collection of weird objects imaginable. There are Franklin stoves, bobsleds, giant dolls, bicycles, broken clocks, automobile parts. Everything's painted psychedelic colors.

On Friday and Saturday nights, people dance mostly barefoot. The floors are an inch thick with sawdust so it smells like a circus: sweat, peanuts and sawdust. The light is pinkish and constantly changing. It's the kind of place I like, a good nonpressure feeling; run-down Victorian; an English pub gone pop. There's something of an old Western bar, too.

So we drive down; it's near the beach about ten minutes from my folks' house. Dad stops in the doorway and looks around.

"My goodness, Johnny, these people are crazy. Look at that."

He points. There's a doll hanging from the ceiling upside down without any hair and somebody painted her blue.

"What's that supposed to mean?"

"Nothing, Dad, it's only decoration."

I pick up a pitcher of dark beer and two cold frosted mugs at the bar. I steer Dad to my favorite booth in back, perfectly located for the sound system. In this spot you feel the sound's coming right out of your head. I get handfuls of popcorn and peanuts, spread them on the table. The tabletop has a laminated picture of a girl in a very tempting pose. I hadn't noticed *that* before. I'm seeing things differently, like going to a zoo with a child.

We look out at the mob. There's a fair amount of pushing and flirting going on; strictly a jeans-and-sweat-shirt crowd. You're supposed to be twenty-one to get into this place and they're strict, but the girls look young. Then again, almost any woman under forty looks like a child to me these days.

Dad's watching all this. He hardly remembers to drink his beer.

"Gosh, Johnny; this is better than Fayes Theatre in Philadelphia, back in the old days."

He swings his head around and laughs. He has a way of putting his hand over his mouth when he laughs, covering his teeth. Both Dad and I have separated front teeth; I mean a significant separation, about half a tooth wide. Dad's incredibly sensitive about this. His father had it too, and I'm obstinate, or vain enough, to be proud of mine. I feel it's a mark of the male line in our family. Still, neither Billy nor Jacky has it; Marty did, cost a small fortune in orthodontics bills. I even like separated teeth in women, but you can't ask a girl to keep something like that if she doesn't want to.

Dad's so embarrassed by his parted teeth he'll never smile or laugh without putting his hand over his mouth; so he's sitting there snickering behind his hand.

We drink our beer slowly, listen to the music and watch the action for about an hour. We get home by ten. We're both tired and manage somehow to climb into bed without turning on the TV.

The next day things start fine. I hear Dad back there fumbling around dressing, making his bed. I do my Yoga and sweep. By nine o'clock he's out. He even finds his own medicine, then sits down for a big breakfast with me. All his movements are stepped up by about half. He's sitting straighter, eating faster. I remember how when Dad was young he used to wolf his food; I wonder if he'll go back to that.

We even have a reasonable breakfast conversation. We talk about painting. Years ago, I gave Dad a box of paints. There was everything he'd need, including two middle-sized canvases.

So Dad took up painting and did some of the most god-awful paintings I've ever seen. He framed them for Mom and they're hung in the bedrooms.

One trouble is Dad didn't use the canvases I'd left. He said he was saving them; saving them for his great masterpiece, I guess. He went out and bought canvas board, crappy cotton canvas stretched over and glued to cardboard. These were all of about six inches by nine inches each. Dad sees paintings as handmade, hand-colored photographs. So he paints paintings the size of photographs. He paints *from* photographs, too. Nothing I say can get him to paint from nature or from his imagination. He wants something there he can measure.

He did one painting of an Indian weaving on a vertical loom in the middle of a desert; all this on a canvas not bigger than a five-by-seven photograph. Dad is probably the twentieth-century master of the three-haired brush. This Indian picture is an outstanding example of eye-hand coordination; but it's a perfectly lousy painting.

He's also done two paintings by the numbers. This is right up his line. The paintings are a reasonable size, maybe twelve by eighteen inches. One is The Sacred Heart, the other The Blessed Mother. He framed these, too; they're hung in the side bedroom beside the bed where I'm sleeping. Again, he's done an absolutely perfect job, perfect color matching, and he's stayed completely inside the lines. These two could be used as models for a paint-by-the-number set.

But this morning at breakfast he tells me his painting career is finished. It turns out he's tried painting one of the San Fernando missions. For him it's a grand affair, practically a mural, fifteen by twenty-four inches. I hope for a minute he's really gone out to San Fernando but it's another photograph. He shows me this photo; has it squared off in coordinates. It's a terrible picture to try painting. I'm not sure I could make a composition from this mess myself. There's a clump of foreground bush, then about half the photo is empty California sky. Between the bush and sky is squeezed a yellowish adobe building, cornered at an angle to the plane of the photo. Worse yet, there are arches running across the near side of the building. It's practically uncomposable, an arrowlike thrust from left foreground to right rear.

Dad tells me how he's had one devilish time with those arches. The composition doesn't worry him but those arches drove him crazy. Perspective is a mystery to him.

After dishes, we go out back and he shows me his painting. It's hidden so Mother won't see it. It's a muddy mess with great green globs in the foreground.

I do a little drawing on it, showing him how to correct the arches and rough in a perspective idea, but it's impossible to make any kind of painting from such a piss-poor photograph. Painting from photographs is never a good idea anyway; cameras have cycloptic vision, the dynamics of bioptic human vision is lost.

I'm dying to write Vron and tell her about the baby but I'm sure Marty wants to do this herself; it's her baby; I'm having a hard time restraining myself.

Dad goes into his greenhouse. He sure spends a lot of time out there.

Soil's just right now, soft enough so the spade sinks to the shaft but not muddy. New dirt opening up, shining where the metal's pressed tight against it.

We visit Mother and tell her Marty's news. Mom takes it easily, as if she'd been expecting it. Maybe when you're almost dying, being born isn't such a big deal. She might even be feeling pushed.

When we come back, I'm still restless so I go back and work some more on my motorcycle. When I'm finished, I get an impulse to take Dad for a ride. It'd be fun rolling slowly down to Venice beach. I think the sensation of riding might help brush away some cobwebs.

We happen to have two old helmets here. I search them out of the garage. Dad's watching me.

"How about it, Dad? How about a slow ride on my motorcycle down to the ocean; it's a fine afternoon; let's go watch the sunset."

He stares at the bike.

"I don't know about that; it looks scary to me."

"If you get scared, we won't go. Let's try it around the block here one time to see how you like it."

I help strap the extra helmet on him. I don't know why he looks so out of it, not like a motorcycle rider, more like Charles Lindbergh in one of those old leather aviation hats. Also, the helmet makes his head lean forward as if it's too heavy for his neck.

I straddle the bike and kick down the foot pegs. I show him how to get on. I tell him to put his arms around me and hold tight.

"Is that the only way I can hold on?"

"It's the best way, Dad. I want you to lean when I lean, as if we're one person."

He grabs hold; I kick the starter, put her in first gear gently. We ease out the driveway and cruise very slowly up and down some of these short dead-end streets. I never get out of second gear. We roll back to the house and stop.

"Well, Dad, how was that?"

"It's no worse than riding a bicycle. I haven't been on anything with two wheels since I was a kid."

"You ready to take a chance going down to Venice? I'll take back streets and we won't hit any traffic."

"It's OK with me, Johnny, but, boy, I hate to think what your mother would say if we have an accident."

He giggles and straightens his helmet.

"There she'd be in the hospital and we'd both be dead."

"Don't worry, Dad, we're not going to get killed. I've been driving motorcycles for twenty years. We're safer than in a car."

He starts climbing back onto the bike. I hook my helmet strap.

"The trouble is, Dad, most people who drive motorcycles are maniacs. If those same people drive cars, they'll have *car* accidents."

I kick but it doesn't turn over. I give her a little choke.

"What kills you in a car is the steering wheel, the windshield and a face full of dashboard; the car stops and people keep going. On a motorcycle, there's nothing to run into; you go flying through the air and slow down some before you hit."

I hear what I'm saying and decide to shut up. It's not exactly encouraging. Dad grabs hold and giggles again.

"John, you could sell holy cards to the devil."

He tilts his head back and laughs; he doesn't put his hand over his mouth; he can't, he's holding on for dear life.

We start slowly along Palms. It's a beautiful afternoon and the sun is low in front of us. There are gentle hills along here, almost like a children's roller coaster. We lift up one side and lower on the other. We go along the Palms golf course and across Lincoln. I roll down Rose Avenue and park on the boardwalk.

We walk out toward the ocean; there are some good-sized breakers; spray is flying up, refracting the sun. There's a bicycle path built along the edge of the sand; it's well designed in easy, twisting curves.

We tuck our helmets under our arms like a couple of beached knights. There are people coming in from the water; kids are sitting in the sand playing bongos and a drunk is trying to dance with the music. It's mellow and I hope Dad's relaxing and not fighting it all too much.

We stop and listen to the music. There are a few guitars with the bongos. It's like the tropics; hard to believe Lincoln Boulevard is only eight short blocks inland, crowded with cars, light industry and thousands of signs screaming for attention. Dad turns toward me.

"You know, Johnny, I've missed my calling. I think I could be a hippy."

We stroll along the boardwalk. It's peculiar they call it a boardwalk, because it's cement and isn't up on piers. It's only a street without cars next to the sand. It might've been boards once or it could be a cross-country carry-over from the boardwalks on the Atlantic shore. Or maybe I'm the *only* one who calls it a boardwalk.

We come on a place called The Fruits and Nuts. A young couple, Tony and Shelly, run it. They take all the time in the world with us. They're interested in Mom and suggest herbs to strengthen her heart. They offer big glasses of carrot juice squeezed from fresh carrots. They make it with 'a blender and it's sweet, not like Mother's pot liquors. Dad's peeking at me from the corner of his eye, drinking carrot juice and smiling away. Tony has a beard with long hair pulled back in a ponytail. This is a surefire hippy, the enemy.

He tells Dad how he has herbs to help with blood pressure. I want to buy these for myself; I'll try anything! But Tony *gives* them to me. I'm feeling so guilty I buy some apples and bananas; Tony assures us they're fresh and tasty. He quarters an apple with a penknife so the four of us can share around.

It's hard to get away. We walk along munching our apple. Dad can make more noise crunching into an apple than anybody in the world; he makes an apple sound like the most delicious food ever invented.

"Goodness, John, those people are nice; do you know them?"

"Nope. I don't know how they stay in business either; they give everything away."

Dad takes a bite into another apple from the bag.

"Maybe they're rich. Maybe they only have this store for fun."

"Yeah, that could be it."

"But they don't *look* rich."

We put on our helmets, climb on the bike and roll slowly back to the house. The sunset is still redding the sky behind us. It's one of those balmy evenings you get sometimes in California, when the coastal fog holds off till dark.

We're just inside the house, and the phone rings. It's Marty. She and Gary want to phone Vron and tell her the news. They want me with them. I say they should come over here, we've got an extension phone.

They arrive as we finish eating. Marty's eyes are bright with excitement. We direct-dial and get straight through. Marty starts crying soon as she gets the words out of her mouth. I'm on the extension in the bedroom. It's so good hearing Vron's voice. She could be crying, too; I am. We spend ten dollars crying at each other over six thousand miles by satellite. When we hang up and I come back in the living room, Dad's pulled off his glasses and is wiping his eyes. He looks up at me.

"What're we crying about, Johnny?"

That cracks us up and we're practically dancing with excitement. We drink some wine together before they go home.

Dad turns on the TV. I'd asked Marty to bring me a book. I try reading it, but every time I start, Dad interrupts me. Reading's a vice in this house. Mother's a great one for burning all newspapers and magazines the day after they arrive. Paper, for her, is like falling leaves, a natural, continual nuisance you have to fight. A book is only paper; after you read it, burn it. Keeping books is like not making the bed. Also, reading softens the brain, ruins the eyes and gives Protestant or Communist ideas.

Dad has something of the same reaction to reading but

for different reasons. His father, my grandfather, insisted bookwork was only for girls. He educated his girls, sent them through high school, but the boys were pulled out soon as they were old enough to learn farming, carpentry and metalwork. He believed men do things; women remember and pass it on. This idea is deep in my father's family.

At about ten-thirty I sneak back into the bedroom. I don't know how long Dad stays up watching Johnny Carson.

Three days later Mother's out of intensive care. Dr. Coe tells me she'll be in the hospital two more weeks. All the tests show she's had a severe heart attack and it's going to be a long uphill recuperation.

In the meanwhile, Dad's been coming along fine. He's practically self-sufficient. One Sunday we even go sailing with a friend of mine and neither of us gets sick. We only sail inside the marina an hour or two and it's an exceptionally calm day.

It's while we're sailing I notice Dad needs a shave. I can't ever remember my father having more than half a day's whiskers. On the way home I ask if he has a skin rash; I think maybe he's missed an item on his morning bathroom list. He looks at me as I'm turning onto Jefferson Boulevard.

"No, Johnny, my skin's fine."

He runs his hands over his stubble. I wait a minute, not knowing how to approach it.

"Well, Dad, I only asked because I think you missed shaving this morning."

He smiles and runs his hand over his face, covering his smile.

"You know, John, I've never seen my beard. I started shaving when I was fifteen, and I've been shaving every morning all my life. Even before I was married, when I went hunting with Dad and the rest, I shaved with cold water. Just once, I'd like to see what it looks like. I think that'd be all right, don't you? Mother's in the hospital and I'll shave it off when she comes home."

I'm surprised at my own reactions. I'm worrying what the

neighbors will say. Maybe they'll think I'm letting Dad go to seed.

Then it hits me. I start laughing. Dad's laughing too; we're still laughing when we pull into the driveway. Sure as hell the neighbors aren't going to think we're completely broken up over Mom's heart attack.

We watch a Dodger ball game on TV. Afterwards, Dad starts up a conversation. He begins with how he's always been an Angel fan because there are too many niggers on the Dodgers. My first impulse is to back off; I don't want to ruin the good feelings we're having. But he wants to talk; there's something bothering him.

"You know, John, when I was a kid and we first came from Wisconsin to the East Coast, we lived down there in southwest Philadelphia near a lot of Negroes. It wasn't safe for us to walk through some parts of town and we'd kill any nigger who came west of Sixtieth Street or north of Woodlawn Avenue. It was like a war going on all the time.

"It's the main reason we moved to Upper Darby. I hated moving five miles from my family but we were afraid of those niggers. Saint Barnabas Church had the only school with no niggers in it and we were proud of that; even the priests used to talk about it in those days."

He stops. I wonder what he wants me to say.

"Now, Johnny, they tell us in church we have to forget all that. Our priest says it's a mortal sin having those kinds of feelings. Honest, I don't have anything personal against niggers, Johnny; it's just a feeling I get down my spine, like a dog's hair standing stiff when he's mad or scared. And I'll bet them niggers have the same feelings about me, too.

"When Bette and I go to church at Saint Augustine's, we always look around for some place away from any niggers or Mexicans. With this 'kiss of peace' business, you're supposed to smile and shake hands with the people near you, and we can't get ourselves to do this with some Mexican or a nigger.

"John, you can't change people so fast. I tell the priest in confession and he tells me to pray for love and charity.

"I pray, Johnny, but nothing comes. I'd sure as the devil

hate going to hell just because I can't work up love for a nig- ger. It's not fair. You do what you're supposed to do when you're young, then they change the rules."

He stops. I still don't know what he wants from me. I'm glad it isn't my problem, not just the race part but the whole business of somebody else saying whether I'm a good person or not. People give up control of their lives too easily.

I fix us a snack: beer, potato chips and pretzels. Dad goes to turn on the TV, checks himself and settles into his platform rocker; I sit in Mom's gold chair.

"You know, Dad, one trouble with your growing a beard is Mother'll have a fit when we visit her. You can't go to the hos- pital looking like this."

He gives me one of his sly smiles, gets up and goes into the bathroom. He comes out a few minutes later with a surgi- cal mask over his face, eyes twinkling.

"Mother wears this when she dyes her hair. We'll tell her I have a cold and we don't want her to catch it."

I choke on my beer and run to the kitchen sink. He fol- lows me, worried. I peek at him again; he looks like a distin- guished surgeon. Considering Mother's fear of germs, it's so diabolically clever.

We work out the mask routine in the hospital just fine. Dad even develops a creditable sniff and cough. His beard grows in a hurry. Within a week, it's past the itchy stage and beginning to curl over. It's curly and compact, a pubic-hair- type beard, wiry. The most amazing thing is it's a grizzled, dark chestnut. Dad doesn't have much hair left on his head, and it's white. There are still a few dark hairs in his eyebrows, all that's left of his original hair color.

But this beard is something else. It's more dark brown than white. He looks at least ten years younger, incredibly vital.

I keep catching him staring in the bathroom mirror. Those split teeth of his are perfectly framed by a beard. I have a hard time adapting myself. It's as if Dad's stepped back a generation and we're contemporaries.

Joan flips. She strokes his beard while he smiles and she gives him a big kiss. She almost laughs herself to death when we show her the trick with the surgical mask. But she's worried Mother will find us out anyhow.

During that last week, Dad and I go regularly down to the Oar House, evenings. We have our pitcher of beer and it's fun watching; one hell of a lot better than TV. We even have almost-conversations. We talk about Mother, her health and all the things we'll arrange to make the house comfortable for her. He's begun having ideas of his own. He rigs an intercom system between the side bedroom, where she'll be, and the back bedroom; even into the garden bedroom. It's a regular *Amos 'n' Andy* "Miss Blue, buzz me" affair, but it works.

Once, he scares the bejesus out of me by ringing in the middle of the night. He says he wants to check if it's loud enough to wake somebody who's asleep. This is at three o'clock in the morning when he gets up for his nighttime pee. There's a strong strain of joker in Dad.

Several times, I take Dad over to visit Gary and Marty. He doesn't say much but obviously enjoys the conversation. Mostly we talk about the new baby or how Mom's doing. We don't watch TV.

The day comes to bring Mother home. We have everything ready. Dad comes out of the bathroom that morning clean-shaven; nothing said. We drive Mom home in the car and she's babbling away ten miles to a minute. She'll have another heart attack before we even get her in the house.

I put her to bed, pull all the blinds and insist she take a nap. I hadn't realized before what a tremendous responsibility it's going to be having her home. If anything happens, it's more than fifteen minutes to the hospital.

I'm having more panic feelings than Dad. He and I share beer and sandwiches on the patio. He asks when I think he can sleep with Mother again. That one I hadn't even considered.

Immediately after her nap, I find Mom sitting on the side of her bed working her arms into a bathrobe. She wants to use the toilet, insists she can't get herself to "go" sitting in bed on a bedpan. Nothing I say will stop her. We move down the hall, slowly. She's holding a wall with one hand and me with the other. I maneuver her into the bathroom, she shoos me out and locks the door.

Dad and I hover outside, hearing her pee hit the side of the bowl, then the flush. We wait but she doesn't come out. Finally, Dad can't take it any longer.

"Are you all right in there, Bette?"

Bette, by the way, is said as in "pet."

"I'm fine. Don't hang over me so, it makes me nervous."

Then she unlocks the door. She's made up, and her hair's in curlers. Guts my mother's got; good sense I'm not so sure.

Things go a bit better every day. Mother's color is coming back or maybe it's only rouge. Our trouble is keeping her down. She's wanting to take over again. At the same time, she's complaining about how hard it is to breathe.

On the third day, we take her out on the patio. It's a warm day with no wind and she's been cooped up for a long time. It seems to help; she lies in the sun and tries to relax.

Dad's doing most of the cooking. He's justifiably proud of himself. Every morning he's out of bed by eight and we take turns sweeping or making breakfast. It turns out he's the mad sweeper, too. This drives poor Mother crazy; she wants us to vacuum; says we're only pushing the dirt around, making everything dusty.

By the end of that week, there's a full load of wash; Dad volunteers to do it at the Laundromat. He wants me to drive him there and show how. Joan's willing to do our laundry but Dad wants to do this himself.

So, while Mom's napping, I drive Dad to the shopping center and demonstrate the machines. He'd gone with Mother before, but hadn't paid much attention.

This turns out to be just the kind of thing he likes. The efficiency and predictability of it all give him enormous satisfaction. I say if he gets bored to look around the Lucky Market or go across to the bowling alley. I leave him there. He'll be off on his own in the big world for a whole hour.

When I get home, Mom's awake. She asks where Dad is.

"He's at the Laundromat doing the wash."

"Oh, Mother of God, Jacky, he can never do that! I take him along, but he's more in the way than anything. He keeps folding sheets so there won't be any wrinkles till I almost go *nuts!*"

"Oh, he'll be all right, Mom."

She snorts, instantly classifying me in the great, growing category of "simps."

"You'll see. He'll put bleach in with the colored things or some goofy trick. Joan said *she'd* do the wash; don't you two worry about it. She isn't doing much of anything else."

"It's all right, Mom, and it's something for him to do. Joan has enough on her mind."

But Mother's lack of trust gets to me. I refuse to go back but I'm checking my watch. It's like the first time you send a young child to the store alone; the temptation is to follow.

When I leave, I tell Mother I'll fix lunch soon as we come back. I can see she's feeling itchy; things are getting out of her control. It won't be long before she'll do something dumb.

At the Laundromat, Dad's sitting with all the clothes dried and piled in the basket. He's even broken down the clothes into Mother's things, my things and his. I can't believe it. And he's so proud of himself; he's sitting there sucking on a raspberry Popsicle.

"Gee, John, I had a fine time. I went over and watched the bowling. I haven't bowled since I used to bowl with Ira Taylor up on Sixty-ninth Street; that has to be over thirty years ago. I'd forgotten what fun it is. Here we are living only two blocks away and I've never even been to this place. You get in the habit of working and then forget how to have fun. It's only fifty cents a line. We can afford it and I have all the time in the world. I'm not too old."

I'm packing clothes into the laundry bags.

"Sure, Dad, maybe we can come up and bowl. I haven't bowled in a long time either."

We pile our clothes in the car and Dad finishes his Popsicle. I don't want him charging in the house with a Popsicle hanging out of his mouth; that'd do Mother in for sure. We drive the car into the patio and start unloading. Mom is out of bed and opens the side door. Dad and I carry the clothes in. When I go into the kitchen, I see she's fixed lunch.

I stand a minute trying to figure how to handle it. I resent treating her as a child; I don't want her seeing me angry, either. I decide to accept. I can't figure any other procedure more likely to discourage this kind of stupidity.

Well, that's the way our days go. Mom's into everything and there's nothing Dad or I can do right. She's even complaining Dad isn't brushing his teeth at night.

"You have to watch him, Jacky; he'll only scrub the front and forget the rest."

This is about a man with every tooth in his head. Mother has bridges across the whole back of her mouth. At first, we keep trying harder. We sweep, vacuum, line garbage pails, scrub toilets, dust, beat rugs, the whole scene; but it's all wrong.

Joan comes and I tell her what's going on. She laughs and sits down.

"Don't you know, Johnny, nobody can please Mom? I thought you knew that. Every week I come here to help with heavy cleaning like washing windows, scrubbing floors. I know she'll do it all over again, wash every window a second time, muttering the whole while. It's Mom's pleasure to convince herself, and everybody else, that nobody's as good at *anything* as she is. The world is filled with two kinds of people, Bette McCarthy and the rest. The rest are incompetent and basically filthy. Relax, Jack, live with it. You and Dad have a good time; you can't win."

Hell, I know all this. Only in my enthusiasm about how well Dad's doing, I forgot.

Joan can't get over how sharp, full of life, he is. It's hard to believe it's the same man. I tell Joan some of the things we've been doing; the Oar House, sailing, motorcycling. She thinks it's all fine but we'd better not let Mom find out.

"She'll make life miserable for him, Johnny. And if she

ever hears about that beard; God in heaven. All the noise I've
listened to about *your* beard; it'd kill her for sure."

We're both giggling. Mom's napping, Dad's out in the
greenhouse.

*Plowing for sod corn, new-cut ground turned close, one row
onto the other, small tufts of grass and reeds marking the
depth of furrows. Jimmy pulls, slowly, easily; and I lean, just
strong enough to turn over topsoil; corduroying the earth.*

The next day when I go to do the bathroom, the tub's been
scrubbed. This is too much. If there's anything a heart patient
shouldn't do, scrubbing a tub must be high on the list. Mother's
in the patio sunning with Dad. I go out.

"Mother! Did you scrub the tub?"

"Jacky, it was such a mess, rings of dirt and water splashes
all over everything, I couldn't stand it anymore. I'm sure you
two step straight out of a tub and never look back; you leave
curly hairs over everything and an inch thick of scum. I may
be sick but I don't have to live in a pigpen."

"Come on, it wasn't that bad. I just went in to scrub it out.
You only had to wait another ten minutes. For ten minutes
with a few hairs in a bathtub you put your whole life on the
line."

I'm working up a stupid mad.

"Dad and I are doing our best while you spend your time
making things difficult. Mother, I'm telling you right now, if
you don't lie back, take it easy and do as the doctor says, I fly
home tomorrow. If what we do isn't good enough, hire a professional nurse. Do whatever it is you have to do but I'm not
taking any more nonsense."

Mother looks at me, then starts crying.

"If I can't even do a little work around my own house,
what's the use of living. You know *he* can't do anything."

She flings her arm in Dad's direction.

"Joan never comes and you're only waiting so you can go
back to Europe with all the foreigners."

I turn and walk into the house while she's raving. Dad comes in after me. I'm getting lunch ready. He's upset; we all are.

"It's not her fault, Johnny; don't be so hard; it's not easy for her to relax, you know how she is."

"Sure, Dad. But remember: this isn't only the usual spoiling, letting her have her own way; she can very easily die. I don't intend to watch her kill herself out of pride, and a frustrated need to dominate.

"And you've got to stand up to her, too, Dad; for her good and yours. It's something we can't put off. If she's going to wash out bathtubs, there's no chance she'll live; I'm not kidding."

I can't tell if he understands. He's so scared he's into his nodding routine, looking serious and doing his worker-boss thing.

"You're right, Johnny. You're absolutely right. I'll talk to her. She's crying out there alone; she doesn't cry much; crying can't be good for her heart, either."

"It's better than scrubbing tubs, Dad."

God, will we have to watch her all the time? I go back out with sandwiches, beer and some Coke for Mom. She's still red-eyed, wiping away tears. She won't look at me.

"Listen, Mom. You've got Dad worried to death with your bullheadedness but I'm not going to say another word. If you want to climb up on that roof right now and start tap dancing, I'll sit here and applaud. If you get a scrub brush and start scrubbing the lawn, that's OK with me.

"Then, when you have your next heart attack, I'll try to help, I'll try getting you to the hospital on time again and maybe they can save you. If they can't, I'll make arrangements for the funeral and help set Dad up. But that's it. I *refuse* to treat you like a baby! You're a grown woman, you're not senile and it's your life. If you want to kill yourself, that's up to you."

I pause to let it sink in. She's looking at me now.

"Do you understand, Mom? There won't be another word from me. It's up to you; you take hold of your own life. I think you have more sense than you've shown so far. I think you really want to live but you enjoy pestering the life out of Dad and me. Eat your lunch."

After this it's better. Now she has to prove she isn't stupid. But her idea of what she can do without hurting herself is bizarre. I feel sorry for Dad because the whole guard duty falls on him. I shake my head in disbelief when she makes a bed or washes out undies, but I say nothing.

Marty calls most evenings and says she'll come over to spell me if I want. I tell her it's OK; I know how much Mom bugs her and almost everything about Marty annoys Mom. Mostly that she's young and has her own life.

After two weeks, it's time to take Mother back for a checkup. I call the doctor ahead of time and ask him to throw the fear of God into her because she's too active.

He does a great scene but I can see Mother sitting inside herself resisting. He shows her the X-rays but she scarcely looks. He gets out the cardiograms, explains her blood chemistry, pulls out charts to show which part of her heart is affected. It's not registering; she doesn't want to know. Afterward, when I'm pushing Mom out to the parking lot in a wheelchair, she turns and looks back at me.

"Jacky, I don't think he's a real doctor. I'm sure he's not a heart specialist. Did you see that belt he was wearing and those tight pants? He's another hippy. They let anybody get through medical school these days. He's probably only a student anyhow, he can't be thirty years old."

I disappoint her and keep my mouth shut. All the way home she stays on the same themes, knocking Dr. Coe and the Perpetual Hospital. Then she starts on the "nigger nurses." She's pulling out all stops.

I keep smiling, nodding like an imbecile and concentrate on the driving. Mother's putting on the brake and clutching all the way. I swear next time I'll slip a sack over her head and put her in the back seat.

At home, she begins telling Dad how she's had a very light heart attack, so light in fact it's doubtful she had one at all. She isn't saying anything of what the doctor told us, only what she wanted to hear. I'll give Dad a straight story later; I don't want to start her crying again. Dad's right, crying can't be the best thing for a heart patient.

After lunch she's at full steam.

"Look how the paint on this house is peeling. The garden is going to pot, nobody's weeding. The windows are filthy. We haven't had any really balanced meals since I've been home. Dad isn't taking his pills regularly, he doesn't look well and he's running around so much he's going to have another stroke."

Far as I know, he hasn't had a first one.

I try to reassure her Dad's doing fine and he's getting good food. But nothing will do. Things are slipping away from her, and she's in a minor panic; her very reason for living is being pulled out from under her.

The truth is Dad *is* getting away, gaining independence. He'll go back, and in his new breezy way ask how she's doing and what he can do. This bugs Mom, the roles have been reversed, so quickly, easily. He's bringing her glasses of water, fixing her medicine, straightening her bed, regulating the electric blanket, giving her massages and trying, generally, to help her relax. Everything he does makes it worse. She's caught in an unplanned double bind.

Dad's cooking is improving, too. It isn't serious cuisine, but then there's never been anything resembling good cooking going on in this house. Dad's opening cans of soup and making sandwiches in the toaster. He makes a couple complete dinners without my assistance; nothing difficult—lamb chops with canned peas and mashed potatoes, or some steaks with canned string beans and defrosted French fries—but it's good.

Sometimes Dad will go into the bedroom to see how Mom is and he'll forget to take off his apron; this drives her up the wall. I almost begin to suspect he does it on purpose; that apron, like his aircraft-carrier cap, has become a badge of authority. And I know all this is almost worse for Mom than her overexertions, but I can't think of any other way. I've got to leave sooner or later and Joan can't do everything.

Joan's concerned, but can't see any way out either. Dad

has to take over. It would be even worse having a professional
nurse. Mother makes no bones about that; no strangers living
in *her* house.

Well, this goes on another week. Dad's getting better
every day while Mom fumes and keeps overdoing herself.
Dad's seventy-third birthday is rolling around. We decide to
have a quiet party for him, just the four of us; Joan, me, Dad
and Mom. We don't want Mother getting involved with the
preparations, but we can't keep her down. I'm baking the
birthday cake and she's convinced I'm going to burn the house
down; wants me to buy a cake at Van de Kamp's. She opens the
oven door so often the damned cake falls. It'd drive *anybody*
bats. I haul her back to bed at least ten times. She's on the
point of tears. Her lines are:

"This might be the last birthday I'll ever celebrate with
my husband and you want to do it all. I know myself; I feel
just fine; you can't know how I feel . . ." and so on.

Joan buys Dad a pair of blue striped flannel pajamas, also
a button-down-the-front sweater from Mom. I buy him a new
dark green aircraft-carrier hat. I want to give him a roller singing canary but there's not one to be found anywhere; the New-
castle blight's almost wiped out canaries in America.

Dad enjoys helping with the cake. We do it from scratch,
no cake mix. He can't believe you can make a cake with only
flour, sugar, eggs, milk, butter and salt, with a little flavoring
and baking powder. It's terrible how far removed from the fun
parts of life most men get. We bake another cake after the first
falls, and put them on top of each other.

The party's a big success. We cut the cake and it's a bit
compact but delicious. Dad blows out all the candles in one
fell blow: seven big ones and three little. He makes a thing
about opening each present, shaking to see if it rattles, making
wild guesses and insisting on untying every knot and preserv-
ing the wrapping paper. He folds the paper carefully before
he'll go on to the next present. He's dragging out the pleasure.

"Come on, Jack, open it; stop playing with the paper; we
don't have all day."

His voice is tremulous but strong and in tune. I don't think I've heard him sing since he used to sing us to sleep when we were kids.

That night they want to sleep together. I move from the garden room into the side bedroom and Mom goes to sleep with Dad in the back bedroom. He smiles and says it's the nicest birthday present of all. This is verging on the risqué from him; Joan laughs and he blushes.

In the middle of the night I hear the buzzer beside my bed. I pick up the receiver but there's Dad at my bedroom door; his face is white in the dim light.

"Mother thinks she's having another heart attack, Johnny. She looks awful."

I jump up and run back to their bedroom. She's pale and sweating but conscious. She says she's having terrible pain and tightness in the chest. She's crying. I give her some digoxin but it doesn't help. Now I have to do all the things I've been preparing Dad for. I leave him with her and tell him to yell if she goes unconscious.

First, I call an ambulance, then phone the hospital to alert them we're coming in.

I go back to the bedroom. She's still conscious but in great pain, crying. I think she's crying mostly from disappointment and discouragement; she'd actually almost psyched herself out of that heart attack. She's also scared.

The ambulance arrives in less than ten minutes. They roll in a stretcher and oxygen; they put her on oxygen immediately. The paramedic takes her blood pressure, shakes his head and says we'd better hurry. We wheel her out to the ambulance; I say I'll go with them and ask Dad if he wants to come along. He says, no, he'll stay home and pray.

We take off in the ambulance, with the orange light twisting and sirens blaring, through the red light on Palms. At the hospital, we go straight through emergency and they move her up to intensive care. I'm left in the emergency waiting room.

Half an hour later, a young doctor comes down and asks for me. He tells me she's having another attack and they're doing everything possible. He says there's nothing I can do

Dad turns to Mom and smiles.

"Oh, yes, we do, Bette; we have all day; today's my day, all day."

He says it nicely and he's smiling but it's the first time I've heard him come back in more than twenty years. Joan looks over and gives me one of *her* looks. Joan's look is to close her mouth, with her eyes wide, so white shows all around the iris. While doing this she nods then tucks her head into her shoulders. It's best translated as "Well, I'll be damned!"

Because I couldn't find a canary, I give Dad the Swiss army knife Billy gave me for my fiftieth birthday. I hope Billy doesn't mind. There's something fulfilling about owning a knife like that. This one has thirteen different blades and instruments, including a magnifying glass, an ivory toothpick, scissors, tweezers, a saw, two blades, two screwdrivers (regular and Phillips), a can opener, a bottle opener, a corkscrew and a leather punch. Dad's fascinated and opens all the blades simultaneously. It bristles like a hedgehog. Mother comes on with the expected "simp" remark, and the three of us laugh.

"You'll see, he'll probably cut off his finger before the day's out."

She's also worried about washing the flannel pajamas; they take so long to dry.

Later, Dad goes into the bathroom and comes out with his pajamas on, his new sweater over them, and the aircraft-carrier cap on his head. He stands there smiling and opens up the Swiss knife to the magnifying glass and peers through it like a lorgnette.

Mom claims this proves he's getting more senile every day and soon he'll be crazy as his son. Dad says he feels like Dagwood, or a prisoner, in the striped pajamas. He sings a few lines from one of his all-time favorites.

> "Oh, if I had the wings of an angel,
> O'er these prison walls I would fly;
> Into the arms of my loved one and
> There I would so safely hide."

and I should go home. They'll call me if there's any major change. He means if she dies.

I need to take a piss something awful, and go into the rest room. I glance in the mirror and I'm almost pale as Mom. I'd no idea how much shock I'm in. I'm also feeling guilty about the birthday party and them sleeping together. She fooled me. She probably fooled herself, too. It's so hard to know where to draw the line.

I take a cab home. Dad's standing at the door waiting. He's still in his pajamas but he's had the sense to put on a sweater and his new cap. I pay off the taxi and go in.

"How is she, Johnny? How's she doing?"

He's close to tears; he has his rosary in his hand.

"She's OK, Dad; don't worry. She'll be OK. They put her back in the intensive care unit. The doctors are doing everything that needs to be done. They have all the backup machinery."

I lead Dad to his bedroom and help him into bed. While I was gone, he remade the bed completely in his meticulous way. I put out the light and close the door. I think of phoning Joan but decide against it. It's out of our hands. There's nothing we can do and Joan needs her rest. I'm feeling wrung out. I go back to bed and somehow do get to sleep.

The next morning I phone the hospital; there's no change. I go over things with Dad. He seems OK; he hasn't gone into any withdrawal symptoms like the first time. He's with it, wanting to help.

"This has to be a lesson for us both, Dad. We can't listen to her. She doesn't want to believe she's sick so she isn't to be trusted. We need to protect her from herself."

Dad nods.

"Yep, it's hard keeping ahead of her, John. You never know what she's really thinking."

I call Joan and tell her what's happened. She's shocked and feels as guilty as I do. She agrees to meet me at the hospital. Dad says he'll stay home, clean up the kitchen and work in his greenhouse. It's best not laying too much on him.

Mother's heavily sedated and all the monitors are on. She's tied into IV and catheter; the whole works spinning to keep her alive. The nurses remember us. They say Dr. Coe has examined Mother and wants us in his office.

We go down. He tells us there's definitely been another attack but it doesn't seem's severe as the first one. He asks if there'd been any sudden shock or stress situation. I tell about the birthday party and Dad sleeping with her. He shakes his head.

"We need to be more careful with her, Mr. Tremont. You've got to see she doesn't overdo herself; she can't take many more of these traumas, her heart's not up to it."

On the way home, Joan and I stop for a pizza. We're both depressed. We try to think out what we can do. Dad can't keep her down any more than we can. I want to remove all the cleaning equipment from the house so she can't get to it. I'll lock the dirty wash in the garden bedroom. It's like hiding razor blades from a potential suicide. Joan shakes her head.

"Look, John, we've got to let her live her own life. She has a right to that, at least."

I can't be so sure. It's hard for me to let go.

Joan says she'll come twice a week and try keeping things impossibly clean. I volunteer to buy her a toothbrush so she can clean out cracks in the hardwood floors.

We talk about my ticket; I'm almost run over the forty-five days. Joan says she and Mario will split the cost of the return ticket if I can only stay on. She knows I want to get home but what else is there to do?

Next day I take Dad to see Mom. She's conscious but still heavily sedated. She's weepy. Dad's crying, too, and in shock seeing her so low. He hadn't seen her at the worst part the first time. Mother speaks in a thin, broken voice.

"If a little thing like a birthday party is going to give me a heart attack, what's the use of living? Just to stay alive I'm not going to be an invalid all my life."

I hesitate, then play my last trump.

"Mother, that's despair; the more you talk and think like that, the less confidence you're showing in God. It doesn't help your chance for recovery and you're endangering your immortal soul. Also, it's cruel to Dad."

I hate using this line, but it's looking desperate to me. If Mother decides not to live, nothing in this world could keep her alive.

Dad looks at me as if the local paperhanger had suddenly turned into an axe murderer.

"Mother, when you talk this way, it's sinful; false pride, an insult to God and his mysterious ways."

What the hell, it probably won't do any good but it's worth the try. Mom's torn between spite and salvation, but gradually settles down. She doesn't have many choices.

Dad and I go back to our old routines. Dad begins perking up. We both enjoy the camaraderie we had before. With Mother home it was a rat race: scurrying around trying to please her; continually feeling inadequate.

First, we build a handrail for the staircase from the side door to the patio. It's healing to work with good tools and oak in the sunshine.

Later, after we store the lounge chairs and turn the sprinkler off in the back garden, we stand staring at the lowering sun.

"Johnny, what would you say if we go down to the ocean and watch that sunset?"

I jump at the chance.

"Sounds good to me; maybe get our minds off things."

Dad goes inside for his coat and I start warming up the car. Dad comes out with the motorcycle helmets.

"No use dragging the car out, John; I thought we'd go on the motorcycle."

So we strap on the helmets and putt on down to Venice. At the beach, Dad takes off his shoes and rolls up his pants as we stroll along the edge of the sea. There's a soft, slow sunset with red approaching purple. The ocean is calm; long, easy rollers. The tide's out. Sunlight reflects on the wet sand as water slides back under breakers.

There are other people walking along; a few joggers. Everybody smiles or says hello. An Irish setter is running and chasing with a young girl; she's throwing sticks, stones or shells out over the breakers. It's a magic moment; a chance to forget how hard life is sometimes.

We don't talk much. Stolen pleasure like this, undeserved, unplanned, you don't talk about.

It's almost seven o'clock and we haven't prepared anything for dinner. I suggest eating at a restaurant called Buffalo Chips next to the Oar House. It's owned by the same people and has a similar general atmosphere. In fact, you can walk from one place into the other by a backstair passage.

We head over and I find a parking place right in front. They're already checking ID cards for the Oar House because it's Saturday evening. These young guys must get a kick seeing a fifty-two-year-old dude riding a ten-year-old motorcycle with his seventy-three-year-old Dad hanging on back. A pair of them come over while I'm pulling the bike up on the kickstand.

"I sure hope you two have your ID cards; nobody under twenty-one's allowed in here."

Dad's slowly taking off his helmet, his feet straddling the bike. He's smiling.

"Well, I'll tell you something, sonny. I've been working on being twenty-one for years. This is the fourth time around but I just can't get the knack of it."

We laugh and shake hands. They say they'll keep an eye on the bike for us.

The restaurant specializes in sandwiches, from pastrami to steak. The hot roast beef sandwiches are something special. We order two with a pitcher of beer. They serve the roast beef with a good dab of horseradish. Dad and I both love it. We talk about the Italian horseradish vendors in the streets back in Philadelphia.

The crowd here is just as informal as the Oar House. There's laughing and kidding around, flirting and counter-flirting. After we eat, we go through the backstairs into the Oar House. We luck out with two seats high on one wall where we can watch the dancing. I get another pitcher of beer and we sit there in the center of chaos.

I see the ID checkers and bouncers drifting toward us. They've been picking on the younger-looking people and checking. They come up to us.

"Ah, here they are."

It's the taller one, a husky guy with a great bushy handle-bar mustache.

"I knew you guys went in the restaurant just to sneak in here."

He smiles.

"OK, let's see your ID there, fella."

Dad looks up, smiles, laughs.

"You'll have to throw us in the clink, sonny; we don't have IDs. I don't drive anymore and my son here lives in Paris, France."

It's good hearing Dad so proud and assertive.

They laugh and move on. We finish our beer slowly. It's getting close to eleven; I figure we'd better be on our way. We go toward the door. Some of the crowd's been tipped off about the motorcycle and come to watch us take off. I help Dad strap his helmet because his hands are shaking. I strap on mine, kick the starter and she turns over first time.

It's a cool, relaxing trip home. Dad's getting to be a good rider; leaning on the turns, not fighting me.

Next morning when he comes to breakfast, I see he's not shaving again. I don't say anything. We're going to see Mom at two and by then it'll be really obvious. Dad does the dishes and I sweep. When we're finished, we go out to straighten up his shop.

He has some of the finest tools I know. They're fitted to the walls with painted silhouettes in white to signal when they're not there. The tools which aren't on the walls are in metal toolboxes with rollered drawers. His old carpentry box is there too, everything in order, including a wood-handled Stanley hammer and three Deitzen saws, two crosscut, one rip. Dad's always been a toolman and knows how to use them. Dad's tools are a biography and description in themselves.

Out there in the shop, I ask Dad what he's going to do about Mother and his beard. He can't pull the mask routine again. He says he's going to tell her he's growing a beard.

"Gosh, John, she gets her hair cut and dyed without asking me; why shouldn't I be able to grow a beard if I want?"

"But, Dad, it'll kill her for sure."

He looks up at me from his bench.

"You really think so, Johnny? I don't want to kill her."

The way he says it, it's as if he's thought it through and decided not to kill Mom after all.

"OK, then, I'll shave. I'll wait till she's in better shape before I tell her."

Afterward, we go inside and he shaves before we head for the hospital.

7

We're still plodding along at a regular fifty-five. Dad seems to think he's in France driving that tin-can Renault 4L of his.

Actually, America's too damned big. We should split into five or so countries. We could have an uptight country for Puritans and phony New England liberals in the Northeast. We could have a down-home farmers' sort of country in the middle somewhere. The South could be an old-fashioned slave-based country for people who go for that kind of thing. Texas would be a militarist, Fascist country and California with parts of Oregon could be the swinging place.

On our map, we're hardly making any progress at all. Dad points his finger to a town called Glenwood Springs and decides this'll be a good place for us to stay tonight. Tomorrow we'll be going through Vail, a big ski resort where Ford used to hide when he was supposed to be President. It's beautiful country around here: pinkish rock outcroppings with shades of purple; even some blue rock, almost black.

We push hard the rest of the afternoon. Once, believe it or not, he actually cracks sixty.

I get thinking about school again, maybe preparing myself for the big knock-down-drag-out discussion.

UCSC; "UCK SUCK," we called it. All the students seemed so dull, placid, weirdly naïve. At the same time, I was continually running into karate black belts or champion archers or chess champions. I played tennis with some schmuck from my biology class and he pounded balls past me so hard I couldn't touch them. It was enough to give anybody a permanent inferiority complex.

In classes, though, I thought I was way beyond the rest. I'm asking the only intelligent questions and the professors are talking directly to me. But then, when we take exams, these freaks wipe me out. Those California robots are tough competition; I almost failed that first quarter. I'd no idea how hard I'd have to work. In their laid-back, casual, California way, they were learning like crazy.

What they knew was how to take exams. They were expert learners for examinations. They didn't bother shit learning anything not likely to be on a test. Also, they were absolutely psychic figuring what would be asked. They'd learn only *this* stuff, not thinking too much about it, then give it back in blue books.

In the beginning, I'm trying to understand. I'm asking questions and trying to think. But there's no room for questions or thinking at UCK SUCK. No way! It takes *all* your brain power passing exams. Maybe some of it's supposed to stick to the sides of your mind when you pour it back, like making pots with slip in a dry plaster mold.

Anyway, I don't want any more. I don't know what all that forced feeding has to do with survival. What good is it having a piece of paper saying you went to college, licked ass and crammed for four, six or eight years?

I can *say* I went. Who checks? I'll *say* I graduated, *say* I have a Ph.D. Who knows the difference? Nobody will call up and ask. Most times you take a job and fill out an employment form. I'll say I have a Ph.D., two Ph.D.s, what the hell, do it right. I have a Ph.D. in physics and another in chemistry.

There aren't enough people in the world who can ask an intelligent question in those areas. Hardly any *physicists* could even trip me up. They all get specialized so soon, none of them know what the other guy's doing. One peon's off tracking down a wee bit of charm from a quark falling off the side of a neutron and doesn't know from hell what an optical physicist might be into. None of them remember anything about general physics. I'll just say, "That's not my area." I'll spend three days memorizing twenty or so of those constants and I'm home free.

I'll get myself a good printer to mock up a beautiful diploma and dingle some names to sign on it. Rupert Crutchins or Part Faley. Or I'll make friends with somebody working in a registrar's office at a university; have them mail off a set of photostat bogus credentials and records for me, give myself a 4.0 average; make it impressive, scare everybody.

Most likely, I'm only going out to work in industry anyway; help Exxon make another billion or two, what's the difference.

The whole thing's so phony. If you can do something, you can; if you can't, you can't. School and papers don't change much.

Up in Oregon I passed myself off as a choker. I faked the name of an outfit and said I'd worked there. They didn't dash out and check.

Sure, I made some booboos the first few days; they must've thought I was a raving idiot. But by the end of a week I was making it, same as everybody else.

The trouble is, choking's one bitch of a dangerous job. You earn that seven bucks an hour. The third week I was knocked cold. When that cat pulls back and those logs roll, you'd better be quick getting out from under; you can wind up smashed into a pancake. Two days later I was floored again. I went in to cash out. But already I was a good enough choker so they offered me more money to stay.

You can get by with anything. I worked as a boatbuilder in

Portland. I told them I'd built boats in L.A. I looked up a boatbuilding outfit in the L.A. phone book at the library.

I've never even built a *model* boat. I get seasick *watching* a boat. But I landed the job. They set me to sanding mahogany pieces of wood and filing rough edges off fiberglass. Then I was promoted to cutting forms out of plywood using a jigsaw. An hour at any of those jobs and you've learned all there is to know.

The thing I *don't* understand is how guys stick all their lives with these jobs. No wonder they wind up stoned, or glued to the boob tube.

We pull into Glenwood Springs before dark. The Rockies stand up in front of us like a wall. The sun, coming from behind, looks as if it's trapped, totally blocked, on this side of the mountain. From here, you'd think it's dark on the other side, all the way to the East Coast.

We find a hotel built into some foothills. It's an old-time place, not a motel. There's a foyer with worn-out rugs, an oaken check-in desk and a punch bell. There's even a regulation-size pool table. The price is about the same as a motel, so we splurge. I can't remember ever staying in an American hotel before.

The room is old-fashioned, with twin beds and paint-thick, cast-metal steam radiators under the windows. This place must be freezing cold winters. In the bathroom there's a genuine bathtub sitting up on lion's paws. We take turns in the tub and there's all the hot water you could ever want. I usually take showers, but there's no shower. I fill the tub till it's at the edge, then let myself float. I make the water hot as I can stand, then gradually cool it off to cold.

I dry myself at the window while Dad takes his bath. It sounds as if he only puts in about three inches and doesn't stay in more than five minutes. He's always in such a hurry about everything.

Downstairs we rent cues for the pool table. I played some in the rec room at Cowell in UCK SUCK; I'm no shark but I'm reasonable. We play rotation. Dad's awkward as hell, looks as back of his chair. Santana is sitting at his desk, still looking at X-rays. I keep trying to catch his eye but can't.

At last he looks up and says, "OK, Mr. Tremont, I've scheduled you for the tenth of March; we should get at this soon as possible."

That's in about two weeks. Dad sits there, nodding his head. This is the boss talking to him again and whatever the boss says is right. Even though he's scared to death, he's shaking his head and smiling, putting his hand over his teeth; doing the whole thing.

I want to confront Santana about his blunt presentation, but even more, I have to get Dad out of there fast. I hate dashing off *again* without visiting Mom, but she'd see right through Dad. That's all she needs.

So what do I do now? Mostly, I want to talk with Joan. But first I need to help Dad settle down. I take him home and pour us both a drink of the muscatel wine. I turn on one of those contest shows. Dad sits in his platform rocker, not looking at the TV.

"Johnny, really; do you think it's serious?"

"Dad, if it were serious, do you think they'd wait two weeks? They wouldn't wait like this. You have an ordinary everyday cyst. You know how many cysts Mother's had taken off. It's nothing at all. Stop worrying."

At least he's listening to me.

"Oh, it's a cyst, just a cyst."

I pick it up.

"Sure, just a cyst, nothing to worry about."

I'm lying like hell. I don't know; it could be anything, but there's no sense having him worry for the next two weeks.

We try to watch the TV. There are people sitting on top of each other in something like a giant three-dimensional tic-tac-toe design. Different boxes light up and they're trying to beat each other answering questions. Dad's mumbling half to himself.

"Just a cyst, that's nothing. Nothing to worry about, only a cyst."

Sometimes he turns his head and looks out the window

at the car and I think he's seeing something, then he turns to me and smiles.

"It's only a cyst. Nothing to worry about there. Nothing at all."

I wish I could get asshole Santana to sit here and watch this. I tell Dad the lie again about the cystoscopic examination only looking for cysts. I don't really know why they call it a cystoscopic examination but I'm glad for the coincidence.

Finally, he begins to relax, to smile naturally sometimes. I go all out for dinner and cook a couple big T-bone steaks. We have beer with them and coffee afterward. We really eat. Dad enjoys this. He's coming around, gaining back some of his confidence, making up lost ground. We try some man-talk, at least as much man-talk as we can manage. It's hard with him. It's not just because we're father and son, but he hasn't had much experience.

Not long after dinner, Dad goes to bed; he's completely pooped. I sit up in the living room and turn on the television. I find an old movie I really like called *It Happened One Night,* with Clark Gable and Claudette Colbert. This might just be the most romantic film ever made.

I'm needing a woman's care, love. I'm lonesome, not just horny, lonesome. There's something about being with a woman, knowing mutual pleasure, sharing the most natural part of being alive. It's been more than a month now, sleeping alone, no one to share with, just alone in a bed.

I fall asleep in the platform rocker and wake at first light. I haven't even kicked off my shoes. That's not like me. I take a shower. I make sure I get all those walls wiped and the tub is spotless. That's how it is living around Mom. You spend your time making sure of everything. It's the story of my childhood, constantly trying to stay one step ahead of recrimination.

I work on Dad not to tell Mom about his operation; to let me break it gently, give her as much time as we can. Then we'll only tell her Dad's having a cyst removed, but not until just before he goes.

When Mother comes home, I put her in the middle bedroom again. I've rented a special mattress attached to a pump;
it's to keep her from getting bedsores. I've rented an oxygen
setup too, in case she needs it. This time we're ready for anything. I have my cuff for her blood pressure and I can take her
pulse or temperature. It's not exactly an intensive care unit but
it's a homemade approximation. I quietly read the riot act to
Mom about taking it easy. She seems willing to go along this
time.

One thing that's haunting Mother is the notion of having
a joint wedding anniversary celebration. I guess she cooked it
up lying there in the hospital. My folks' golden anniversary
was three years ago, but Joan and Mario's twenty-fifth was in
January, while Vron and I will have been married twenty-five
years in June. Mother is determined to put on some kind of
event while I'm here, even though Vron is still in Paris. Joan
thinks it might spark her up; it's just Mom's kind of thing.
Joan made Mom a wedding dress for the fiftieth celebration.
There was a mass, renewing of vows, the whole thing. I didn't
come; spending money that way seems stupid; so I'm feeling
guilty and go along with it.

Two days before Dad's to go in for his operation, we
get dressed up. Mario, Dad and I wear suits with white shirts,
ties. Joan and Mother are in wedding dresses. Joan's baked a
three-layer cake and she still has the bride and groom dolls
from the top of her original wedding cake. She also has the
decorations from her wedding, silver collapsible bells and
white crêpe-paper streamers. We decorate the dining room.

Mario and I take turns snapping pictures with a Polaroid
camera. We take pictures stuffing cake into each other's
mouths. We keep faking it as if Vron's there. Both Joan and
Vron were married in the same dress. We were married five
months after Joan and Mario, so Vron saved on a dress.

Naturally, Joan still has it and that's the dress she's wearing. She stays out of the frame and shoves wedding cake in
my mouth. Since it's Polaroid, we see the pictures right away.
It always seems like an accident Vron's not there. One time,
Mario takes a picture with my arm out as if I have it around

Vron's shoulders. He says he'll frame it so nobody will know, but he doesn't correct for parallax and it looks as if I have my arm around somebody invisible.

We do this Tuesday night and Dad's to be operated on Thursday. Looking back, it's weird; maybe Mother had some kind of premonition. You'd never know we were virtually lifting Mom out of bed, snapping pictures, then lowering her, wedding dress and all, back into bed. I hate to think what Dr. Coe would say.

Over my objections, Dad and Mom sleep together that night in their own bed. Dad promises to behave himself; I'm almost ready to rig a bundling board. Of course, in the morning, Mom knows about Dad's operation; he couldn't keep his mouth shut. I imagine after more than fifty years' confiding it's impossible to hold back.

She wants to know what it's all about. I tell her he has a cyst, that some blood showed in his urine and I took him to the hospital. I tell her there's nothing wrong except a cyst on his bladder they found in the cystoscopic examination.

Mom sucks in her breath when I mention the cystoscopic; this is something she knows. She's had trouble with her bladder since I was born. It's something she's never let me forget; "I ruined her insides." I remember as a kid feeling guilty, wishing I hadn't done it. I've heard a hundred times about my "big head." I'd look at myself in the mirror and was sure I had a head half again bigger than normal people. I do wear a size 7½ hat but I'm not exactly macrocephalic.

As a result, Mother's bladder dropped and had to be sewn up. It's always been small and she's constantly having it stretched, a painful process.

My birth was such a trauma she came home and told my father she wouldn't have any more children. One's enough and she's had it. He's to leave her strictly alone. They're rigid Catholics, so contraceptives are out of the question.

At first Dad goes along; she's scared the daylights out of

him; they stay immaculate for six months or so. They're sharing a single-row house with my Uncle Ed and Aunt Mary. I was born in early November and all through the winter, Mother's hanging out diapers and having them freeze on the line, fighting diaper rash, and I have colic for the first three months.

But Dad's a normal guy with more than normal sex drive. This is something I've only recently realized. After six months, he comes home from work and hands something wrapped in a piece of paper to Mother. Inside, there's a beautifully carved wooden clothespin, not the spring-clip type but the old squeeze kind. Dad's good with a knife and he's carved a small man from this clothespin. It has arms, hands, fingers, everything. Written on a slip of paper is "This is the kind of man you need. I'm not it."

Mom got the message. She's carried that clothespin all her life and the note is in her cedar chest of valuable things, along with baby books, birth certificates, baby bonds, war bonds, defense bonds, savings bonds.

But she's still scared, so she worms a contraceptive remedy out of a Mrs. Hunt down the street. Why this is going to be all right with the church and Dad wearing a rubber isn't, I don't know. But she's only eighteen years old. She's still nursing me, so she's probably not going to get pregnant anyway.

The remedy is to drink a teaspoonful of bleach every morning. After a few days of this, I start turning green and sickly; I don't know how Mom feels. She rushes me to the doctor when I go into a convulsion. The doctor can't figure the trouble. He asks what she's been feeding me. She says she's only been nursing and giving me a little baby food. He decides to check her milk. He asks what she's been eating, if she's been drinking heavily. She admits she's been slugging down bleach. I'll bet that doctor flipped.

As soon as she stopped the bleach, I improved. I don't know what they did after that. They didn't get pregnant for three years, so they must have been doing something. If Dad put on a rubber before he went to bed, Mother could just pretend it wasn't there.

You read this kind of stuff in all the Irish-American

novels but it keeps going on, over and over. Nobody seems to learn; humans must want to torture themselves in as many ways possible.

But to go back. Mother does know a lot about cystoscopic examinations and isn't nearly as panicked as I thought she'd be. But Dad is scared deep inside.

That day I drive Dad to the hospital for tests and pre-op things, Mother gets weepy and Joan comes out to stay with her. At the hospital, I take Dad to his room and help store his clothes in the closet. I show him where the john is and assist him with getting dressed in the hospital gown. I speak to some of the nurses and try telling them how scared he is, but they're mostly only professional. They listen but have their routines and are too busy to do much in the way of personal care.

Dad's embarrassed by the hospital gown and wants to wear his pajamas but they won't let him. The gown is a long shirt with a neck-to-bottom opening in the back and no buttons.

"Do I walk around in this, Johnny; with the back open and all these nurses here?"

I want to reassure him but can't; I don't know why hospital gowns are made that way. It's basically degrading. There must be another solution. They spend billions of dollars on hospital buildings and doctors. They charge hundreds of dollars a day, but they still use the same gown they used during the Civil War.

I settle Dad in bed and show him how to work the TV. He finds a program he likes, and it all doesn't seem so strange. I leave and tell him I'll be back as soon as possible.

The nurse tells me they'll begin sedation tonight and operate in the morning. At home, I tell Mother everything went fine. She doesn't want to stay in bed now; says she lies awake thinking; she wants to come out and watch TV.

I could move the TV back there but she wants to sit in the platform rocker.

She's lonely and is being so good about things, I help

her out and stack some pillows behind her head. I prop her feet on another chair. It's Lawrence Welk night.

He really does bounce up and down saying ". . . and a one and a two and a three . . ." I try projecting myself. How will I feel when I'm seventy? What will be the equivalent then that I'll enjoy? There'll be something, some gimmick which will interest, comfort me, but will seem ridiculous to my kids and impossible to my grandchildren. I watch and listen. Mother laughs at all the corny jokes and sight gags. She keeps repeating how young Lawrence Welk is for his age and how beautifully he dances; and how he's the same age as Daddy.

After that, we watch a movie; then I move her to the bedroom. I ease her into bed and give her some Valium.

I go back to the living room. I don't want to watch TV anymore.

I write a letter to Vron. I try telling her my feelings of lonesomeness, of feeling disconnected. I need my own place, familiar things. I feel like a grown bird crawling back into last year's crap-encrusted nest. I also feel ineffective, helpless; Vron could do these things ten times better than I can.

I go check Mother. She's sleeping fine. I put on my sleeping suit and climb in bed. I think about Dad alone in the hospital. I think about how fast things have gone downhill.

Next day Joan comes. We decide to spell each other and go independently to see Dad. I go in first. He's sitting up in bed and seems OK; says he didn't feel a thing, didn't know anything; he's sore down there but that's all.

He wants to know how it went; does he have cancer. He's very anxious.

"Find out for me, will you, John?"

I tell him I'll go talk with Dr. Santana, but I'm sure everything's fine. I go to the urology clinic and catch Santana in his office. He's wary seeing me, but we get right into it.

"Well, Mr. Tremont, I've just gotten the lab reports; there were several malignant tumors. I think I got them but we'll have to do some chemotherapy. We won't radiate, not with a man your father's age."

"But it's definitely cancer."

"Yes, a very virulent form. It's a good thing we went in and got them when we did."

"Please, whatever you do, Dr. Santana, don't tell my father. He's terribly anxious and frightened."

"Come, Mr. Tremont, you'd be surprised what these old people can take. Their children tend to underestimate older people."

His attitude worries me. He doesn't seem to understand or want to understand.

"Doctor, this is not so in this case. My father's deathly frightened."

"There should be no shock, Mr. Tremont; this was a relatively simple excision; it hardly qualifies as an operation."

I repeat, as forcefully as I can, how I'd appreciate it if he would hold off telling Dad he has cancer. I thought he was listening.

I go back to Dad and say the doctor feels everything went off fine. He doesn't ask me again directly if it's cancer, so I don't need to lie but I'm ready to.

At home, I tell Mother how bright and chipper Dad is. I go into the living room with Joan and explain what the doctor told me. Joan's more worried, as I am, about how Dad will take it than about the cancer itself.

After Joan leaves for the hospital, Mother wants to know what Joan and I were talking about; I lie and say I told Joan the same thing I told her.

"Tell me the truth, now, Jacky. Is there anything really wrong; does he have cancer?"

I'm usually a fair-to-middling liar but Mom has super antennae.

"Mother, I'd *tell* you if anything were wrong! The doctor said they got out the cyst; that's all there is to it!"

It's close, not too far off; but I know she's still suspicious.

Joan comes back. Dad asked her what she knew and she told him the same thing I did. He accepted and was glad it's all over.

Mother's insisting she has to go see Dad herself. Here

she's only been home less than a week and she wants to visit the hospital. Joan and I succumb; if that's the way she wants to die, OK. Joan needs to go home and cook for her mob; I say I can manage it myself.

I make dinner, keeping an eye out so Mom doesn't come out of her bedroom checking to see her idiot son isn't burning up the kitchen.

Mother doesn't comment on the food but she doesn't complain. After dinner we go back to her room and she tells me what she wants to wear. I get clothes from drawers and off hangers. She says she can dress herself while I do the dishes. I'm wiping off the dining table when I hear her shuffle into the bathroom. I phone the hospital, and ask if a wheelchair can be ready in the lobby.

When I put down the phone, she comes out of the bathroom. You wouldn't believe she could possibly be sick. Mother is a master of disguise. Her hair is fluffed out and she's wearing high heels. She's tickled pink with herself; the way things look means a lot to her. I'm almost ready to call back and cancel that wheelchair. It's going to look ridiculous pushing her through the hospital glowing like this.

But it only lasts a minute. She's made her show, now she's getting pale under the color. I help her into the platform rocker.

"You sit here, Mom, and get your breath. Have you taken a Valium?"

She nods her head. I'll never know if she did or not.

"Do you have your digoxin with you?"

She pulls a bottle out of her purse. She doesn't talk; she's still too fatigued, or in pain. Mom's a tough cookie.

I go warm the car and roll it out of the patio. I close the doors and sit there gunning the accelerator, giving Mom a chance to calm down. I go in and she's up; I help her into the car. She doesn't want to lie out in back, wants to sit in front. She pulls out the eyeshades she uses for sleeping and puts them on. Damned smart idea. She's way ahead of me. So long as I don't do anything sudden, she'll be fine.

I drive like a one-man funeral cortège through the back-from-work traffic. A couple guys look in to see what's up with this jerk driving in the right lane at twenty miles an hour. What they see is an old lady with the darkest, opaquest sunglasses, sitting straight up in the front seat ignoring everything. I try talking with her but she's holding herself in. It finally dawns on me she's just holding back from crying. Maybe Mom *is* a witch; it'd explain a lot.

The wheelchair is waiting; I help her in it and wheel her through the parking lot, past the reception desk, to the elevator. Mother turns her head.

"It scares me just being back in this place, Jacky. When I think of being sick, I think of niggers and Japs."

We get to Dad's floor and I'm hoping he's asleep or under sedation. If only she can visit him, see he's OK, then we can go.

I roll her into his room and immediately I know something's wrong. I'm tempted to twist the chair right around and push Mother out of there. I should have, but I'm going into light shock myself.

Dad's awake. Boy, is he ever awake! His eyes are wide open so you can see the blue isolated in the white. He glances at us when we come in but there's no sign of recognition. He's twisting the sheet in his fingers and staring at the door to his room.

I quickly go to Dad and take his hands; they're ice cold. He looks at me, briefly; nothing; tiny concentrated pupils. He turns away with a jerk as a nurse goes by the door.

When he looks at me again, his lips start trembling. His whole body is shaking; he's trying to speak. I bend close to listen. His voice comes out, rattling, juicy, deep, scared.

"What's that! What's that out there?"

I'm torn between getting Mom away and comforting him.

"It's nothing, Dad. You're here in the hospital and there's nothing the matter. You're fine."

He looks me in the eyes without belief, neither in what I'm saying nor in me. Mother has pulled herself up beside me. Somehow she's gotten out of the wheelchair and reaches past me. She leans over and kisses Dad. He kisses back, lips puckered big, like a child kissing, burlesque of a kiss. Mother isn't crying yet; she whispers in Dad's ear.

"Hello, Jack, sweetheart; are you all right?"

She holds his face in her hands. He stares that same round-eyed, childlike stare at her. He smiles but it's not a real smile; it trembles, a smile of a child smiling on command. Mom holds his head against her breast and runs her hands over his bald head.

"Baby, what's the matter?"

She looks at me in despair, tears starting to roll down her cheeks. She mouths the words, "What's the matter with him, Jacky?"

I don't know what to do. I lean out, signal to the desk frantically. Mother could just up and die right here. How much can a heart take? My own heart feels as if it's jumping into my mouth. I can't make myself pull Mother away from Dad.

No nurse comes. I hold Dad's hands while Mom holds his head. He makes no resistance. We hold him like that, hoping he'll come back. He's gone, this is only a shell; whatever he is is gone.

He keeps trying to see past me out the door. The reflection in the glass has him frightened. I go over to show him it's nothing, only a glass door reflecting light. I run my hand in front of it, explaining all the time. He's not comprehending. He's frightened at a level beyond anything rational. Finally a nurse comes. I stop her at the door.

"What's happened?"

She looks at me, coldly, disdainfully.

"Why? Is something the matter?"

"Is he under heavy sedation?"

She looks at the chart.

"No, not really. It's not necessary in a case like his."

"Then what's the matter with him? He doesn't recognize us and is in terrible shock."

She comes in past me. Mother's still holding on to Dad's head. She glances at the wheelchair.

"What's that doing in here?"

I hold myself back. No scenes.

"My mother's a heart patient, only five days out of the hospital."

She looks at Mother, then leans forward to hold Dad's wrist for his pulse; she slips on her cuff and takes his blood pressure. I'm having that terrible smothering feeling you have when you know you're not getting through.

But the BP and pulse mean something to her. She looks into Dad's eyes and feels his head. Mom is starting to sob. I go to her.

"Whatever can it be, Jacky? He doesn't even know me. What can be the matter?"

"Come on, Mom, sit down over here. The nurse can handle this. They probably doped him up so he's half asleep; after an anesthetic you know how it is."

God, I wish it were easier lying to her. But she lets me take her back to the wheelchair. I know I need to get her away and home. Or maybe I should leave her here in the hospital. If she doesn't have another heart attack now, she's never going to have one. I go close and whisper to the nurse.

"I'm taking my mother home, then I'm coming back. I want to see Dr. Santana immediately."

She looks at me, low-level authority brimming in her eyes.

"Dr. Santana was already here to see your father this afternoon. He's not in the hospital right now."

I begin to smell the rat.

"Look, you have the hospital call Dr. Santana. Tell him there's been a tremendous change in the condition of Mr. Tremont and that his son Dr. Tremont wants an immediate consultation."

I figure now's the time to get some mileage out of that dumb Ph.D. Her eyes light up at the word "doctor."

Twenty years ago, I helped run a study on nurses. We were trying to find out what made some nurses stick it and others drop out. The ANA was financing the study; they wanted to avoid training nurses who didn't have it. It was a three-year study in depth and breadth. The two factors we found most highly correlated to long-term professional continuance were a father fixation and sadistic tendencies. The ANA didn't publish our results.

But I can see I've automatically fitted myself into the father role with this girl. I'm now one of the white coats. I'm sure she'll call Santana.

In the lobby I phone Joan. I give her a quick idea of what's happened and ask if she can come stay with Mother. She'll be there in half an hour. Mom cries all the way home and I'm trying to calm her. I have a hard time keeping panic and anger out of my voice, so I'm not much good. It'll be better with Joan; she hasn't actually seen Dad.

I get Mother into bed and give her two Valium. She insists I'm making a drug addict out of her but I know somehow I need to get her to sleep. Joan comes just after Mom's swallowed the pills. She walks into the bedroom and Mother breaks down again. Joan looks across the bed at me while she's hugging Mom. She begins to look scared too; it must be in my face. I leave them alone and go into the bathroom. I look awful. I comb my hair, wash my hands and face. Joan comes out of the bedroom as I leave the bathroom.

"What is it, Jack? Mother says Daddy's crazy. What's happened?"

"I don't know, Joan. I'm going back. If my suspicions are right, Santana told Dad he has cancer and Dad's gone into shock. I asked them to get Santana there."

I put my coat back on.

"Keep an eye on Mom. I don't know how she survived this. I don't know how *I* did."

"Now, you take it easy; you're fifty-two years old, you know. Don't go around playing macho-hero."

When I get to the hospital, Santana is in Dad's room. There are two nurses with him. He turns to me.

"What is this, Mr. Tremont? I don't see anything drastically wrong with your father."

I look at Dad; he's grinning and nodding with his "Yessuh, boss man" smile.

I hope he really is back in contact, but he still seems traumatized.

"Dad, do you remember seeing Mother today?"

He stares at me, no response. He isn't even blinking his eyes. He begins nodding his head up and down again. He's staring and smiling at Santana.

"That doesn't look like normal behavior to me, Dr. Santana. I consider it serious. He doesn't recognize me and he didn't recognize his wife."

This gets to Santana. He uses his light to look in Dad's eyes, checks his pulse. He leans forward toward Dad.

"Mr. Tremont, this is Dr. Santana. Do you know who I am?"

Damned if Dad doesn't start it again, nodding, smiling, saying, "I'm fine, yes, I'm just fine, Doctor. Thank you."

Santana leans back, turns to me.

"Yes, he's in shock."

He sends the nurse out to get some medication. He motions me to go outside the room with him. He's being more reasonable now.

"This is standard with older people, Mr. Tremont. They often go into delayed shock like this even after minor surgery. He has a history of arteriosclerosis, you know."

I nod. I'm trying to hold back, trying to think it out.

"Well, this is a form of senility—"

I interrupt.

"But he wasn't senile when he came in, Doctor. Why should he suddenly go into senility?"

Santana runs his hands through his hair, sighs.

"Senility is a strange thing; it can go on and off. You get a stress situation like this and it crops up. We don't know as much about these problems as we'd like to."

I figure now's good a time as any to ask.

"Dr. Santana, today did you tell my father he has cancer?"

He stares at me and steps back. He doesn't have to say anything.

"I told you before, Mr. Tremont, I have an ethical obligation to be honest with the patient."

"Do you mean, even after I warned you of what might happen, you disregarded my advice completely and told him?"

I point to Dad.

"Just look what your ethical honesty has brought about!"

I stare Santana in the face. I'm talking in a whisper but I'm furious. Santana is a little guy and steps back again; maybe he's worried about his surgeon's hands.

"It could also be physiological, Mr. Tremont. Perhaps as a result of the operation, or the anesthetic, there was a reduction of blood circulation to the brain. That could cause this kind of reaction. I'm sure rest and proper medication will correct the situation; don't you worry."

My impulse is to attack, but I back off. I'm too emotionally involved to be effective.

I stay with Dad for another half hour, trying to make contact, but he's unavailable. He's not my father at all. Whatever Dad is as a person is not there. There's a monkeylike quality in the way his head is hunched inside his shoulders, something he never did; he's using his hands to caress and feel everything. He's rubbing his lips one over the other, grimacing, smiling and muttering in a totally unrelated way. I've watched my share of mentally disturbed people but never one I love.

I go home. I tell Joan Dad's still the same, that I've seen the doctor. I want her to visit; maybe he'll recognize her. She says Mom is being reasonable but is terribly shaken up; she's convinced Dad's crazy.

Joan leaves and I go back to see Mom. Joan has pulled all the blinds and Mother has a cloth on her head. This is an all-purpose family remedy for anything; even if you don't have a fever, put a wet cloth on the head. I think it's more a signal "I'm sick" than anything else. But Mom looks bad. I sit on the bed beside her. Now she starts with the theme that becomes a common one.

"There's craziness in that family, Jacky. Daddy had a cousin who was deaf; Orin, his brother, wasn't quite right in the head."

This is one of my uncles, who is very eccentric, I must admit.

"Joey's another one, a drummer in a jazz band. They finally had to put him in a crazy house, too."

Orin's son, called Joey, had a serious motorcycle accident,

causing a skull fracture, so he had to retrain his motor skills.

Mother goes on and on. She's apparently kept a careful list of all the Tremonts back three generations. She even brings in my grandfather's first cousin, who, as a young man, climbing through a fence in Wisconsin with a shotgun, blew off his lower jaw so he could never eat properly. He lived his life out as a hermit in the woods.

She doesn't miss one variant. Everyone in my father's family who has been in any way abnormal is on her list.

I don't argue with her, but my father's family is, at least, normal. There is no suicide, no divorce, no crime. They generally work hard all their lives. There's no real alcoholism. Uncle Pete might qualify but he worked till he was seventy, so he's not exactly an alcoholic; he just drank a lot. All my first cousins on my father's side, and there are almost thirty of them, work for a living. The state has made money in Social Security off this family.

Now Mom starts her story about Dad. How he was always peculiar; how when she was about to marry him, Aunt Trudy, Dad's oldest sister, warned her.

I can imagine the warning. The Tremonts are a great bunch of kidders, and Mother has never understood teasing or kidding. Vron's the same way. It isn't worthwhile because they don't play along; they get mad. Also, sometimes Mother will pick out something said in fun, treat it as serious, then use it to her advantage. I suspect Aunt Trudy calling her brother Jack "peculiar" is in this category.

And—oh, God!—Mom's convinced Dad isn't quite white. My granddad, Dad's Dad, was half American Indian: Oneida, one of the Iroquois nations. But to my mother he wasn't Indian, he was nigger. My father does have a darker-than-Irish skin and beautiful full lips, shovel-shaped teeth. He also has a prominent eye-socket ridge, and high cheekbones. As he's gotten older, he looks more and more like the Indian on an old nickel.

Also, Mother has a friend named Fanny Hogan. This might be one of the most vulgar women in the world. They've been friends since they were twelve. Fanny has a loud, deep, fruity voice. She divorced her husband after driving him into a loony bin, then kicked her only daughter out of the house at sixteen. She's lived alone since. As a child I hated and feared this woman.

For years, Fanny ran Mother's life, told her what clothes to wear, picked her boyfriends. Mother likes having somebody tell her what to do, so she can complain. That's probably not too original a pattern. When Mom met Dad, Fanny Hogan was jealous.

Fanny told Mom Dad was most likely a good part nigger and she'd have little black pickaninny kids. Somebody'd snuck into the woodshed was the way she put it. She insisted Mother could make sure by looking down Dad's backbone; it would be a deep yellow or brown at the bottom. Mother's dragging Dad to the shore when they're dating so she can get a look, but they wear one-piece suits, all one piece top and bottom.

The night they're married, and finally in bed, Mom keeps turning on the light, looking down Dad's back to see if she's married a nigger.

Mother's always nourished the idea she's married a man with a genetic deficiency. And now, finally, it's beginning to show.

I don't want to get angry. I know Mother is only trying to protect herself. She has such a terrible insecurity about her own value, about her own continuity, about everything she is, she strikes out in every direction; and the more frightened she is, the worse she gets.

I wish I'd understood this better when I was a child. So long as everything goes well, Mother is generous and kind. But if she feels threatened, she turns into a holy terror. If she feels jealous, or unloved, or ignored, it's impossible.

I sit for an hour and listen. I hold back; this is something Mom needs to do. She's preparing to have Dad die. If she can make him seem unimportant, she'll be able to bear it. At least that's my rationale as to what her rationale is. Who knows what's really going on?

Joan comes back from the hospital. Mom's finally asleep and I go out to the living room. Joan's crying.

"It's awful, Jack. What can be the matter with him?"

I tell her what the doctor told me.

"No, Johnny, it's more than that. There's something seriously wrong. He's scared to death; I've never seen anybody so scared."

Joan calls me Johnny on stress occasions; the last time was when she miscarried at five months visiting us in France. I was Johnny when we were kids.

Joan gradually calms down. I go over everything I can think of to reassure her. She needs comforting so badly, she's willing to believe almost anything.

Finally, we decide it's best if she go home. I'll take care of Mom. In the morning I'll visit Dad and let her know right away how he is.

Later, I call Marty and give her some idea of what's happening to Dad. She starts crying, so Gary comes to the phone. I tell them to stay out of all this. Their job is having the baby. This is my job now.

"Mom and I aren't going to be having any more babies and the best favor you two can do us is having yours."

They try to argue but I insist. I tell them I'll yell for help if I need it. I promise on a stack of Bibles. This whole business is between Joan and me.

9

In the morning, we have ham and eggs at the Pizza Hut. While Dad's paying, I roll the car down to a gas station. They have eight-tracks for sale on a revolving rack. I make the big move and buy a Dylan tape.

I check the water, oil and battery. There's enough motor to power a locomotive there. The battery's big as a box of apples; the dipstick's so long I could break my neck holding one end looking for oil on the other. Then, the damned machine drinks twenty-two gallons of gas.

We've beaten most of the trucks out and start winding through beautiful country. I pull my tape out, fool with the dials and slip it in. I balance the speakers and we're wrapped in sound. I look over to see how Dad's taking it, but he's hunched hard-eyed over the wheel, as usual.

I lower the reclining seat, and watch the scenery float

past. The sky gets bluer as we get higher and the air is sharp clear. The trees are more pine, less deciduous. The sound system is so great it's almost like earphones. I'm drifting along.

We go through the tape a couple times. The breaks aren't bad. Trouble with eight-track is each part's exactly twenty minutes; breaks can come anywhere.

We're into the second song again when Dad asks if we could turn it off for a while. OK. I don't want to make a scene, but I can't keep my mouth shut.

"What's wrong with Bob Dylan, Dad?"

He looks up quickly and smiles, one of his Yoga-meditation guru smiles.

"Nothing much, Bill; only two hours solid is pushing it."

"Gee, Dad, these songs are important. He's singing about things we should all put our minds to."

"Please, just for a while, Bill. We can listen some more later."

We cruise along quietly; packed silence.

"He's better than those Mafia-type moaners, Dean Martin, Bing Crosby, Frank Sinatra, Perry Como, those guys you and Mom like so much."

He doesn't say anything.

"Christ, all they do is take some dumb simple idea like 'I love you' or 'kiss me' and grind away at it."

I'm not sure he's heard me. He can block off completely when he wants to.

"Well, Bill; let's see if I can explain my feelings.

"First, it's been so easy for so damned long. My generation started marrying, settling down at the beginning of a thirty-year boom. Most of our friends are semiretired, with a house on a hill, a pool and a Cadillac.

"Hell, anybody white and half bright who even tried could make it. And you kids grew up in the middle of this. Nobody can get excited struggling for something they've always had. We're accustomed to twenty-minute showers, thick, six-foot-long towels, clean underwear every morning, wheels, freezers full of food, stereos, the whole thing. And, on top, there's the business of 'having' to go to school."

Boy, he's getting close. Billy boy, you'll never learn!

"Now, today's kids want to hear about *hard* times, *hard* people. Guys like Bob Dylan tell them. You know, Dylan's name is Zimmerman, comes from Hibbing, a town outside Duluth, Minnesota. He's singing Tennessee because Tennessee is supposed to be manly, poverty, earthy talk. Actually, he's imitating Woody Guthrie imitating an Appalachian dirt farmer. And he's not out in a corn patch singing those songs, either. He's in a recording studio, surrounded by technicians. There are different specialists with blenders, dampers, amplifiers; mixing, putting together all the honky sound. It's totally computerized; not even Dylan ever hears himself sing the way it sounds."

Now he's the technical genius. Hell, he can't play "Jingle Bells" on a harmonica without making mistakes. I dread Christmas. Every year he whips out his harmonica and massacres all the Christmas carols. How far is it to Philadelphia?

"But that's OK, Bill. It's just *I* don't want to hear about hard times; it doesn't interest me. Dylan's only another entertainer like Crosby, Sinatra or Como. It's what he's paid for; singing things people want to hear. Dylan's worked up a voice that's just right, black enough but not too black, red-neck but not hick, an acceptable squeak of poverty. Here's a nice bourgeois Jewish boy who's been turned into an event."

He's quiet. I'm praying he's finished. I'll hide the tape in my knapsack, forget about it.

"One more thing, Bill. There's the voice. I'm not talking about the Tennessee accent but the voice itself. It violates me. There's something tight-jawed. I don't feel this is a rational person with whom I can talk, work it out. There's hate in that voice, just generalized hate."

Oh, boy! I can see there isn't going to be much Dylan played on this trip. I only wish I could get my eight dollars back.

We're behind a whole line of trucks on the way up Loveland. The old man isn't about to pass, either, so we lug along at thirty, thirty-five. The car's heating up. At this altitude, in midsummer, any water-cooled engine is in trouble.

At last, the road widens and we come to Vail. It's the American idea of a picture-postcard town, like the place in Austria we skied when we were kids. Only it's blown up five times normal size. It reminds me of Santa Cruz: Twentieth Century National Forest style, everything wood and glass.

We stop for gas, then go into a restaurant. We have flap-jacks with eggs and real maple syrup. I lay it on, all over the platter and let it soak in; lots of butter, too. We don't have maple syrup in France.

When we're back on the road, I push in the tape again. What the hell, I've got eight bucks invested. I can't just throw the damned thing away. I balance the speakers, low, and I'm inside that harmonica. Outside it's beautiful: clear sun and deep drops on both sides with pine trees all around. I watch huge cumulus clouds booming ahead and let that music come into me.

I don't know where Dad's mind is. We're in the same car but it seems as if he's a thousand miles away. There's no sense keeping up a conversation; it doesn't go anywhere. He's prob-ably still sweating all that crap in California.

I don't know why it is but I don't seem able to save money. I get a chunk together and it disappears. Sometimes I think I have holes in my pockets; I have it, then when I reach for it, it's gone; like I dreamed it.

I'm working in that boatbuilding place, sleeping in a sort of flophouse, trying to get a bundle together when I get a letter from Mom saying Dad's in California and Grandmom's had a heart attack. I hitch down there, figuring maybe I can help.

By that time Grandmom's out of the hospital but Grand-dad's totally bonkers. He's gone, flipped. He doesn't know who I am, doesn't know who my father is. And Dad looks awful; he must've lost fifteen pounds since I last saw him. He's pale, balder, grayer; worried-looking. I move into the garden room; Dad's sleeping in the side room.

I stick it for more than a week, then Tom comes down from Santa Cruz. He's cut out, too, and has a car. My folks own a forty-acre hill in Topanga Canyon, so Tom and I move up there. Tom has a terrific battery-driven stereo and a tent.

We haul water in the car and shop at the Topanga market. I borrow Dad's little Honda 175 and we ride it over those fire trails, ducking the fire department. I take a few spills and knock in one side of the gas tank, bend the brake pedal and break off the clutch handle, but I pound out the tank, spray it with some paint, bend the brake pedal back into place and replace the handle. When I'm finished, you'd hardly notice.

While Dad's with Granddad in the hospital, I come down and sit with Grandmom. That woman's absolutely insane. All day long, it's "Why don't you shave off your beard; what're you hiding from?" or, "Why do you wear that long hair?" or, "If you must have long hair like a girl, at least wash it."

God, it's a constant hassle. One day she comes at me with a pair of scissors. "Here, Billy, I'll just cut off this one part sticking out over your ear." I duck away. "Come on, don't be silly; let me trim your neck anyway."

Then sometimes she comes into the back bedroom while I'm sleeping, after she's supposed to be in bed. She comes sliding in, snooping into everything.

One day she goes through all my underwear; throws them into the bathtub and washes them. She's supposed to have a heart attack and she's washing *my* underwear. She tells me no girls like boys with dirty underwear. What a mind!

Then she asks if I know how to wipe myself properly. I almost expect a demonstration. She tells me to use several sheets of paper folded over and wipe from the outside, not between the legs, and to wipe at least three times. I can't believe it; she has no idea of privacy. I don't know how Dad takes it; imagine having her for a mother.

Finally I blow up. Dad's out painting and she's been bugging me all afternoon, wanting to know if I go to church, if I'm still a virgin, do I have a steady girl. I tell her she's driving me crazy, she's driving Dad crazy and she probably drove Granddad crazy. She has a crying fit, goes into her bedroom and slams the door.

When Dad comes home, I tell him what happened.

"What the hell, Billy, you know she's sick."

He doesn't sound mad, only discouraged. I feel like a shit, but I've about had it. Tom's gone back to Santa Cruz; he left me his tent. If it gets too bad, I can always move back on the hill again. Tom's going to be a psychologist.

Hell, there're already too many psychologists; too many everythings. Too many engineers, too many chemists, too many doctors, too many dentists, too many sociologists. There aren't enough people who can actually *do* anything, really know how to make this world work.

When you think about it; when you look at the way it really is; God, we've got—well, let's say, there's 100 percent. Half of these are under eighteen or over sixty-five; that is, not working. This leaves the middle fifty percent. Half of these are women; most are so busy having babies or taking care of kids, they're totally occupied. Some of them work, too, so let's say we're down to 30 percent. Ten percent are doctors or lawyers or sociologists or psychologists or dentists or businessmen or artists or writers, or schoolteachers, or priests, ministers, rabbis; none of these are actually *producing* anything, they're only servicing people. So now we're down to 20 percent. At least 2 or 3 percent are living on trusts or clipping coupons or are just rich. That leaves 17 percent. Seven percent of these are unemployed, mostly on purpose! So in the end we've got 10 percent producing all the food, constructing the houses, building and repairing all the roads, developing electricity, working in the mines, building cars, collecting garbage; *all* the dirty work, all the *real* work.

Everybody's just looking for some gimmick so they don't have to actually *do* anything. And the worst part is, the ones who *do* the work get paid the least.

I know I'm not the first one to figure this out, but I think even Marx was only looking for a way out of work; Lenin, too —two more middle-class slobs.

So Tom's going back and be a psychologist. He can join the vast army of psychologists catering to all the people feeling guilty because they aren't doing their part. Not only that, none of them can even take care of themselves anymore.

I wonder where the hell *I* fit in with all this.

10

The next day I phone Dr. Ethridge. He's been Dad's doctor at Perpetual the past fifteen years. After being put off several times by switchboard operators and nurses, I get through.

I explain what's happened. Ethridge goes into his act.

"Ahh, Mr. Tremont, this kind of thing happens all the time. Dr. Santana knows exactly what he's doing; he's a fine young surgeon. I'll go see your father this morning; he's been a patient of mine a long time. You know, we both come from Wisconsin.

"We might just have to accept it, Mr. Tremont, this could be the onset of senility."

He's giving me the same bullshit as Santana.

"So fast, Dr. Ethridge, instant senility? I've never heard of such a thing."

"Well, Mr. Tremont, you know he was getting forgetful."

I keep at him.

"But, Dr. Ethridge, he went in for the operation perfectly aware and now . . . well, wait till you see him."

I pause, he doesn't say anything.

"Dr. Ethridge, would it be all right if I come with you when you see him this morning?"

There's a pause again. He could be reading or writing something at the same time he's phoning.

"Oh, no, that won't be necessary. I'll see him on the morning rounds and phone you after lunch."

He hangs up.

I tell Mother I've talked to Dr. Ethridge and he feels everything is going to be all right, we aren't to worry. Of course, she wants to go see Dad.

"No, Mom, the doctor says we're not to visit; he needs rest and sedation. Dad's nervous and anxious about the operation; an older man like him doesn't adapt easily."

"Jacky, if we can only get him home, he'll be all right."

She's convinced if we can get him out of the hospital, he'll be perfectly fine. She can take care of him and that's what he's used to, "instead of niggers pawing him over."

"Mother, *you* can't take care of him. If we bring him home, I'd have to do it and I'm sure they can do a better job with him at the hospital."

Dr. Ethridge finally calls at four.

"Mr. Tremont, I saw your father and at this time he seems confused. I also talked with Dr. Santana and he feels you've attacked his professional judgment."

This gets me.

"Dr. Ethridge, Dr. Santana was absolutely wrong telling my father he had cancer after I'd warned him repeatedly concerning his unnatural fear of this disease. The result is there now. My father fell into this state immediately after Dr. Santana told him."

"Mr. Tremont, these are decisions we doctors make. If your father uses our hospital facilities, you must trust our judgment in these matters."

Then he goes into a harangue on the theme "we know our business." I listen till he winds down.

At this point, I'm ready to drop Ethridge, Santana, Perpetual, the whole mess, and start over. But I don't; I'm too unsure, angry, scared.

Dad's in the hospital five days. I spend all the time with him I can. Joan spells me with Mother. I talk to Dr. Santana every day and he's getting more and more nervous. I never let a day go by without asking for neurological and psychiatric testing, observations. I'm combing a new copy of the *Merck Manual* I bought at the UCLA medical library, looking for some reasonable explanation to what's happened.

I'm up against stone walls with the hospital staff. At the same time, I'm trying to stay calm at home around Mother, assuring her everything is proceeding fine.

At the hospital they keep telling me it will all go away when he recovers from the shock. But Dad continues in his deep, disturbed, anxious, removed condition. He's lost control of his bowels and bladder. He needs to be hand-fed and it's very difficult feeding him. He doesn't have any desire to eat, and is beginning to waste away. All his senses seem cut off.

The nurses are too busy to get sufficient food into him. I take over the feeding; they don't mind much. It can be two hours just getting half a small meal down. It's worse than feeding a six-month-old infant. He bites down on the spoon so it's hard to get out. He twists his head back and forth. A good part of the time I'm waiting for him to swallow. He'll tuck the food into one side of his mouth or the other like a squirrel, or sometimes spit it out. He avoids my eyes or stares at the spoon, or nothing, but not my eyes. I talk to him about the food, about Mom, about Joan, anything I can think of, but there's no response.

Now the hospital starts taking up Mom's idea he might "come around" at home. I'm beginning to agree.

But I know it would never work with Mom there. She'd have to live with Joan and that would be hard. But something happens which decides me.

A part of Dad's dilemma is he's constantly twisting, turning, trying to escape. He's also continually pulling at his catheter. After the first few days, they lace him into a sort of straitjacket. It's tied behind and has straps attached to wristlets which can be slipped over his hands. He has relative freedom but can't reach down to the catheter.

He fights against this; it's pitiful watching him struggle, like a puppy on a leash. When I feed him, I take it off but keep an eye on his hands.

The nurses are also afraid Dad will develop bedsores. He's losing weight fast and with the constant twisting-turning of his struggle, he's rubbing his butt and back sore; the skin is wearing off.

Starting about the fourth day, they sit him in a chair beside the bed while they change sheets. They leave him out there an hour or two to get air on his back but he's secured by his straitjacket.

I come in one evening for the dinner feeding and find Dad still tied to the chair. He's defecated and somehow pulled out the catheter so he's soaked in his own urine. He's twisted and one of his hands is caught under the handle of the chair. The circulation is cut off; the hand is blue. Also, he's wiggled around so his hospital gown is twisted up to his waist and he's naked from there down.

I'm shocked. I kneel beside him and his legs are ice cold. This is all happening in the surgery ward of a modern hospital, not in a nineteenth-century mental institution. I don't know how long he's been this way but his legs and feet are mottled red and white and the urine is drying on them.

I ring and holler out. A nurse comes running in and I lay it on her hard. She helps me untie Dad and change his gown. We slide him back into bed. I yearn to comfort Dad but he doesn't seem to realize what's happening.

Next day I plow into both Ethridge and Santana. They say it's difficult to care for somebody in my father's state at a normal hospital. I tell them I'm taking him home; he's not getting proper care at Perpetual.

I go home and try to avoid Mom. I sneak back into the garden bedroom with a can of beer. I drink in the quiet and try to think. I want to do the right thing for Dad and Mom, not just work off my own anger.

I get Mom down for her nap and phone Joan. I want to tell it straight, not too much artist-type exaggeration, no heightening for effect. When I finish, there's a long pause. She's crying.

"That's awful, Jack. We've got to do something. Mom's right; we must bring him home. Could you take care of him there if Mom comes out here with us?"

"I think I can do it; I know I'll do better than they're doing at the hospital. But can you handle Mom there with Mario and all? You know how she is."

"We'll manage. I'll put her in Maryellen's room; it's next to the bathroom and I'll keep her in bed as much as possible. Mario can work out in his garage or in the garden. With playground supervision, he's not home till six anyhow. Mario understands; don't you worry about it."

So it's decided. When Mom wakes, I tell her. She wants to stay with me and help. I'm firm. I tell her it's impossible. She'd have another heart attack for sure and I can't take care of them both at the same time. She can come visit when Dad's better.

I help her pack. We get in the car, she puts on her eyeshades, and I drive her to Joan's over Sepulveda, not the freeway.

When I go get Dad next day, the nursing supervisor comes tearing out. She's a big matronly type and gives me a time about telling off the nurse yesterday, but I'm not so easily managed. I tell her to get out of my way. All these people are only thinking of their own prerogatives.

She calls in the security man. I explain to him what's been going on. He nods and pretends to listen. Together we get it worked out. He helps me dress Dad in his pajamas and bathrobe. I gather the rest of his personal effects in a paper bag. I tell the supervisor to hurry it up, to get me discharge papers and a wheelchair.

The security guard gives me a wink; perfect man for the job. Together we maneuver the wheelchair into the elevator. Dad's sitting there shivering, jibbering, worrying his bathrobe with his fingers. It's hard to believe this could ever have been a functioning human being. Even his fingers and toes are curled under, practically cramped; his head hangs as if it's too heavy. He looks like the drawing van Gogh did in an insane asylum, the one with a man pushing his face into his fists, only Dad doesn't even have enough control to do that.

I roll him across the parking lot in the wheelchair and struggle him into our car. He has no idea what's happening. I drive him home.

I almost have to carry him across the patio, up those steps and into the house. He puts one foot in front of the other but they don't take any weight; it's like walking a giant doll. He's wearing his old aircraft-carrier cap and it gets twisted around to the side. He's nodding and mumbling, not noticing where he is.

I decide to dress him in his regular clothes. He's not actually sick, only debilitated. I'm sure if he can regain the feeling of being his own self, he'll recover. I take him into the back bedroom, sit him in the armchair and dress him. I choose slacks, a blue shirt, a button-down-the-front sweater and his other cap, the one I gave him.

He reaches up, takes the cap and throws it on the floor. Then he almost falls off the chair bending down for it. I put it back on his head. This time he leaves the cap on. I think maybe a warm head will increase the blood circulation and rejuvenate some neurons in his brain. I'm grasping at any straw.

I guide him into the living room and sit him in his platform rocker. It's a comfort for me seeing him sit there after all the days tied to that sterile hospital bed. I don't know if it's doing him any good, but it's great for my morale. Appearance means much to me, probably too much; could be why I'm an artist, redoing things to the way I want.

I'm hoping if we can only go on as if there's nothing wrong, he might slip a gear and get it all on track again.

I go into the kitchen and start making my parents' classic lunch. It's a toasted cheese sandwich, served with relish, about ten Ritz crackers and a glass of beer. I run back and forth checking him. He's sitting there, more or less calm, staring at their clock over the TV.

I bring the sandwiches into the living room and set up a collapsible tray between his chair and Mother's. They use these trays when they watch TV. While I'm running back and forth, Dad leans forward a few times as if he's going to get up, but the rocking action of the chair defeats him and he falls back.

I turn on the television and find one of their favorite "Crying Annie" shows. That's what they call them themselves. Dad stares at the TV but with blank incomprehension. He leans slightly forward, reaching slowly with one hand as if to pick something out of the air about two feet in front of his face. He does this several times, then gives up.

I slide the glass of beer into his hand but he doesn't do anything. He looks at it, then at me. It's as if we have no relationship, nothing of being the same species, let alone related. I've seen circus acts where chimpanzees have been trained to drink out of a cup and eat off a plate. Those chimpanzees looked more human than my father. He stares at that glass of beer, no idea what to do with it. I put my hand over his, around the glass, and bring it up slowly to his lips; his hands are cool, trembling. I tilt it so the beer goes into his mouth. About half runs out the corners but he gets some and swallows. I lower his hand and wait to see what happens.

Nothing. I take the beer out of his hand and fit half a sandwich into it. Then I bend his arm again, moving it up to his mouth, but he won't open his lips. His jaws are locked tight.

So I cut the sandwich into small squares and have more luck. He opens his mouth to take the squares, chews and swallows. This way, I get half a sandwich down. He's tasting and it's something he likes. I try the beer again. It's easier this time but he hasn't worked out the difference between eating and drinking; he chews the beer. He almost bites off the edge of the glass. Next time I'll use a mug.

City Hospital comes on TV. This is one of my parents' favorites but I'm not up to watching it right then. Dad doesn't seem to notice what's on; he's only staring at the movements and colors. I flip around until I find the Dinah Shore show. Dad is watching TV the way you'd look in a kaleidoscope. He's watching the movement, hearing the sounds; it calms him, holds him in one place but that's about all.

I chatter on, about the TV, about anything, but he doesn't pay attention. I'm getting restless; patience is not my strong suit, especially when there's no feedback. I talk about Joan, her kids, about Vron, our kids, about Mother; about what I remember from the work he did at G.E. and then at Douglas. Nothing.

The television is fine in the daytime, but when evening comes, things get difficult. There's something about colored TV light flickering on the rug.

My parents have the weirdest damned pattern in their living-room rug. Mother bought this rug because she said it wouldn't show the dirt. It's different colors: red, green, brown, orange, yellow in tiny dots, like a mad pointillist painting but with no image.

The flickering of TV colors on that rug drives Dad crazy. He keeps sliding off his rocker to the floor; feeling the surface, or trying to pick up the lights and shadows or smoothing them out.

I kneel with him. I run my hand over the rug saying it's nothing and trying to calm him. I help him back up on the rocker several times but then inevitably he slides down again.

Finally I let him do it; he isn't hurting himself and it's something to do, better than sitting in the rocker like a vegetable. He crawls along on his hands and knees, touching and wiping the rug. It's night by now and eerie. He doesn't make any sound, nothing but the rubbing of his hand on the rug. It reminds me of when he taught Joan and me to shine pennies.

It's painful seeing him reduced to walking on all fours; but I don't know what else to do. Nobody'd ever prepared me for anything like this. I'm totally spooked sitting there in the dark while he crawls along the floor in the quiet house. I know I should be starting dinner but I can't get myself to move.

Whenever there's a sudden sound or a change in light coming from the TV, he springs back and cowers, pushing himself into a sitting position. This is primitive man, man before he's gotten up on two legs. He's frightened by any change and doesn't understand what's going on around him. It's as if he's come from some other planet, another star; this world is totally unfamiliar to him. Here he is a grown creature with a certain motor skill and no idea what to do with it. Whatever he is, whatever his intellect might be, he's unrelated. His world-wise, rational capacity is gone. He's back there in the furthest part of his mind.

I squat and stare at the new light. I think of everybody still sleeping up at the house, still safe in that other place inside themselves. Meadowlarks start from the grass, they fly just over the reed tops. Twisting, turning, catching early insects. Almost like barn swallows.

I begin to feel maybe some kind of serious cerebral accident has happened, that he's stroked and a big part of his brain is permanently lost to him.

I'm thinking if he can only regain control of his bladder and bowels it'll be a big step. Every hour, I lead him to the bathroom. This works, sometimes, at least for peeing. I take his penis out and aim but he wants to hold it himself. He mostly makes the toilet but sprays the wall when he loses concentration. I'd rather wipe up than take away this one pleasure. The urine is a fairly normal color, not bloody, but it stinks to high heaven.

We don't eat much for dinner, French fries and hamburger. I feed him French fries one at a time and chop the hamburger into small pieces. He eats about half.

At ten o'clock, I lead him into the bedroom. I've arranged the room to make it safe for him to sleep. Normally, everything in that room is symmetric. The bed's in the center of the wall with night tables on each side. The dresser is on my mother's side, the closet on my father's. The cedar chest is at the foot of the bed, with a desk under the window. It's been this basic arrangement in our house as long as I can remember.

But I've changed it around. I've put both night tables on one side of the bed. Then I shoved the bed against the wall. I've lined up three dining-room chairs to block him from falling off the open side. He'll be safe this way, I hope. In the hospital he's had a high-sided bed.

I get Dad undressed and into his pajamas. He doesn't fight me, he's nervous and twitching, but he lets me lift his arms or legs. He's very sensitive or maybe I'm rougher than I think, because, several times, in my shifting around, getting trousers off, or an arm in a sleeve, he moans or grunts as if I've hurt him.

I pull back two chairs and ease him onto the bed. It's hard getting him to relax and lie back. I slowly lower his head till he's resting on the pillow. He stares at the pink ceiling, his eyes wide open, hardly blinking, as if he's watching something.

I begin to think lying down is a major event for him; maybe he's lost his ability to compensate movements in space. Maybe, lying down, he's seeing everything sideways. What used to be on top is straight ahead, and he can't adjust. It's as if a motion picture camera were tilted up. I try to think that way, get inside him somehow.

His eyes have begun drifting over the light-and-shadow patterns on the ceiling as if it's a whole new world, at least as interesting as the sidewise world. He's seeing the way an infant sees. If it weren't my own father and I weren't so emotionally involved, this could be fascinating. It's amazing to see how he's participating in this world with such intensity. He's probably seeing forms, shadows, colors and movements in an original, personal sense, the way an artist tries to see and never can.

So I tuck him in, folding his hands across his chest. I pull the covers up. To protect the bed, I've put a plastic tablecloth under the sheet; but I'm not sure about an electric blanket. If he urinates in the night, can he electrocute himself?

I take off the electric blanket and throw on a couple regular blankets from the cedar chest. Before I leave, I get some water, tilt his head with my hand and give him his regular medicines plus five milligrams of Mom's Valium. I say good night and hope for the best.

In the side bedroom, I change into my sleeping suit. Then I go out into the living room. I'm looking for something to read; the only thing around is that lousy Hearst paper the

Herald-Examiner. I make a snack, and sit in the rocker letting myself be worked through several articles about murders, rapes and Communist plots to destroy the moral fabric of America. Half an hour later, I go back to see how Dad is. I peek through the door carefully, trying not to make a sound. He's gone!

I can't believe it. I push the door open all the way and turn on the lights. The bed's empty! The room's empty! I dash back down the hall and look in the bathroom. Nobody! I look in the middle room but he isn't there either. He's vanished! I stop for a minute and try to breathe. I look in the kitchen, then back in the living room.

I don't know what gives me the idea, finally, to look under the bed but that's where he is. He isn't asleep, he's quietly moaning to himself under there. I should've heard this when I was looking but I was looking so hard I wasn't listening. He's moaning and trying to turn onto his stomach. He's up on his side pushing his shoulder against the springs of the bed. The bed's too low and he can't turn over.

I try to get hold of his feet but he kicks my hands away. I can't pull him onto his back because he's wedged. I try pulling on his arm but he moans louder. I'm getting wedged under there myself, and feeling claustrophobic. I wriggle out for a fresh start.

I'm afraid to slide the bed for fear I'll crush him. I try lifting one corner and holding it up, hoping he'll roll onto his stomach. But when I lower the bed carefully, it's worse. He's rolled up on his side in a fetal position and is jammed tight by the springs. He moans louder and grunts in pain. I quickly lift the bed again.

"Turn over, Dad, turn over!" I yell, and let the bed down again. He's moaning and screaming now; I'm crushing him! I lift the bed. I have a sacroiliac condition and I don't know how long I can hold up.

I stretch out a foot and hook one of the chairs. I edge the chair toward me and muscle the bed up at the same time until the bedspring rests on the chair. I'm shaking and sweating like a hog. I sit on the floor to get my breath.

I look under; he's still curled up but the bed isn't on his shoulder. I can't tell if he's asleep, but at least he isn't moaning. I consider pulling the covers off the bed and wrapping them around him under there. If he's asleep, I certainly don't want to wake him. This room is warm and the carpet is thick, especially under the bed where nobody's ever walked.

But then he starts moaning again. I slip off my dripping sweat-suit top. I check to make sure the bed is secure on the chair. I wedge another chair against the bed just in case. It'd be a scene if we both got trapped there; nobody could ever explain a thing like that. I slide under with him.

I squeeze close and fit myself tight against his back. I put my arms around his waist and start pulling backwards. I inch myself back, pulling on him, watching out for the chairs. He doesn't resist except to moan and curl deeper into his fetal position. I'm afraid I'll pull too hard; he seems so fragile I might break him. His coordination is shot; he could easily get an arm or leg twisted without my knowing it. After ten minutes' struggling, we're out from under. He's still curled up on himself. His eyes are shut, squeezed shut.

We're both covered with streaks of dirt and dust. Mother might be one of the world's greatest housekeepers, but nobody dusts the springs under a bed, not at seventy anyway.

I take off Dad's pajamas, twisting and pulling to get them loose from his clamped-down arms and legs. I pull the chairs from under the bed and lower it to the floor again. I lift Dad in my arms; he starts to uncurl. I maneuver him to the bathroom.

I sponge him, wipe the dirt off his head, hands and a few other places. I guide him back to the bedroom, prop him on the side of the bed. Now his eyes are full open, pinpoint pupils, watching me carefully. I get new pajamas and wrestle him into them. It's exactly like dressing a giant ten-month-old.

Then, slowly, I straighten him onto the bed again, lower his head to the pillow. When I get him down, I sit and watch. He's so incredibly nervous; his lips, his whole mouth is twitching; his fingers and hands are shaking and rubbing on the edge of the sheet where I've pulled it to his neck. He's in a total state of negative anticipation.

I run fast into the bathroom, fill a glass of water and come back. He's still there, he hasn't moved. I tilt his head with one hand again and slip a Valium between his teeth; another use for that space besides long-distance spitting. I slip it through there because his jaws are locked tight. He chews and swallows it like candy. I pour water gently between his teeth and he swallows that, too. I hope I'm not killing him with Valium. What the hell would I say at an inquest? These aren't even *his* Valium pills; they're Mother's. I gently settle his head on the pillow, put out the overhead light and sit.

I fall asleep, half naked, dirty. I wake up with my head in my arm on the bed. He's asleep. It's so good to see him relaxed, his face smooth, absolutely quiet, in a dead sleep; but he's breathing. It gives me some hope. I didn't see him asleep like this even once in the hospital. I quietly sneak away. I wash myself in the bathroom and spread my sweaty sweat suit over the shower-curtain rod to dry. I put on jockey shorts and a T-shirt, then climb into bed. It's past one-thirty.

I don't know what wakes me, but it's almost five o'clock. I decide to check how he's doing. I tiptoe down the hall and try pushing his bedroom door open quietly. It won't open! I push till it's open enough for me to stick my head in. He's on the floor against the door at my feet, curled up naked, covered with shit! His face, hands, feet and legs, everything smeared with it! The smell almost knocks me down.

There's a moment then when I'm not sure I can go on. There's a strong animal impulse to just close the door and run. I want to run as fast and far as possible, get on a plane and go home. I want to call Joan, call the hospital, call anybody and ask for help.

I push the door open carefully. Dad's chattering, muttering and shaking. He's ice cold. He isn't asleep. When I lean over him he looks at me with locked eyes, as if somebody'd turned on a light, but no recognition. I take off my T-shirt and lift him in my arms. As I said, I have a bad back; I'm amazed at what I'm doing. Dad's not a heavy man but he still weighs over a hundred and forty pounds.

I ease him into the bathtub and turn on the water. God, he's a mess. It's in his hair, in his pubic hairs, all over. I fill the tub and scrub as best I can. The smell fills the bathroom.

Mother'd have two fits. I drain the brown water when I've got most of it off and fill the tub again. I rinse him, try to wipe off what I've gotten on my chest and arms while carrying him.

Dad only watches me. I drain this tubload and dry him in the tub. I dash into the bedroom to grab his last pair of pajamas. One pair is covered with bed dust, the other with shit. Then I lift him from the tub and sit him on the toilet, just in case. I want to get out anything left; it can't be much, but I'm taking no chances.

We're into flannel pajamas now, the ones Joan bought for his birthday.

I stagger with him back to the bedroom. The bed's clean, thank God. He must've fallen or gotten out first. I put him in the bed, this time on his side and curled in his fetal position. Maybe that's the way he likes to sleep. I pull the covers over him and watch for five minutes or so; he doesn't budge.

I go back to the bathroom, fill a bucket with warm water and pour in a cup of laundry soap. I take one of the more ragged towels and hurry back to the bedroom. He's still quiet but I can't tell if he's asleep. The smell is overwhelming. I'm usually good with things like shit, garbage or vomit but this is at the limits of my endurance. It's on everything. It's on the walls, the woodwork, the door and, worst of all, the rug. I scrub, wipe and scrape. Mom is always so worried about dirt; boy, this is the end of dirt. She has a special thing about shit, anyway.

Now, I'm an anal personality by Freud's or almost anybody's definition. I like to preserve things, hold on, I'm a nest maker, husbander and conserver; but I think there's good reason.

There was an event when I was two years old—not even that. Mother likes to brag about it. And it's strange, while I'm wiping all this up, it comes to me clearly. To be honest, I don't think I ever really remembered this incident, but there on the floor against the closet door, it comes back; I have a memory, not a memory of Mother telling the story, but a real memory of it actually happening.

This memory draws open a curtain and allows me to have some empathy with Mom. I've always felt I should have remembered because it must have been a terrible shock but I'd never been able to.

My mother had me "trained" by the time I was eighteen months old. One day she dressed me in a white suit without diapers and was taking me to South Philadelphia for a visit with her mother and some of her sisters. She was going to show me off: "Look, curly blond hair; look, no diapers." My mother was twenty; I've got to give her credit; at least I was alive.

Mother has me ready and stops to take a pee or put on some powder. She comes out and I'm standing there, red-faced, smiling, legs apart, proud. I've crapped in the white pants. The story at this point goes, "I'll tell you, I gave him the best smacking he'd ever had. I take those pants, filled with it, pin them around his face and lock him in the hall closet."

I'm remembering this. There's something about the combination of the smell, the woodwork, the door and Dad's helplessness which brings it all back. I'm crying. I'm scrubbing and crying. I could be crying for my father but I think I'm crying for myself, still crying out a fifty-year-old event. I might also be crying for Mom. I hope so. There's something of wanting to tell her I won't do it again.

I wipe things up as best I can. I dump the bucket in the toilet, wash out the tub, rinse and soap everything down. I spray pine deodorizer. I change jockey shorts and put on my T-shirt. I go back to Dad; he's still curled up. I'm dead tired. It's about six-thirty now. The lack of sleep, the strain is getting to me.

This time I decide to do it differently. I close off the side of the bed with chairs again. Then I lie out across the foot of his bed with my hand on his left foot. I don't want to tie him down. I go to sleep like that, at the foot of his bed. When I wake, it's light. Dad's still there. I look at my watch and it's almost nine o'clock. He's asleep.

Everything still smells shitty so I go in and take a shower. I don't take a bath in the tub, even though I've cleaned it out with Ajax. I swear I have the smell of shit caught in my nose hairs. I take my shower fast, running back and forth to check while I dry myself, brush my teeth and get dressed. I'm like a mother with a young baby. Now I know what Vron means when she says that for seven years she never went to the bathroom without a baby on her lap.

At about ten, Dad wakes up. I get him dressed. I want to try giving him breakfast as if there's nothing wrong. I sit him in the armchair at his end of the table.

But he won't eat; all he does is play with it. So I feed him. He doesn't fight me; just keeps opening his mouth. We get down two eggs, some roll and orange juice; at least he won't starve today. I watch him carefully. When he reaches for anything, he misses. It's almost as if he's half blind. Then, when he tries to compensate, like as not, he moves his hand in the wrong direction.

I turn on the record player; Guy Lombardo this time.

Dad's just as interested in the table, the legs of the table, the pattern on the tablecloth and, of course, the rug as he is in food. He keeps leaning over trying to touch the floor. So, while I do the dishes, I tie him to the chair lightly with the belt from his bathrobe. I can't think of any other way.

Just after I've gotten the dishes off the table and put them in the hot water, I look out and see he's leaning so far he's tilting the chair over with him. I run fast as I can, but he hits with a thump before I get there. He looks up at me in noncomprehension, probably thinks I'm standing on my head. He makes no effort to get up, only whimpers.

I feel terrible. I untie and lift him to his feet. I look him over and there's a big, black-and-blue mark rising on his hip and elbow. I never knew old people bruised so easily. People are going to think I'm beating up my own Dad.

It's a gorgeous sunny day. I finish the dishes and take Dad out to the patio. That's one thing Dad and Mom like to do, sit out there and sunbathe; it's part of their dream come true. I lower him into one of the redwood chaise longues he made. I have him in his button-down sweater, gray trousers, socks, black shoes, and he has the cap on his head. If you just looked at him lying there, you'd never know anything was wrong.

I settle into a chaise longue beside him and start up a running conversation. I try remembering everything of my childhood with him. I ask questions, and when he doesn't respond I go on. I talk about his brothers, his sisters, his mother and father, all his life I know of. I feel he's beginning to listen; in some passive way, he's tuned into it; but I don't think he understands. He's listening as a dog or a child listens; for the tone of voice only, without comprehension.

I close my eyes and listen to the sounds. There's the beginning hum of insects and the twitter of ground thrushes. I hear the sound of the screen door slam; must be Johnny going out to feed the chickens before school. I'd better be getting on up there with this water.

After more than an hour, he stirs, and tries to speak. I lean close. He speaks in a deep breathy voice with a heavy stutter. It's as if he's forcing his voice out.

"They'll get mad at us if we stay here. Where's the owner of this house?"

It's such a wild, crazy thing for him to say; still it's something, words with sequence. But it breaks my heart. He's built this house, nail by nail, from the ground up, foundations, framing, electricity, plumbing, the whole thing. Now he thinks it's somebody else's. He can't claim for himself this one visible proof he's even lived.

He reaches out tentatively with his shaking hand and pats me lightly on the knee, very tenderly; I can barely feel it, a ghost tap. He lifts his head again, looks left and right, then up at the sky. He almost seems to sniff the air the way I've always thought the groundhog would on Groundhog Day. He leans toward me again and whispers excitedly.

"They're going to throw us out on our ear! Let's get going."

I put my hand over his and try to look into his eyes; the pupils are somewhat dilated but he won't look at me.

"Relax, Dad, you own this house. Nobody's going to throw us out. This whole property is yours."

He looks at me quickly, a fast, sneak look; a faint quivering smile goes across his face. I can't tell if the smile is saying, "Is that so, isn't that marvelous?" or, "You must be out of your mind."

That's the only contact all morning. The rest of the time I'm mostly talking to myself. Dad once rigged a little loud-speaker system connected to the record player in the living room for music in the patio. I go put on a big stack of Bing Crosby, Perry Como and the Hawaiian music. Dad and Mom have a passion for fake Hawaiian music. We listen to Bing Crosby sing "Sweet Lailani," then something about a little grass shack. Dad seems to relax; he even falls asleep some-times. But each time he wakes it's the same nervous shaking.

At two I make lunch; we get most of the beer down and a whole sandwich. I'm starving so I have two sandwiches and a second glass of beer. I'm bored out of my mind. That sounds terrible but it's the truth. I don't know how people who do this professionally stick it. It's so discouraging, and by nature I'm not the endurance type.

At three, I take him in to try for a nap. He falls asleep with me holding on to his foot again. I'm worrying what we'll do for the coming night.

That evening I get Dad to eat a reasonable amount but he's not drinking much. I'm worried about dehydration. It's hard getting fluids in him, and he definitely has diarrhea. I tried giving him hot chocolate but I almost burned him, a combination of his shaking and my lack of skill pouring liquids down another person's throat.

I lean him back in his rocker before the TV. I run back and forth, clearing dishes and washing, watching him.

He's having the same damned problem with the rug. He's lowered himself onto the floor and is crawling on all fours picking at the pattern and the flickering TV shadows.

I settle in Mother's chair and watch. He crawls on his knees to investigate a vase of fake flowers on the coffee table. He's very careful, touching lightly, studying, trying to under-stand. I keep up a running commentary, explaining the things he's looking at, but he doesn't react.

Then he kneels with his knees on the floor, his head and

shoulders on the couch. He stays that way for almost ten minutes till I think he might be asleep. I sneak over to look in his
eyes; they're wide, unblinkingly open. God, I'm glad Mom
isn't here to see this! I wish I weren't!

I sit at the dining-room table where I can keep an eye on
him and try writing a letter to Vron. I tell her Dad's been operated on, so I have to stay longer. I tell her I'm taking care of
Dad, now he's out of the hospital. Then I can't stop myself, I
spill all the beans. I'm practically crying, writing that letter
and knowing all the time it isn't fair.

After the letter, I call Joan. I don't want to upset her, so
I just say things are going OK. I tell her Dad hasn't changed
much but we're getting along. She tells me how Mom's been
playing hearts with Maryellen; no big scene with Mario, yet.

I'm dreading the night. Something happened to me the
night before. I'm not afraid of the dark. I really have this advantage, I like the dark. I like being alone in it; there's something about darkness that comforts me. Billy's afraid of the
dark and so's Jacky. Marty's petrified.

For a long time at the mill we had our john in the cellar.
Marty wouldn't go down unless somebody went with her.
She'd seen a Dracula film when she was about fourteen and it
got to her. After that, Marty even kept a crucifix over the
head of her bed. She has no religious convictions but she had
a crucifix. I'm sure if I could've gotten her a gun with a silver
bullet, she'd've slept with it under her pillow.

That crucifix made a great impression on Mom the one
time they came to visit us in Paris. She's always been worried
about the lack of religiousness in our family. We've never had
The Sacred Heart or pieces of palm hanging over religious pictures, all the paraphernalia of a primitive Catholic family. But
Marty had a crucifix over her bed, so we weren't completely
lost.

Now *I'm* seeing things out the corners of my eyes, just
beyond vision. I keep turning my head fast. I'm jumpy all
right.

I undress Dad and sit him on the toilet hoping for the
best, but nothing comes. I put on his pajamas and lead him

back to the bedroom. He doesn't know what's going on, he's gone.

I put him in bed. What can I do to avoid last night's catastrophe? I decide I'll sit on a chair beside him and read. The only book I find in the house is a book on different ways to psych yourself up when you're about to crack. It's Mom's all-time standby. It's filled with mundane solutions but it's not bad, written in an easy-to-understand style, not too far off the mark; sort of front-line therapy.

This is the first night Dad starts reaching out as if there are butterflies going across in front of him. He's reaching up with his fingers, very gently, very delicately, trying to catch something out of the air in front of him. There's nothing I can see, but he's tracking with his eyes and closing his fingers carefully, like a child picking motes from the sunlight.

I put down the book and lay my head close to his on the pillow. He continues his graceful plucking. I try to see what he's seeing. Whatever he's reaching for, he isn't catching it. He reaches with the frustrated movement one makes when unsuccessfully pulling a piece of thread through the other side of a needle. Whatever they are, he can't get hold of them. But he isn't complaining; only gibbering away with his chattering teeth and lips; saying nothing, expressing extreme concentration.

I slip my hand over his as he reaches, strokes, grabs.

"What is it, Dad? What are you seeing?"

He doesn't look at me. His eyes are focused two or three feet in front of him.

When someone is with you and seeing something you're not seeing, you begin to feel invisible yourself.

First, I turn on the overhead light; maybe this will help; maybe the dim light is causing some kind of hallucination. He pauses briefly and stares at the light, then one of his "things" catches his eye and he reaches for it, his hand carefully inching up.

I turn out the overhead. He slows for a few seconds, then starts again.

I turn off the bedside lamp to see what will happen. In the near dark we watch each other. There's enough light so I can see he isn't reaching anymore. Whatever it is he's trying to catch doesn't fly in the dark. I listen to his trembling, babbling—"bebebebedebdedebgegbebe—"

God, it's scary! I run my hand over his forehead, over his shoulder and down his arm on the outside of the blankets. He's as tense as if he's on the mark ready to run a hundred-yard dash. You could do an anatomy lesson on his tensed-up body. You don't expect those kinds of muscles in a feeble old man. Also, I haven't had much experience feeling a man's arms or shoulders. Except for drawing or painting the figure, I have practically no experience with what a man's body is like except my own. It certainly feels different from a woman's.

I stroke him like that for maybe fifteen minutes and the chattering dies down. In the dark I can't see if he's asleep. I lean close; his breathing is shallow but I'm not sure.

I reach back and turn on the bed light. He's staring at me when the light comes on. Somehow, in the dark, he knew just where my eyes were all the time! He's boring into my eyes with those unblinking, pinpoint eyes. He's looking at me the same way he'd look at anything else, including his butterflies. He's not looking with any recognition, only with a vague curiosity. He looks as if he has a desire to understand or know, but no expectation of doing so. He looks at me the way I might stare at the Milky Way on a starry night, not being able to put together what I see with what I know.

I smile; it doesn't mean anything to him. He watches and seems satisfied so long as I don't move too fast. After what seems forever, his eyes blink a few times. Then they start flickering, then closing slowly, like the sun going over a hill. He looks dead when they're halfway down and the pupils turn up under the lids. I listen for breathing and he begins to breathe long, staggering breaths. I settle back in the chair to read but can't hold concentration. I vary between anxiety and falling asleep; there doesn't seem to be any comfortable place for my mind between those two.

Then I think, What if I fall asleep? I don't want to find him on the floor again. What am I going to do? I can't leave him and I can't sit up all night. I decide I'll get in bed with him. It might help if he feels somebody close. He's slept all his life with someone; it must be a terrible change sleeping alone.

I slide him against the wall so he's blocked in, put on my sleep suit, spread out on my back and listen to his breathing. It isn't long before I'm asleep.

I wake scared. What wakes me is the smell of him. He's on his hands and knees straddling me in the bed. I'm flat on my back and he's on top of me with his head directly over mine. He's looking straight into my face in the dark, his nose practically touching my nose.

I jump so hard and fast I thump his head with mine. It takes me a minute to know where I am, what's happening. I grab his shoulders and carefully roll him back into place on his side of the bed. My heart's going blubablubulub in the dark, and I'm convinced I'm about to have a heart attack. God, how much strain can a fifty-two-year-old heart take? I'm completely freaked out.

Dad's lying tense beside me. I put the bedside lamp on again and look at him. He stares back at me with empty eyes, then starts after the butterflies again. Lord!

I get up and go to the bathroom. Going back in the room, I still catch the shit smell.

He's picking away at his butterflies. I lie beside him and breathe slowly, trying to relax. It's then, lying there, I figure out what he's doing. He's picking the pattern off the wallpaper across the room. Something's wrong with his perception and he's seeing that flower pattern hanging in front of his face. He's picking flowers. I watch some more and I'm sure of it.

I roll out of bed and pull one of the extra white sheets from the cedar chest. I drape it over the two small photographs hung on the wall. One is of Joan in third grade, a school picture at Saint Alice's, back in Philadelphia. She has her thumbs pressed onto the desk in front of her. The other is me, seventh grade, same position. Those pictures have been on that wall since my parents moved into this house, over twenty-five years ago. I drape the sheet over them so it covers that whole wall. Then I get in bed beside Dad.

Almost immediately he subsides. What in hell can be wrong with his perception?

I put my arm over top of him, across his chest. That way, I'll know if he moves. So I lie on my side, one arm over his shoulder. I can feel his body tense, shivering, jerking, kicking; like a dog dreaming.

I can't get to sleep. About the time he seems to settle down and I'm drifting off, he'll jump, kick a foot or push out an arm. But he must have settled down because finally I do sleep. I'm to the point where I could sleep on a pile of nails.

This time I wake and I've been punched in the eye! What he's done is throw out his arm in a violent swing and smashed it across my face. My nose is bleeding, my lip is cut. He's really given me a good one.

I go into the bathroom and look. I could be in for a shiner. The nose stops bleeding and the lip is cut inside my mouth. It's eight o'clock in the morning; I don't feel I've gotten any sleep at all.

But Dad's been in bed for nine hours and he's slept most of that time; it isn't all bad. When I go back to the bedroom, he's awake. I walk him to the bathroom. He takes his own weight and I only have to guide him. He goes to the toilet, both a piss and a shit. I'll never get used to wiping the ass of a grown man. I'm not tuned to being a nurse. It's something I'm finding out about myself. I take him back to the bedroom and help him get dressed. He's better than he was last night, more with it. He even helps some with the arms of his shirt and lifts himself so I can pull his pants on.

I feed him breakfast, take him out to the patio, tuck him into one of the chaise longues and turn on the music. I'm talking all the time but nothing's coming back. My chatter means no more to him than the chatter of a squirrel.

Then, sometime in the afternoon, and I can't tell what the turning point is, he sits up straighter and takes notice. He turns and looks at me, straight in the eye, with a weird twinkle of recognition. Surprised, I lean forward and he points into the garden.

"Mandy's out of the pasture, Ed."

Who's Ed, who's Mandy, what pasture? My mind spins. There's just that; then he nods his head a few times to reassure himself, a habit he's always had, then settles back. I try to think. Ed has to be his brother, an even year older than Dad. They grew up as farm boys together in Wisconsin.

The best thing is go along.

"Don't worry about it, Jack; it's OK."

I want him to stay in there. I wait. Then, about fifteen minutes later:

"Hand me the eighteen wrench there, Jim."

"OK."

He starts the business of putting two things together. He's holding something invisible in his left hand and pushing something invisible in his right hand against it. He's pressing hard as he can, applying full strength and gritting his teeth. He's pushing from one direction or another, grunting with the effort and completely concentrated.

"How's it going there, Jack?"

But he only keeps grinding away and won't answer.

Those are the two big moments of that day. I put him down for a nap and climb in with him again. I sleep, I don't know whether he does or not. He doesn't clobber me or anything and we get in two peaceful hours.

After that, I cook dinner and we eat. Then I turn on the television. This time I leave the lights on. I put him in his platform rocker and sit a little behind it. I rock his chair the way you would a baby's cradle, the way he always did himself; he'd keep it rocking with a slight body movement while he watched. I want to reproduce things as much as possible.

But it doesn't matter. He begins leaning forward; then he falls to his hands and knees on the floor. He starts scooping up those phantoms of his and picking at the patterns on the rug. He crawls down the hall and into the bathroom. He looks into the toilet the way a dog does; I half expect him to push his head in and take a drink. He pulls himself up, using the sides of the sink, and stares at himself in the mirror, not moving, not doing anything; just staring. Then he grabs hold

of the hot and cold faucets and pulls on those. He isn't trying
to turn them on, only tugging. I lead him back into the living
room and put him in his chair.

It starts all over again. He does the doorjamb-inspec-
tion routine several times. I'm watching, trying to get some
idea of what's going on in his mind.

*Silken ears filled with seed, every shining hair connected to a
single kernel. I gently squeeze drops of oil in each ear. Some
stalks have four or five, it should be a fine crop.*

*The sky's hot but the ground's still moist on my feet,
sheltered from the sun and wind. The glistening, blue-reflect-
ing, green, wide leaves and pollen-heavy tassels rise around
me. I step carefully, slowly through my self-made jungle,
shaking new pollen into open crotches of waiting leaves. A
slight breeze blossoms. I stop and listen to the rattling clatter
as tassels and twisting leaves bend into each other.*

What can be the matter? Who is this giant infant? Is this
the way he was as a child? Is he back there with no memory
of his entire life? Is nothing left? Can a whole lifetime be lost
just like that? It's as if somebody passed a gigantic magnet
over the memory tapes of a computer and wiped it all out. The
computer, the tapes look the same, but there's nothing in
there anymore.

He ends up on the floor stretched in front of the TV like
a dead Indian from a cowboy movie. Do I wake him? What do
I do? I'm having a hard time making decisions. I bring some
blankets out and cover him. I slip a pillow under his head
carefully not to wake him. He's sleeping deeply.

I'll sit there in the chair and keep an eye on him. I close
and lock all the outside doors; pull the venetian blinds. There's
no door to the hallway or the kitchen, but I close all the doors
in the hall. I feel safe enough, even if I do drop off.

I also do the same kinds of things you'd do with a baby.
I move the junk from the coffee table and low tables, things
with which he might be able to hurt himself. I sit back in the
rocker, call Joan and tell her things are OK. She tells me Mom

is behaving herself, Mario's keeping out of sight. I hang up and then don't last five minutes.

When I wake he's gone again! For a minute it doesn't register. I try to hold down the panic. Well, he can't have gone far; he's probably in the kitchen. I go in there but it's empty. I go through and look in the hall. He isn't there. The doors to the bedrooms and bathroom are still closed. I dash down the hall and look in each of them. He isn't to be seen.

Hell, it isn't a big house, I don't think it has a thousand square feet. I make a quick check of the front and back doors; they're still locked. Then I run back and look under his bed; I look behind the door; I look in the closet and under the cedar chest, the dresser. I'm getting desperate. What will I tell Mother and Joan if I've lost him?

I go into the middle bedroom, I look under that bed; *in* that closet, under everything. I'm about ready to start pulling out drawers in chests and looking there. I run into the kitchen, look under the table, in the oven. I go back to the living room. I look behind the couch, behind the chair. There's no place left. It's one of those locked-room mysteries. What happened to the body? It walked away, that's what; maybe right through a wall. Maybe he's turned invisible! I'm thinking *all* these things. That "invisible butterfly" business has made a deep impression.

I collapse on the platform rocker. Should I call the cops? No, I've got to think this out. I take some deep Yoga breaths. I get up and carefully go over all the doors. There's no way he could've gotten out, the screen-door latch is still on. Even if he'd suddenly come back to his full strength and sense, opened the doors and walked away, closing the doors after him, there's no way he could've latched the screen door behind him!

Then I notice there's one door I haven't checked. In the hallway, on the left, just after the kitchen and before the bathroom door, there's a louvered door opening into a tiny two-by-three closet with the heater in it. They also keep the vacuum cleaner and brooms in there. It takes all my courage to open that door.

I open it, not really expecting he'll be there. It's the only place left, that's all.

He's standing with his back to me, fully clothed, leaning against the heater. I don't know how he got the door closed behind him. I don't know how long he's been in there, but long enough to have crapped his pants. It's amazing I didn't pick up the smell; then again, the nostril hairs inside my nose are still coated.

I stand there, my heart's pounding away, and I feel light in the head.

"Hi, Dad. What're you doing in here?"

He turns at the sound of my voice. He looks through me for several seconds, then turns back to the heater. I gently take him by the arm and lead him toward the bathroom. He doesn't resist actively but there's a low-level reluctance. He'd like to stay in that closet.

It's two-thirty in the morning. I undress him, clean him off, fill the tub and throw the dirty clothes in. I wipe him off as best I can and put on the washed pajamas. I lead him back toward the bedroom. My nerves are on the very edge; it wouldn't be hard for me to start bawling.

Now I've got him in my arms leaning against the hall wall and I'm afraid to open the bedroom door. Opening any door is getting to be a traumatic event. I tell myself I've got to call Joan in the morning. I need time to recuperate.

Dad lies out stiff on the bed when I finally get him in the room and stretched out. He lies there chattering and whining or whimpering sporadically like a puppy. What to do? I think of tying his hands so he can't whack me again. My face is swollen and sore; I'd hate like hell to get hit in the face again. I bring my sweat suit into the bedroom, get undressed and put it on while I'm watching him, hoping he'll go to sleep. I climb in bed with him. This time I do what I do with my wife.

Vron typically turns her back to me in bed and I tuck in behind her, knees behind her knees and my arm over her. I don't sleep all night that way but that's the way I start.

I find it a great comfort to sleep with someone. Sleeping with another human is one of the great life pleasures, maybe even a necessity. I'm sure it's only recently humans have been sleeping alone. The single bed and separate rooms are probably partly responsible for our anxiety-ridden world.

Especially, asking children to sleep alone in the dark is cruel; time is different for a child, longer.

And, right now, Dad is like a child. I sleep with him. Small as he is, he seems monstrous. I've never slept with a man before. I'd slept spoon-style in a pup tent or in a foxhole, but we were in separate fart sacks and there was no direct physical contact except bulk. The smell is different, the feel, the height of shoulders, the breadth of chest, the all-over hardness, feeling of density; it's entirely another thing.

But I figure I'll *hold* him down if I have to.

We sleep! He sleeps; I sleep! We sleep through the night like mice. I never move and he doesn't either. God, it's nice!

I wake at nine o'clock and he's still asleep, snoring lightly. I carefully unwrap myself. He's in a tight, curled, fetal position again, still on his side. I pull the covers up over his shoulders. I'll let him sleep long as he wants. If he sleeps through thirty-six hours, that's OK with me. I take his pulse, it's slow and regular.

I go into the bathroom and the shitty clothes are still in the tub. Maybe I expected the brownies would wash them. I run in hot water, scrub and rinse till the water is clear, not yellow. Then I hang them on the line in back. I Ajax out the tub and fill it to near the top. I keep peeking back at Dad; he's dead to the world. I lower myself into the tub and try to relax.

After a ten-minute soak, I check him again and get dressed. I cook up *my* kind of breakfast; three eggs with cheese on top and some pieces of Canadian bacon. I organize Dad's medicine and it's coming onto ten-thirty. I keep checking but he's still sleeping. I do the dishes and pick up around the house, sweep the living room, kitchen, bathroom and hall. I sweep off the patio. It's almost noon.

So I begin to get worried. Maybe he's had a stroke. Maybe he's in a coma. Maybe I haven't been getting enough food or liquid into him and he's dying.

I calculate he's been asleep for over twelve hours. That's not counting whatever he was doing when he was in the closet draped over the heater.

Quietly I go in the bedroom. I pull back the curtains and
open the venetian blinds. They're always closed tight; even in
the day you need to turn on a light back there. It's a conviction of the poverty mind that bedrooms should be permanently
dark. Maybe it has to do with working swing and graveyard
shifts in factories. Dad's done a lot of that in his time. I think
he worked swing shift most of the time he's been in California.
Or maybe dark bedrooms are Irish or French.

But I want to let some light and air into that room. Otherwise, I'll never get rid of the shit smell. Also, I want to let out
the dark, poor spirits, let in the good fairies and sunshine.

I sit in front of the window. Sun's streaming in so I open
my shirt; I drift off in the chair with my head leaning against
the wall.

When I wake, it's two in the afternoon. He's awake and
I don't know for how long. He's on his back. He isn't trembling
or shaking, his eyes are more relaxed; but then I see his face
is wet. He's lying with his head on the pillow, crying. His whole
face is wet with tears. Tears are running down the sides. I go
close. The pillow's soaking wet too. He's crying quietly, not
sobbing, only a long, continuous, uncontrolled crying.

I run my hand over his head, then put my hand on his.
For the first time, he grabs my hand and holds it.

"What's the matter, Dad? Everything's OK."

He begins crying harder. He cries so hard, so *hard,* and
now he's sobbing. He won't look at me. His eyes are open, staring at the ceiling and he's sobbing deep, twisting sobs. I keep
talking to him, rubbing my hand over his, his other hand
clutching mine.

What can it be now? What's brought this on? I carefully
lift, shift him to the edge of the bed so I can dress him, and
he cries the whole way. It isn't often you hear a man cry
deep, sobbing non-hysterical crying like this.

I bundle him up and take him out on the patio. He leans
his head back on the chaise longue and cries. I watch a few
minutes and go in to make something to eat. I'm feeling completely helpless. I whip up a quick cheese sandwich and a

glass of beer. When I come out, he hasn't moved and he's still crying. He's going to dehydrate from tears alone.

I can't get him to eat. He won't open his mouth, he won't chew when I force a bit of sandwich into his mouth. He isn't resisting, he just isn't paying attention, isn't noticing the food. I try pouring beer between his teeth and almost drown him. He doesn't clear the path to his stomach and it goes down his bronchial tube. I'm liable to bring on pneumonia! I sit there for half an hour holding his hands and hoping it will stop, that he'll cry his way through whatever it is. But it goes on and on.

I dash inside and pull out the phone extension so I can sit on the steps and keep an eye on him while I'm talking. I call Joan. She's psychic or something; before I open my mouth, before she even knows it's *me,* she says, "What's the matter, Jack? What's happening?"

"Joan, I don't *know* what's the matter; Dad keeps crying. He woke up crying and he's been crying ever since."

"Mother of God! Is there anything I can do?"

"Could you come over, Joan? I'm at the end of my rope."

"OK, I'll be right there. John and Maryellen should be home soon, they can watch Mom. Have you called Dr. Ethridge?"

I'm listening to Joan and watching Dad. He isn't paying any attention to me or what I'm doing.

"Good idea, Joan; I'll call Ethridge. I hate to bother you with all this but I'm definitely not cut out for nursing. Thank God, I never got involved with clinical work; I think if I worked with abnormals for a month, I'd be the most abnormal character on the ward."

"This is your *father,* Jack. Even *doctors* don't treat their own families."

It's so good to hear her sane, calm voice. I hate to hang up.

"OK, Joan. I'll call Ethridge and wait for you. While you're here, maybe I can shop, and do some wash. I'm out of underwear and socks."

"I'll bring the wash I've already done; some of your things

are in it. I'll be there at about four; that way I can beat the traffic."

"OK, but be careful. We don't want any more casualties; the emergency ward's full."

"All right, 'Mother Hen Jack.' I'll be careful."

She laughs lightly, privately, over the phone. There's something so soothing, healing about a mild, content laugh, even when everything's upside down. If I could bottle that laugh, or record it, and play it up and down the corridors of mental institutions, we could empty half of them in three months. I hang up.

I pull out the Perpetual card and dial Ethridge. Dad's still crying in front of me.

After the usual runaround, I'm put through; I tell Ethridge Dad's home with me on Dr. Santana's suggestion. I get a very cold response; he's still on his high horse, playing "boss man."

"Dr. Ethridge, I don't know why it is but my father keeps crying. He's been crying the whole day; he won't eat and is not responding."

There's a slight delay.

"Does he seem depressed?"

I guess that's a logical question but it sounds stupid. No, Doctor, he's not depressed, he's only crying.

"I would say he is, Doctor. He seems terribly depressed."

"Well, it sounds as if we should try some Elavil; that will bring him around. These kinds of severe depressions are not unusual with older people after surgery."

He's talking as if we're discussing a puppy with a case of worms.

"Mr. Tremont, if you can come into the hospital I'll have a prescription left at the pharmacy."

He has "hang up" in his voice, so I let him. I sit there with the phone in my hands for several minutes, not able to move. I feel cut off. I need more of Joan's magical laughing.

I sit with Dad out there on the patio holding his hand. I have Hawaiian music playing and I take off my shirt to get some more sun. I'm going to get something out of all this, if it's only a tan. I hold Dad's hand and pretend I'm on the deck of a ship sailing to Hawaii on my honeymoon. I'm distinctly going kooky!

When Joan arrives, she has the clean clothes and a roast she's prepared. I tell her what Ethridge said. She latches on to that and wants me to go for the medicine right away.

She sits beside Dad, watches him cry and starts crying herself. She holds on to his hands and tries to get his attention but he won't look at her. The exception is when she kisses him. Then he puckers up his lips for the kiss as usual. It's almost instinctive, the way an infant will start sucking when you touch its lips. He stays puckered after the kiss for almost five seconds. There's no change in his facial expression, just the puckering up.

Joan says the situation at her house with Mother is getting impossible. Mom has cast Mario in the combined role of Mafia chieftain and Nero. She calls him the "big shot" and keeps talking him down to the kids. Joan doesn't know how long she can keep Mario from blowing up. She's convinced Mother can't live in any environment without dominating it.

"You know, Jack, if Mom had only been born thirty years later, she'd've made a great feminist."

I go over some of the things that have happened with Dad. She's deeply sympathetic, laughing when it's funny, reaching out to touch my arm, crying at the sad parts. Dad sits next to us, weeping away almost silently. You can't believe a person could keep crying continuously for so long. He's been crying over three hours I know of.

I dash to the hospital, get the Elavil. When I come back, Joan's sitting close beside Dad. She shakes her head.

"This is terrible, Johnny. He won't look at me. He's like a little boy who's been bad and feels guilty. What can be the matter?"

I smash two tablets of Elavil in a glass of water. He'd for sure choke on pills. I don't know what to tell Joan. She sees me as the one in the family who's supposed to know something about psychology. I don't know, can't figure, what's the matter. Joan tips Dad's head back, I hold his nose and we pour the Elavil slowly between his teeth; thank God, he swallows this time.

I sit and wait. I have no idea how long this stuff takes. Joan's inside getting dinner ready. After about fifteen minutes, Dad stops crying. The tears seem to dry on his eyes. He stops sobbing and begins with the chattering lip-bouncing again. He has brief spasms as if he's reacting to small sudden pains.

I call out.

"Wow, Joan; look at this. These modern drugs are incredible. Less than half an hour and he's stopped crying completely. He doesn't seem sad anymore."

She comes out and leans over Dad.

"He doesn't look happy either. He looks as if a whole war's going on inside his head."

About ten minutes later he gets to be— Well, it's hard to describe. He becomes supersensitive to every sound, every change in light, every movement, everything. Even his own breathing sends him off. He's in a continual state of agitation; every part of him is moving, vibrating, twitching, twisting.

It's like the time in California our washing machine broke loose from its mooring and I tried holding it down. The machine was jumping around while I was grappling with it and hollering for Vron to pull the plug.

I lean across to hold him. I'm afraid he's going to wear himself out. He hasn't had anything to eat all day and here he is giving off calories like crazy.

"My God, Joan! He's elevated all right. Maybe this is what Elavil is supposed to do but it can't be good for him."

Joan wraps her arms around his legs. We're both talking, trying to soothe him, holding on.

I need to give him a tranquilizer before he totally shatters; he can't keep on like this. I run in to get Valium from Mother's room. We smash it and force some through his teeth. I take his blood pressure. It's two twenty over one ten. His pulse is so fast I can't count it, a fluttering.

Joan holds on while I call the hospital and fight my way through to Ethridge. I tell him what's happening and what I've done so far.

"Mr. Tremont. Who took your father's blood pressure?"

"I did, Dr. Ethridge."

"What do you think you are, a doctor, Mr. Tremont?"

Somehow, by having taken Dad's blood pressure I've threatened this schmuck. Then he comes on with the next thing.

"And do you have the right to prescribe medication, Mr. Tremont?"

I figure now's the time to do a little lying. In fact, I don't even think it out, I just do it.

"*Dr.* Tremont, Dr. Ethridge. Yes, I do have the right to prescribe. It's well within the range of my prerogatives as a member of APA. And I do not like your attitude, Dr. Ethridge, it is distinctly unethical and inappropriate in a moment of emergency."

Actually, I haven't been a member of APA for over twenty years. It's one of the little luxuries I let slide. There's a pause. I give him his chance but he doesn't say anything.

"All I want from you right now, Dr. Ethridge, and as quickly as possible, is a recommendation as to what we should do to compensate for the results of the Elavil *you* prescribed over the phone."

I know I've got him. There's another long pause. I swear if he hangs up we're going to have a shoot-out.

"Well, Mr. Tremont, I don't like your attitude either. For the moment, with your father, perhaps you should wait until he calms down or shows further signs of depression before you give him any more Elavil. The Valium you've given him should calm him but he's liable to become depressed again. Experiment till you find a balance. If that doesn't work, bring him in."

I say thank you and hang up. It's best to get off the phone before I say what I'm thinking.

It takes a while, but Dad slowly unwinds. Joan and I sit and talk with him or with each other. We recognize we can't go on like this. With Mom acting crazy at her place and Dad not getting any better, we're stymied. It's not only that Dad hasn't shown any signs of improving, but he's physically and mentally deteriorating. I can't get him to stand straight on the scale in the bathroom to weigh him, but he's wasting away. His elbows and knees are like ball-bearing sockets and his muscles are stringy.

We decide we'll take him back to the hospital. I call and tell them we're coming in.

But first we want to get him clean. Even with all my care, he definitely smells. He smells the way my grandparents used to smell when I was a kid and we went to visit them in Philadelphia. It's the smell of age: old sweat, constipation and dried urine. Maybe it isn't bad as that with Dad, but Joan and I have a compulsive mother so we need to clean him before we take him into the hospital. We're embarrassed because he smells.

We slide the plastic cover from the bed and spread it on the living-room floor. We take his clothes off and turn the heat up. He lies back, watching us, not resisting in any way. Joan takes one arm and rubs all along it with a washcloth, soap and warm water; then she does the other; he lets her do it, not helping, not resisting or even watching. Joan washes his hands, rubs between his fingers and cleans his fingernails. Then she cuts them.

I'm doing the same things with the bottom parts. I'm cleaning his toes and between his toes, the bottoms of his feet. I cut his toenails with the big toenail clippers from the bedside table. I clean out his crotch, wipe him and pull the foreskin back to clean his penis. I'm lifting his legs up and down as I do these things, exactly the way you would with a baby. It's so hard putting this together with Dad.

We dress him in a clean pair of pajamas and his terry-cloth bathrobe. It takes the two of us getting pajamas on him. He's disintegrated to a point where he can't help. He can't walk, either. He won't put one foot in front of another. He stands and rocks.

Joan makes up the bed in her VW camper. I scoop him up and carry him out there. Joan gets in front and I stay back with Dad, sitting on the edge of the bed and trying to comfort him. Through all this he's anxious, chattering his lips, fixing us in a helpless way with his eyes or staring at whatever happens to be in front of him.

When we get to the hospital, I run around trying to get a wheelchair but when they come out and see the condition Dad's in, they bring a stretcher. We roll him into the emergency ward. Two doctors and a nurse begin working him up right away. I explain the situation while they're working. They put him on IV immediately. The doctor is a concerned young guy. It turns out Dad's BUN is up; blood tests don't look good; he's definitely dehydrating. The BUN, he explains, is the amount of nitrogen and urea in his blood.

They say Dad needs to stay in the hospital. We sign all the forms. By now, Dad's been given a sedative and looks more relaxed. We stay with him till they roll him upstairs. We kiss him goodbye but he's asleep.

When we get home, Joan and I eat the dinner she's cooked. Then I drive over to the Valley, following Joan in Mother's car. We tell Mom that Dad took a bad turn so we brought him back to the hospital.

This springs off a whole scene. It would all've been fine if we'd only let her look after him. It's her he's missing.

"After all, it's *my* husband! You kids have no idea what a tender man he is; he can't do without me. Now look what's happened."

Joan and I nod, agree; we don't need another heart attack. It doesn't take much to talk Mom into going home with me. You'd think staying with Joan was some kind of penance she's having to pay for the heart attacks: five Our Fathers, ten Hail Marys and a week at your daughter's.

Thank God, Mario isn't there; he takes an awful beating. I think Mario's gotten more or less inured to it all but you can't ask anybody to put up with this kind of nonsense.

I feel sorry for Joan. I'm sure it hurts. I know from bitter, personal experience it hurts. I know also how that kind of poison does get into good relationships; you can't completely wipe it out. Mom's just a smart enough amateur psychologist to pick up minor dissatisfactions, vulnerabilities and lean on them. But she'd better be careful; better yet, I'd best get her out of there.

· · ·

I drive her home. It's getting late and she still hasn't eaten. I don't feel like cooking and I don't want Mother in the kitchen, so I take her to one of her favorite restaurants, a crappy place called the Williamsburg Inn. I can always eat a second dinner, especially when I'm anxious and feeling pressed or depressed.

This Williamsburg Inn is a phony colonial-style place on the corner of National and Sawtelle in West Los Angeles. It has a red-brick façade with colonial white woodwork and thin, fake, wooden columns across a narrow porch. It even has one of those intolerable little statues of a black boy in a red suit with knickers where you're supposed to tie your horse. Hell, there isn't a horse within twenty miles, but there are a lot of blacks.

Then there's all the superpatriotic business with flags draped over everything. Fake copies of the Declaration of Independence blown up fifty times are on the walls along with about twenty copies of Stuart's George Washington. It's awful. The waitresses are dressed in Martha Washington-style costumes with a deep decolleté. They must hire these girls by bra size. Also, the whole place is pervaded with a vague, anti-black feeling, very superpatriot, very Virginian.

They probably have several not so subtle ways to discourage any black who might walk in by mistake, little things you can't quite put your finger on: smaller portions, overseasoning, slow service—that kind of stuff.

Normally, this is a restaurant Mother loves. She says things like "Such a nice type of people eat there," or, "It's so 'refined.'"

But now she's into complaining. Nothing is any good. Nothing is good as it used to be. Jews must have bought the place. The drink before dinner is no good; they didn't put any alcohol in it, just fancy ice, water and fruit. So what else is new? That's why the cocktail was invented; people can think they're drinking without using much alcohol.

Then it's the service. That poor girl with her boobs falling into our plates can't do anything right for Mother.

The food is mediocre at best, and expensive. I listen to

Mother gripe through each course. I let her go on; she's enjoying herself, at least it keeps her mind off Dad. I listen again to all the details of their visit to Williamsburg in Virginia with the Barlittles. It must have been ten years ago and I'm sure I've heard about it five times. Williamsburg is a town the Rockefellers fixed up the way it never was so people won't ask for the money robbed from them by crooked oil deals.

When we get home, I tell Mom I'm going to sleep out in the garden back bedroom. I show her the signal system Dad's rigged and how to use it. She wants to know why I'm not sleeping in the house. I know if I'd said I'd sleep in the side bedroom, she'd want me to sleep in the garden. I know that. I'm not evasive enough to deal with Mom.

But I do sleep. Mom gets through the night without any problems, too.

But the next day I have to stop her five different times from doing crazy things that could kill her. Also, she can't believe I can cook dinner.

Mom has the ultimate put-down when everything goes wrong; that is, when somebody else is doing anything right without her help. It goes like this.

"My God, look what my idiot child can do, he can boil an egg! Who'd ever believe it? I didn't know you had so many talents, Jacky. Soon you'll be the best water-boiler for men over fifty on Colby Lane."

We work through various versions of this during the entire dinner process.

Afterward, we go in and watch TV. Mother sits in Dad's chair with a stool pulled up to put her feet on. She has a habit of crossing her legs or feet, and the doctor has made a point about how this is bad for her circulation. It's one of the things heart patients aren't supposed to do. She's always forgetting and I keep reminding her. I spend more time watching her feet than watching TV. Probably I'm trying to get even for the dinner put-down.

Also, the back-seating on the dishwashing was overwhelming. I happen to know she's a sloppy dishwasher, sloppier than I am, and that's saying something. But you'd swear we were preparing those dishes for brain surgery.

At about eleven o'clock, I get so tired I go back to the bedroom. She's still sitting up in the chair and says she's not sleepy yet. I don't feel like fighting her.

11

Next morning, Billy really wants to drive. What the hell, he should feel I have confidence in him. If we have an accident, we'll change places with each other just before we die.

Today we'll be coming down the eastern side of the Rockies and it'll be tedious driving. We leave early, but no matter how early you take off, it's one long line of trucks. Not many trucks take Route 70, because of the pass, but enough do; so it's a drag and the road isn't wide enough for passing.

I make a rule, no passing unless we both agree. I've driven with Billy before. Also, I'm in charge of music. I don't want to be nervous about his driving and at the same time have "Bobby boy" singing through his nose; telling me how he has exclusively discovered the meaning of life.

It's a gorgeous day. The pass is twelve thousand feet and we're starting down. We curve along in the sunshine; massive trees and rocks, crisp creeks shining at the bottom of deep cuts. The road meanders through hairpin turns. All along are sections being built for the big highway to go through here someday.

We're never going to agree on passing. Billy can't see more than seventy-five yards along the road ever, and those semitrailer trucks are at least thirty yards long. They're lined up in front of us far as we can see.

So after he's put on the direction signal a couple of times and I've shaken my head no, Billy pushes back his seat and drives with his arms straight out. His head is tilted as if he's looking through bifocals. Thank God, we can't go more than thirty miles per hour.

There isn't much in the way of music. We're out of range for Denver and there's nothing but Country Western from small towns.

I'd like to find a Glenn Miller eight-track. I wonder if they've made any tapes of that music. I'll bet there're a lot of people, people my age, who'd enjoy hearing those old tunes again . . . "Moonlight Cocktail," "Sunrise Serenade," "In the Mood" . . .

I could tell Miller from the first bar. He'd set up his woodwinds to carry the theme; then his brass and percussion would move in, blend with some kind of magic weaving to pick it up. I could almost see it in my mind. It was like watching a dancer, or slow-motion pictures of a basketball player dribbling, making a shoulder fake, springing and pushing off a jump shot while fading.

I had every record Miller cut. When I was fifteen I bought one of the first portable record players. The replacement battery was the size of a motorcycle twelve-volter. The thing cost a fortune. I'd play Miller out there in the aviary for my birds. It was heaven playing those old 78s, three minutes on a side, listening to Glenn Miller having a concert with my birds. I even wrote him once about it but didn't get an answer.

While I was in the army, my folks moved from Philadelphia to California. I'd packed my collection carefully and put it in charge of Joan; she was fifteen.

Joan tried to keep them on the floor of the back seat with

her but that space was needed for suitcases to go in and out of motels, so they packed them in the trunk of the car.

They drove right across the desert in midsummer. When Joan unpacked the records, they were baked together into one solid wavy thick record, the thickest Glenn Miller record in the world.

During the war, I'd dream about those records. When I got home, I was going to play them for at least two weeks getting myself straightened out. I'd make up different concerts in my mind, trying to remember the music.

So I came home. After about an hour of welcoming, I ask where my records are. Joan motions me to follow her. Nobody says anything. She takes me into her room and from the bottom of her closet brings out this black, round lump. I cried. At that time I could cry easily. I was having a hard time keeping myself from crying about almost everything.

I was in a tent in the middle of a muddy field being transported back to my outfit after being wounded the first time when we got the news Miller had disappeared. I'd been being shuffled from hospitals to repple-depples for almost a month. This place had a genuine old-fashioned bed-check-Charley type who'd come over our field at chow time and bomb the tents from an antiquated monoplane. There wasn't any anti-aircraft unit around, so we'd all run out to fire M1s and BARs at him; our before-chow evening target practice.

I think this nut dropped those bombs by hand over the side like W.W.I. They were handmade jobbies built from strapped-together masher grenades; about half didn't go off. Another fanatic doing a German-style, old-man-Hemingway scene.

He's just done his little circle and dropped two bombs. They both dudded in a muddy field and we didn't hit him. I'm going back to the tent for my mess kit when the mail clerk of this transient company comes by, passing out copies of *Stars & Stripes*. I open mine and there is it. "MAJOR GLENN MILLER MISSING IN ACTION OVER CHANNEL! SEARCHERS INDICATE PLANE IS PROBABLY LOST!" I can't believe it.

I go back to my tent and let it soak in privately. All the

music, the church dances, what seemed my wonderful ab-
breviated childhood, finished. I felt cheated; cut off from the
best part of my life; knowing it would never be the same again.

Sure, this is true for everybody and everything, even
without a war or critical deaths. But I'd been sustaining myself on the illusion I'd be going back; not only going back in
the geographic sense but going back to the way it was, con-
tinuing where I'd left off.

Squatting there in the tent, in that spring evening, I let
go. I was almost late for chow.

The cowboy music on the radio is incessant. There can't
be more than ten different tunes they use; only the words are
changed. I try listening to those words and they're American
all right, upside-down America or maybe inside out.

I reach over and switch it off. Billy smiles.

"God bless you, kind sir. Five more minutes and I'd've
pulled out the trusty six-shooter and put one right through
my Stetson."

I started laughing. God, it feels good to laugh. It seems I
haven't laughed out loud in six months. And normally I'm a
big laugher, with a terrible snuffling walrus guffaw. I laugh so
hard I worry I might be getting hysterical. Billy's laughing
too, I think mostly at my laughing.

"Dad, what this world needs is some new cowboy songs,
maybe porno lyrics closer to the way it is."

We go through tunnels and there are incredible rock
formations, beautiful as Bryce. Probably somewhere along
in here we've crossed the Continental Divide.

You can tell we've passed over something. From here on,
everything's different. It's the first long step east. It's a giant
step to Europe when you go over that big rock hill. This side
is more civilized, tame. It's less exciting, sure, but a hell of a
lot easier to live with.

Here's where tame animals start. The people aren't tame
yet, neither are the plants much, no real agriculture.

Back on the other side it's all wild: wild plants, wild
rocks, wild people, wild skies, wild water and wild animals. The

only exceptions, a few people-ghettos like Los Angeles or San Francisco.

We'll be going through some of the most extensive tame-animal country in the world, straight across Kansas, four hundred miles of prime tame-animal country. When we cross the Mississippi, tame plants really start; and on the other side of the Appalachians tame people.

We've come out of the mountains and are on straight four-and-four highway. This is our payoff. Billy seems hypnotized. I look over and we're going eighty. Christ, there's a fifty-five-mile speed limit.

"Look at the speedometer, Billy; heh, heh, heh, we're really moving."

I don't lay it on, just say it the way I'd say, "Look at that yellow cow out the window there." But he does slow down, *slows* to sixty-five. After eighty, it feels as if we're going thirty.

There's nothing out the windows; the road doesn't curve an inch; like a flat railroad. And tame animals, cows, steers, are out there all around us.

Billy's started laughing and giggling to himself. Sometimes he hums and then marks time with his left foot.

"Listen to this, Dad; the first meaningful set of Western lyrics since 'Bury Me Not on the Lone Prairie.'"

He starts singing, a blend of Johnny Cash, Bob Dylan and Arlo Guthrie. He's using number three of the cowboy tunes.

> "In the valleys and the hills of the Oregon wood,
>   Not a chain saw screams like Frieda's could.
>   Fightin' and acussin' are a logger's game
>   But they all go quiet at Frieda's name.

"Then there's a chain-saw solo. I could do it on a guitar easy."

He starts humming and razzing, making noises that are supposed to be a chain-saw chorus.

"Then it goes—wait a minute— Yeah!

"Frieda has elbows like an elephant's knees;
  Some people say she stands when she pees;
  She just ain't much for the birds and bees,
  But you oughtta see Frieda fellin' them trees."

He does his buzzing, humming, razzing again. There's a long quiet while he's putting the next part together. He's still beating it out with his bare foot and giggling.

"OK, here it is, I think.

"Frieda met her end one dark, gray day,
  Fellin' two at once or so they say;
  The logs cut easy and she wondered why,
  Then saw the saw sticking through her thigh."

We have some more mouth noises. I never knew he could make so many different sounds; he almost does sound like a guitar. I've heard him make all the motorcycle noises but this is something new to me.

He pauses briefly, but then he's off and running. We're both laughing now.

"Frieda fell to one stump, then to the other,
  Some even say she muttered MUTTHUH!
  She looked straight up at the trees spinning round;
  Then, with a sigh, Frieda hit the ground."

He's buzzing and laughing so hard he can hardly drive. He even forgets to keep his foot on the accelerator and we're doing a legal fifty-five for the first time all day. I've got tears in my eyes and my sides hurt; definitely working up a hysterical laugh. I've got to watch myself.

About five miles farther on we pull up for gas and some lunch. The lunch stand is a converted trailer chocked up on railway ties. A lightweight swinging aluminum door latches shut behind us.

Along the back is a counter and there are two tables on the side we came in. We order hamburgers, then sit at one of the tables. There are no other customers. It's almost two, late for the lunch crowd. We order milkshakes with the hamburgers.

Now, there's something about an American hamburger in America; it's like French bread in France. Maybe it's the atmosphere, or the grass the cows eat, but an American hamburger in America is something special.

And these hamburgers we have in this jacked-up trailer are sensational. We spread them with everything: relish, mustard, catsup, mayonnaise. Those hamburgers *leak* out our fingers. The milkshakes are solid ice cream, stiff enough to hold the straws straight up. If there were an American equivalent to the *Michelin Guide*, this place deserves three stars with an asterisk.

Counting the milkshake, I'm probably putting back on three pounds in one sitting. I lost almost twenty over the past five months, twenty I could well afford to lose, and now I'll be packing them back on.

Pizzas, hot dogs, hamburgers, milkshakes; by the time we get to Philadelphia I won't be able to squeeze behind the wheel.

I'm still waiting for Billy to elaborate on his reasons for leaving Santa Cruz. I didn't even know he'd left school till he showed up at Mother's. I asked then if he'd walked out in the middle of the quarter but he said he didn't even start.

He's been up in Oregon working as a choker, living out Kesey's *Sometimes a Great Notion*, I think. I only wish he'd told me, for income tax purposes at least. I'm carrying him as a deduction and if he's getting W-2 forms I'm in trouble. All I need is the IRS on my tail.

I can just see Billy up there in the woods, no experience with that kind of life or even work itself, and he's choking: hooking cables on felled timber. Lord! It's like me going into the infantry when I'd never even had a BB gun or firecrackers. I know Billy did get hurt; he told me that much.

We drive on, skipping all the big towns. Once you get off the highway, you're dumped into local traffic. None of these towns have any real interest. When you've lived in Paris for over fifteen years, it's hard to work up a big interest in Abilene, Kansas, even if Dwight D. Eisenhower did spend his profitable boyhood there. The most you can hope for is a town like Denver, which is a smoothed-over Westernized imitation of Chicago, which is an imitation of New York, which is an imitation of Paris or Rome or Athens or London.

For dinner we stop and have another pizza. We haven't had a pizza for over twenty-four hours. We get a big, green salad too, because we're plugged up. The salad's more expensive than the pizza, but we both definitely need grass-type food. Later, we find a motel well off the road.

This is a true Midwest town, all separate houses with porches, everything wood or fieldstone; sidewalks.

After dinner, Billy and I walk around. The people on the porches stare at us.

There are locusts or crickets in the trees, making the most god-awful noise. It sounds like an electric generator gone mad; the buzzing comes from every direction.

At the edge of town we see a lit-up baseball field with cars parked all around it. Now, Billy has never played baseball. He doesn't even know the names of the positions. If I said shortstop, it wouldn't mean anything to him. Like as not, he'd think it's some soft drink or a deodorant for men.

But, God, as a kid, I lived, breathed, died for baseball. There was no way I could've survived in my neighborhood if I didn't play. Our year wasn't spring, summer, fall, winter. It was baseball, football, basketball and ice hockey. We squeezed the kite, roller-skating and swimming seasons in the spaces.

By March I'd be down in the cellar taping up balls and bats. Soon as the snow was gone we were throwing balls against steps, getting our eyes and arms in shape. We had more damned varieties of games we played against cement steps with tennis balls. Then, all summer long, it was baseball. We went from after breakfast till nine o'clock at night. We'd keep games going when you could only see the ball if it was against the sky.

We'd play three or four nine-inning baseball games every day. The second game was at lunchtime and the unchosen usually got to play then. Bringing your lunch was an admission of defeat.

Mornings, I'd put on my ragtag baseball uniform, crowned by my Philadelphia A's baseball cap, fill a milk bottle with water, hang my glove on the end of the bat, tuck a ball in my pocket and go down to the baseball field. There'd always be a bunch there ready to play. It was usually choose up; we rarely had regular teams; but we always had more than enough to make two full nines, and it was tough competition getting chosen. There were whole rituals for the choosing process, involving swinging a bat round your head three times after catching it and then hand-fitting around the bat. After the teams were chosen, there were backup jobs for the unlucky: scorekeeping, umping, shagging fouls and hunting lost balls.

It was interesting how the slotting happened, how you found out just what you could play according to your skills and abilities. At first, I caught because I wasn't agile or quick enough to play infield and I wasn't a good enough hitter to play outfield, even right field.

But I wasn't strong enough to be a good catcher either. When Ray Ziggenfuss moved into the neighborhood, it wasn't long before I knew my days as catcher were over. Ray was strong, quick with his hands and he could hit. He could hit well enough to play outfield but he wanted to catch. A kid named Mickey Mullens was the other catcher and he was good, too. I was about to be slotted as foul-chaser and lunchbringer.

I took my carefully saved Christmas money, and bought a genuine first baseman's mitt. I practiced tagging and making all the combinations, day and night, for weeks. My left foot could stretch back the full length of my body. I could reach and grab with that glove like a lizard catching flies. It was the one place in the infield where I might make it.

Only I wasn't left-handed. A left-handed first-baseman has a tremendous advantage; his gloved hand's to the infield so he has a bit more reach toward the ball. Also left-handers had an advantage on right-handed pitchers.

So I still didn't make it. I worked my way from foul-chasing to scorekeeper but I wanted to play more than one game a day.

I decided to become a pitcher. In our neighborhood, pitching was the nonathlete's job. I worked for hours pitching to Ziggenfuss or at a circle on a brick wall, and developed into a fairly accurate thrower with a reasonable slider. In those days we called it a drop or a hook. Today they call a hook a curve and what we called a curve, a screwball. Even baseball changes.

Now here Billy and I are in this little Kansas town and two college teams are having a game. I'm excited; Billy says he'll come but he's not enthusiastic.

We pass some motorcycles in the parking lot. The local thugs are racing each other fifty-yard sprints. I have a hard time getting Billy past this but we do get inside for the beginning of the game.

There's the smell of cigarettes being smoked outside, of wire, fresh paint and the overall odor of peanuts and hot dogs. This is an American baseball game complete with handles.

But the quality of play isn't so hot. We've probably all been spoiled with so much professional-level ball on TV.

Billy's bored out of his mind, anyway. I keep trying to explain what's going on but it doesn't mean anything to him. It's no secret baseball's a subtle strategy game. If you can't go along with the minor shifting decisions, it can be a drag. If you don't know how the infield should play with men on first and third, two out, actionwise, it's only one guy throwing a ball past another with a stick.

Billy sees it as really dumb.

"Christ, look at that guy standing way out there, Dad!"

He points to the right fielder.

"Nobody's hit one ball to him all night. He's either standing, waiting for nothing, or running back and forth. And that fat one, squatting behind the guy with the club, is liable to find his left ear growing on the right side of his head."

I give up and enjoy the game. It's too late, too many years in Europe. When the game's over, we head back to the motel. I didn't realize how tired I was. I lie there thinking about what different lives Billy and I have led. We've lived together most of his life but we haven't actually shared much. It's too damned bad.

12

That evening Billy shows up. I'm asleep and Mother's still up watching the Johnny Carson show.

It's amazing she didn't drop over dead. The first thing I know is the damned intercom beside my bed buzzes. It's Mom, practically hysterical.

"Jacky, come! COME! *Billy's* here!"

My brain's spinning. "Billy *here*? Billy's in Santa Cruz. He can't be here." I come staggering out in my sleeping ex-running suit, portrait of the lost athlete.

But there he is. I haven't seen Billy since he left Paris for school. It's damned nice to see him. We give each other a semi-hug. My God, he smells like a whore's shoes. I step back and he's a sight! He looks undernourished, pimply. When Billy doesn't eat right, he breaks out. His clothes are filthy, his shoes falling off his feet.

Mother's standing there, her hands in little fists over her mouth. I have to admit, he's enough to make anybody cry. He looks like an overgrown edition of a drawing for a Boys' Town Christmas seal.

He tells us he got a letter from Vron saying Grandma's sick. He asks her how she's feeling, but she still can't talk.

I tell him Dad's sick now and is in the hospital. I'm trying to maneuver Mom into a chair. I don't know how much to tell Billy about Dad here in front of Mom.

I'm figuring where to put him. The best is the garden room where I've been sleeping. Out there it's less chance he'll bug Mom. I'll move up here to the side room. I'll give him a key and tell him to keep that place locked up. The way he slops his stuff, beds unmade and all, it could be too much. I can see she's already working up a scene.

I'm somewhat disturbed myself. If he looks bad to me, he must look ten times worse to Mom. Before I know it, she's dashed into the bathroom and started a bath. I drag her back to the chair. I ask her to go to bed but she doesn't move.

"Please, Mother. It's late."

I know every minute she's out here looking at Billy she's digging her grave. I help her from the chair and lead her to the bedroom. I ease her into bed, get a glass of water and Valium. I put these on the nightstand.

I dash back and tell Billy to get those clothes off, and take a bath.

"Put the clothes you're wearing and any clothes in your sack into the clothes hamper. I'll wash them tomorrow. Here's a bathrobe and a pair of Granddad's pajamas."

I'm not waiting for Joan, I'll take those things to the Laundromat myself; if they're around the house too long, we'll need to fumigate.

"Bill, you take a good long bath, wash your hair and relax while I help Mother get to sleep. There's some shampoo under the sink."

I go back to the bedroom. Mother's having a fit. She hasn't taken the Valium. Her head's on the pillow but she keeps lifting it to talk. I sit on the edge of the bed and insist she take the Valium.

"What's the matter with him, Jacky? He looks sick. What's he been eating? Is that the way they dress in college these days? He looks like a hippy. Does he take drugs, Jacky? Ask him, Jacky, you ask him! I won't have any drug addicts in my house!"

On and on.

"He isn't even's clean as a hippy; he looks like a bum. I'm amazed the police let him walk the street like that."

I listen and wait for the Valium to take effect. Everything she says is vaguely true. That's the way with Mother. She doesn't actually invent so much as she grabs onto rag-tail ends of things and elaborates them into personal fantasies.

Finally she settles down. I quietly sneak away. Billy has just finished his bath and comes out of the bathroom, dripping wet, wearing Dad's second bathrobe. He comes into the living room, turns on the TV and plops into the platform rocker with his feet on the other chair. Billy's expert at moving in, making himself at home.

I go into the bathroom. Everything's soaking wet and the tub's still full of dirty water! I guess when you're into taking showers, you don't know how to handle a tub. I'm sure he wouldn't leave it on purpose; he just doesn't think. I wipe up the mess, throw his clothes in the hamper and clean the tub. I'm not going to say anything. Mostly, I want to find out what he's doing here, why he isn't at school.

When I come back to the living room, I turn the TV down so it won't wake Mom. Billy needs everything two decibels higher than I can take. At the station break, I get up and turn it off.

"Billy, Grandmom isn't in very good shape. She's had two severe heart attacks and is barely holding on. Every day she gets under her belt now is to her advantage. She's had what's called an occlusion. She can't have any shock or strenuous exercise.

"But Grandma isn't the real problem, bad as that is. Dad's the one."

I tell him what's happening and I can see his face turning white. All our kids love Dad. He has a knack for playing with little kids. He'd always have something new for them to play with, a new trick or a toy he'd made, or darts, Ping-Pong, a BB gun; something. This was part of Mom's proof he wasn't "quite right. That's where Joan gets it; it's part of that crazy Tremont streak."

Billy's stopped rocking, and leans forward. I don't want to make it hard, but I want him to know the problems.

I tell how Dad doesn't know us, can't talk, has to be cleaned and fed. Billy wants to know what's wrong. I tell him what Ethridge and Santana have told me, how it's a sudden onslaught of senility.

Then I let out my own feelings about the kind of care he's been getting. It's something I haven't talked about to anybody, not even Joan. I express my doubts about both Dad's treatment and the diagnosis. I'm feeling strongly it might be something truly physiological, more complex than simple senility. I'm also thinking in terms of some fault with the anesthetic or perhaps a blockage in the artery feeding his brain, perhaps a clot formed as a result of the operation. I'm only fishing; I know it; I don't have enough knowledge.

I reveal my doubts, my worries; I need to talk. I hadn't realized before how, after Vron and Joan, he's the next closest person to me. It snuck up.

"I tell you, Bill. Dad's shown less evidence of senility than most men his age. Sure, he isn't fifty, but senile he isn't."

Finally, I ask what he's doing down here. He says he's dropped out of school; it wasn't meaning anything to him.

I can live with that. If you don't know what you want, school's only another way to put in time. But Billy was always such a good student.

I ask what his plans are: job or what. That's when he mentions coming back to France.

Now, Vron and I'd be happy having him near us, but if he isn't going to school he's got to work; he can't hang around the house. Billy has his own life-style; and it doesn't fit ours; no more than *my* ways fit here in California. He's flown out of our nest.

But we drop it there; neither of us is ready to go into it. We talk about Dad and then he goes out to the back bedroom.

I go in the side room and I'm asleep faster than I thought possible; maybe just anything not to think.

The next day Joan comes; she gives Billy a hug and a tug on his long hair. Billy and I throw his laundry in the car. Joan says she'll clean house while we're gone. She's brought food and will cook supper for us, too.

After the Laundromat, we drive to the hospital.

Billy stares at Dad, lying flat out with his eyes open. Dad doesn't recognize either of us, even when Billy gives him a hard hug and kiss. Billy's so positive, so violent, he almost pulls off the IV. Dad stares at Billy, his head and neck stiff, his lips moving.

He's on catheter again. I peer under the covers and it's indwelling. He's becoming a living piece of meat. If he were anything except human, we'd let him die. He's going fast and it seems there's nothing to do; I don't think he could've survived another day of my amateur care.

Billy's badly shaken. He goes out in the hall while I stay with Dad; I'm stroking his head, talking to him softly. Dad watches me passively, without emotion or interest. Billy comes back; he's stopped crying but his light blue eyes are rimmed red. We go down in the elevator and out to the parking lot without saying much. The daylight is glaring out there. I take Dad's sunglasses from the glove compartment and give them to Billy.

"What's happened, Dad? What could've happened to make him like that?"

I go through it again. I tell him I don't know and I'm not sure the doctors do either.

We get the clothes at the Laundromat. Together, we fold Billy's things, also the sheets and towels. We still aren't talking.

At home, I tell Joan it isn't worth going; Dad won't even know she's there. She's going anyway. I know how she feels. It tears you apart; but you have to.

Mom wants to know what we all want to know.

"What's the matter with him, Jacky? Is he crazy?"

I try convincing her he's not crazy. Mom gives me what's meant to be one of her long, penetrating looks.

"He never was exactly right in the head, I know! I've lived with him over fifty years! He is *not* an ordinary man."

What floors me the next days is Billy with TV. Maybe all those years without it in our house is catching up with him.

He spends hours watching. It doesn't make any difference what's on. I swear he doesn't bother changing channels, he keeps staring right on through the commercials. He watches soap operas, talk shows, cowboy movies, the police series; he even watches a baseball game. He watches as if it's an eyeball marathon.

Mom's happy having somebody to watch with her. She brings Billy up on what's happened so far in the soap operas; who's been sleeping with whom and who has an illegitimate baby by what and who's trying to steal whose husband or wife. Billy stares straight on through it all.

I know where I've stashed an old box of paints. I roust it out, clean the brushes in turpentine and go through the tubes. I might keep some sanity if I can paint. I hate to admit this, but there *is* a therapeutic aspect to my painting. It shouldn't be that way for me, a professional, but it's there.

When I can control my private world, take things from out there and recast them the way I want, it heals me.

I ask Billy to keep an eye on Mother; I go in back, find a pair of old-time white dungarees, a sweat shirt and cap. I'll use the canvases I left for Dad.

I have the box on my back and I'm on the motorcycle before I even think to ask what I'm going to paint. I'd completely forgotten where I was. One possibility would be to paint the insides of garages. But I want to be outside in the sunshine; I've had enough looking inside at people's personal garbage. I want to see long distances.

I don't want to paint these rows of suburban houses either. I know it's a big part of America, but I don't want to paint it. I know from experience I only paint well things I want to paint. If the push doesn't come from inside, it's only work.

But there's one thing that *has* turned me on; it's those Venice beach-front stores and old houses. I roll down and park where Rose Avenue runs into the beach. I rock the bike up on its stand and stroll along in my dungarees, deep pockets for nails, small pockets in front for a folding rule and flat carpenter's pencil. I lean forward with the box on my back. My insides are settling slowly like a glass of beer going flat.

I stop at an old brick motel, a strange-looking building with an up-slanting courtyard. It's got dark green faïence tile roofing with tiles missing. French doors close off the courtyard from the wind. The sun is trapped, held in that courtyard. It's something to paint. It's a California version of Mad Ludwig's Neuschwanstein Castle in Bavaria; not some grotesque imitation like Disneyland but the same kind of mind, a romantic mind, a mind that didn't want to build another ordinary motel.

This is a fantasy in brick and tile. There's even a tower in back with wooden stairs leading up to it. I'd love living in that room back there on top of that tower, and once I'm inside this painting I will.

It's amazing how fast painting comes back. It's as if I'd put down the brushes yesterday. I'm right into it, no loss at all.

I'm putting the last licks on the underpainting when I look up and the sunset is happening. I can't believe it. Holy cow, they'll think I've run out on them!

I pack my box and jump on the bike. It feels like old times, smelling of turpentine, moving on a motorcycle with the box and a wet canvas flapping on my back. In Paris nobody pays much attention to me; I'm part of the scenery. But here I'm getting hoots and hollers from passing cars; I guess they think I'm another California clown. I pull over and turn the painting upside down on the holder.

At home, they're still glued to the TV. I go out back and change into my regular clothes. I use the garden hose and a brush to scrub the paint out of my hands. I start dinner and tell Billy he can eat with us or take off and do whatever he wants. I give him five bucks, the keys to my motorcycle.

Dinner doesn't go too badly. Billy stays and is on his best behavior. There's no overt lip-smacking; no farting, not out loud anyway, no belching. He claims he gets stomachaches if he doesn't fart and belch on schedule. Mom's behaving, too. We get through the meal fine but I develop indigestion waiting for something to happen.

After dinner, Billy leaves. I wash dishes and sit with Mom in the living room. For some reason, the TV isn't on. Maybe Billy's maniac approach satiated even Mother. I want to talk about how it was when she and Dad were young, how they met, what they planned. I know I'll never get it anything like straight. I know too, she won't actually be lying either. Her fantasies, even more than with most people, get realer, truer, to her with time.

I'm interested in listening. I'm beginning to realize I'll soon be the oldest branch on the male end of our particular genealogical tree. With Dad gone, I'll have no more direct access to tribal, family information. I should've talked more with my grandparents to find out what they were like, what they thought. I'm needing cementing. There's something tenuous about being male, nothing in line, all so zigzag. I want some Mother glue to help stick myself together.

It's astounding what Mom doesn't know. She doesn't know how many brothers or sisters her mother had. She knows a bit about her father's family, the black Protestants, but nothing about her mother's. My God, we all disappear so quickly, so easily.

She tells how she met Dad under an awning outside Wanamaker's in Philadelphia. She was fifteen and it was raining. She'd snitched her older sister Maggie's hat to look dressed up and older. The rain was ruining it and she was crying. Dad shared his umbrella with her.

I can't imagine Dad carrying an umbrella, especially at eighteen, but times change. For the greater part of his life, Dad wouldn't even wear a hat in the rain; said it was good for his hair, made it curl. That all changed when he went bald.

At this time, Mom is only a year out from under her nervous breakdown and working in a candy factory. According to Mother, from the beginning she knew Dad was the man for her. I wish I'd talked with Dad about what he remembers.

Mother had been dating another fellow, "a very nice Jewish boy from a very well-off family," to use Mom's exact formula. I've heard of Sidney Parker often enough all my life. "He didn't have a Jewish name, but he was Jewish." Probably every woman has some man she brings up as the one she might have, should have, would have, married. Maybe men do this, too, and I just haven't noticed it.

Mom switches on the TV. She has a fairly consistent evening schedule of particular shows. There's also a Dodger game, but Mom doesn't like baseball. We compromise. I see the second inning through two out in the third, then all of the seventh and eighth. By this time, the Dodgers are behind eight–three, so I imagine they lost. Johnny Carson takes preference.

Between the third and seventh innings, we watch a show called *All in the Family*. Mom insists the star of this show looks like me. He's called Archie Bunker, a sort of hard-hat, hard-nosed jerk with all the racial, cultural prejudices of the poverty mind. I think he's supposed to be basically sympathetic.

Maybe it's like seeing yourself by accident in a three-way mirror at Sears. You see things you don't let yourself see usually: the thickness of your neck, the real extent of your pot, the generally crappy posture; but I can't accept myself that way.

Sure, we both have blue eyes, OK, but then so did Adolf Hitler. We're both cursed with turned-up noses; how about Bob Hope? But Bunker has white hair and I don't. Maybe it would be white if it hadn't fallen out; who knows? The main thing is, he looks so stupid, tight-together pig eyes. But I might look stupid, too, if my hair hadn't receded, making me look as if I have a high forehead. I hope my soul isn't as hidden from me as my physical identity.

"See, doesn't he look like you, Jacky? Doesn't he? Even the profile; see that? If only you didn't have a beard."

I triple-resolve to never never shave off my beard. Also, I start on an instant diet. It lasts three days.

I like to eat; I won't look in mirrors. What the hell, fifty-two *is* fifty-two; I have to look like something; I can't always be a boy.

It's amazing how much they squeeze into those situation comedies. Eleven minutes of any half-hour show is reserved for ads and station breaks. So they work it all out in nineteen minutes.

No wonder everybody's anxious and feeling there's no meaning or continuity to things. You watch TV long enough, you get a warped view of the world. Normal-paced living seems slow, boring.

After Johnny Carson, I put Mom to bed, with Valium beside a glass on the bedside table. I don't want any more of the drug-addict business. If she can't sleep she can take them; it's her life. I'm learning, but slowly.

Now I can't sleep. I find myself staring at those "by the numbers" paintings Dad did of The Blessed Mother and The Sacred Heart. For some reason they're hung the wrong way. Usually they're hung with The Sacred Heart on the left as you look at them.

I can't say I've ever consciously noticed a special way to hang these pictures but it must have seeped in during nine years of parochial school.

I don't think enough, ideas come out of nowhere. Maybe that's what thinking is. But right then an idea comes. At my age now, I'd consider Jesus, even at his oldest, thirty-three, as a snot-nosed kid, a hotdogging post-adolescent. I lie there in the semidark. Johnny boy, you're getting old all right.

When I was a kid, the beard made Jesus look older, like another breed of human being, more serious, a grandfather or father figure.

Now the kids are the ones with beards. Having a beard is the same as wearing jogging shoes or sweat shirts, a cheap shot at staying young.

I look at Mary. She couldn't've been more than sixteen or seventeen when she had Jesus. Now, let's say the archangel Gabriel really did come down and tell her about God being the father and the baby being God, too, and telling her what to name it; would she still be believing that seven, eight months later?

And Joseph, if he'd really had nothing to do with her, what's he thinking?

And what happened to Joseph? You never hear about him

after Jesus is twelve. Even if he isn't Jesus's father, they could at least say he died or ran away or got run over by a rampaging donkey; something.

And what a lousy day they chose to celebrate Saint Joseph's birthday, two days after Saint Patrick's. They don't actually know when either of them was born, so they could've picked any day. Joseph is limited to holding off donkeys and cows while Jesus is being born; then to giving a few carpentry lessons.

Next, there's the marriage feast of Cana. Mary's all of forty-six, forty-seven; nice age for a woman, fully mature and no real decrepitude set in yet. So Mary pushes Jesus into his career before he's ready; wants to show her friends what a hotshot son she's got. I wonder if he did a few parlor tricks at home first, to practice.

Or maybe Mary was tired of having a thirty-year-old galoot of a son still hanging around the house.

I'm looking at these two pictures and spinning. I'm for fantasy but this was supposed to be real. This whole mystique invades the psyche and changes you. I'm wondering how much of it's left in me; I'm sure there's a lot. I lie out there in bed having these sacrilegious thoughts, wondering what it's all about.

The next morning we get a call from Ethridge. Mother takes it; she's holding the receiver against her chest, making exaggerated whispering mouth movements. "He wants *you*, Jacky." I pick up the living-room phone. She can stay on her line and listen.

Ethridge comes on in cool, masterful tones. This call must have been fairly high on his list; it's only quarter past nine.

He goes through the basics of Dad's condition, spreading the old medical jargon. I listen. Finally he comes to the crux of the matter.

"I'm scheduling your father for release today, Mr. Tremont. You can pick him up after twelve o'clock."

I'm stunned. I can't believe it.

"You mean he's recovered, Doctor?"

"Well, no, but he's in a stable condition."

"Then how can you release him? As he is, he can't live outside a hospital."

"Well, Mr. Tremont, your father's condition is stable, medically; there's not much we can do for him. He's basically custodial."

"What does that mean, Dr. Ethridge? What does custodial mean in this case?"

"Mr. Tremont, we just cannot hold hospital beds for patients who can't profit from medical care."

I'm still having a hard time believing it.

"But, Dr. Ethridge, we tried having him home. I slept with him, fed, bathed him, spent all my time with him and still couldn't keep him alive. He *does* need hospital care."

There's a slight pause. Ethridge is gathering his limited patience.

"Mr. Tremont, your father should probably be in a convalescent home. I'll give him an extra day so you can have time to find a place. The social-services personnel here should be able to help you."

He hangs up.

I sit there not knowing what to do. I hear Mother shuffling up the hall. She's in a state; shaking her fist.

"I always knew that Ethridge was an SOB! Daddy liked him just because he came from Wisconsin. I know he made a mistake on that gall-bladder operation!"

I lead her to a chair.

"Take it easy, Mom. Having another heart attack won't help anything."

"Who's been paying money for over twenty years so they could build their big new hospital? We pay and pay; now when we need them they throw us out. A bunch of kikes and niggers, that's all they are."

She's crying.

"Jacky, I don't want Daddy going to any old people's home. Think of it. All the years we've worked and saved, taking care of you kids, and now he winds up like this."

"It's a convalescent home just like the one down the street here, Mother, not an old people's home."

"Don't tell me; I know. It's only a fancy name for the same thing. Daddy and I would look in at those poor souls down the street and we'd feel sorry for them. We were so glad we had our own place and now it's happening to him."

She's crying now. I wait. I want to phone Joan but things here need settling first. What choices do we really have? I don't know how I can force the hospital to keep Dad. I know there's no way I can sustain him, especially with Mother here. He has to go into a home, that's all there is to it. Finally I calm Mom down; and phone Joan.

I explain the situation, tell her how upset Mom is. Joan asks me to put her on the phone. I sit back.

After about five minutes nodding and saying yes, bringing up complaints but backing off, Mother passes the phone to me.

"I think Mom understands, Jack. It's psychological more than anything else. There's the whole Irish business about the poorhouse. She'll be all right. You go to Perpetual and talk to the social-service people."

It gets resolved just like that. I make breakfast for Mother and myself. She's still vacillating between acceptance and resistance. Billy comes in from the back and I tell him what's happened. He's set to go burn down the hospital. He starts Mom up again. Behind her back, I desperately give him the signal to cool it. Lord, it's hard enough.

After being shuttled around the Horn three times, I find social services in the hospital basement. The woman who's assigned to me is a nice person; a listener. She phones and verifies, calls for Dad's records. She's not rushing or pressing in any way. She explains the nature of Perpetual-run homes for members. She shows me the names of other places accredited by Perpetual.

I'm shocked by the prices. Mother'd be wiped out in short order. I ask how Dad can qualify for one of the Perpetual-run convalescent extensions. These are covered by the insurance plan. I'm feeling like a cheapskate copping a plea.

She smiles, speaks with a little Scottish brogue or something, is about my age, maybe younger; graying-black hair, light blue eyes.

"Well, Mr. Tremont, if he needs medical as opposed to custodial care, he could qualify." She goes carefully through Dad's records, looks up, smiles.

"It shows here your father has an indwelling catheter; that would definitely be classified as medical. If he's dismissed with that catheter, you should have no trouble."

She's happy for me, for Dad. My stomach sinks. Am I willing to keep a catheter on for maybe thirty dollars a day? Is it my decision to make?

I thank her and say I'll be right back. I slink upstairs and hang around the urology clinic till I catch Sam at an off minute. He remembers me immediately.

"It sure is too bad about your dad, Mr. Tremont. I've never seen anybody take such a bad turn so fast."

I ask about the indwelling catheter. He says Santana has scheduled it to be removed this afternoon. I ask if it can be left in. He looks at me. I explain the situation. He shakes his head.

"You'll have to check with Dr. Santana. He'll be right out; talk to him."

When Santana comes, I step up. He backs off two steps.

"Dr. Santana, could you leave the indwelling catheter on my father for another week or so?"

He looks at me; wishing me away.

"Medically speaking, that could make sense, Mr. Tremont. Do you have a special reason?"

"The convalescent home where I'd like to place him would prefer it."

I leave it at that, hoping he's not up on the details for this kind of thing. He looks at me again. He has papers in his hands he keeps going back to.

"All right, Mr. Tremont, we'll leave it in."

He walks away. I go to Sam and start explaining. He's leaning against the urology sign-in desk, holds up his hand.

"I heard. OK. He's scheduled for discharge tomorrow, right?"

"That's right. Thanks a lot, Sam; thanks for everything."

We shake and I head back downstairs.

I tell the lady, whose name is Mrs. Trumbull, the catheter will stay in. She glances over her cards.

"There might just be a place available at Cottage Villa. I'll call."

On the phone, she goes over Dad's situation. She looks up at me and smiles as she hangs up.

"There's no opening right now but there will be soon. They want you to come for an interview."

She pulls out a card with an address and signs it. Cottage Villa is about a half mile away, on top of a hill near the San Diego and Santa Monica Freeway Interchange. I drive there.

From the outside, the place looks great. It's built with an open U-shaped front enclosing a large lawn with flowers. There are colored umbrellas spread around and picnic-type tables. It could be a low-priced golf club in Palm Springs.

Extending back from the turns of the U are two long corridors. The wheelchair in all its variations is the main theme; stainless steel and strained faces, pale wrinkled skin, white hair, everybody in dressing gowns. I work my way to the office.

The lady there tells me how convalescent homes are 70 percent women; the men die young. I'm in luck because there's a man who should die within the next forty-eight hours; Dad can have his place.

She asks if I want to see the room but I don't have the courage. She shows me another that's exactly the same. It looks like a small motel room with high-sided beds. There's a door on the corridor and a window to the parking lot. A man is sitting in a wheelchair by the window playing with himself.

She says she'll call the hospital and tell them when to move my father; the hospital will supply the ambulance. I tell her about the indwelling catheter and ask if it can be removed soon as possible without Dad losing Perpetual coverage.

"Don't you worry, once he's here we do what we want; the doctors are very understanding."

I'd hoped it would be something like that.

God, it's good getting outside again. I look up at the sun, then across the green to an almost motionless scene on the patio. I feel footloose, carefree, potent. I swing without pain into the car, gun her up and charge out of the parking lot, something nobody back there will ever do again.

At home, Mother comes shuffling up the hall. Before I open my mouth she starts. She can't accept the idea of Daddy in a home. Couldn't we hire a professional nurse and have her stay here with Daddy in the house? We could fix up the back room so she could live there.

It's something I hadn't thought of. I'm just feeling I have everything settled, now this. I sit down to get my breath, listen to her, nodding, trying to make it fit.

I pick up the phone and call Joan. It's the best way to tell Mom about the home without being interrupted. There's something magic about a phone. Most people will interrupt if you're talking to them or talking to somebody else in the room but won't interrupt if you're talking to someone else on a phone. I explain the situation to Joan, including the indwelling catheter. Joan agrees to it all.

"Remember, Jack. It isn't the end of the world. If we don't like it, we can always take him out."

I bring up the new idea of having a nurse. Joan says she'll talk to Mother. I hand over the phone, go back in the bedroom, stretch out on the bed, pick up the receiver and listen.

Joan's doing it again. She's already worked out an angle.

"Look, Mother. It's no different from having him in the hospital, only it's closer. He's getting medical care, something we can't give him. It's not so far to visit. While he's there we can start looking for a nurse to stay at the house. We can't just find somebody overnight, it'll take time. We'll call the Catholic Welfare Agency."

I put down the receiver and try to relax. I've been tense all day and my blood pressure's pounding. One of Mother's Valium and a glass of water are beside the bed. I slug it down, stretch out and wait.

It's amazing how fast it works. Maybe it's all in the head but I feel myself unwind. The creeping worries around the edges of my unconscious recede and fade. I don't feel like sleeping but only staying in this rested, as opposed to restless, state.

Mom comes back to me after she hangs up. Just walking down the hall, it seems, she's changed her mind. She starts off with how nobody cares about old people.

"Even if you have money, they only want to tuck you away somewhere with strangers. It didn't used to be that way. Oh, no! My sisters and I took care of *my* mother for seven years when she was half paralyzed. Then when she died we shared Pop around too.

"And you sure can't count on a visit or a phone call from grandchildren, even if you've had two heart attacks and your husband's dying in the hospital; they couldn't care less. Nobody cares about you when you're old."

She isn't crying, only tolling off these facts as if she's repeating some kind of litany. I can't argue with her.

I'm still riding loose on Valium. I'm listening to Mom but she isn't bugging me at all; I'm almost enjoying it. I feel like the master guru, ready to advise the world.

Next day, Joan begins looking for a nurse. Mother's willing to pay eighteen dollars a day, room and board; but she's never going to get any trained person at that price.

And Mother has so many restrictions. This person has to be Catholic, can't drink or smoke; of course, can't be black or Mexican or Cuban. Mother has a special category for Cubans. In fact, it can't be anybody with a foreign accent of any kind. And nobody too young or too old. We're looking for an ugly female, over forty, under fifty, who's competing for sainthood. I'm glad this is Joan's end of things.

I'll spend as much time as I can at the convalescent home. I want to see what kind of care Dad gets. I've heard the usual horror stories of mistreatment, oversedation, neglect. I'm hoping he'll only be there a week or two till Joan finds somebody.

. . .

The next morning I get a call from Perpetual; Dad's being released to Cottage Villa. He'll arrive there before noon in the hospital ambulance. I tell Mother, give her breakfast and go over.

He arrives on a stretcher. He has the indwelling catheter. I walk beside the stretcher while they wheel him to his room. I help the nurse settle him into bed. He's anxious, jerking his head around, watching but unaware. He doesn't recognize me and doesn't respond.

The attendants start with the lunchtime meal. It's on Dad's chart that he's to be spoon-fed. A lovely, pale brown woman, with one brown, one almost green eye, settles down to the job. We crank up the bed; Dad's wearing a restraining belt attached to his waist and wrists. She opens up the containers, talking to him all the time in a soft voice. She's gotten his name from the chart but pronounces it "Mr. Truman." I give her Dad's pronunciation. She asks for his first name and starts feeding, calling him "Jack" to get his attention. Dad's eyes are riveted on hers but he opens and closes his mouth when she touches his lips with the spoon and he's swallowing.

"That's the way, Jacky, that's a good boy; now let's have some carrots."

She has a sweet voice and a lovely body. I wonder why she's taken a job like this, what she feels about all these old people. I hope she can work up some commiseration for the people here, that it seems worthwhile.

I stand on the other side, watching, trying to pick up pointers. She smiles at me between bites and we talk.

She pushes some custard into Dad's mouth.

"You don't have to hang around here if you don't want; I can feed your daddy just fine; he's no trouble at all."

"Is it all right if I watch?"

She smiles a quick smile.

"It's perfectly OK with me if you want to watch. I don't mind."

I talk to Dad as she feeds him. He pays no attention. His eyes are on the girl and he's cooperating with the feeding. He begins opening his mouth for more food soon as he's swallowed, even before she touches his lip with the spoon.

I watch her. Her arms are full but not plump or fat; the white uniform is crisp and presses against her body. It's a lightweight material so I can see the difference where the hem is turned up at the end of her sleeve compared to where the cloth is directly against her skin.

When she's finished, I ask if I can take Dad outside to sit on the patio.

"I think that'd be real nice for him."

We take the restrainers off, get him tightly bundled up in his dressing robe and transfer him to a wheelchair along with his urine bottle. There's a little holder for the bottle on the bottom, under the seat. He looks better sitting up; any stimulation is better than lying in bed, scared.

I push him through the halls. He's gotten into the habit of hanging his lower lip open; it's so unlike him. One of Dad's characteristics all his life has been a firm mouth and tight jaw. Now, with his lower jaw slack, his lip out in a pout and his head down, eyes peering from under eyebrows, he's like Charles Laughton playing Captain Bligh. He doesn't look like himself.

Outside, I find a table with a sun umbrella and park Dad in the shade. I sit down in the sun beside him. I talk about how relaxing it is, how good the sun feels. I talk about the flowers, naming some of them. We sit there for almost an hour. I'm tending to run down, letting the dead calm of the place leak into me.

Then he begins talking. First, he's talking to himself, mumbling; his voice is so low, so rusty, I can't catch anything. I lean close from behind not to distract him. His eyes and head are moving, tracking. He's seeing something across the lawn, out the gate toward the overpass to the freeway. I lean closer.

"You know, Ed; we ought to start picking them cucumbers."

He looks back at me, through me, looking for affirmation. I nod my head. I want to keep it going.

"You're right there, Jack; we'd better do that."

"The pickle factory's payin' seventy-five cents a barrel; now's the time to sell."

"That's right, Jack; do you think we can get them in to-morrow?"

He looks at me closely. There's more Wisconsin twang in his voice.

"Don't forget, Ed, we gotta help Dad muck out the barn tomorrow. Remember that."

"Yeah, that's right, Jack. I forgot."

"But we can start soon's we're done, then get the last after milkin'. We can borrow the rig and haul 'em in Saturday."

"Good idea, Jack. We'll do that."

He sits there, leaning forward, shaking his head, smiling. I wait but that's it. Nothing I say can start it up again. When it begins to cool, I wheel Dad in and fix up his bed for him. The nurse helps. We work on either side of the bed, tucking and buckling restrainers. She says her name's Alicia.

I tell her mine's the same as Dad's. I tell her about living in Paris, about being an artist, about coming because Mom's sick. I know it doesn't sound real, not even to me anymore.

"How do you like working here?"

She makes a face, shrugs, sighs.

"It's so depressing. I been working in different places like this for five years. You always lose; nobody gets better from being old."

She goes around to the end of the bed.

"But when you're alone and have a little girl, you gotta work, and jobs just aren't all that easy to find. Here I can usually make my own hours, too. It ain't so bad."

She looks at her watch; says she's going off duty. The other nurse will feed Dad dinner. I ask if I can give her a lift anywhere. She looks at me quickly.

"Thanks a lot, that's nice, but Missus Kessler, the lady who runs this place, would blotch the ceiling if I went out with you."

She giggles, looks at the floor, shakes her head. I think she misunderstands.

"It's only I'm going home to check my mother, then come back here to help with Dad's dinner. I thought maybe I could drop you off someplace."

She looks at me, cocks her head.

"Man, you sure are nice to your folks. Nobody comes to

see these people here. There's some I know haven't had a visitor or even a letter for years."

She turns, pauses at the door.

"Even if you was black, Missus Kessler would make us a scene."

When I get home, everything's OK. Billy's slumped into Dad's chair and they're watching some show. I tell him I'll be back soon as I feed Dad and he can take off for the night. Mother insists she's perfectly all right and doesn't need people baby-sitting her all the time.

In back with Billy, I help clean things up. Billy says he doesn't know how long he can take it. Mother's bugging him about his hair, his bare feet, his uncut toenails, his pimples, his smells, his farts.

He tells me a friend of his from Santa Cruz is coming down and is it all right if they stay in the back room. I tell him I'll check with Mom. I feel it's going to be hard. Probably his friend will also be barefoot, bearded and play the same damned twenty songs on the guitar. I won't have much to say about how he acts around Mom, either. Things are getting away from me and I'm running down.

The third day I go help Dad with his midday feeding. I find him tight and tense. His lips are quivering, he's chattering madly and his eyes are flickering.

I can't get him to eat. It's hard to get his mouth open; then, when we do, he bites down hard on the spoon. It's the way it was when he had the Elavil.

I ask Alicia if they've been giving him his blood-pressure pills, or maybe he should have some Valium; anything to get him off this crazy high. She gets his charts, comes back and shows them to me. There's nothing about medication. Perpetual didn't forward his medication records or his medicine!

I go out and tell the head of the home to phone the hospital. I run to the car where there's some Valium I just picked up for Mother; my cuff's there, too, and I grab it. When I get back, Dad's practically trying to fly away. He's pulling at his straps, straining to get up, being jerked back again. He's gritting his teeth and groaning.

I work the cuff onto his arm and pump up. He's two forty over one twenty. Alicia goes to get the RN.

The RN whips out her own cuff, gets the same reading. I want her to give him some Valium, a sedative, something. He's liable to stroke. But she's afraid without a doctor; she's waiting till the records get here from Perpetual.

I charge out to the office phone and bulldoze my way through to Ethridge. The alarm must have gone out, because I get through fast. I tell Ethridge what's happened.

"That's too bad, Mr. Tremont. We'll get on that right away. The medical records are being forwarded."

The bastard's still very arrogant, just the peasants getting in the way of the leaders with the great mission.

"This is too much, Dr. Ethridge! Nobody's giving my father proper care! What is it; are you all hoping for him to die to get him off your consciences?"

"Come now, Mr. Tremont; let's not be hysterical."

"God damn it, I'm not hysterical; I'm only trying to keep my father alive and I'm not getting much help from you or the rest of the Perpetual staff."

That does it. He blows his stack. He starts off very coldly identifying himself as a doctor of medicine committed to the Hippocratic oath. He rolls on self-righteously for about two minutes. I interrupt him.

"Look, Dr. Ethridge, could you settle down long enough to prescribe for my father? He might well be dying while you're telling me how great you are."

There's silence. I'm expecting another "hang up."

"I'm informing you now, officially, Mr. Tremont that I am no longer your father's doctor. I disassociate myself from his case. I shall make arrangements for another doctor to be assigned."

I shout back before he can hang up.

"You're already disassociated, Dr. Ethridge! And don't bother looking for another doctor, I'll find one myself!

"I'm warning you now, *officially*, that you'd better check if your malpractice policies are paid up because you're going to need them! It was your direct responsibility to have those records forwarded and you are definitely in tort!"

I hang up. Mrs. Kessler is staring at me, her lips pulled tight together. She doesn't want trouble. She wants to keep her relationship with Perpetual. It's all in her eyes, in her mouth.

I say to myself, "Now what have you done, fool? God! How does this help?"

I go into Dad's room, tell Alicia not to watch, and pop ten milligrams of Valium into Dad's mouth. He chews it but swallows.

I sit there holding his hands and wait. He gradually subsides. I keep the cuff on and take his pressure every five minutes or so. It slowly goes down to one eighty over a hundred. He drifts into sleep and I take it off.

I'm stinking with nervous perspiration. I hate to leave but I have things to do. I need to find a new doctor at Perpetual or, if I have to, change hospitals altogether.

I go home to Mother's. Tom, Billy's friend, has arrived; terrific timing. He's everything I expected, only Jewish and quiet. He has even more pimples than Billy and wants to be a psychologist.

Mother's having fits. She's not running a flophouse and so forth. It seems Tom came in, dropped his backpack on the floor at the door while Billy and Tom hugged each other.

Do I think Billy's queer? You never know with those hippies. They've got everything all mixed up. I'm hardly listening.

First things first. I take Billy and Tom out back. I suggest they'll be more comfortable camping on the forty acres in Topanga. Billy's worried about leaving me alone with Mom. I assure him it'll be all right. Maybe he can come down once in a while to spell me for an afternoon or an evening. I tell him he can take my motorcycle up if he wants.

Tom has a tent and sleeping bags in the back of his car. I'm wishing I could go with them.

I use the phone in the bedroom. I call some medical friends. One's the head of medicine at GWU. I give him a brief rundown of what's happened and ask if he knows anyone he can recommend here at Perpetual. He doesn't know anybody. He does know somebody at Wadsworth General and suggests I call her. Her name is Dr. Smith. She's in internal medicine and urology. He says I can use his name.

I make another call to a neurosurgeon friend in Cincinnati. Max listens to the whole story. He tells me just what neurological procedures should be followed. He volunteers to fly out if it gets desperate.

I call Dr. Smith at Wadsworth. I give the name of my friend at GWU and review the problem. She's very sympathetic and says she'll ask around for someone good in the area and phone back within the half hour.

After fifteen minutes fending off Mother, the phone rings. Mom picks it up before I get to it.

"It's a *woman* for you, Jacky."

It's Dr. Smith. She's found a good man named Dr. Adam Chad at Perpetual. He's young but everybody recommends him highly. I thank her and promise I'll forward her best to Jens at GWU. I hang up, take a deep breath and phone Perpetual. I ask for Dr. Chad. His secretary says he'll call me back.

I go out and tell Mother I've canned Ethridge.

"But, Jacky, Daddy'll have a fit. You know how much he liked Dr. Ethridge. Why, he's been Daddy's doctor for almost fifteen years."

You never know with Mom. I explain what happened at the convalescent home. I tell her I'm convinced Dad has not been getting the kind of treatment he needs. I admit I've just made two long-distance phone calls consulting doctor friends and now have the name of a good doctor at Perpetual.

Mother wants to know what Dr. Ethridge did, what he said. I tell her I accused him of just letting Dad die and not really trying. This fits her prejudice, so now she's with me. The phone rings.

It's Dr. Chad. I explain who I am and that my father is a patient in a Perpetual convalescent extension home. I mention how highly recommended he is by Dr. Smith. I ask if he'll add Dad to his case load.

He asks who Dad's doctor is now. I tell him Dr. Santana

recently operated but Dr. Ethridge is his regular doctor. I tell how I've already spoken to Dr. Ethridge and he's in agreement with the change.

Chad won't commit himself but says he'll look at my father's record and check with Dr. Ethridge. That's OK with me; Ethridge'll yammer but he'll be glad to get off the case.

I sit down at the typewriter in the middle bedroom. I normally use an electric at home and it takes awhile adjusting to pounding the keys of this old, stand-up Underwood. I think best on the end of a broom, second best on the end of a brush and third best at a typewriter.

I try to put it all together, all that's happened to Dad, all that I've noticed. Then I retype the whole thing to make some logical sense. It goes to ten pages single-space. It helps, just getting it out and looking at it.

I call up a friend from UCLA student days. Now he has his own practice in Santa Monica. I make an appointment to see him.

I think about calling Joan but decide against it. I'm not ready for any calm advice or the reasonable approach.

The next day I go for my appointment with Scotty, my lawyer-ex-art-student friend. He's gotten fatter, grayer; looks old. I imagine I look old to him—Archie Bunker without hair. Time is a bitch. Mother keeps saying "old age isn't for sissies"; middle age isn't either. None of it is.

Scotty goes over what I've written. He asks some questions and takes a few notes. He peers up at me when he finishes and bounces the papers against the desk.

"It looks like a malpractice suit to me, Jack; but I'm not an expert. Perpetual is a big outfit and has some tough lawyers. Also, they have control of the records; doctors will lie like hell to protect themselves. This is an in-house situation, none of them are going to testify against each other."

I'm feeling he's giving me the brush-off, but he goes on.

"Still, it looks as if they're vulnerable."

He gives me a lawyer's cool stare, razor smile. God, think! They can do this even to an ex-art major.

"Look, Jack, two of the best malpractice lawyers in the

country operate right out of Santa Monica here. Both doctors, both lawyers; husband-wife team. They don't lose. If they'll take your case, you'll win."

That sounds more like it; I'm tuned to fight.

"How do I get in touch with these people?"

Scotty phones and makes an appointment right there, now. I thank him. He won't take anything.

"Save it for Knight & Knight, Jack; you'll need it."

The Knight & Knight offices are in a dark brown glass professional building on Wilshire and it's a huge suite. I'm ushered past a row of secretaries, through ankle-deep rugs, past solid mahogany walls covered with first-class decorative paintings.

In the inner office, the pair of them look like an ad for yachting clothes tucked behind those enormous black leather-topped desks.

We shake hands and I give them the résumé. She sits and he stands to read over her shoulder. These are California beautiful people. I'd hate like hell to have them on the other side. They look lethal, smooth and invulnerable.

She finishes first, looks at me through her tan, through sea-crushed eyes.

"What is it you actually want, Mr. Tremont?"

This seems like the dumbest question in the world. Then I realize it is *the* question and I haven't thought it through; I've been too mad to think. I'm slow responding.

"Well. First I want my father to stay in the hospital where he can get the kind of care he needs."

She stares at me, calm as a hunter. Her husband looks up now. They glance at each other. Now he speaks.

"There's a suit here but it would be a long and hard one. We've entered into litigation with Perpetual eight times so far and won each time; the first three, in court; the last five, settlements. They'd probably settle out of court with this, mostly on our track record."

His wife looks up; they thin-smile at each other, bridge partners with all the trumps. She takes over again. It's like

one of those mind-reading acts where the wiggle of a fingernail
or an eyelash tells your Social Security number and how much
money you have in your left pants pocket.

"We can assure you, you will get good care for your father;
you'll be able to request and receive any treatment necessary.
Is that what you want?"

I quickly write off a half-million-dollar settlement; it could
pollute my mother, me and our descendants for generations.
I couldn't live with it either; Perpetual's wrong but not that
wrong. I hear myself say it out loud.

"That's all I want."

She reaches into a small space hidden behind the pen-
holder. She pulls out a card with her tanned hand, well-veined,
slightly liver-spotted and garnished by a silver-set emerald
worthy of Paulette Goddard. She signs it. He takes the pen
from her hand, somehow a subtle act of intimacy. He signs
too. She hands the card across to me.

"Take this to Dr. Benson, the administrative director of
Perpetual. Tell him you have engaged us concerning a potential malpractice suit; show him this document you've written,
just as it is. Tell him we've seen it. Also, write out any and all
treatment or consultation you want for your father and mail it
by registered letter to his physician in care of the hospital."

During this speech, her husband has strolled silently from
behind the desk and around beside me. I'm having a hard time
keeping my eyes off him; I know he isn't going to pull out a
silencer-extended Luger and fit it cross-armed in the crook of
his elbow but I think of it. He's only anxious to make a quick
trip in the Maserati to the courts; tennis, that is. He snaps a
brief stiff bow.

"We're certain this card is all you will need, Mr. Tremont."

I take the card. She stands. This is it; I'm dismissed all
right.

"Thank you very much for your time and consideration.
What do I owe you for your services?"

She's pulling a hand-knit Irish sweater over her shoulders.

"The secretary will bill you. Please let us know if you wish
to pursue this matter further. And would you have the secre-

tary nearest the door make two Xerox copies of this statement for our files?"

"Goodbye, Mr. Tremont. I don't think you will need us anymore."

They usher me to the door, smile as they pass by: empty-handed, no sails, no rackets, no golf clubs, no Luger.

The secretary makes the copies and tells me I'll be billed at the end of the month. It turns out to be a hundred dollars for that little card, a hundred dollars well spent for an ace of spades I can stick in my sleeve, a card I can shove up Ethridge's ass.

I go home and try explaining things to Mother. Now she's afraid Perpetual is going to throw them out of the plan.

"You know, Jacky, they don't have to keep us on. The union pays most of the insurance, we only pay twenty-three dollars a month."

I try convincing her they can't throw them out just because we insist on proper care. And actually it doesn't matter. With Medicare they're mostly covered anyway. I listen to her hammer away. I'll think she's stopped but she'll start up on it again.

Another thing about the poverty mind is there's so much shadowboxing, threatening, but when it comes to standing up to some "boss" figure, the poverty person usually collapses completely. They've been so brutalized, dominated by life, they get deeply scared at the first sign of combat. The fear of losing what little security they have totally incapacitates them.

I go feed Dad. I'm holding back with my card. Let Ethridge simmer some, and I'll concentrate on Dad.

I decide to paint him. That way I can get something done at the same time I'm sitting with him. I'll do it out on the patio. I can't see how Mrs. Kessler or anybody can object to that. Also, I can prove to Alicia I really am a painter from Paris, France.

Alicia's already feeding him when I get there. The medical records and medicine have come.

"Man, you really threw it through the roof, didn't you? Gawd almighty, Missus Kessler was fit to be tied. Now look, Jack, your Daddy here's a nice man; don't you go and mess things up for him."

I take over the feeding. She has others to do and now she knows I can do it.

Dad's in much better shape. His attention still wanders but he's not trying to get away. He half watches me, or at least my hands, as I put a bit of food on the spoon and tilt it into his mouth. I do it the way Alicia does, the way you do with a baby, mixing the bites: a bite of peas, then a bite of chocolate pudding, then one of meat; next a drink of milk. Constantly changing around seems to work better than feeding one thing at a time. I get it almost all down in less than an hour. I have my cuff and take his pressure: one ninety over a hundred, still high but better.

When I'm finished, I put a light sweater on under his robe and move him into the wheelchair. I tie him in with the belt of his robe and wheel him outside. I've left my painting box beside the main door to the patio. I set up my box, keeping an eye on Dad. I'll do a three-quarter view, just the head.

I start the drawing and as I do it, I see how much he's changed. It's as if a whole layer of civilization, of superego, has been wiped off his face the way an actor wipes off makeup with cold cream. It's his face, but much younger, much less used, not lived in. The face isn't my father. I want to paint it true, true to what I think I'm seeing and true to what I'm feeling.

I'm getting into the underpainting when Dad begins mumbling, then talking. I slide closer to hear. He turns to me and speaks quite clearly.

"Ed, what do you think we're going to do?"

I'm Ed again.

"I don't know, what do you think we should do, Jack?"

"Geez, I hate seeing us lose the old farm; I can't even remember any other place. I don't want to live in Manata and go to a town school. I know I won't like that at all."

I wait.

"Yeah, Jack, that's right."

I look to see if anybody can hear us. Nobody's near and nobody's looking.

"What happened, Ed? Dad always works so hard. He's out in the fields before sunup and works till dark; even in the wintertime, he's always working. Nobody could ever say Dad's lazy, nobody."

"That's right, Jack."

Dad peers toward me, into me, as if he's trying to see through a blur of time and memory.

"What'd he do wrong, Ed? Why's he have to sell out to Uncle Bill? I don't get it."

We're into something I know a little bit about. I know my grandfather sold his farm and started a store in Manata, but I'd always been told it was so the girls could go to high school. I never knew he sold it to his brother. I try staying in there; I nod with him. The last thing he says I can barely hear, like a radio station drifting off band.

"I'll never understand it, Ed. Dad's a good farmer; he don't want to run no store; he'll never be no good being a store-keeper in a town!"

And that's the end of it. Dad sits staring at his lap, hands turned up. I wait awhile, then go back to painting. Dad looks as if he might be on the edge of crying but he doesn't. I keep working. I finish the underpainting and get into the impasto. I want to finish the whole painting in one sitting if I can.

I'm about halfway through the impasto, picking up some light in the penumbra, when Alicia comes out. She's in her street clothes, going off duty. She stops and looks over my shoulder.

"You certainly got him there, Mr. Tremont. Man, you really are an artist; I never knew no *real* artist before."

I stop, push myself back and look up. The sun is low behind her; I can see light between her legs through the nylon dress she's wearing. She's not wearing a slip. She catches me looking and crosses her legs standing up.

"You want to paint me?"

She laughs and puts one hand behind her head.

"I'd make a just fine model. You don't see many girls my color with one green eye, do you, now?"

She's absolutely gorgeous in that setting-sun light.

"I'd love to paint you, Alicia, but what would Mrs. Kessler say to that?"

I put another touch on the backlighted wing of Dad's nose.

"Not here; oh, no, not here! Ol' Missus Kessler'd have cat conniptions, wouldn't she? Oh, yes! You'd have to come to my place. Little Jessica'd love seeing a real artist paint her mother."

She laughs again and crosses her legs the other way.

I add more burnt sienna to the background over Dad's head. I'm too stirred up for any real painting. I look at Dad. He has no idea what's going on; I don't myself. She must figure me for a capital dud.

"Well, now there; don't you keep your daddy out here too long, now. It's beginning to get cold."

I smile up at her into the sunset.

"I'll bring him in soon, Alicia. You have a nice evening and I'll see you tomorrow."

She looks into me, pinning me with that green eye.

"That's right."

She looks back over her shoulder, already on her way. She's laughing.

"I'll see you."

I watch her walking away; even in flat shoes she has nice moves, long, sure strides. I watch till she turns in to the parking lot.

I finish the painting in another half hour. There's something so sad there, so lost, I can hardly look at it anymore. I definitely can't show it to Mom. It's a good painting, though; too good.

During the next week, I come twice a day to feed Dad. Things are going reasonably well with Mother, but Joan is almost out of her mind trying to find a nurse Mom will accept. It begins to look hopeless after she's interviewed twelve and Mom has turned thumbs down on every one.

Mother takes on a little more herself every day and I'm

mostly trying to hold her back. One day I come home to find her weeding the backyard. Her argument is she can't bear seeing Daddy's flowers get overgrown by weeds. Besides, she's sitting down and only pulling easy weeds. What can you do? After that, between feedings, I'm weeding.

I don't know whether it's because Mrs. Kessler catches on to the little flirt Alicia and I are having, or it's part of the regular rotation cycle, but Alicia is moved to the evening shift. It's probably just as well. Her vivacity and joy are getting to me. One day she told me how she was raised by her mother without a father, too, just like little Jessica. There's something about women who've never been dominated by males turns me on.

I wonder how much I worked my way into Marty's feeling about men. I tried my damnedest not to make too many waves but you never know.

Saturday evening, at eight, I'm going out to dinner with Sandy and Pat Mock, longtime friends. Billy's staying with Mom for the evening. I decide to stop in and see how Dad's doing, at least that's why I think I'm stopping in. I've already given him his six-o'clock feeding.

When I go into Dad's room, I see right away something's drastically wrong. Dad looks dead except he's breathing with a loud, deep, rattling snore. I've only heard the death rattle a few times and that was over thirty years ago but it's a sound you don't forget. He's pale, greenish white, and there's perspiration on his face. I quickly run out and Alicia's coming from the other hall, smiling at me.

"Alicia, would you check my dad? There's something seriously wrong!"

I run on to the desk looking for Mrs. Kessler but she isn't there. The RN is in the other wing, giving medication. I run for her.

"Please come with me, Nurse; my father might be dying!"

She's fat and at least sixty years old. She wobbles after me down the hall.

When we get there, Alicia's rubbing Dad's wrists. The nurse takes his pulse with one hand while I take it with the other; it's weak and fluttery. She wraps on her cuff, pumps and watches. There's no movement of the dial over fifty. She looks up.

"Alicia, call the hospital. Get an ambulance here quick."

She turns to me.

"Can you do cardiopulmonary resuscitation?"

I nod. I think of my trying to teach Dad, his squeamishness about my putting my mouth over his. I'm wondering why they don't have a resuscitation unit here at a convalescent home.

"Does he have any dentures?"

I shake my head. I'm going into some shock already.

Now we can't get any pulse. Time for cardiopulmonary resuscitation. She pulls him by the legs down toward the end of the bed so I can position myself over him. I tilt his head back and start the mouth-to-mouth. At the same time, I begin the cardiac compression. I'm holding Dad's nose and blowing in hard, two breaths every eleven seconds. Then I stop the breathing and do the compressions. I'm pushing down on his sternum about sixty times a minute. Then I go back to the breathing.

Alicia comes in and says an ambulance is on the way. The RN puts her to rubbing Dad's legs. They're already mottled and blue from lack of circulation.

I think of the autopsy painting by Rembrandt in Amsterdam, or was it the Vatican? I'm trying hard not to think about what I'm actually doing. Alicia moves beside me and assists with the cardiac compression. I concentrate on the breathing. The RN keeps taking the blood pressure and frequently pulls open Dad's lids to check his pupils. She says we're up to eighty over fifty now; also he seems to have better color.

I'm beginning to wonder how long I can keep it up. I'm dressed in a suit and shirt with a tie. Sweat's soaking through my shirt. I'm beginning to feel dizzy from hyperventilation. I try thinking of something else besides when in hell the ambulance's ever going to come.

DAD

Alicia slides her hands under mine on Dad's sternum and takes over the compressions. That way I can concentrate all my attention on the breathing.

I keep on with the mouth-to-mouth; Dad's lips are slippery with slobber. The nurse says he's up to ninety over sixty. I look over at her; she looks like a candidate for cardiac arrest herself, but we're keeping him alive.

Now the moisture is drying around Dad's mouth; his lips are drying and so are mine. Between breaths I take several deep breaths for myself and try working saliva into my mouth. I'm sweated down to my socks; black spots drift in front of my eyes like dust motes on the cornea. We keep working in silent desperation but nobody comes. This is a minimum Saturday-night staff and the rest of the patients are unattended.

We've been at it over twenty minutes when we hear the ambulance siren. It rolls up to the back door. Alicia leaves and an attendant comes running with her up the hall. The RN tells him to bring in a resuscitator. While we've been working, it's gotten dark and there's no light on in the room. It isn't exactly dark but more bluish twilight.

He runs back, and two of them come in with the resuscitator. They lift Dad's head and put the mask over his face. They get the oxygen going and Dad continues to breathe. They roll in a black leather stretcher and we lift Dad onto it while I keep up the cardiac compression.

One of the ambulance guys moves in beside me and takes over. I help roll the stretcher down the hall and into the ambulance. I go back to the room for my coat I'd dropped on the floor.

I'm absolutely dripping sweat. The RN is gone and only Alicia's there. She hands me the coat, then leans into me. She lifts her head and we kiss, deep, a mouth-hungry, wicked-tongued, active kiss. My lips are numb and dry; I can't feel anything.

"I hope someday somebody loves me the way you love your daddy."

I slip my coat over my shoulders. It presses cold sweat against me.

"He's a wonderful man, Alicia, he's easy to love. You would be, too."

"Come and tell me how he is, will you, Jack? Come see me, huh?"

I nod. I know I won't. My mind is somewhere else, partly in that ambulance, partly in Paris.

I turn and run down the hall. I jump into the ambulance and we're off. They have the light turning and the siren whoop-whoop going. I take over cardiac compression while the attendant adjusts his resuscitator and prepares an IV of what looks like a simple saline solution. When he gets it taped on and running, he takes over again. His forehead is breaking out in sweat. The driver signals for me to come up front with him and I climb into the passenger seat.

"How the hell do I get to Perpetual from here, anyway? I'm lost."

I look out the window and we aren't on the freeway! We're on Washington Boulevard, too far south. I get him aimed in the right direction. He tells me they aren't a regular Perpetual ambulance; they got an emergency call. I'm too scared, too tired, too exasperated to comment. I keep watch as we go through red lights; we're making good time. But we'd've been there already if we'd taken the freeway.

They're expecting us when we arrive. Dad's moved into one of the emergency cubicles with a doctor and two nurses; they pull the curtains around him. I'm told to go outside in the waiting room. The pros have taken over; I'm ready, I'm not fighting. I'm so strung out I feel gutted.

I keep wondering if Dad'll ever regain consciousness. I'm sure he can't live long after a shock like this. I wonder how much brain damage he suffered; I don't know how long he was alone in that bed with a diastolic under fifty before I found him.

Half an hour later, the doctor comes out. He motions me into a small room. I figure this is where he tells me Dad's died. I'm ready. There comes a point where you're ready to give up.

"How is he, Doctor?"

The classic question, the dumb question.

"Well, Mr. Tremont, he's still alive and that was a close one. Could you tell me exactly what happened?"

I give him the details, but I don't exactly know what happened. This is a young doctor, probably doing his residence and he's taking notes of what I'm saying. He has Dad's charts there. I imagine Saturday-evening emergency is not "top gig" for a doctor.

As I review what's happened, I find myself getting mad again. I begin ranting about how my father can't live outside a hospital and inform him I've already told Dr. Ethridge this but was ignored. I lay it on about the ambulance driver getting lost. This doctor writes away, then looks up at me.

"Don't get upset, Mr. Tremont, you're overwrought."

I'm having a hard time holding on; I don't have the energy. Just then I remember the Mocks. I look at my watch and I'm already over an hour late. I ask the doctor for a phone; there's a booth in the waiting room.

I call Pat and Sandy and tell them what's happened. They're most sympathetic and I'm needing sympathy. It's beginning to register what's been happening. I've been so busy fighting I haven't had time to think.

I call Joan. I tell her as gently as I can. There's a long pause on her end of the line. When she starts talking, she's crying.

"Mario and I will come to the hospital; you stay there. Don't call Mother yet."

I hang up but I don't want to come out of the phone booth. The space of a phone booth is about all I can handle right then.

Finally, I go out and sit in the waiting room. I don't know what I'm waiting for, except Joan. Before Joan arrives, the young doctor comes out again. He looks tired but not so grim. I swear he's grown half a day's beard while I was phoning. I wouldn't be a doctor for anything. He doesn't sit down, so I stand up.

"Well, Mr. Tremont, he's out of danger for the moment. We'll need to do more tests to find out what's wrong. His BUN is up again and he's dehydrated; that's all I can tell you now.

I'm putting him in intensive care. You might as well go home; there's nothing more you can do."

He looks at me carefully. I must look like hell; at least that's the way his eyes register.

"You came in the ambulance, didn't you? Do you want us to call a taxi?"

I shake my head.

"I've called my sister; she should be here any minute; she'll take care of me."

He stares a few more seconds.

"All right, you rest here and if you feel faint, let one of the nurses know. Don't worry about your father, he's comfortable now. Dr. Chad will call you in the morning."

He turns away. That's the first time I know for sure Chad's taken the case.

About fifteen minutes later, Joan and Mario come in. She sits beside me; her eyes are red from crying. Mario is playing impassive male, but he's breathing shallowly and has a bluish color under his half-day beard. I go over everything.

Joan wants to see Dad. I know why; she's afraid he'll die without her seeing him a last time. It's amazing the way the living mind works about the dead. Joan persists with the nurse, who finally summons the doctor. He calls intensive care and explains the situation.

"The two direct relatives may go up for a few minutes; but he's unconscious, so he won't know you're there."

Christ, I think; you don't know where it is, Doc; he wouldn't know we were there if he *were* conscious.

We go up. For some reason, the Muzak isn't playing. Maybe they give the machines a rest on weekends. Maybe they only play music during visiting hours. It's the same, though, small rooms opening onto a large monitoring center.

There's the smell, the repressed silence, the instrumentation. They've pulled the curtains on Dad's room and we can just make him out in the dark. He does look peaceful; he almost looks dead, but he's breathing naturally. The IV is still on, the catheter in place, the oxygen tube fitted into his nostrils. He looks like one of the men in a capsule in that *2001* film. He doesn't look as if he's in this world anymore. He's lost so much weight his cheeks have sunken in. He's like a mummy, yellowish, Nile-embalmed.

Joan goes over and kisses him on the forehead, runs her hand over his head. When I kiss him, caress him, he's dry, silky smooth, almost parchmentlike with a feeling of graphite powder over his skin. Joan's crying beside me, then she turns and comes into my arms. I hold her and she's sobbing deeply. Her sobs trigger me and I can't stop. I'm looking over her head and crying.

The nurse comes in. She shoos us out and we go slowly past all the overhead lights and bottles surrounded by black faces in white uniforms. Joan's still holding on to my hand.

When we get to the lobby, she says she wants to use the ladies' room. Instead of standing, waiting, I go into the men's room. In the mirror, I look cut out, as if there's a slight space all around the outside of my head and I vaguely don't fit somehow, like a poorly done photomontage. I stare and let warm water run over my hands. I'm still soaked with sweat.

Mario drives us home. By this time, we have ourselves fairly well in control. Joan says she'll tell Mom. I keep wanting to be with Dad, even though I know there's nothing to do.

At home, I sneak past, back to Mom's room, snitch one of her ten-milligram Valium, go into the bathroom and swallow it. I'm a wreck all right. I hope Joan's OK.

I strip and fill the tub, hot as possible, until I'm practically floating. I dread getting out and going into the living room with Mom. I'm not ready.

But by the time I'm out, the Valium's hit, the hot water's hit and a sedating shock has settled in. I'm calm when I join them in the living room. Mario's in the platform rocker with his hands locked across his stomach, staying neutral, out of it. Joan's biting her lips to keep from crying. Mom's crying. I tell Joan and Mario they'd better get back home; I can take over now. Joan's more than ready to go. She'll be crying all the way over the San Diego and Ventura freeways. I'm glad Mario's with her.

Believe it or not, Mother's convinced Dad's dying because we canned Ethridge. I wonder if she brought this up with Joan or she's saved it for me. The temptation is strong to walk out to the back bedroom in the garden, lock the door and just forget it all.

Instead, I go over everything once more. I explain all the things they didn't do, the fact that it was Ethridge who insisted Dad leave the hospital. I'm talking to a wall. She has something to blame it on and I'm a logical victim; she's not going to let go.

I tell her the neurological tests Max in Cincinnati told me should have been done and weren't. I try to convince her concerning Max's credentials as chief neurologist at a university hospital, but he's only one of my hippy quack friends. There's nothing to be done. I look at her there crying and striking out.

Then I remember. When I was a child, my Aunt Helen died of peritonitis after an appendix operation. It was my mother—over the objections of Aunt Helen's husband, Charley, and her father, my grandfather—who insisted Aunt Helen have the operation. At the funeral, my grandfather turned on Mom.

"It's your fault, Bess. If you hadn't talked her into that Goddamned operation, she'd be alive today."

This triggered Mother's second nervous breakdown.

I look at Mother and say quietly:

"It's your fault, Bess; if you hadn't talked Helen into that Goddamned operation, she'd be alive today!"

I get up slowly and walk out of the house into the garden. I know I'm being a shit and a theatrical bastard but it feels so good. I halfway turn back to apologize but don't; I go on into the garden bedroom and lock myself in.

I stretch out on that big pillow of a bed and submerge myself in the smell of Billy's dirty feet. How the hell did he get the smell of his feet into the pillow under my head? Maybe he sleeps with his head at the foot of the bed and his feet on the pillow. Maybe he's trying to get some blood up to his brain. Maybe my father isn't dying.

No matter what, Dad's going to have every one of those

neurological examinations he should have had. He's going to have all the medical backup he needs. I get to sleep at last. The final thought I have as I'm going under is about Mom.

I discover I wouldn't be too heartbroken if I go in the next morning and find her dead on the living-room floor. That's a rotten thought but I have it.

13

Soon's we get out of Kansas, two things happen. One, we start getting into nice little hills, not mountains, not even hilly as the Morvan, but it isn't just one great, checkered table-cloth anymore. The second thing is everything turns green and humid.

When we stop for gas and I step out of the car, the air's so thick, hot and heavy I can't breathe. I climb right back into the joy of canned air. Out there looks just fine through cool air and tinted glass. This luxury tank makes sense now.

We drive along across Missouri toward St. Louis. I'm at the wheel. Dad pulls out a notebook and starts scribbling. I figure he's toting up how much we've spent so far with gas, motels and eating. Boy, is he in for a surprise; it'd've been cheaper going first class in an airplane.

We've gone maybe thirty miles when Dad clears his throat.

"Listen to this, Bill; tell me what you think. It's called 'God's Joke':

> "Adam lived alone on the old ranch Eden
> Just playin', thinkin', sleepin', and feedin'.
> He was pickin' flowers in his garden one day'n'
> God came down to teach Adam about prayin'.
>
> Adam didn't know God was making up sin
> And wasn't quite sure just how to begin.
> 'Pray hard,' God said, 'Pray with your life,
> Pray for money, or power. Pray for a wife.'
>
> 'What's that, God?' says Adam, scratchin' his head,
> 'Some new kinda fruit, somethin' soft for my bed?'
> 'That's right,' God said, smilin' and grinnin',
> 'Cause now he knew how to start Adam sinnin'.
>
> Adam woke next mornin' with a stitch in his side
> And a cute little critter sayin' she was his bride.
> This critter, named Eve, had two bumps and a hole
> And knew just how to steal a man's soul.
>
> Adam fenced off the ranch and took up the hoe,
> Planted taters 'n' cotton and corn in a row.
> Eve raised Cain, then Cain slayed Abel,
> And God laughed his ass off all the way to the stable."

We start laughing. He's proud of this crazy song; he's going over it, making corrections, improving it; laughing to himself. Maybe all that shit with Grandma and Granddad was too much. I might be delivering a basket case to Mom.

We start seeing big advertisements for caves along the road. One's called Meramec, the other Onondaga. Dad wants to visit one, only he isn't sure which. It's a good fifty miles out of the way, however we go.

It seems, fifteen years ago, my parents drove cross-country and visited a cave. All these years, he's carried in his mind the idea I was too young to appreciate it then but he's convinced I'll like it now.

When he gets an idea like this, there's no stopping him; it's only a question of which cave; Bryce and Zion all over again. Somehow he decides it's Onondaga. I'm sure it'll be the wrong cave. But it doesn't matter. We're in for a cave.

We drive through rolling green countryside; he's manning the maps. We go along small roads, then come down on a place fixed up like one of the national parks.

They've got rocks squared off and cemented together, with rough-cut signs hanging on chains. These have burned-out letters like brandings. Everything very woodsy. All these signs have arrows pointing toward Onondaga Cave.

But it turns out this isn't a national park at all. This is a bit of free enterprise. Somebody bought these caves and developed a tourist attraction. They figured people are going stark raving mad driving cross-country with only Stuckey's peanut brittle to break the monotony, so they'll come in to see anything.

There's a gigantic parking lot three-quarters full and seething with Americana in Dacron colors, checkered shorts and kids in Keds.

We've hardly gotten the car stopped and the motor turned off when an old guy, in what looks like an ice-cream-salesman costume, comes over and collects fifty cents for parking. Before we can move, he's whipped out a sticker with an Indian arrowhead on it and stuck this thing on the back window. I dash to scrape it off but it's practically vulcanized by the heat. That Mafia stud in Philadelphia will want some reason for an arrowhead named Onondaga; imagine explaining to the mob. He'll probably cover it with a decal of crossed American flags.

This place is notorious for two things. Jesse James and his band are supposed to have hidden gold somewhere in the cave. That's got to be good for at least an extra thousand admissions per year. The other thing, Mark Twain is said to have used this cave as a model for the one where Tom Sawyer and Becky get lost.

Can you believe it, three bucks to walk into a hole? But Dad's a follow-through type so he plunks out the money.

A six-foot-tall Boy Scout herds us into the cave, passing out gems like how to tell a stalagmite from a stalactite. Would you believe it? A stalagmite *might* reach the ceiling, a stalactite holds *tight* to the ceiling; so much for geology.

First there's the James brothers' hideout. This is competition for the Knott's Berry Farm Award of the Year. Even Disneyland is better than this. There's one part with gigantic "gold nuggets" sticking conveniently out of the ground. They also have a section with fluorescent rock and black light beamed on them, probably gathered those rocks from all over America.

But the cave is damned impressive in itself, as a cave. I see what Dad's excited about. We're down hundreds of feet in the ground. There are parts bigger than a whole wing of Versailles. It's dripping with calcite in an enormous range of subtle colors. And it's cool. It's almost worth six dollars just to get cool. It's a constant fifty-seven degrees, winter and summer; I can feel the cold sinking into me. I want my bones to get cold so I can hold on till we get back in the car.

But things are so hoked up. There are colored lights shining on every interesting rock so you can't tell what color anything really is. Then, they have names for each geologic formation. One is called The Golden Horn. This is a stalagmite bathed in gold light to make it look like a huge golden horn sticking out of the ground. Everybody is shuffling past in the dark hanging on to ropes. There's a hush over the crowd as if we're going through Notre Dame.

Another place is called The Organ of the Giants. Some stalagmites and stalactites have run together so it looks a bit like a giant pipe organ. There are constantly changing colored lights playing on this. It's something like old-time vaudeville or a funky light show. Come to think of it, what a great place this could be for a rock concert; call it the Underground Rock.

We finish in a huge natural amphitheater, bigger than any movie theater, with wooden seats all around. Our guide leads us in and we sit there till the place is about filled. Then they turn off all the lights.

A voice comes out of the dark from at least ten speakers; we're surrounded by this voice. He talks about the primal dark and how it's been dark in these caves for thousands of centuries. An organ begins playing and colored lights come up slowly on a beautiful display of arches, water-washed caves, stalagmites and stalactites. Well, that's the way it's been all along so I settle back.

But then comes the kicker. A projector behind us flashes the American flag onto the stalactites. They wiggle the projector so it looks as if the flag is blowing in a breeze. Worse yet, fat Kate Smith, one of Grandma's all-time favorites, comes on singing "God Bless America"!

I stand up to leave. Everybody stands with me. They think it's the national anthem. They're standing, staring at that monster jiggling flag. I walk along the bench to the aisle, up and out.

Going outside into the wet heat again is miserable but it's better than staying inside. I'm an American and all, but it doesn't have anything to do with that kind of commercialized bullshit.

Dad comes out with the others. We don't say anything as we work our way two hundred yards through air sludge to the car. He turns it over and the air conditioner starts pushing blessed cool air around. It's just getting bearable when we pull past the last little stone pyramid with an arrowhead sign on it. Dad turns toward me.

"Well, Bill, I think we're both about ready for Paris."

We start laughing. We go over it all and we're getting at least six dollars' worth in laughs.

We're laughing along when suddenly we get two coughs; that big boat of a car gives up. We barely get it to the side of the road. The gas gauge registers almost empty. We meant to buy gas at the station outside the caves but, in our hurry getting away, forgot.

Still, I can't believe we're actually out of gas. The needle definitely lifts when we turn on the ignition; that should mean something. But Dad's convinced it's gas. We latch up that gigantic hood and there are four of the biggest Stromberg carburetors I've ever seen in my life. Just pushing down on the accelerator is like flushing a toilet with gasoline.

Dad digs the gas can out of the trunk and insists on walking back. He's so sure we're out of gas he doesn't even want to check. I think we're both afraid of fooling around with this monster.

It's got to be two miles or more back to the caves but he says he'll hitch. There's a fair amount of traffic and with the gas can he shouldn't have any trouble. I say I'll go but he insists he needs the exercise. He crosses to the other side and starts slogging along. He's going to be dripping wet with sweat before he gets there.

Just out of curiosity, I begin playing with the carburetors. There's not much you can do with that kind of equipment when all you have is a pair of pliers and a screwdriver. At least, I can find out if fuel is getting to the carbs. It could be the fuel pump.

I pull off the gas lead lines and turn it over. Gas comes from somewhere; those lines pump gas like cut arteries. I look back for Dad but he's gone; he must've gotten a lift right off.

I'm afraid to fool around with the jets so I hook everything up again.

Then, when I turn her over, she fires up like downtown; probably only a vapor lock from all the heat. I think of tearing off after Dad but I'm afraid we'll miss each other. He'll get a ride back from the gas station easy, Americans are great that way.

I figure now's a chance to top up my suntan; I stretch out on the grass verge.

I must've fallen asleep; the next thing, Dad's there. He has a can full of gas and looks fresh as a shrimp. He says he got a lift almost right away to the caves and a lady at the pump took him back. He's pouring gas into the tank. He's so pleased with himself, I don't have the heart to tell him the car's already working.

Also, at the gas station, he bought two pairs of sunglasses. We've been driving into the morning sun every day and our eyes are almost burnt out. We both have light blue eyes and can't take glare. But these are some sunglasses he buys.

Of course, the car turns right over. We're both smiling

like lunatics. These sunglasses have mirror lenses, and are curved so they wrap around the face. With our beards and these glasses on, we look like monster insects from *The Lost World,* or gangsters or hip drug addicts.

But they do keep the sun out, they practically keep *air* out; be great for motorcycle riding. He must've paid a fortune for them. That's the way he is, tight as a witch's cunt; then bango, big-shot spender.

The rest of that day we beat our way across Missouri. Late afternoon, we reach St. Louis. We manage to get ourselves lost in a complex series of overpasses, underpasses and cross-over exits.

We're going round and round as if we're on a roller coaster and getting nowhere. Looming over all is the most god-awful thing I've ever seen. It's some kind of steel rainbow. It curves up in the air hundreds of feet, but doesn't go any-where. It looks as if the people in St. Louis decided to build their own Washington Monument and got confused; or the damned thing melted in the heat so it bent over and the top stuck into the ground. The Disney approach has totally in-vaded American thinking.

After we go through the loop-the-loops at least six times, we give up. We cruise off our roller coaster in the shadow of that towering steel rainbow and into one of the most desolate black ghettos I've ever seen. There's nothing but boarded-up brick buildings, cracked streets and thousands of people hang-ing loose on corners. Here's this monstrosity looming over them, costing millions of dollars, and these people live in filth.

We stop at a gas station and ask how we get on the main route east. After half an hour twisting through St. Louis, we're on the open road again. America is clots of people, joined by gigantic straight highways. Most of this country is prac-tically empty.

We start looking for a motel when we're fifty miles into Illinois on the other side of St. Louis. We stop at twenty differ-ent places but they're all filled. We move on another thirty miles, going off at each little dink of a town, drifting up and down tiny streets in our Batmobile, looking for lit motel signs.

Finally, we pull over on the roadside at a picnic place to camp out. I have Tom's tent and a blanket. It's so hot we won't need the blanket; this air's stiff with humidity.

I'd half hoped we'd leave humidity in Missouri but it goes all the way to the Atlantic. I don't know how people stand it. Sure I do. They run from air-conditioned houses to air-conditioned cars, drive to air-conditioned movies, shopping malls, restaurants. They move between air-conditioning machines like people living on the moon or a hostile planet where the air's unfit for humans. It just about is.

It's dark when we unpack the tent. It's tangled and still has dirt from Topanga Canyon wrapped in it, our own forty acres here in Illinois. There are some tough knots to untangle. I just pulled up and rolled it when I packed. Dad isn't saying anything, only struggling in the dark with the knots.

We aren't there five minutes when the mosquitoes hit. They must come out of the grass. At first it's only a few, along with some lightning bugs, but then there are swarms.

I wrap myself in the blanket to fend them off. Dad slaps once in a while, but keeps at those knots.

The tent is a simple pup tent with a floor. We'll be crowded but it's better than sleeping in the car or driving through the night.

At last we struggle ourselves inside the tent with the mosquito netting pulled across. We beat down twenty or so of the beasts we've closed in with us. I hear thousands outside trying to chew their way through. I'm slippery with blood from the ones I've squashed, *my* blood.

We stretch out side by side. I never realized what a thick, broad-shouldered old dog Dad is. I've slept in pup tents with other guys and there was plenty of room. I peek to see if he's got extra room but he's pushing against his side, too.

And now we begin hearing the trucks. I'm sure they've been going by all the time but we didn't notice. One passes about every two minutes; there's hardly any time between. One roars off east and we start hearing another, west. Just our luck, we're on a slight grade. All the eastbound trucks are shifting

down to make the hill while the westbounds are double shifting up a gear.

We lie out like that for an hour, neither of us saying anything, hoping the other guy is asleep but knowing he isn't.

Then the wind starts. It quickly blows up into a real Midwest thunder-and-lightning storm. We didn't exactly do a
merit-badge job putting up our tent, either. What with knots,
dark and mosquitoes, it's sagging in every direction, mostly
front to back, like a swayback horse.

Bam! Crash! Flash! Thumble! Rumble! Crack! Flash!
The lightning and thunder are almost simultaneous. It goes
on and on. At least now we can't hear the trucks. And some
rain! Some wind! The tent slowly begins collapsing against us.
Anyplace we touch, the rain leaks through. What do mosquitoes do in a rainstorm? Drown? Swim? Dig holes? They
can't fly, that's for sure.

We begin edging toward each other. Then we roll up on
our sides and tuck spoon-style away from the tent. The whole
wild world is doing its damnedest out there. Dad reaches over
my shoulder.

"Here, take this, Bill. Otherwise, we'll never sleep."

In a flash of lightning I see it's a "reddy," Seconal. Where
in hell did *my* father get a thing like that? And what's he doing
carrying it in his shirt pocket?

I have a hard time swallowing any pill even with water.
But I slug it down with some apple juice in a bottle at the head
of the tent. Dad pops his like a true pill freak.

Imagine, him popping reds; shows what you don't know.

14

I'm up early. When I telephone the hospital, they say Dad's condition is critical but stable.

I take my notes from Max and sit down at the typewriter again. I type out a formal request for all the neurological examinations he said should have been done. They include an LP, or spinal tap, a brain scan, an EEG—electroencephalogram —certain blood tests and psychiatric consultation. I make a clean copy of this letter and mail it registered to Dr. Chad at Perpetual. The original I put on my clipboard along with the statement of Dad's case and the Knight & Knight signed card.

At the post office I make photocopies of all these for record. After that, I go back home and type out a recapitulation of last evening's events at the convalescent home. Mother is curious about what I'm doing. I put her off as best I can; I'm barely holding myself together.

I go to the hospital. I stop at intensive care to see Dad but he's still wired, taped up and unconscious. God, he looks so pitiful! It gives me strength to go through with all this.

I ask the nurse at the desk for the administrative offices. They're on the top floor of the building; I take the elevator up. I find the office of the administrative director and tell the secretary I'd like to see Dr. Benson. She gives me a look as if I'd asked to see God.

"Dr. Benson is very busy, sir. Dr. Benson is preparing for a conference in Boston. Who are you and what is it you want?"

I go for broke; give her a quick summary of the situation. She listens with her pasted-on smile but doesn't interrupt.

She sees me for what I am, crank. I'm getting nowhere. I pull the Knight & Knight card off the clipboard.

"Give this to Dr. Benson, please. Tell him my attorneys have suggested I present this card before action is taken. I'll be downstairs in the intensive care unit with my father; the name is Dr. Tremont."

I don't stay while she's reading the card; it'll work or it won't. I walk out. This part of the building doesn't smell like a hospital. It has the ordinary office smell of typewriter ribbons, erasers, used perfume, starch, paper and the electronic smell of computers. I take the elevator down to Dad in the nether regions.

I sit in the room with him. I check to see if the IV, catheter, monitors, oxygen are all in place. I tuck in his bedclothes; all meaningless moves, just puttering around, trying to hold myself in. A few nurses look at me but I'm so deep into grief and anger they turn away. I'm half expecting a security guard. If he does come, he'll need a submachine gun to get me out. I stare at Dad; he seems miles away, in another world.

The water's hot. I pour some in the washbowl and dip my shaving brush to soften it. I spin the brush on the soap and start lathering up. I work myself a thick soap beard, open my razor and strop it a few times on the strop hanging beside the mirror. That mirror has a crazy crack through the middle so I can make myself look as if I have a thick nose with three nostrils. I keep promising Bess I'll buy a new one but always forget. I start scraping away, wiping the suds and cut stubble off on my finger.

Ten minutes later, a large, tweedy man comes strolling onto the ward. I watch him stop at the nurses' section. Even if I didn't see abject panic on the nurses' faces I could tell this is top dog. He has proprietorship written all over him.

The nurses point and he heads over. As he comes in the room, he switches on the overhead light. I walk past him and turn it off again.

"I think we can see well enough for what we have to discuss, Dr. Benson. My father is in a very sensitive condition and the light might bother him."

Two points for me and the lines are drawn. He pauses, gives a benevolent grandfatherly grin and pulls out the other chair in the room. I've taken the armchair for myself; he's stuck with the armless one. He turns the chair around to straddle it, the knight talking to the peasants from his horse. It's tubular steel frame with black seat and black padded back. It helps him maintain his Marlboro-Chief Surgeon role.

"My secretary says you want to see me, Mr. Tremont."

So that's the way we play it. OK.

"That's right, Mr. Benson."

No accent, just lay it out quietly. He wants me to go on; I wait.

I'm wishing it all weren't so important so I could enjoy our little farce. There's something crazy in me. I desperately avoid this competitive confrontation nonsense; it's unrelated to my ideal of the good life. But when I'm in it, I enjoy myself. He waits as long as he can.

"Well, Dr. Tremont, I'm a very busy man; my schedule is tight and I fly to Boston in three hours. Just what is it you want to see me about?"

I pick up my clipboard and pull off the statement I showed to Knight & Knight; I include the write-up of what

happened last night. I hand this to him, switch on the small
light beside the bed and tilt it away from Dad.

"I think you'd better read this first, Dr. Benson."

He takes it from me, riffles through the pages; it's up to
thirteen single-space now.

"Really, Dr. Tremont, I don't have time to go through all
this. Couldn't you abstract this manuscript for me?"

"No, I don't think so, Dr. Benson; this is as succinct a
statement of the situation as I can possibly present. I'm sure
reading it now will be to your advantage."

He sighs, pulls his glasses from his coat pocket. The
Knight & Knight card is dislodged, lifted a bit, as he slides
them out. He quickly tucks it back, eases his glasses free. That
quick move verifies Knight & Knight. He adjusts his glasses
and tilts his head back to read through his bifocals. He'd like
to move the papers closer to his chest, but he's stuck trying to
read straddled around the chair.

"Dr. Benson, I presented this statement to the firm of
Knight & Knight; they suggested I show it to you."

He shoots a full double whammy over the top of his
glasses. That, combined with his graying cowlick forelock,
gives him the look of a mean Will Rogers.

I'm not going to wait around while he reads, so I go over
and fuss with Dad some more. I feel his head, cool; take his
pulse, irregular, racing; and tuck the bedclothes in. I stare at
the monitors, pretend to make some notes on my clipboard,
then stand leaning in the doorway watching the nurses.
They're all in a semi-catatonic state. Here's Dr. Benson, himself, on their floor in a patient's room with a wild-eyed,
bearded man.

I wait till I'm sure he must be almost finished, then go
and play with Dad again. His breathing is deep, his mouth
open.

I hear Benson putting the papers together; he clears his
throat. I sit in my chair again. He hands the statement to me
and I lock it onto the clipboard. I slip the letter with my list of
requests on top. I wait. He pulls the card out of his pocket
now.

"I suppose this means you intend to institute a suit against the hospital, Dr. Tremont?"

I wait, staring at him, through him, for perhaps five seconds.

"I'd rather not, Dr. Benson."

"It seems to me, Dr. Tremont, that all your complaints, though serious, would not constitute a malpractice suit."

"Knight & Knight disagree with you on that, Dr. Benson."

He's pissed all right. I'd love to be there when he rips into Santana and Ethridge. He stares at the card again. I know he's repressing an urge to call that security guard and have me thrown out.

"Just what is it you want, Dr. Tremont?"

Knight & Knight primed me for that, God bless their reptilian hearts.

"Dr. Benson, here's a copy of a registered letter I mailed to Dr. Chad this morning. It lists some of the things I'm asking for."

I hand the letter across to him. It's in the envelope unsealed. He reads it through carefully; looks up.

"Are you a neurologist, Dr. Tremont? These are rather specific requests."

"No, Dr. Benson."

He stares at me again; let him stew; he's about to burst but he's keeping his administrative cool. This guy earns his money for Perpetual.

"I see nothing amiss in arranging for these tests if they haven't already been performed. Most are somewhat superfluous in this case, but I can approve these procedures."

He looks over at Dad.

"But the condition of your father is rather critical, some of these tests are rigorous."

"Naturally, Dr. Benson, I don't want these tests given until my father is in a condition to support them; I assume Dr. Chad has the medical judgment to determine that. I've chosen him on the recommendation of medical friends in this area not associated with Perpetual."

"Dr. Tremont, I assure you Dr. Chad and *any* doctor here

at Perpetual is fully qualified to make these kinds of decisions."

I almost expect him to stand and salute; for God, Perpetual and the AMA.

"I disagree, Dr. Benson, but that isn't the question here. The issue is whether or not I bring a malpractice suit against the Perpetual organization, against Dr. Ethridge and against Dr. Santana. My attorneys await my decision."

I sit back. There's sweat in the hollow of my back and it surprises me when I press against it. It's his move again. He goes to the door and one of the nurses scurries over.

"Would you get me the records for Mr. Tremont, please, Nurse?"

She practically does a full Oriental bow and a back flip. She runs off.

When he comes back, Benson turns the chair around, sits down in it and crosses his legs. We're through with the cowboy act.

The nurse comes in. She hands the records to Benson. He opens them on his lap and starts from the front. He's either a quick study or he's only going through the motions. He could be thinking of something else. I couldn't care less. I hope he doesn't skip over that gall-bladder operation. I wait. He closes the record and looks up at me.

"Well, Dr. Tremont, your father is a very sick man. I'm not sure Dr. Ethridge isn't correct in his diagnosis of a sudden decline to deep senility, or there could be some stroking. Just what is it you want from the hospital?"

I'm ready. I was awake two hours last night spinning my head on that one.

"First, Dr. Benson, I want to be the one who decides when my father is ready to leave this hospital."

I let that sink in. He half nods his head.

"Also, I want full visiting rights any time of day or night."

I pause but he doesn't respond. I go on.

"I want my father to stay here in the intensive care unit until it's absolutely clear it is no longer necessary."

He looks sidewise at me on this one but I charge on.

"I want all tests or any treatment that I or a consulting physician deem necessary."

That one hurts too, but he dips his head slightly. He doesn't know what's coming.

"Dr. Benson, I've lost confidence in your nursing staff. You've read about the disgraceful incident where my father was tied to a chair here in this hospital with his wrists lacerated, his hands swollen and his catheter torn out. I don't want anything like that to happen again. If I consider it necessary, I want the right to sleep with my father in his room and care for him or see that proper care is given."

"Come, Dr. Tremont, we do have hospital rules. You could never stay in the intensive ward here, for example."

"Let me finish, Dr. Benson. Here in the intensive ward I'm not worried, there's sufficient nursing coverage, but in the regular wards, this cost-saving technique of a central station for a large number of patients is not adequate."

Benson stands up. He puts his hands in his pockets, bends his knees and rocks on his toes. He's into *his* dismissal routine. I remain seated and cross my legs. I lean forward.

"And when I decide my father can come home, leave the hospital, I want whatever support equipment I consider necessary, including Perpetual-supplied nursing aid."

He goes into a head-shaking routine. He pastes on an old-style "ain't this ridiculous" smile. Maybe he *is* Will Rogers.

"I'm not sure all that can be arranged. It's completely against hospital policy, especially your staying with the patient at the hospital."

"Dr. Benson, I'll be here with my father the rest of the morning; if, after consultation and reflection, you decide you can fulfill my requests as I've described them, would you have them typed out, signed by yourself and delivered to me here?"

I pause.

"If not, you have the card from Knight & Knight; you may contact them or they'll contact your attorneys."

I stand up and do *my* dismissal routine, a slight Peter Lorre bow from the waist. We do some more eye-to-eye staring. He could still throw me off the floor and lock me out of the hospital but I can see he isn't going to. He can't afford it. He walks past me, out the door and off the floor.

An hour later a nurse scurries in with signed approval for everything.

During the next week, I stay with Dad a good part of the time; Billy comes and sits Mother most days.

Dad continues in a coma. I see Dr. Chad every morning; he's kind and concerned. There's nothing said about the confrontation with Benson. Chad does an LP; there are some red cells in the spinal fluid but nothing to indicate serious stroking. He takes an EEG, but it's hard to tell anything while he's comatose. These things should all have been done a long time ago. The brain scan shows no sign of a tumor. But he remains unconscious. His BUN stays high. His eyes are dilated and his pulse irregular. It looks as if there will be no problem about Dad leaving intensive care.

On Thursday afternoon, Dr. Chad sits down in the chair beside me in Dad's room. He pulls out the record and goes over the medical evidence. He looks at me.

"Mr. Tremont, I think your father's dying. I'm still not sure just what happened. It could be any of a number of things, but his condition looks irreversible. If you want to have another consultation on this, please do."

I look at him. It's hard to accept. I look over at Dad. If they took off all the support—IV, oxygen, monitors, catheters, all the hardware—he'd die in hours. I can't say anything.

"Mr. Tremont, you should probably start considering arrangements for your father's death. I know your mother is very ill and perhaps you should try to prepare her. I don't think he will last much more than a few days."

I go down to the lobby and call Joan. I tell her what the doctor said. She's shocked but not surprised; that best explains the way I'm feeling myself. Joan says she'll meet me at Mom's.

I go home. Billy's in back working with the motorcycle. He took a spill on it riding the fire trails and he's trying to straighten the forks and knock out some bumps in the gas tank. The headlamp and direction-signal lamps are broken, too. Mother's watching TV. I sit beside her. If the show is over before Joan gets here, I'll break it to her myself. This is another hospital show. I'm beginning to think everybody's dressed in white, blue or green gowns. The show ends with a freeze shot of a woman screaming. Some fun.

I walk over and turn off the set. Mother's in her dressing gown after taking a nap. She has her hair in curlers and some cream worked into her face. She's a full subscriber to the "don't let yourself go" theory of survival.

"Mom, I just talked to Dr. Chad."

She's onto it right away.

"What did he say, Jacky; is he going to die?"

I think her mind is still half in the soap opera; we're acting out another episode. *I* should complain; it makes things easier for me. I take on the role of kind, loving, concerned son.

"Dr. Chad feels Dad doesn't have much longer. He wants us to make the arrangements."

That sounds appropriate to the genre. I'm feeling disengaged, thirty-six-plottish. Then Mother puts her fist into her mouth and starts crying, really crying. The soap opera is over.

She throws her arms around my neck. Mom's such a tiny woman, I always forget except at times like this. If a man were her size, he'd be totally marked by it, at a terrible disadvantage. I wonder if I could be five feet tall and cope.

I hold on to her until we hear Joan's camper roll into the driveway. Joan climbs down and comes in. Mother and Joan fall into each other. I'm empty, bare, cold inside. I'm surprised to find I've been crying. I'm the one it hasn't reached yet. I've been so busy, arranging, arguing, fighting, I haven't allowed it to happen to me. My father's going to die.

It's hard for all of us to talk about it but we need to do something. Except for an insurance policy, my folks haven't made arrangements. Like most people, they didn't want to think about it. Mother says she and Daddy agreed they wanted the simplest kind of funeral but buried in the ground together, in the same grave. That's all. We decide on the Holy Cross Cemetery, about two miles from my folks' house; no showing of the body or any of that. Mother wants any money beyond the minimum to be used for mass cards, prepaid masses said by priests in different places for his immortal soul.

I'm all primed to fight against embalming. It seems I need to fight something through these hard parts, something to keep me from thinking.

When I was fifteen, my Grandfather Tremont died. I was known in the family as the one who was good at school and I'd noised it around about wanting to be a doctor. My grandfather was to be embalmed in his own bedroom for the laying out. Friends of the family, the Downeys, who had a funeral home around the corner, were doing it. I was elected to help with the embalming.

By the time I'd watched the draining of the dark, thick blood, the cutting out of the insides, the stuffing of cotton into the sides of his mouth and into the eye sockets, it was the end of my doctoring career. I also swore nobody I loved would ever have that happen to them.

This is the first time I've had to check out that resolve. I've had thirty-seven lucky years since then, not being forced to make any of those decisions, but now it's here.

The next day, Joan and I go to Bates, McKinley & Bates, a mortuary and funeral home on Culver Boulevard. It's a sad business for a sunny California day but it's good doing anything with Joan.

The mortuary home is tan, plaster-covered cement, with smoked glass windows you can't see into from the outside. I stop at the parking meter to wind in a quarter. When I turn, Joan is standing, appraising the building.

"What do you think, Jack; they're afraid the corpses might escape?"

It *does* look like a camouflaged Nazi bunker.

She opens her purse, rummages around in it.

"Darn, I forgot to pack my silver-plated, pearl-handled twenty-two."

From then on, we're into it.

The doors are dark glass, too; swinging, metal-latched. Inside, the décor is virtually colorless; blacks, pure grays and whites. Everybody's dressed to match. It must be weird spending your days in a place like this, dealing with sad people; death on the dotted line. I want to turn around and walk back into the clean pollution and glare of Culver Boulevard.

There's a lady at the reception desk. She's wearing a white carnation in the lapel of a gray suit. Her hair is a muted gray but she looks young, not more than thirty-five. Joan does the talking; I'm not paying enough attention. The lady smiles and asks us to wait. I lean toward Joan.

"I think she dyes her hair."

I get a smile and cautioning finger.

We're ushered into a small room with a non-view tinted window on the street. I'm shocked to see a pinking beige automobile float slowly past outside. Maybe there's something special in this glass to make things move slowly.

Inside it's so still. A young man with undyed blond hair in a comb-line-visible pompadour is sitting at a desk. He has very white, detached hands folded on the desk in front of him. He brings off the saddest smile I've ever seen. It's the smile of a man with freckles who's just been told the sun has burnt itself out.

We sit down. I'm into the act now. I'm even appropriate in a black suit with a gray tie. Mother and Joan dressed me. The suit was designed for Joan's father-in-law to be buried in. He was dying of emphysema and spent his last gasping months planning his funeral. He had this suit designed for the laying out. It's black with a silkish paisley, almost invisible pattern and is lined with black silk. There are narrow lapels, trick slant pockets and three buttons in places you wouldn't expect them. Mr. Lazio, Joan's father-in-law, Mario's father, was Italian, Sicilian actually, and liked things fancy. He was also only five feet seven inches tall. I'm wearing the trousers as hip huggers, held up by a pair of Dad's old suspenders let out to maximum. I'm showing about two inches of cuff and can't breathe deeply.

The reason Mr. Lazio isn't buried in this suit is because the last week before he died, he decided to change the game plan. Now he wanted a gray suit with a gray casket and a black pillow to set off his gray hair. So they had a new suit cut for him to the dimensions of this one. Carmen, Joan's mother-in-law, gave this suit to my father, who is also five feet seven, but Dad would never wear it. He said he was afraid somebody would shoot him. So I'm the first one to wear it; probably the last. Some kind of hunched-over, hobbled pallbearer I'm going to make.

We tell the man we want the least expensive funeral possible. We try to make this sound as if it's a deep religious conviction but I can tell he pegs us as cheapskates. He moves a small pad from the corner of his desk and starts writing down the figures. He asks questions, we answer. "Yes, burial, not cremation." "But cremation is so much less expensive." "That's all right." We'll blow it on a bit of ground. "No, we don't have the plot; we'll buy it after we're finished here." . . . No, the corpse isn't dead yet. But he's working on it; we'll deliver, don't worry.

There's some complication about burying them in the same grave on top of each other. There has to be a cement vault, California law. OK, we're in for a double vault, cheaper in the long run and appropriate.

Then he quotes the price for the embalming: not much, about seventy-five bucks. Up to this point Joan has done most of the talking, very refined, very capable at keeping things on an even keel. I come drifting in.

"No, please, we don't want him embalmed."

A small squall passes over the unlined, calm, passive features.

"But it's customary to embalm, sir."

"We don't intend to have a showing of the body, so there's no reason to embalm."

"But, Mr. Tremont, it's a California state law; the deceased must be embalmed before burial."

"How about the ones you cremate?"

"They're embalmed, too. It's the California state law."

He smiles. I figure he's got us, I don't intend to do time over an unembalmed body. But then Joan comes on.

"I have a friend who's Jewish Orthodox; she was allowed

to bury her mother without embalming because it's part of her religion. Is this true?"

He folds his fingers, interlacing them the other way.

"Yes; it's an exception to the law; a question of religious freedom."

"Well, we want a Jewish burial."

She turns to me.

"Don't we, John?"

I nod. I can see us making arrangements at the local temple, running around sticking up crosses to confuse Mother, *Oy veh!* But we're past the embalming part for the time being. We're into caskets. He leads us down a corridor. I peek in several doors on the way. There are little metal name plaques over each door. Two I can remember; The Everlasting Peace Room, and The Eternal Truth Room. The room at the end has wall-to-wall caskets, three deep, hung on hooks and tilted slightly forward so we can see into them. They look like gigantic jewel cases. Most of them are lined with quilted silk in light colors from white through pink to gray again. The outsides of some are armored like Brink's trucks.

Our man is going along describing each coffin, its advantages and disadvantages, quoting prices. There's no stopping him, this is grooved-spiel time. He has instructions to give us the full treatment even if we are cheapskates.

We go along beside him, listening, waiting till he's finished. He's doing his best to make us feel that if we don't buy a foam-rubber-lined coffin so Dad'll be comfortable, with Duralumin or stainless-steel exterior to keep the worms out, we don't really love him. Joan looks at me. I don't know what she expects me to say.

"Sir, do you have anything in the line of a plain pine box?"

He looks down at his shined shoes, then up at us.

"No, the least expensive casket we have is this one. It is *pine,* sir, and painted metallic gray. It's priced at only one hundred twenty-two dollars."

"Would it be all right if I *built* a casket? My father was a carpenter, so he has all the tools. I'm sure I could build a box he'd like in two days or less."

He brings up a hand to smother a cough, probably a smirk or, hopefully, a smile.

"I'm afraid not, sir. *We* shall be responsible for the funeral, transportation, ceremony and interment; the reputation of our establishment would be involved. We couldn't allow a thing like that."

I know I'm being ornery, dumb; maybe I'm taking it out on death. Joan pulls me by the arm and turns toward the door. She whispers.

"That's enough, Jack, you've had your fun. You know how Dad is. He wouldn't want anything out of the ordinary. We're not going to have a hippy funeral."

She turns and goes back to the man.

"We'll take that one there."

She points to the one with the metallic gray paint.

"Is it possible to have it unpainted?"

He smiles and leans forward. Joan can get just about anything she wants. She's such a handsome woman. When you're her brother, it's easy to forget.

"I *am* sorry, madam, I don't think there are any in our reserve without paint and if there is to be no embalming—well —we can't wait very long."

Oh, he *is* a son of a bitch but it doesn't faze Joan; she smiles and nods.

"All right, we'll take this one just as it is, paint and all."

She grabs my arm and we follow him to the office again. As we go along the narrow corridor, I fall back and take a closer look into one of those rooms. There's a casket on a little platform, surrounded by vases of flowers. There are indirect lights and baby spots on the casket and it's open. An old lady, dressed in orchid, is sleeping in the casket. There's a smell of beeswax and floor polish. I run back out and catch up.

We sit down. He opens his pad and writes in the price of the casket.

"And where shall the services be held? We have lovely chambers for private services here in our own chapel."

I'm completely boggled again. That little smiling lady did me in; but Joan sticks with it.

"We'll have a funeral mass at Saint Augustine's and then the burial will be at Holy Cross."

He looks at her. What kind of a Jewish funeral is this? I half expect him to start talking embalming again. But he's given up; we could ask about hiring a five-piece band and he'd go along. There's more talk concerning the hearse, the number of limousines and a police escort. I'm not fighting anymore. It's going to be a funeral like any other funeral and Joan's right, that's the way Dad would like it.

The total bill comes to something over a thousand dollars. That was the maximum we'd set when we talked with Mother. We plunk down a two-hundred-dollar deposit and say we'll notify him when Dad dies. He also wants us to let him know soon as possible the exact location of the burial plot at Holy Cross.

We walk out, through the glare, to our car. The parking meter is almost run down. We climb in and I sit there watching the meter.

"What in heaven's name are you doing, Jack? What are we waiting for?"

"I'm getting the rest of my money's worth from this meter. Spending a thousand dollars—bam, like that, throwing it into a hole, shakes me up.

"You know, Joan, what I can't understand is why I'm not crying. Inside I'm like soft water flowing, going nowhere, but I can't seem to cry."

Joan turns and looks at me, a glint in her eye.

"Do you really want to cry? I can make you cry."

She folds her hands in her lap, clears her throat and starts singing:

> "Where is my Mommy, where can she be?
> I'm so awfully lonesome, lonesome as can be.
> Papa is brokenhearted, Mother left us alone,
> So if you see my Mommy, tell her to come home."

She hasn't gotten into the second line before my sobs start, softly, openly. I'm crying, scared, and ashamed as I always was. I stare through my tears at Joan. She stops. I get back some control.

"Did Mom really hide from us when we were little? Sometimes I think I made it all up; it's so hard to believe."

"Yep, she really hid. She even recommended the idea to me for my kids. She'd hide behind the hedge or sometimes go over to Mrs. Reynolds, for a cup of coffee.

"She thought it was funny how she could make you do anything she wanted by threatening to sing that song. You really were a 'simp' when I think about it."

"Well, why weren't you scared?"

"There *is* a song that makes me cry, too, you know, Jack. I never let Mother know about it and don't you snitch. I only hope I can sing it without crying now.

"I don't know why I love you like I do;
I don't know why I just do.
I don't know why you thrill me like you do;
I don't know why you just do.
You never seem to like my romancing;
The only time you hold me is when we're dancing. . . ."

I pick up the melody and we sing together. There on Culver Boulevard, under clear California sunshine, we cry our way through the rest of my quarter.

I pull out and we head toward Jefferson Boulevard. This part of town is cemeteryville. There are three cemeteries within three square miles: a Protestant one, a Jewish one and a Catholic one. I don't know what you do if you're an atheist or a Moslem. I wonder if there are still black cemeteries in America? There were when I was a kid. We called them colored cemeteries.

The Catholic one we're going to is built over what used to be a riding stable.

It has an entrance gate like Mount Vernon. The main administration building is a studio-set blend of a Howard Johnson's and a Bavarian chapel. Californians come up with the weirdest combinations in architecture. Except for Spanish-adobe style, there's no indigenous form, and they have no fear.

Inside, it's a more practical setup. On the wall is Pope Paul VI staring down at us. I wonder if they'll ask for our baptismal and confirmation certificates. Who's to know if Dad's Catholic?

We're ushered into a cubicle in a row of cubicles. A woman comes with a sheath of folders under her arm. We explain what we want. Again, we're going for the cheapy but it doesn't bother her. She puts aside two leather-bound folders and opens the folders in cardboard.

This cemetery is laid out like a golf course. There are no gravestones except flat plaques set in the ground. She shows us some plots which are still available. It's like working with a real-estate agent, choosing a lot in a development. In a sense, that's what it is, only the lots are tiny, the habitation subterranean, the neighbors very quiet.

Each part of the cemetery has a name. There's the Immaculate Conception Section, the Communion of Saints Section, the Resurrection Section, the Crucifixion Section, and so forth. Joan speaks up.

"We'd like a view in the direction of Palms."

The lady takes this in her stride. A view from your cemetery plot? It must have been asked before, because she's got her geography in hand. She turns the folders and points to several uncrossed-out plots.

"This is the Resurrection Section here. Palms is in this direction." She points on her map. "You could look around in here."

She makes a circle with her pencil without touching the map.

"I think you'll find what you want. It's on a little rise and has excellent drainage. There are some in the middle, here, in your price range because they are relatively inaccessible."

She indicates a wiggly circle with a dot in the center.

"This is a tree. The four graves around it are slightly more expensive."

She refers to a chart.

"There's one left under the tree and it's six fifty instead of five fifty; you see, the tree makes it easier to find."

We get the numbers and go out to look. There are winding, turning roads going all over the cemetery and she's given us a small map to find our way. It reminds me of driving toy cars in an amusement park. There are white arrow signs pointing to the different sections and we find Resurrection with no trouble. I park, we get out and locate the cross-section markings on the edge of the road. We work our way down across graves.

When we were kids, we had a big thing about not walking on the graves in the graveyard but here you're more or less encouraged to. Actually, the graves are so close together, and without gravestones, you can't tell whether you're walking on a grave or not.

We find the plots she pointed out to us, including one under the tree. This tree is a young jacaranda and that does it. Dad has always loved the jacaranda trees in California. We'll blow the extra hundred bucks and not tell Mother. We sit under the tree, look out and search for what we think is Mom and Dad's house.

"We should've brought a picnic with us, Joan. This is a cemetery I could come visit anytime. I wonder if they'd let somebody pitch a pup tent and camp here? After all, it's our own property; how could they stop us?"

"Jack, don't you dare mention that idea to any of the kids; you know they'll do it."

Then we start crying again.

When we're recovered, we go back to the office. Our lady picks us up and leads us to our cubicle. It brings back the time Vron and I were buying our first new car at Central Chevrolet in Los Angeles. We made the deals in cubicles just like this. I'm almost expecting talk about a trade-in.

We tell the lady we want the one under the tree. She's so enthusiastic you'd think she's the one who's going to be buried there. We tell her the plot is for two. She asks if we want a plaque. We decide to buy one at seventy-five dollars. We're caught up in the spirit of things. We give Mom and Dad's names. We'll have Dad's name first and both the year of birth and death cut. There's something final about putting down the year of death like that when it's only early April. We just put down the year of Mom's birth.

The lady asks if we want a flower holder installed. This is twenty dollars more. It's a metal holder set in the ground for flowers. I insist on having one; Joan thinks I'm crazy but goes along. All together, we drop about another seven hundred and fifty bucks at the cemetery. It looks as if the funeral's going to cost somewhere around two thousand. It's worth staying alive.

Outside in the car, Joan wants to know why I bought the flower holder.

"Gosh, Jack, we could bring a trowel, dig a little hole and stick flowers in the ground if you want. Mom's never going to go up there and visit; she's never visited her mother's or father's or any of her sisters' graves. She's afraid of cemeteries."

"I know, Joan, but someday I might want to do a little putting."

We go back home and explain to Mother what we've done. She doesn't want to know too much.

"When he's dead he's dead and that's all there is to it. The only thing makes sense is buying mass cards and praying for him."

I don't think it's truly hit yet. She knows he's going to die but not that he's going to be dead. The first is an event, the second is a fact of being. There's a big difference. It's only beginning to sink in to me. Dad isn't going to *be* anymore. We've said the last things to each other. I've seen him move around the garden or fix things in his shop for the last time. He'll never plant another flower or laugh again. He'll be gone.

Billy is there during all this. Thank God he doesn't say anything in front of Mother but out back he lets me know his feelings. I sit in the rocking chair and he flops on the bed.

"Christ, Dad, it's barbaric. Why don't we rent a rowboat

at the Santa Monica pier and dump him in the water? Who needs all this funeral crap?"

"There are California laws, Bill. It took some doing just not having him embalmed."

We still haven't told Mother about not embalming. We told her there wouldn't be any viewing of the body, but there was no reason going into the rest of it.

"You mean you got out of embalming him?"

"That's right. Joan quoted some obscure rule about Jewish religious custom and he's getting a Jewish non-embalmed funeral."

Billy stands up and starts pacing.

"That's great, that's really great! It'll be almost like a real funeral. Remember how when Mme. Mathilde died we packed ice around her in the bed till M. Didier could get the coffin made? Then we lowered her into the box and walked her up hill to the church, then to the churchyard. The gravediggers were M. Perrichot, M. Boule, the mayor, and Maurice. There was an extra shovel, so I gave them a hand. We had that grave filled and tamped down in fifteen minutes. That's my idea of a funeral."

"You're right, Bill, but it's not enough of a funeral for your grandmother. She's being terrific about the whole thing, and we've got to give her credit."

"Dad, I don't have a suit of any kind, let alone a black suit. What do you think?"

"Look in Granddad's closet, Bill; maybe one of his will fit you. I'm wearing one."

"You mean you're going to the funeral in your dead father's clothes?"

He sits down. I'm too tired to explain about Mr. Lazio.

"I don't think I could do it, Dad. That's too creepy. If he weren't my own granddad, I could, maybe; but I couldn't do that."

He shakes his whole body and closes his eyes. Sometimes I forget how young he is. A young man like him looks so grown up, it's easy to forget.

"Then go to the Salvation Army, Bill; they'll have something in a dark suit that'll fit you. Here's fifteen dollars. See if you can pick up a pair of shoes for a buck or so, too. You can wear them for the funeral, then toss them if you want. Your feet are too big for either Dad's shoes or mine."

Billy says first he'll wait till Dad's dead. I think again about our putting the year of death on that grave plaque. I hate to be superstitious but it's there in all of us; from books, movies, TV, the games we play as children. I ask Billy to stay with Mom. I want to be with Dad as much as I can.

The nurses are definitely different. Somebody tipped them off about me as a troublemaker. But they're polite. I feel like an accountant in a bank who's come to examine the books. I don't care; I'm not running a popularity contest with nurses.

Dad's the same. When I go in the room, I kiss him on the forehead and speak to him but he only continues his deep sleep. I wonder how they can tell a coma from sleep; maybe it's only a question of depth and length.

I'm just finished washing up when Lizbet comes wobbling into the kitchen. She has on her nightgown and her eyes are half open. I pull my suspenders over my shoulders and pick her up. She cuddles against me and I carry her to the maple rocking chair Gene made for Bess last Christmas. He sure has a knack with hardwoods. I sit and rock softly in the slowly lightening room. Lizbet tucks her toes into my crotch and sticks her middle two fingers in her mouth. Bess is afraid she'll pull her teeth out of straight but I let her suck, a nice sound like a calf nuzzling a teat. I breathe the smells of hay and child through the red gold of her hair.

The nurses are in and out every fifteen minutes. Dad's getting the royal treatment all right. I ask one what medication he's being given. She shows me the chart. I pretend I can read the squiggles, lines and abbreviations; smile and give it back. I don't see any narcotics listed and that's what I'm looking for. I don't see any hydrochlorothiazide or Zaroxolyn either, so I figure they've discontinued his diuretic for the blood pressure.

While you're in a coma, I don't imagine high blood pressure is much of a problem.

I'm getting nothing but bad vibes all over the floor. I don't know it then but the LVNs, kitchen help and all maintenance people are voting right that day to go on strike. In a little while these RNs will need to take over the whole hospital by themselves. I think they're pissed at me but actually they're pissed at the world in general and I'm only part of the world.

Dr. Chad comes in twice a day, once at ten-thirty in the morning and again about four in the afternoon. Each time he sits beside Dad, takes his pulse, listens to his heart, takes his blood pressure, looks at the catheter bottle and, with his stethoscope, listens to Dad's breathing. Each time he speaks softly, then more loudly, calling Dad's name.

"Mr. Tremont? How are you, Mr. Tremont?"

He pinches Dad's shoulder and slaps his face lightly, then harder. Each time there's no response. It's like trying to wake a drunk.

On the afternoon of the third day, there's a slight response when he slaps Dad; his eyes flicker open briefly, he turns his head, lifts his right arm slowly, then settles back. Dr. Chad slaps him again, calling, but there's no more. It's so like Jesus calling Lazarus back from the dead, especially since Chad has a full, black beard.

Every day, Chad explains the situation and what he's doing. He's running continual daily checks on the blood, urine, sputum and feces. He's beginning to think a big part of the problem might be metabolic. He doesn't know what set it off or how to re-establish life functions. When I ask, he still says he can't give me any hope; he's doing what he can but it looks terminal.

He's willing to tell me, exactly, everything he's trying and he's a natural teacher. I feel he's glad I'm interested and wants me to know.

The big thing is he's moved the IV from Dad's arm to the superior vena cava on his neck. He's giving nitrogen as protein hydrolysates, backing up with 150 calories for each gram of nitrogen. Chad tells me all this as if I should know what he's talking about. I feel he's truly doing something and it makes sense as he explains it.

After juggling around a few days, he settles on 165 grams of anhydrous dextrose plus 860 milliliters of 5 percent dextrose in 5 percent fibrin hydrolysate. To this he's adding 30 milliequivalents sodium chloride and 50 milliequivalents potassium chloride and 8 milliequivalents of magnesium sulfate. He says it's a delicate balance he's trying to establish. He explains all this but admits he's only taking shots in the dark.

But he's trying and I let him know how much I appreciate it. I only wish this kind of care had been given from the beginning. The nurses need to prepare these brews for the IV by filtration sterilization because they'd be destroyed by heat. This is a lot of additional work and they're not happy.

Still I hang in there, Chad hangs in and, most important, Dad's hanging on.

15

In the morning, we're soaked. The tent's sagged so it's on top of us. We crawl from under like worms slithering in the grass.

The sky is blue and warm with large drifting clouds, but the grass and trees are water heavy; drops sprinkle every time we move.

Dad stretches and almost falls over. It's past nine-thirty; those reds sure sent us off. There are huge water puddles on our tent where it sagged the most. We carefully pull out the tent pegs, ease down the tent poles, then try to roll the biggest puddles off without soaking the blanket more. We each take an end of the blanket, wring, then spread it on the car roof. The car's already so hot the blanket steams.

At the other end of the lay-by there's a rest room we didn't see before. We head there, wash, scrub our teeth and work on getting our eyes unglued. We're still wobbly. Our clothes are wet and wrinkled, so we come back and pull clean clothes from the suitcase. Aunt Joan washed for us just before we left and the clothes smell clean, dry and Californian.

When we come out of the rest room, the tent's half dry but the blanket will take time. We roll up the tent and stash it. Dad's carefully making a neat roll of each rope. We spread the blanket over the tent in the trunk.

Dad takes our wet clothes and puts them on hangers from his suitcase. He slips these hangers over little hooks on the inside of the car by the back windows. We're beginning to look as if we might be bushy reps making our yearly tour for a lingerie company.

It's ten-thirty before we get rolling. Dad takes the wheel. I put on the Dylan tape but keep the volume down. I'm still sleepy, so I recline the chair and close my eyes. It's amazing how much better you hear with your eyes closed.

We resist two Pizza Huts and eat on the other side of Vandalia, Illinois. It's a diner in a Quonset hut. We have fried chicken and dumplings. There's also little lumps like French-fried mothballs.

It's half a chicken each and I switch a leg for Dad's breast. He'll eat any part of a chicken, including the heart, liver, lights and the pope's nose. I only really like white meat. In our house, the whole mob, except Dad, are white-meat eaters. The rest of us scramble for scraps while he gorges himself on thighs.

We finish at three, then head off toward Indianapolis. I want to check out the Indy 500 track but Dad isn't enthusiastic about getting all tied up in city traffic. I'm driving now, but he's boss.

We're about ten miles past the Indiana border when we see a bunch of cars pulled over on the verge. People are jumping out of cars and some are running. The grass divider between the east and west lanes is crowded. There's been an accident on the westbound lane. I'm so shook I pull over and stop. It's the worst accident I've ever seen and it's just happened. The front wheel of an upside-down car is still spinning. There's only the one car and it's slammed against an embankment where the highway cut through a small hill.

A whole family is spread along the road. The father is farthest forward, farthest west. He's about Dad's age, husky with a little pot like Dad's. He must've slid over forty yards on the asphalt and is half sanded away. He's not bleeding much but you can see the bones in his shoulder and arms. His shirt's torn off and his pants are in rags with the belt pulled down over the top of his butt; he's barefoot and his toes are worn off. He looks more like somebody from a motorcycle than a car accident. Two men are on their knees beside him but he's not moving.

There's a woman about his age and she's bent against the dirt embankment with one leg twisted the wrong way under her. She's on her back and one arm is half ripped off. She's covered with blood and still bleeding. Three people are trying to stop the blood. From the way she's twisted, her back must be broken.

Trailing behind, going east, are three little kids and a dog. The dog is up on two legs spinning in circles, like that dog we hit, only this one's not barking or growling, just spinning and whining.

One of the kids is a skinny little boy, maybe Jacky's age. His guts are spilled over the road in circles as if he stood up and they all poured out. The guts look plastic in the sunlight. He's wearing shorts with a striped shirt and is covered with blood. He's spread out on his back so you can see the edges of his ribs where they've been cracked in. His eyes are open and somebody covers him while I'm watching.

There's a little girl and she doesn't look hurt much. There's no blood. People are standing around, but she isn't moving. I get closer and there's a deep dent in the side of her head just above her right eye.

Farthest east is a tiny kid still standing up. He can't be four years old. Just about all his skin is scraped off. He's red, raw and bleeding. He's crying and yelling for his mother. People are kneeling around him, trying to hold him, staunching blood in the worst places.

I turn away and vomit up that chicken, dumplings and mothballs. Dad's white and running around checking if anybody's called an ambulance. On the ground, I see I'm not the only one who's lost his cookies. Dad comes back.

"Are you all right, Billy?"

I nod my head. He's all hyped up.

"I'm not sure anybody's called an ambulance. Let's head down the road till we find a place with a phone. That little one might make it if they get him to a hospital fast."

I see somebody's taking the kid with them in a car but I don't say anything. I just want to get away. They'll need an ambulance anyway, even if it's only to settle for sure all those people really are dead. I climb in the passenger seat and stare out the window. How can such a rotten mess be happening under such a beautiful sky?

Dad's driving like a crazy. Now he has a mission, there's no stopping him. He pushes this crate to almost ninety. In about three miles, we come to a group of stores. He skids to a stop, jumps out, runs into a liquor store. I wait in the car. Three minutes later he comes out.

"Somebody's already called and they're on the way. I told them I thought there were five people critically injured, probably fatal."

He climbs in the car. He sits and doesn't start the engine. I look at him; he's white and breathing shallowly. He looks awful, pale, face all over shining wet.

We start hearing a siren. It's barreling out of the east and goes past us with that *heehhoouuughhh* sound a siren makes when you're sitting still. A minute later, another one screams by. Dad watches till they disappear. He turns on the motor.

"Well, Bill, I guess there's nothing more we can do."

He puts her in gear and waits till the highway is empty end to end before he pulls out. Now he's driving all of thirty-five miles an hour; but I'm not fighting. I'm considering *walking* the rest of the way.

We stop at the next gas station and tank up. There's a small snack place there, so we go in for a cup of coffee. My stomach's so empty now the back's hitting the front. I buy a piece of blueberry pie. I'm beginning to feel better, but Dad's still white.

"Billy, would you drive for a while?"

I nod.

"And take it easy, please, I've about had it."

He takes out a bottle of Valium from the glove compartment and pops one.

"Boy, Bill, I can feel the blood pumping through my heart like a hydraulic press."

I keep it at fifty-five and the old man lies back in the seat the way I left it. He isn't watching the road at all, just lying back staring at the headlining. It's the first time he hasn't had his eyes glued on the road. It's spooky, as if he's given up running things.

"What do you think happened, Bill? There wasn't any other car. It's the middle of the day; I can't see the guy falling asleep. I checked the tires; there wasn't any blowout. What the hell could've gone wrong so this guy ruins everything, his wife, his children, even his dog? What the hell did he do wrong?"

He gives a big sigh and I look over at him. There are tears in his eyes. He *really* is about ready to crack, but he's not finished.

"Maybe his kids were bugging him and he leaned back to give them a whack and lost control. God, I hope not, that'd be an awful thought to have at the last minute. Maybe the steering wheel cracked or the brakes gave out. So many things can go wrong, no matter how careful you are.

"I only hope he never had a chance to look back and see it all, wife twisted like a pretzel against the dirt, his son gutted, his daughter poleaxed and his baby standing there like a walking piece of hamburger on the road crying, surrounded by strangers. It's enough to make you hope there isn't any life after death. How the hell could you live any kind of life, anywhere, doing anything, if you had to live with that?"

Oh, God, I wish he'd only shut up. I'll be upchucking that blueberry pie and coffee if he keeps on with this.

"And damn it, Bill, there's no way to get out of driving. It scares the hell out of me. I hate getting into one of these metal boxes and I'm glad every time I step out alive. I know I'm too tense when I drive but I keep seeing that kind of thing, only it's us. It's us, publicly dying on hot, or wet, or icy asphalt with strangers pawing over what's left."

Jesus, you think he's the iron man, getting things done, carrying through; then he collapses. I've slowed down to forty-five! I juice her back to sixty. He doesn't even notice; only stares some more at that headlining.

"It's just destiny, Dad. Accidents are a question of bad luck. You can only do so much. There's no sense sweating it; you can worry yourself straight past any fun in life."

He doesn't move. Maybe he isn't listening. It's getting dark so I switch on the lights. It's not that late but some big black clouds have blown up between us and the sun. I'm hoping we can make it to the other side of Indianapolis and find a motel. I'm pooped. We slept last night but it wasn't real sleep. I was only unconscious; some part of me was fighting rain, thunder, lightning and trucks.

Then he starts in again.

"I used to feel that way, Bill; it's part of being young. It's also a question of recklessness. I looked up the word 'reck' once to see if there really was such a word. It means worry or care. As people get older they get more 'reck.' Bad experiences, accidents, near misses—seeing things like we just saw—pile up, accumulate in the brain. A person becomes more 'recky' every year; continuity, survival, gets bigger and bigger.

"Also, the brain itself is changing. Certain kinds of mental and physical skills begin declining as early as seventeen.

"I've watched myself becoming less sure, Bill, less capable of making decisions. When I'm driving, I feel caught between the reckless, the twenty-year-old, and the inept, the fifty- or sixty-year-old, who might not have the skills to cope with an emergency. And I can't help projecting *my* limitations onto others, like you, Bill. I can't be comfortable when you drive in ways I couldn't handle."

It goes dark fast and then the first big raindrops start. The road here outside Indianapolis is packed with giant semitrailer trucks. I pass one about every quarter mile. Thank God Dad's all cranked up on the decline and fall of the human animal. He'd be a raving lunatic helping me get around these big bastards.

When I turn on the windshield wiper, there's only a humming sound. I look at the dash to check I've pushed the right switch. I joggle it on and off a few times.

Man, this is going to be fun with the dark, the rain, the trucks and the voice of doom beside me. He leans forward, leaving the chair back. He fiddles with the switch; it's kaput all right. I'm sure glad this bucket of bolts isn't mine; I'd need to work full time just keeping it running.

The rain is coming down in sheets now; I aim on the taillight of the truck in front of me; it's the only thing I can actually see. I can't pick up the white lines *or* the edge of the road. I've only got the two red lights repeated about a hundred times by each water splash on the windshield; and I'm afraid to stop.

"Can you see at all, Bill? I can't see a thing. Maybe we'd better pull over!"

"I can see OK, Dad; I'll just stay behind this truck. Long's I see those taillights we're all right."

He's quiet. I know he doesn't want to go on but what the hell else can we do? There's no real shoulder on this road and it's beginning to go under water already.

"Look, Dad, you keep watch for a turnoff. If you see one, yell."

He rolls the window down two inches on his side so he can see out. The rain comes pouring in and swishes around the inside of the car. Even with the window open he can't see; and with that big truck in front of us, there's no way to pick up signs till they're almost behind us.

I'm tailing my truck at less than fifty feet; if I get farther behind I lose him. I'm going to get wet anyway so I roll down my window. It pours in like a boat sinking in a catastrophe movie; in one minute I'm soaking wet. I hang my head out to see if it's any better, but the rain whips in my eyes so it's worse than with the smeared windshield. I pull in my head and roll up the window.

I catch some blinking lights coming up behind. I hold on to the wheel and hope for the best. It's another semi who's impatient with this big Lincoln tailgating one of his buddies. He steams by, and I lose whatever vision I had. The semi is throwing up dirty water and mud faster than clean water is coming down. I hold the wheel tight, keep up my speed and wait till I can see the taillights again. Our whole car gets a tug in the semi's slipstream. I'm doing forty-five and he must be doing sixty. It's almost a half minute of absolute blind driving, the windshield tinted brown mud, before I pick up the taillight again.

But I'm getting the hang of it. If he puts on his brakes, the brake lights come on and I put on mine. The problem is I'm getting hypnotized by those two lights. They shimmer on the road and on the windshield; no hypnotist could think up a better gimmick.

Just then, Dad hollers; more like yelps. There's an exit coming in one mile. I put on the direction signal and ease to the right. I hope to hell I can pick up the turnoff. It's pouring horse and elephant piss now. The roof of this crate's howling with sound.

Dad sees the turnoff arrow just in time and I turn. There are no lights behind so I slow to fifteen. There's a dim marking along the edge of the exit road; we curve off and down to a stop. There's a sign across the road. I kick up the highs and roll out till we read "BROWNVILLE FIVE MILES." I swing hard right and start that way.

It's a high-crown, narrow road, and the white line's almost invisible. I ride the crown; if anybody comes speeding along without headlights, we've had it.

We cruise into town looking out blurry windows for a motel sign. I'm hoping the cops or sheriffs or whatever they use for law here are inside. They'd never appreciate this Lincoln with no wipers nosing blind up and down the main street. We're about to give up when we spot a sign, "HOTEL," at the other edge of town. God, I hope there's a room; spending the night wrapped in a wet blanket for two doesn't exactly turn me on.

This place is brick with a colonial porch. There are coach lamps with yellow bulbs on both sides of the door. Dad jumps out and dashes through the rain. He can't get any wetter than he is, but people run hunched over in the rain as a natural thing. I know if they have a room he'll take it even at fifty dollars a night.

In about five minutes he comes out; he opens the door and smiles in.

"I've got us a great room. The manager's convinced I'm a bank robber just off the job and we've got the trunk filled with gold bullion, so let's live up the part; at least put your shoes on."

He's hyped again. Maybe he's only glad to be alive, with a warm bath and dryness waiting inside. I give him the keys. He opens the trunk and struggles out his suitcase with my duffel bag. He hauls our bags onto the porch while I back the car into a parking area behind.

I walk slowly through that warm rain. I'm smiling as if it's the most natural thing in the world to walk through teeming rain in the night. There are hydrangea bushes off the edge of the porch and I lean over to sniff the flowers, no smell. Dad's rocking back and forth squishing in his shoes. But he's laughing.

"Come on, Bill, you don't have to overdo it. I'm sure this pussy's already alerted the sheriffs in three counties."

We sashay into the lobby, dripping genuine Indiana or Ohio rainwater all over maroon rugs. We carry our own bags up to the room and it looks beautiful, two gigantic double beds.

We take turns wringing clothes and taking showers. I'm completely out of dry things, so I borrow a shirt and trousers from Dad. I even borrow a pair of his jockey shorts and tennis shoes. Going down we look halfway presentable; I'm loose in his clothes and my feet are cramped in his size 8 sneakers, but we're clean.

Would you believe it, the manager comes over and casually introduces a gentleman who's wearing a half-Stetson white hat. It really is, it's the marshal for the town. He must have jumped up from dinner to come see the masked bandits without their masks. He starts polite conversation about where we're coming from and where we're going to; and, of course, about the car. Even if we'd gotten out of that car clean-shaven and in tuxes, this hotel manager would've called his friend the marshal.

Dad looks him in the eye and asks if there's a Colonel Sanders in town. A sheer stroke of genius. The marshal shakes his head, all sorry about that. Just for the hell of it I ask if there's a Taco Bell, another mob franchise. He shakes his head and smiles again. He could be half catching on.

"But there's a Pizza Hut, fellas; just on the other side of town, toward 80."

He nods and smiles. He leads us onto the porch and points the only direction the place could be; it's dark every other way. Just gives an idea how hard that rain was coming down when we went past a Pizza Hut without stopping.

We bow and bend, thanking the marshal as he tips his hat to us; Spade Cooley saluting his horse.

We board the Philadelphia Express and float our way blind to the Pizza Hut. It's like coming home. We order a giant cheese pizza and a pitcher of beer each. We're going all out. The pitchers are glass with curved glass handles like gigantic mugs, only with spouts. We drink our beer straight from the pitchers as if they're beer steins. We wipe out the pizzas and an Italian salad. I can't say I ever enjoyed food more in my life.

There are two cute waitresses having a ball watching us drink from pitchers. If I were with any other guy except my father, I'm sure we could talk them into coming to the hotel with us; give that manager something to worry about.

16

Next day the strike hits. All RNs and doctors are put on full time, two shifts. Everything's on emergency basis. The hospital accepts no new patients and they're discharging or shipping patients to other hospitals.

The RNs are forced to do all the bedside and dirty work normally done by LVNs. I volunteer to help wherever I can; there's no way they're going to move Dad out.

I'm concerned he'll be neglected with all the confusion, so I move in and sleep next to him. Over half the beds in intensive are empty anyhow. A little redhead nurse shows me what to look for with Dad and I change his sheets, his Pampers; give general bedside service. Except for renewing bottles on the IV, there's not much medical involved. Chad's cleared things for me to stay, so I'm having no trouble there.

When I tell Mother about the strike, she wants to shift Dad to another hospital. Joan and I talk her out of that. Perpetual knows his condition and Dr. Chad seems to care. The move alone could kill him.

Mother's at home. Billy's sleeping in the back garden room to keep an eye on her. He's being great about it.

It's strange living in a hospital when you aren't sick, especially sleeping in an intensive care unit. Most of the patients still here are desperately ill, too far gone to move, so the line between the well and ill is even more exaggerated than usual.

After I've been around several days and haven't bitten anyone's head off, the nurses are more reasonable. Several times they use me as an extra hand, holding a patient still for an IV insertion or lifting and holding or shifting while they make a bed. I also help with the feeding of other patients.

Early in the morning of the fifth night, I wake to the usual jingling of glass and metal, the main sound in a hospital. There's a pale gray light coming through the window and I listen to the early going-to-work traffic. It's the time when I usually have my most depressed thoughts. I'm lying in bed, half thinking, half in suspended animation.

I glance over at Dad. His eyes are open and he's looking at me! I mean he's looking *at* me, not past me, or through me or around me! He's looking into my eyes!

I slide out of bed on his side and approach carefully. At first, I think maybe he died in the night, but his eyes are live, they follow me, keeping me in focus. I come to the edge of his bed. His mouth opens twice, dry pale lips, paper-frail. But he gets out a sound, a thin, high voice almost falsetto.

"Where am I, Johnny?"

I can't believe it! He's still looking into my eyes, waiting for an answer.

"You're in the hospital, Dad, you've been sick."

He nods his head slowly. He looks down the length of his bed and smiles.

"I think I could've guessed that one, Johnny. But what are you doing here? Are you sick, too?"

God, there's something so clear, so young-sounding! I reach out and put my hand on his head.

"Just take it easy, now, Dad; don't force yourself. You're doing fine."

He lifts one arm, his right, discolored with IV punctures and tape marks. It's so thin the muscles are like ropes over bones just under the skin.

"I don't look so hot to me, Johnny. What's happened any-way; was there an earthquake or a car crash or something?"

I don't know what to say, how much to try explaining. Just then, the morning nurse comes in. It's the redhead again. Dad looks at her and smiles. She stands there staring, as shocked as I am, but recovers quickly.

"Well, hello, Mr. Tremont, how are you feeling this morn-ing?"

Dad looks over at me.

"Isn't she pretty, Johnny? I always wanted a redheaded daughter; left-handed like your mother and redheaded."

Now the nurse stares at me, bewildered. There couldn't be a more drastic swing from death to life.

"Nurse, I think you should page Dr. Chad."

Dad closes his eyes. I'm afraid it might only have been a moment's clarity before some horrible final descent into death but I don't want to disturb him. I pull my chair close.

When Chad comes in, we're still like that. Dad must not have been asleep, because he opens his eyes as the doctor and nurse bustle into the room. Dad looks at Chad and smiles.

"My goodness, it's like the House of David baseball team."

Chad looks at me, eyes wide.

"He woke this way, Doctor. What do you think?"

Chad's taking Dad's pulse; he puts a thermometer in his mouth. Dad keeps an eye on him; a quivering smile flashes around his eyes, his lips. Chad takes his blood pressure and looks at me.

"One twenty over seventy-five."

He checks the thermometer.

"Normal."

"Hello, Mr. Tremont, how are you feeling?"

"I don't know. How am I supposed to feel? I'll say I feel mighty tired."

Chad's leaning forward, peering into Dad's eyes, feeling his skin. He looks under the bed at the urine bottle.

"Well, Mr. Tremont; you've been sick but you seem fine now. What can we do to make you comfortable?"

Dad looks down at himself in the bed.

"Well, to start with, could you take off a few of these tubes and wires; then can I have something to eat? I'm hungry."

He holds up his withered arms.

"It looks to me as if you've been starving me in this hospital. I'd say I haven't had a good meal in a month or so."

I take his hand. It's something I never would've done when he was well. We take liberties with the very ill.

"It's been more than that, Dad."

He loosens his hand, interlocks his fingers, looks at them, turns them over.

"Say, I must've really been sick."

Dr. Chad stands and backs to the door. He signals me with his eyes to follow. The nurse tucks Dad in; she has a basin of water to wash his face and hands. Chad's face is a cross between perplexed and elated.

"Don't ask me to explain it, Mr. Tremont. I've never seen anything like it. It could have been the metabolism all along."

"Dr. Chad, it's more than that. He's different. He's so clear, so calm, somehow younger than he was even before his operation. What can it be? Is it permanent?"

Chad shakes his head and we go over to the counter. He writes a long time in Dad's medical record. Finally he looks up.

"Mr. Tremont, I really don't know. He could go back into a coma anytime. We'll stay with the metabolic approach and be careful of his diet. I don't want to take the vena cava off too soon. We'll let him eat but keep the IV so long as he remains rational."

After I get dressed, I start feeding him soup. He takes the spoon away and feeds himself. He has all the control of a young man; he's weak but he has control. He drinks some

orange juice and is still hungry. He complains about the catheter and IV again. I explain what Dr. Chad said. He wants to
know what's been happening to him.

The last he remembers is coming to the hospital for his
operation. He can't believe that was six weeks ago. He remembers Mother's heart attacks and wants to know how she
is. I tell him she's fine. I tell about the strike here and how I've
been sleeping in the room with him.

He accepts all this. He wants to know when Mother and
Joan can come visit; when he can go home. I tell him they'll
come soon as possible but he should stay in the hospital until
he's really on his feet again.

The nurses are all in and out of the room. They're almost
as pleased as Dad and I are. A pretty Japanese nurse takes
Dad's hand and he puts his other hand on top of hers.

"Gee, you look so well, Mr. Tremont."

There are tears in the corners of her eyes. Dad looks up
at me.

"Maybe I *will* just stay on here in this hospital, Johnny;
it's not so bad."

At nine o'clock, I call Joan. I try preparing her for what's
happening and insist she come immediately. She's there within
the hour.

She holds on to Dad and sobs. He looks past her at me; he
can't really understand why she's crying.

It's the same thing when we bring Mom; she cries so hard
we need to take her straight home. Joan stays with her that
night.

Three days later, Chad takes off the IV. Five days later,
off goes the catheter. Dad hates to use the bedpan and urine
bottle, so I carry him into the toilet and back. There's a little
handrail beside the toilet; he hangs on to it and insists I leave
the room while he "does his business." We've started him on
light, solid food with a backup of pills and medication Chad
has worked out. Chad keeps an eye on the blood pressure but it
stays stable. He says he doesn't want to start medication for
the blood pressure unless it's absolutely necessary. He's willing

to let it go high as one sixty or one seventy over a hundred; he wants to guarantee blood circulation in the brain. He also continues all his measures on intake and output. Chad admits he's still only flailing around, guessing; he has no real explanation as to what happened or what's happening now. The strike is still on and I stay at the hospital.

Dad's taking on some weight but still doesn't weigh a hundred pounds. It was bad enough when he was lying still in bed; now he's so active, he resembles a living skeleton and it's frightening. But his color is improving and he's hungry all the time.

On about the tenth day, when the food comes into the room, he sniffs like a dog catching a scent.

"You know, Johnny, I can smell that food. I haven't been able to smell anything for over twenty years."

I take his tray from the nurse and put it in front of him. He puts his head down close and sniffs each dish.

"I can even smell spinach; it smells something like the Atlantic Ocean. I'd forgotten how good things smell."

He starts with the veal cutlet, chewing carefully and long before he swallows. He's like a TV ad for food.

"It's exactly the way it was after I quit smoking, John; food tastes so good, so strong. Each thing is different."

The next day he asks about Dr. Ethridge. I tell him I changed doctors because I'd lost confidence in Ethridge. He looks at me.

"You mean you fired him?"

"Well, no, Dad. I only had him removed from your case. He still works for Perpetual."

"But I've had him as a doctor for fifteen years, Johnny. He's from Wisconsin, you know."

"I know, Dad, but I became convinced he wasn't giving you the kind of medical care you needed. I truly believe you'd be dead today if we hadn't changed doctors. Dr. Chad seems to have figured out your problem; at least you're here."

He stops eating; he looks me in the eyes, smiles, shakes his head and starts eating again.

"You're a boss, all right, Johnny. I don't know if I like having a boss for a son."

"Well, you're stuck with it, Dad. You were too far gone to fight me, so I took over. You can always go back to Ethridge again if you want."

He stops with a forkful of spinach in front of his mouth.

"Oh, no. I believe you. I've always felt he made a mistake with that gall-bladder operation. They didn't need to take out my gall bladder."

I'm glad Dad can admit it. He begins cutting his veal cutlet. It's wonderful to see his mechanic's hands working.

"It's just the idea of '*firing*' a doctor; I could never get the nerve to do a thing like that."

"Remember, Dad, they're here to serve you; you're paying them, just the way you'd pay somebody to fix your car."

He waves his knife at me, shakes it.

"Oh, no I'm not; it's Douglas and the union pays."

"Sure you're paying, Dad. The money they give to Perpetual comes from somewhere. It comes from the money you earned for Douglas, money they made off you and your work. It's not charity, you earned every dime. They made a fortune off your work over the years, don't forget that."

"OK, Johnny, OK. We'll fire Ethridge, maybe take over this whole hospital. That's just fine with me."

I'm enjoying watching him eat. After all the feeding— trying to get his mouth open, then get the spoon out; catching the drivels—it seems like a miracle to watch him shove food in his mouth.

I've always liked watching Dad chew anyway. When he chews, there are tight muscles at the juncture of his jaws which flex with each bite in a way I've never seen on anybody else. They flex into a hard round nutlike muscle under his thin skin. It's the same way when he bears down to tighten or loosen a bolt or nut. I remember as a kid trying to develop that chewing muscle; it never came. It's like his hammering muscle.

"Dad, let's see if you still have that old hammering muscle of yours."

He puts down the fork and looks at his withered, wrinkled right arm. It's liver-spotted and the skin is somewhere between something a snake would discard and old parchment. Even most of the hair has rubbed off. But when he bends his wrist, it's still there. A bump about the size of a marble rises in the middle of his lower arm. He pushes on it with the index finger of his left hand.

"Soft as a lump of pig fat. I'd never get a job now with a hammering bump like that."

He peers at me and smiles.

"But you know what, Johnny; I don't need a job. I'm retired. I own my own house, I've got money in the bank, a pension and Social Security. I don't ever have to work again. Hot dawg!"

He picks up his spoon and starts scraping, cleaning the corners of the dishes. I think he could eat another whole meal.

Before he was married, Dad worked as an outside carpenter in Philadelphia. He and his brothers worked for their father, who did the basic contracting. Sometimes they'd get a big job and hire extra people. Dad told me his dad never asked about apprenticeship papers or recommendations. He'd only ask to see if the guy had a hammering bump. If it was there, he'd touch it the way Dad did just now and if it was hard the guy got the job.

My granddad refused to pay a salary. Everybody who worked with him was a free agent. He'd offer a job like sheeting a roof and promise a certain amount of money if it was done well in a certain amount of time. Dad said if you worked your tail off and were good, you could make a lot of money working for him but if you loafed on the job you'd wind up broke.

This way Granddad got the best carpenters in Philadelphia and was known for getting a job done quickly and well.

The trouble was he couldn't expand with his "no salary" system, so it was mostly job carpentry. Then too, just when he did get things rolling for him, building six houses on speculation, the Depression hit. He lost everything, worked ten years paying off his debts and died within the year.

I never developed a hammering muscle. I've rebuilt three

houses, adding a total of six bedrooms and two baths as well as building a two-car garage, but that hammering muscle never came. Once when I was helping Dad build his place I asked about it. Then he was about my age now; I was maybe twenty-five, just finished my master's.

"You have to work years, Johnny; eight hours a day, hammering. Don't worry about it; you've got your hammering bumps in your head."

It was that same day we were putting shingles on his roof. Dad'd showed me how to fit the shingle and nail, working up. He started on the right half, and I'm working on the left. After about an hour, I look over and he's done four times as much as I have. I stop and study to find what *he's* doing I'm not.

He has his mouth full of roofing nails and works them out between his lips, point first, as he needs them. He fits the shingle with his right hand, still holding on to the hammer, reaches up to his mouth with his left, pulls the nail out, holds it in place and hits twice, once to settle it in, the second time, hard, to drive it home. He's already working that new nail between his lips, without pausing, shifting and getting the new shingle. It's sort of: pause—bang-BANG—pause—bang-BANG. My sound has been: long pause—pulling nail out of can, fitting shingle in place, starting nail—then bang-bang-bang-BANG-BANG; start over.

So I watch a few cycles, then fill my mouth with nails. I cheat by starting with three already in place between my lips. I work the shingle in with my hammer hand, then try to get the rhythm with him: bang-BANG—nail shingle—bang-BANG—nail shingle—bang-BANG. I'm trying to concentrate on hitting the nail hard enough and at the same time working a nail with my tongue into my lips. The nails have an electric, galvanized taste. Nail shingle—bang-BANG—nail shingle—bang-BANG—YOUUWWWWW!

I've hit my thumb with a full swing of the hammer! I stand up and almost fall off the slanted roof. Dad looks over at me. I've spit out the nails with my holler. Vron and Mom run from inside where they've been painting. I manage to get down the ladder and put my thumb in cold water but that thumbnail is smashed and already on its way out. I still have a bump in my left thumbnail. I didn't develop a hammering bump but I developed a thumb bump in one fell swing; a twenty-seven-year-old reminder that I'll always be an amateur carpenter.

Every day Dad grows stronger. He's a big favorite with the nurses. The strike ends, the main crew comes back and I start sleeping at Mother's. Billy, who's been going stir-crazy, moves up onto the forty acres again.

But Billy does come down almost every other day to visit Dad at the hospital. Dad's been moved to a regular ward and has a whole new set of nurses to play with. They've given him a walker and he's getting up out of bed a little bit every day. He tells Billy he has the walker to keep the nurses from attacking him. Billy stays long times with Dad and tells me he can't believe it's the same man, his *grandfather*. Billy never knew my father like this; I can hardly remember him this way myself.

One day I'm sitting and joking along with Dad when he says:

"You know, Johnny, I might not have to go to hell after all."

I don't know what he's talking about. Maybe he's slipping gears again.

"Heck, Dad, if you're not going, then I'm not going either."

"No, John, remember I was worried about going to hell 'cause I couldn't work up any feelings of love for niggers? We were talking about it one day before I went into my tailspin. Remember?"

"Yeah, I remember now, Dad."

Oh boy, here we go again.

"Well, John, I've been having some visits from one of the nicest people in the world and she's almost black, a medium soft brown, but definitely a nigger for sure."

"You've got to admit, Dad, some of these nurses here have been awfully kind to you, no matter what color they are."

"Oh, this isn't a nurse, Johnny. Well, actually she is, sort of. Sometimes she comes in her uniform, but she doesn't work here."

It still doesn't register. I'm thinking he's confused.

"She says she's a friend of yours, John; she has one green eye. You wouldn't think anybody could be pretty as she is with one eye a different color like that."

I can feel the blush rising over me, but Dad isn't noticing.

"She tells me she was a nurse in some hospital I was in that I don't even remember. She brought them African violets there; raised them from cuttings. She has seventeen different varieties of African violets alone; I only got eight myself.

"You are keeping up the watering on my plants and things, aren't you, Johnny?"

I nod.

"I've been watering, Dad, and staying up with most of the weeding, too. Alicia's a fine person all right; one night she helped save your life."

"She told me all about that, John. I could hardly believe it. She sure thinks the world of you, says you were better'n a doctor. You know, this is a peculiar thing to say, considering everything, but that girl reminds me of my own mother, your grandmother, Mary Duheme, more than any person I ever met in my life. That's why I'm not going to hell, John, I can love that woman, nigger or not, just as much as I can love my own mother."

He smiles at me and I smile back. I think of asking what time she comes but I don't. Before leaving I say if she comes again to say hello for me.

Dad tells the nurses he doesn't want to be shaved anymore. The nurses talk to the doctor and Chad comes to me. I talk to Dad.

"We've been through all this before, Dad. You know how Mother feels about beards. Here she's got a bearded son and three bearded grandsons; don't you think a bearded husband might be too much of a good thing?"

"Don't worry, let me talk to her, John. After all, I almost died; I have some rights. I'm an old man; old men should be allowed to have beards if they want. Besides, I have a very tender face. Since I can't grow hair on top, I'll grow some on my chin."

There's no stopping him. I tell Chad it's OK. He smiles out of his bush. He thinks this is one of the funniest things happening in the hospital. He tells the nurses and they don't fight. It's no fun shaving an old man with a heavy beard and folds of neck wrinkles. I go home to prepare Mother.

"I tell you, Jacky, he's gone completely crazy; he isn't the same. He's turning into some kind of Don Juan. I think he's senile; going into his second childhood. You wait till I get him home, we'll see about that beard; nobody with a beard is going to kiss me, I'll tell you that much!"

I try calming her down. I call Joan; she's convinced I've talked Dad into it; she's going to the hospital and discuss it with him, then she'll come over to Mother's.

Mother's still raving when Joan drives up. Joan comes in the door laughing. She goes over and gives Mother a kiss and a hug. Before Mother can get in a word, Joan lets it out.

"Mother, you'll just have to try living with Santa Claus for a while. He's got this bug to grow a beard and he's as excited as a kid."

Joan throws her purse on the couch and flops beside it. She's still giggling.

"I had no more chance with him than I did with Jeff and Ted. He's convinced you'll like it, Mother."

"Do you think he's gone crazy, Joan? Tell me, is he crazy?"

Joan spreads her arms along the top of the couch, spreads her legs, kicks off her shoes. She looks at me.

"He's no crazier than this one here, or Billy, or Jeff, or Teddy; he's only doing some kind of 'man' thing on us."

I get up, go in, and bring out some of the muscatel. I pour us all a glass and pass it around.

Mother begins to see the humorous side.

"My God, Joan. How will I ever explain it to the neighbors? They'll all think I have a hippy boyfriend."

Joan takes a sip of the cold wine.

"Maybe you do, Mother; he's so different. He's like a seventeen-year-old and I don't mean he's senile; his mind is young. He's making jokes, smiling at everything, at everybody in the hospital."

She sips again, looks at me.

"You know, it'll give him something to think about. He's always been a farmer at heart, now he can grow a garden—on his face."

Mother laughs, almost spills her wine.

"You're crazy too, Joan; it's in that damned Tremont blood."

I know Mom can laugh because she's convinced she'll talk Dad out of the beard.

I help her back to the bedroom for her nap. Joan and I sit out on the patio. It's a fine sunny day, not too hot but with strong sun and a soft breeze. There's practically no smog. It's the kind of day L.A. is supposed to have all the time. I've rolled out the two redwood chaise longues. Joan stretches herself on one and I lower myself onto the other.

"Tell me, Jack, what does the doctor say? What's going on? It's like Dad stepped into a time machine; he makes me feel older than *he* is."

She has the back of her hand across her eyes against the sun. She takes the hand away and leans forward.

"I think he's got that beard mixed up in his mind with getting well. I'm sure he sees himself coming out of this whole thing a new man."

"That could be a big part of it. That show of color when he let it grow maybe reminded him of his real life locked in there."

Just then it hits me.

"Holy God, Joan! What'll we do about the dates on that tombstone?"

She sits up.

"Oh, my goodness! I forgot. We'll have to call and ask them to leave off the final date."

"Do you mean the last seven or both sevens?"

"Jack, at the rate he's going, maybe we should think twice about the nineteen!"

When I finally decide Dad should come home, he weighs a hundred ten and his beard's well grown in; thick, dark, grizzled brown.

Chad goes along with everything I ask. This includes a

deluxe pneumatic mattress to help with healing Dad's bedsores, a wheelchair, one of those walkers and a cane. We also have a special chemical toilet and an oxygen tank with the nose attachment. I figure Mother can use the oxygen while napping, even if Dad doesn't. Perpetual is footing the bill for all this and a nurse will come once a day to check on Dad. I get Dr. Coe to sign a procurement slip allowing the nurse to check Mother, too.

I must admit I'm laying it on, but it's a small revenge.

I'm half tempted to walk the senile corpse in on Ethridge but I'm not sure this would be good for Dad. Ethridge wouldn't care anyway; just so long as his stocks keep going up and his golf game doesn't deteriorate too fast.

Dad comes home and Joan joins us to help with the settling in. There was never anybody more pleased to be home; but then he's happy about everything. He sits in his platform rocker with his leg cocked under him and comments immediately on the African violets blooming in the window box. I've added his new ones from the hospital. Alicia's given him five different varieties. I'm praying Mother won't ask about them but I'm ready to lie.

He wants to check his garden and the greenhouse. Billy and I've been keeping things in the greenhouse tended, also the grass cut and trimmed. It isn't up to his standards, we know, but it isn't a jungle either.

Mom watches Dad as if there's a stranger in the house. Already, he can get along with a cane if somebody holds his other arm, so we take him out to the patio, help him into a chair. It's another good day but a bit warmer and there's a touch of smog. Still, out there, with the greenery and the recently watered grass, it's beautiful.

Dad stares up.

"Boy, it's easy to forget how wonderful the sky is. I haven't been out where I could look up and see blue in a long time. I must say, though, I do miss clouds here in California. We had beautiful clouds in Philadelphia and Wisconsin."

Mother's in the redwood chair. I know she's stewing. It's the beard, all the attention Dad's getting, his talking so much. It's a lot of change, too much.

"Don't forget, Jack, those clouds used to be full of rain. You remember in Philadelphia it would rain sometimes for two weeks straight, even in summer. Don't forget the rain."

"That's right, Bess; but rain's good for growing things."

Dad's been calling Mother "Bess" since his recovery. I don't know whether he's doing it on purpose or it's automatic, or he's forgotten she wants to be called Bette. She's been Bette for almost thirty years, since they moved out to California, and now he's back to Bess. Mother's real name is Elizabeth but she's never been called that. Mother hasn't said anything about the "Bess" business yet, but I know it's bugging her.

"Jack, I remember once we took your two weeks' vacation in Wildwood and it rained the entire time. We were locked up in one room with two beds and two kids for two weeks. I'll never forget it."

Dad's still staring at the sky, eyes wide open; blue as the sky, but clearer. A smile works its way across his face.

"Well, well, rubber ears!"

He says this, then looks around. Mother looks at Joan, then at me; there's raw fear in her eyes. I get up, go over to Joan and pull her ear.

"Well, well, rubber ears!"

Joan yanks away, then laughs. She leans over toward Dad and pulls on his ear.

"Well, well, rubber ears."

She leans close and kisses him on the cheek.

"Dad, I'd forgotten; was that the time it rained so much? It's the time at Wildwood I remember most."

Mother gives a vintage snort.

"You're all crazy. You and your 'rubber ears.'"

Then she laughs.

"If anybody ever saw you three pulling ears like that, they'd be sure you were insane.

"And it all came from the funnies, you know. He'd read the comics to you two with different crazy voices even after Jacky could already read himself.

"Popeye pulled Sweetpea's ear once and said that; then you *all* got started. I couldn't relax without one of you sneaking up and pulling my ear."

She's laughing so hard now, she's holding her hand on her chest.

"It's a wonder I didn't have a heart attack or go completely crazy a long time ago living with such a bunch of nitwits."

Within another week, Dad can get around with only a cane. He starts getting cocky, using the cane to investigate growing plants without stooping. He's smiling all the time and singing or humming to himself. He drives Mother nuts hanging around the kitchen. And he's asking questions, just like a kid. I'm caught between fires. Dad doesn't want Mother working in the kitchen and she doesn't want me to cook. I tell Dad I'll watch Mom to see she doesn't do too much. Dad's all over Mother; he hardly lets her go to the john alone.

The other thing is: he, who all his life has been so reserved in physical signs of affection, is continually coming over to rub Mother's neck or her back, or leaning down to give her a quick kiss. Mom doesn't know how to take it. A couple times, when he gets up from his chair, unannounced, to plant one of his kisses on her, she gives me her "here comes the simp" look; also there's fear.

One day Dad asks if I'll take him to the Salvation Army thrift store, just the two of us. He shows me his wallet; he has three twenties and a ten. I never remember Dad carrying more than five dollars in his life.

Mother's in a tizzy wondering what we're going to do. Dad says it's a secret and he'll tell her when we come back. I suggest she take a nap while we're gone. She's been complaining she doesn't have a minute to herself with Dad hanging over her. So, quietly, while Dad's getting out the street version of his aircraft-carrier hat and a sweater, I whisper to her.

"Look, Mom, here's your chance to have some time for yourself. Relax and enjoy."

"How can I relax when he's acting like this, Jacky? Where are you going, what's he doing now?"

"I don't know, Mom, and he doesn't want to say. Don't

worry, it's all right; I'll be with him all the time. We'll be back before five; try to get a good rest."

We drive over to the Salvation Army on Eleventh Street in Santa Monica. When we get there, Dad goes sniffing around like a bird dog. He and I are back in the old days routing around in the dump for something to salvage and fix up. Dad's convinced, has been all his life, that people throw perfectly good things away because they're only tired of them or because there's some little thing wrong he can fix.

We spend half an hour on the thrift-shop side. This is stuff that's so far gone even the Salvation Army won't try to fix it. Dad finds himself an old pair of Adidas running shoes. The laces are gone and the toe is coming out the left shoe but they're his size and he gets them for twenty-five cents. They're light blue with three dark blue racing stripes and Dad's pleased as punch. Those shoes should've tipped me off.

In the main store, I talk him past an enormous burnt-gold colored couch. It costs seventy-five dollars. Holy cow, if we come home with something like that strapped on top of the car, we can bury Mother the next day.

After I work him away from the couch, he noses around for a while in women's purses, then blouses. Next, he looks up and sees the stock of Salvation Army furs. They look like a backwoods hunter's private cache of last year's killings. Dad heads directly for them, his eyes glowing.

"Your mother's always loved furs, Johnny."

During the next ten minutes, he's taking fur coats off hangers, holding them up, turning them around. He puts two on himself, strokes the fur, looks in the mirror. Thank God none of them strike his fancy.

I steer him over to the sweater section. A sweater shouldn't cost much and Mother can hide it or give it away. Nobody can buy clothes for Mother. She even takes back half the clothes she buys for herself.

I tell Dad I'm looking for a pair of pants, and I head for the pants racks. I'm looking for anything reasonable in 33- or 34-30 under a buck and a half. If you don't care much about being in style, you can get great buys. Dad follows along behind me. He pulls out a pair of violet velvet pants and holds them against himself. They're size 38-34.

"Are these too big, John?"

I try to keep a straight face; I won't fall into Mother's role here.

"Yeah, probably. What size do you wear, Dad?"

He looks down at his waist. He's lost so much weight his pants are folded under his belt and the trousers hang slack around his legs. He's already gained back fifteen pounds but doesn't weigh one twenty yet. He opens his belt and holds up the pants. I look inside the waist seam; 32-29.

"But you're more like twenty-eight-twenty-nine right now, Dad. The thing is, who knows how much you'll weigh three months from now; the way you're eating you could be the new Tony Galento."

Dad tightens his belt, checks his shirttail and smiles.

"Do you remember that fight, John?"

"I sure do. I even remember where we were when we listened to it. It was the furthest I'd ever been from home. We were in Upstate New York with Ira Taylor and his wife, Kay."

"You're right, Johnny; I almost forgot. Gee, that was a fun trip. I remember I promised you you'd see a mountain. Every time we'd go over a hill you'd ask if this was it. We had the '29 Ford then."

Dad pulls out a pair of red, blue and purple striped Picasso pants. They're 28-29 and only a dollar. He holds them against himself. My God, with the beard, he looks like Cézanne in his last years. All he needs is a field easel on his back.

"They look great to me, Dad, but do you think they'll fit next week?"

"I don't care; if they don't, I'll give them away. I think I'd feel fine in a pair of pants like this. I'd feel like somebody special, as if people could see me. All the rich people I've seen on television wear crazy clothes. They don't have to please anybody except themselves and they don't care what people think of them; they're already rich. Now I don't need anything from anybody either. I'll buy them. I feel like I'm buying Baltic in Monopoly; it's purple, cheap and how can I lose?"

"OK, Dad; I think they look great. What do you suppose Mother'll say?"

"Well, she'll laugh and call me crazy, but she'll laugh. We haven't had enough laughing around our place the last ten years."

During the next hour, Dad buys the most outlandish combinations of pants and shirts. I jump into the spirit of things and help him color-match. He's laughing and having great fun making up wild costumes; nothing is too much.

Against my advice, he buys a shot silk shirt for two dollars. I know how impossible it is to get a shirt like that clean without killing the shimmer effect. Dad says when it gets dirty he'll throw it away. He's fascinated by the feel of the cloth and the way it changes color at different angles to the light.

All together, we spend under twenty dollars. I don't remember ever enjoying shopping so much. I even buy myself two rather insane outfits. I hate to think of Mother's reaction when we show up with these clothes.

On the way home we talk about which costumes we'll wear first. Dad decides on a pair of ochre-golden ski pants with the shot silk. The silk is a golden thread interwoven with a deep blue. We also buy shoelaces for the Adidas running shoes.

When we get home, Joan's there. I don't know whether Mother panicked and called her or Joan just stopped in. We smuggle our bags of clothes through the side door into the back bedroom. I go into the living room to tell Joan and Mother we're giving them a fashion show. Mother's punch-drunk and doesn't know how to react anymore.

We come out, me first in my almost pistachio-ice-cream shirt, Jack Nicklaus golf pants, Stan Smith green-and-white tennis shoes. Joan whistles between her fingers, a skill she mastered before she was five years old, one I've always envied.

Dad comes out behind me, no cane. He walks to the center of the living room slowly, carefully, and turns around with his arms waggling loosely in the air. Joan and Mother crack up totally. I begin walking and turning around Dad. Joan breaks out with "A Pretty Girl Is Like a Melody" and Mother joins in.

They start clapping to the song. We all get giggling and Dad turns back to the bedroom. I bow.

"Keep your seats, ladies. The show has just begun. You ain't seen nothin' yet."

I disappear down the hall before they can say anything.

Dad's laughing and giggling. His hands are shaking so I help him with the buttons. This time, he puts on the Picasso pants and a dark blue, almost navy, flared blouse with three-quarter sleeves. All he needs is a beret to go out and paint in Montmartre. He looks at himself in the mirror, turns his head each way.

"This is my retired-artist's costume."

He takes the brush off the dresser and brushes his beard into a point, turns up the ends of his mustache. He looks more like an artist than I ever will.

I slip on a pair of striped Italian no-belt pants with a brown, long-sleeved, three-button-at-the-cuff shirt. It even has a lion as a monogram on the pocket. I look somewhat like the Prince after the Princess got drunk and ran off with the butler. Dad stares at me.

"Boy, if you ain't the cat's meow."

He whistles between his teeth, another skill I've never managed.

"Johnny, you should dress that way all the time. You look like a man who's never done a day's work in his life."

We take a last peek at ourselves in the mirror. This combo just might be too much. I go out and peer around the doorjamb.

"Ladies, our next showing is what they were wearing in Paris fifteen years ago. Time and tide wait for no one."

I step forward and Dad follows; Mother bursts out.

"Oh, no! Joan! Oh, no!! They're both simple. Oh Lord!"

She's between crying and laughing. I stand in the center this time with my hands over my head and Dad walks around me lifting his thin arms up and down so the sleeves slide past his elbows each time. Joan starts clapping and Mother picks it up. They're belting out "A Pretty Girl" again as we troop back to the bedroom.

I'm out of costumes, but Dad has two more. I don't fit into either his shirts or pants. I help him get undressed and dressed again. This time he has flared denim striped pants in a rather subtle range of tans and browns; he wears a sailor shirt with brown-and-white horizontal stripes and a small white collar. He looks slim and trim like a faggy old cabin boy. I quickly slip into Mr. Lazio's black burial suit, a white shirt and tie. I go out very serious; Joan and Mother roar. I wait till they stop laughing. While I'm waiting, I bow slowly, smiling falsely at each of them in turn. Dad's pushing behind me.

"What is it, John? What's going on?"

With one hand I signal Dad to stay back and I step out.

"Ladies and gentlemen, the house now presents the star of the show, the late sick man and almost corpus delicti, just back from a successful tour of the Caribbean, Gorgeous Jack."

I hold out my arm and Dad comes shuffling past me, all smiles, no hand over his mouth. This time Mother screams when she laughs. She can't control herself.

"Stop them, Joan. I'm dying. They're trying to kill me! Stop them; I'll pee my pants!"

Joan's rocking back and forth, laughing, on the couch.

"I never heard of anybody dying laughing, Mother, but wouldn't it be nice?"

Dad walks over, leans down and kisses Mother. Her cheeks are wet from crying and laughing.

"Are you all right, Bess? We're just having a little fun."

"You two are crazy and where in heaven's name did you get those clothes? They must've cost a fortune, Jacky. And who in their right mind would sell them to two old kooks in beards anyhow?"

She leans back, still laughing, to look at us again.

"With those costumes and those beards, people would cross the street just to escape! Somebody's going to lock you two up for sure."

Then she starts laughing again. Dad straightens, puts his hand on his chest.

"This is my costume for bicycling in Venice along the beach or maybe roller-skating."

He says this biting the smile off his lips; at the same time, trying out the idea. Mother turns to Joan.

"I wouldn't put it past him; neither one of them. The way he's been acting since he came out of that hospital, he's liable to do anything."

Dad insists on dressing by himself for his last costume. I'm to join the audience. I can't remember just what's left. We looked at so many crazy combinations I've lost track. In about five minutes, he sticks his head around the doorjamb.

"This here's my baseball-watching outfit. Mostly I'll only wear it around the house, watching Dodger or Angel games, but I'm also going to actually go see a few games, but not in my costume."

He comes out, and somehow—maybe it's because he's by himself and having such a good time—we get laughing so hard none of us can breathe. I'm on the floor with my knees bent up, rolling on my back, trying to get air. Joan's prostrate on the couch and Mother's rocking uncontrolled in her chair. Sometimes she leans forward with her head almost on her knees.

He has on a pair of white flannel trousers with a pale blue pinstripe. The shirt is short-sleeved with the colors in reverse, blue with white pinstripes. He's wearing the aircraft-carrier hat I gave him for his birthday with the bill slightly cocked to the left. He looks like a sixty-year-old Dennis the Menace. The point is he doesn't look seventy-three. The boyish figure and grace have somehow come through the illness, the years, the awkwardness of self-consciousness. Mother gets her breath first.

"My God, Jack. You make Lawrence Welk look like an old man."

Dad smiles and tries a little buck-and-wing, stumbles, catches himself.

Nothing will do but that this is the costume he'll wear the rest of the day. The Dodger game's on at six and he wants a can of beer and some pretzels. He tells us he's liable to do some loud cheering, so we're not to get scared.

Joan calls home. Mario says he'll take the kids out to

McDonald's. Joan whips up hot dogs and potato salad. We have a great time watching the game. Dad turns down the sound and imitates an old-fashioned radio announcer recreating a baseball game, giving all the details—touching the resin bag, looking for the sign, all kinds of things that aren't even happening. Joan and I laugh till it hurts but Mom's quiet. She's afraid of him. This man's been away too long and came back too fast. I'm hoping it will work out all right.

17

We're on the Pennsylvania Turnpike when we start hearing the noise. I think we've stripped a gear or maybe the transmission fluid's low. Dad insists I shift out of drive to second and then to first. The sound's the same in all gears. He thinks it's the universal joint. How the hell would he know? As a mechanic, he makes a great painter. But what else can it be?

"Bill, hold her in second and we'll limp on to the next garage."

I keep her at a constant twenty-five for the next fifteen miles. The grinding gets louder so we're beginning to sound like a cement mixer. Dad's nervous as a mother cat, listening; opening a window, hanging his head out. He puts his ear onto the drive-shaft hump. He even climbs into the back, rips up the seat and jams his head in there.

I'm beginning to think we'd be better off calling a tow

truck. After all, the cost would be picked up by this Scarlietti we're delivering to.

We limp into a garage making such a racket it stops everything. It's always fun seeing some bomb of a car crap out, and this clunker sounds as if it's doing the death rattle.

Dad goes looking for somebody. I'm afraid to turn off the motor, but I keep it in neutral to hold down the racket. Dad comes over with a mechanic. They signal me to roll her onto the grease rack. When I put her in first and start lugging, she sounds as if the bottom's about to drop out. We just might need to phone and tell Mr. Scarlietti to kiss off this bucket of bolts. But if we do that, they're liable to send somebody here to kiss *us* off.

I climb out and the mechanic pushes the hydraulic-lift button. Up she goes, an elephant in an elevator. The mechanic shakes his head.

"Sounds like your universal's shot to hell, all right. You fellas keep prayin' that's *all* it is."

When the car's up, he stops the lift and walks under. He moves along pushing his hand on different parts, shaking his head and muttering. I'm ready for the worst. Even if it isn't anything important, this clown could rob us. He sees us in this wagon, he's sure we're touring millionaires.

He fetches a wrench. Doctors and mechanics like to be mysterious. He twirls off four bolts and starts struggling to pull clear the front end of the drive shaft. He works it out and lowers it to the floor; wipes his hand into the crotch of the differential and shows it to us. His hand is covered with small silver, metal filings. He shakes his head but still doesn't say anything. Then he pulls out the rest of the drive shaft, carries it over to his bench and knocks off the universal joint. It's gored, silvered and generally chewed up. He wipes it with a grease cloth hanging from his back pocket.

"Well, there she is. You ain't goin' much further with this baby."

We both stare. It's an amazing chunk of metal sculpture; it looks like a giant pair of kids' jacks, joined in a ball socket.

After some palaver, it's costing us a hundred fifty bucks.

He needs to buy the joint in New Stanton. New Stanton is the name of this stop on the turnpike, but New Stanton, the town, is about ten miles away. There's nothing else to do.

We go into the hotel beside the garage and spend half an hour trying to reach the car owner, but can't get an answer. We have to let the mechanic know right now so he'll have time to get the piece tonight. Dad goes out and tells him to start, we'll have to take the chance.

The motel here's in colonial style again, brick and white wooden columns again; there's a restaurant attached. The mechanic says no matter what, we can't have the car till tomorrow morning.

"I'll go check the prices, Bill. I think we're in for an expensive night. You watch them take this thing apart so we can save ourself some money next time."

I go back in the garage and sit on a used oil drum. Two mechanics about my age are undoing the rest of the bolts, cleaning and greasing the drive-shaft seat for the yoke and joint.

Dad comes back. He's got us a room, twenty-five bucks. We sit there in the garage watching, and before I know it he starts.

First he says something about how glad he is not to be a mechanic. Sounds simple enough, but I'm already suspicious. He's leaning against a wall and I'm still sitting on the oil drum. These young guys are in front of us working. It's one hell of a messy job. There's oil dripping and crud from the bottom of the car keeps falling in their eyes.

"But at least you're doing something important and you get good pay, Dad."

I'm only being ornery; I could never be a mechanic, I'm not good enough. You watch a real mechanic at work and you know.

"I'll bet neither of these guys makes more than seven bucks an hour. If you work forty hours a week, fifty weeks a year, that's less than fifteen thousand and you wouldn't take home twelve after taxes and Social Security.

"You can't keep a family on that in America today, Bill, and there isn't much chance of making more unless you open your own garage; then you're a businessman.

"And you're always dirty, the kind of dirt you never get out of the cracks in your skin and under your nails; it gets driven into the cuticles. You've got banged fingers and hands all the time; and I'll tell you, you're dead tired at night. My dad used to come home nights filthy and absolutely bushed when he worked at G.E."

It's coming all right; what did I say or do to bring it on? Maybe nothing. Maybe he's been sitting back in his mind waiting.

"Bill, what are you going to do in France this year?"

There it is. OK.

"Well, Dad, I'll go down to the cabin, finish it off, then do some writing."

"How are you going to live? Do you have money saved up?"

I tell him about the hundred fifty.

"That's nothing, Bill; a hundred and fifty dollars won't last two weeks."

So I tell him Debby might come.

He's quiet a long time. We concentrate watching these poor bastards cleaning out the crap that got chewed off the universal joint. He's not happy but he doesn't know which way to go.

"God, Bill, a hundred and fifty dollars won't go anywhere at all with *two* of you."

"Her Dad's chipping in. He doesn't like her quitting school, but he's giving her money so she won't starve."

Dad's quiet again. I'm hoping it's finished. If I'm not getting help, I sure as hell won't beg for it. We watch awhile but then he starts. He's apologetic but firm, as if he's taking a thorn out from under a fingernail.

"Well, Bill, you're nineteen now, an adult; so you'll have to figure some way to earn money while you're down there. I don't know what to suggest. It's hard finding work in France without papers. I really don't see how you can make it."

"Well, the guy in Huez who hires for beet-picking said he'd take me on. I can make four thousand francs in two months. Along with Deb's money, we'd have enough to live on."

I should leave it there.

"But I could sure use the money you sent me when I was at Santa Cruz. Hell, I'll be working to improve myself; writing's a respected profession."

He looks up and stares me in the eyes.

"Bill, it's probably not good sitting back knowing for sure money's coming in. We have friends who've lived off money from parents all their lives. It ruined them. They have a child-like dependence combined with an arrogant ignorance. They're never members of the real world."

So we leave it there. I don't need to be insulted.

It's almost six when the garage closes down. We eat dinner at outrageous prices, then head up to our room. The only thing going is cars whizzing past on the turnpike. We watch a movie called something like *It's Tuesday, This Must Be Amsterdam*. It's about traveling in Europe. Dad and I get to laughing. We need something after all the heavy stuff.

It's past eleven when the movie's over, and we crash. I'm pooped from all the *Sturm und Drang*. The lights are off and his voice comes out of nowhere.

"Look, Bill. I hope you don't feel bad about the money business."

He pauses. I don't say anything. Let him think I'm asleep. I don't want to talk about it.

"It worries me, Bill, you might take the easy way. There are so many pressures to 'take it easy,' 'cool it,' 'be groovy.' I'd hate to have you be a twentieth-century dilettante. To me, that's the enemy. I can cope with mere Communists—Russian, Chinese or Cuban—the Nazis, the Calvinists, the Baptists, the Catholics or the KKK, any ordinary group of dogmatists, but the real enemy, for me, the dangerous ones, are the leisured, advantaged dilettantes who have dominated and clogged the machinery of creativity and invention for centuries."

I wonder if he expects me to say something. No, I'd better keep my mouth shut.

"I'll tell you what, Bill. The mill needs a new roof. If you and Debby take off all the old slate, repair the slats and rafters where they're rotted, then turn the slates over and put them back, I'll give you five hundred bucks plus materials. If you both work hard, it shouldn't take much time, and that kind of work could be a break from writing. Inner searching can be more tiring than you think; climbing over a roof will seem like a picnic. That way you'd get through the winter and have something to start sending around to publishers."

So this is what he's been working up to. He knows I'm scared of heights. I'll probably fall through that rotted, slanted roof and break my neck. I keep quiet but he *still* isn't finished.

"Another thing, Bill. I'd appreciate it if you don't push it into everybody's face down there how you and Debby are living together; don't violate their idea of what's right. OK?"

Of course I say OK. So now he knows I wasn't asleep.

I think I'm home free, but just when I'm on the edge, he's back at it.

"Bill?"

I don't answer.

"Bill, this thing with my dad and mom has been tough. I only now realize I've been in a kind of shock for the last three or four months."

I wait.

"It's been a long haul and it's the sort of thing I'm not good at. If I've been too critical, don't think much about it."

I wait and hope he's finished.

"I feel terrible leaving Mom and Dad. But I can't justify staying away from Mother and Jacky any longer. It's been hard for them, too. I had to leave."

Shit, I don't know what to say. I keep pretending I'm asleep. I lie there quietly and listen to him lying there in the dark. He's not sleeping; I can tell by his breathing. I lie still and listen. I think about what it is to be alive.

18

Next day, Dad really does dress up in his different costumes. He watches the Dinah Shore show in his dancing costume. He wears the bicycling-roller-skating costume to putter around in his greenhouse. More important, he hangs these clothes back in his closet after each change. He's in the bedroom often and I'm sure he's checking his wardrobe.

Two days later, he wants us all to visit the Salvation Army again.

He's been making notes on his clipboard cards. Just before we leave, while Mother's in the bathroom, he shows them to me.

Each card has a different title, printed in capital letters with the "I"s dotted. These are his ideas for new costumes. One is his "Confession-Going Costume"; another is his "Having Tea with the Queen Costume"; then there's his "Jogging Costume." He also has one titled "Singing and General Fooling Around." He's written below what each costume should be like. The "Confession Costume" is a black shirt, black pants and a cape. There's a note, "sort of Dracula-like." It's hard to know how serious he is.

"I wouldn't show these cards to Mom, Dad."

"Oh, sure, John. But you know, Bess used to like fun as much as anybody. It's been too serious around here lately. Our trouble is we keep thinking of ourselves as retired people. Life has gotten boring and we didn't even notice."

He looks at me, streams of waving light passing through his eyes; he's staring at me, serious on the edge of his new perpetual smile.

"I think you're right, Dad. But remember Mother's not well. She's had some terrible heart attacks and we've got to go slow."

He nods his head and looks down.

"You're right there, John. We'll go slow."

He pauses; Mother is coming along the hall.

"But, I'll tell you, we'll go somewheres."

He pushes himself up with his cane and we head for the car. It's already on the driveway warmed up. Dad helps Mom in back. He can't actually help much, he has a hard time standing up himself; but he puts his hand under her arm and helps get her feet straight on the floor. This bugs Mother; the worst thing for her is feeling like an invalid. I stay out of it and slide into the driver's seat. Dad climbs in front with me.

"I hope you don't mind, Bess, but I want to sit here and see if I can pick up the knack of driving again. When I'm back on my feet, I'd like to take that driving test. It'd sure be fun if I could drive; maybe visit the bowling alley."

He pulls out his clipboard.

"By golly, that's one I forgot. I want a bowling costume, something in black-and-white stripes for a shirt, then black pants like an official at a basketball game."

He writes on his clipboard. I glimpse in the rear mirror, backing out, and see Mom's face. She's not putting on; nobody's watching her, but her face is set tight. She's worried, scared, critical. She doesn't know what to say, what to do.

Dad turns around, lifting his knee onto the seat as he does it. It's hard putting together some of his moves with his age, his physical condition.

"You know, Bess, you ought to get yourself a few costumes, too. I don't mean just more ordinary clothes but real costumes. Maybe a wig; they've got some fine wigs there at the old S.A. I'm liable to try on a few myself. I was too embarrassed last time but with the two of us we could have some good laughs."

I don't look back. There's a long silence. I definitely must talk to Dr. Coe, or at least have a long talk with Mother. She's overwhelmed. Even if she were in perfect health, I don't think she could cope.

"All right, Jack; I'll look with you; but remember, after all, we are in our seventies."

Now Dad swings himself up on two knees, leaning over back of the seat. He seems to have forgotten the things you're not supposed to do when you're grown up. Maybe it's part of being so light and lean; he could have some feelings of being physically thirteen or fourteen years old.

"Honest, Bess, you still look like a girl to me. Nobody'd think you were even *forty* years old. You can wear anything you want and look great. We need to get over the idea we're old fogeys and stop worrying what people think. You sure as *hell* don't see any of the young people asking *us* what to wear."

We're both shocked. Not so much by what he's said, not even by the strength and youth in his voice, but by the fact he said "hell"! I take a quick peek in the mirror. Mom seems fine, better than the last time I looked. The compliment from the mouth of a man who never compliments has completely undone her. There are tears in her eyes. I have a strong feeling I shouldn't be there. Dad hasn't used "hell" except as a place description during the past forty years I know of. But he doesn't seem to notice he's said anything out of the ordinary.

It's right here Mother decides to make a stand about the "Bess" business. Maybe she figures he's caught out on language and now's the time to strike.

"Jack, couldn't you call me Bette again? You know how much I hate Bess. I don't know what's happened; you've been calling me Bette since we came to California and now, suddenly, you're calling me Bess."

There's a long silence. Dad's still up on his knees; I'm driving along Sepulveda Boulevard toward Olympic.

"Well, Bette. I married you as Bess and I've always liked that name. It's a name you don't hear very often; it's a strong name, like you. Every time I call you Bette I'm afraid somebody else might answer."

I sneak a quick mirror look. Mom has her eyes on it and catches mine. My mother, in a rearview mirror, where I can only see her eyes, gets across a full gamut of emotion. She's telling me she's afraid, confused and asking what she can do. That's expression! Dad goes on.

"But honestly, Bess, if you want to be Bette, OK. I'll concentrate on it. I'll call you Bette and you call me Jake. Say, I like that! It sounds as if we might be Prohibition gangsters or drug runners. It'll be fun! We're Bette and Jake. I have as much right to be called Jake as anybody. Maybe I can take up smoking again, get some of those little cigars Edward G. Robinson used to smoke."

He turns to me.

"Do you think they might have any old derby hats at the S.A., Johnny?"

I look to see if he's playing Machiavelli. No, he's only having a good time. He's all excited about being Bette and Jake, suspicious characters. He can't realize how he's stripped Mom's pretensions to the bone in one fell swoop. I don't think he even knows how effective his threat to take up smoking again is. He's playing. He has all the ego isolation and drive of a twenty-year-old.

The rest of our ride to the Salvation Army he goes over his lists and tries to interest Mother in his costume plans. He keeps calling her Bette and when she calls him Jack he corrects her every time, saying in a low, reminding tone, "Jake."

I'm torn between commiserating with Mom and breaking

up. I can see why Mother devoted her life to dominating him. He must have been totally irrepressible as a young man. No wonder his sisters warned her. He's worse than either Uncle Orin *or* Uncle Pete. This is a strong, impish Rabelaisian id that's been cooped up for thirty or forty years. Whatever could have unstoppered the bottle?

At the Salvation Army, I cut Dad off from the thrift shop. I know we only have so much time before Mother will flag; she's already taken enough of a beating. Dad's giving me signs behind Mother to make sure I steer her by the gold couch. He hasn't forgotten. It's so unlike him to even notice, let alone care, about what kind of furniture is in a house.

We slowly move Mother near the couch. But she's still too much in shock to pay much attention. We're almost past when Dad stops suddenly.

"Johnny, we're probably wearing Mother out with all this coming and going; let's sit down on this nice-looking couch here and take a little rest."

With that, he lowers himself onto the far end of the couch. I help Mom sit down and I sit beside her. Dad's running his hand lovingly, possessively, over the nap of the couch. Mother's holding herself in, exasperated.

"We've been sitting in the car for the last half hour. I'm fine."

Dad sneaks a little kiss on the side of her neck; Mother swings around to see if anyone's seen.

"Just look at this couch, Bette. You know, this is the kind of couch I've always wished we had for our living room."

Mother looks down at the couch. She's only doing it to shut him up, but then looks more carefully, her furniture-appraising eye in action. She struggles herself to a standing position. I stay seated. Dad watches. It's like watching a very rare bird flitting around a trap. She goes to the back and pulls at an edge of the upholstery. She finds the price tag and reads it.

"There must be some mistake here, Jacky. It says seventy-five dollars."

We both get up and look at the tag. Dad peers at it, looks at me and smiles.

"Maybe it's supposed to be seven hundred and fifty. It looks like a seven-hundred-and-fifty-dollar couch to me. They could have left off a zero by mistake."

Mother goes around lifting all the pillows on the couch and turning them over. She does the same with the back pillows. It's the kind of thing Dad and I would never think of. There could be a hole in every one of those cushions and we'd have bought the couch, holes and all. Mother leans close and gives me one of her conspiratorial whispers.

"Jacky, go over casually to that nigger there and ask if this is the right price. Don't let her suspect you're really interested."

She leans down and begins smelling the couch. I can't figure what she's smelling for. I ask the woman at the counter; she comes over and looks at the ticket.

"That's right, ma'am, seventy-five dollars. It certainly is a pretty couch, ain't it?"

Now Mother starts her pensive consideration. Every aspect of the living room must be considered. Yes, it goes well with the rug, yes, the drapes, yes, the dark wood of the Chippendale-style dining furniture. She's onto the lamps when Dad slips off. He's convinced she'll buy it now; that part of his mission's accomplished. I stay with Mom. I'll go help with shirt selection after he's found the pants.

Now Mother's wondering what she'll do with the sectional couch she has.

"Maybe Jeff and his wife would like it, Mom; they're just setting up house and don't have much money."

She goes hmmm, smiles and nods. That's that. Next.

"How could we ever get it home, Jacky? Do they deliver?"

I go over and ask. They'll do it but it costs twenty dollars.

"Don't worry, Mom, I can do it myself."

"You'll scratch the roof of the car and you know how Daddy is about that car."

I tell her I'll put it on the roof upside down; we'll take the back streets home; they'll give me rope to tie it down; somebody will help me get it on the roof; no, the roof won't collapse; we'll put the cushions inside the car, it isn't likely to rain, there will be enough room for all of us; I'm sure the guy

next door, or Billy, can help me get it off the roof; don't
worry, I have my checkbook with me. These are the answers.
Then she breaks into a smile; it's so nice to see her smile.
Now it comes out. She's been dying to change those big, old
clunkers for ten years but never found anything she really
liked. Daddy never wanted to spend any money on furniture.
She sits down again, spreads her hands on each side, strokes
the nap.

"Isn't it beautiful, Jacky?"

I agree. It really is beautiful, a beautiful couch and
beautiful to see her smiling. I sit beside her. She leans over
impulsively and kisses me on the cheek.

"You're such a good boy, Jacky. I don't know what we'd
do without you."

That's the way Mom is. All the fear, the dissatisfaction,
the anxiety is forgotten. I even think she's almost forgotten
about her heart in the joy of getting this new thing. I'm happy
it worked out. I'm half afraid that in loading the couch, I'll
find something seriously wrong, like sprung springs, a broken
frame or missing legs. I start checking surreptitiously, but
nothing seems amiss. I go over and write the check. I make
arrangements to drive the car up close. I tell Mother to go with
Dad while I get this done.

We push the couch onto the roof and tie it down. It's a
real brute. I shove five cushions in the trunk and pile three in
the back seat. This is one hell of a couch; it overhangs both
front and rear a couple of feet. I'll stay on back streets. If
some cop stops us, I'll tell him Mother's a heart patient and we
carry the couch along in case she has to lie down.

It's half an hour later when I go back to the clothing
section. I can hear them laughing from the door. Mother's
letting loose with what I've always called her vulgar laugh.
It's deep, hearty, juicy and sounds like a laugh you'd expect
to hear coming from the window of a brothel in New Orleans.
It's the laugh you want to hear when you tell a dirty joke.

I go back. They've got the most outlandish clothes spread
all over the counters. They're setting up "his and her" cos-

tumes. Mother's moderating Dad's more bizarre impulses, but not much. They really *do* have confession-going costumes. If they ever wear them, they'll look as if they're going to a public execution. Dad has a Gothic flair, Gothic in the Hawthorne or Poe tradition. They've also selected some light, Eastery, pastel getups. Mother's entered into the spirit of things and is masterminding the his-and-her bowling costumes. She gives me one of her stage whispers.

"After all, Jacky, we're not spending more than twenty-five dollars all together. The cloth in these clothes is worth that, and he's having such a good time I hate to spoil it."

But she's having a good time, too. Together we work on our having-tea-with-the-queen costume for the three of us. We'll invite Joan over and pretend she's the queen. We keep adding new touches to these costumes, sometimes including hats and shoes. We laugh ourselves sick imagining how Joan will react.

I'm beginning to feel it's going to be all right; that Mom will learn to enjoy her new "crazy" husband.

The next day, Joan calls and says she's coming in the afternoon. We set out the best dishes and silver. We cover the dining-room table with a white tablecloth—the works. I make a crown from gold paper I find in the Christmas decoration box. The new couch is in and it's beautiful. I've even maneuvered the old sectional jobs back to the garden bedroom.

That new couch gives a golden light to the living room, a glow. We're all pleased as pussy cats about it. Dad and I talk Mother out of pinning her little crocheted antimacassars on the back and arms.

"What the hell, Bette, if it gets dirty, we'll buy a new one."

This is Dad, exercising his newfound largesse and expanded vocabulary.

We get dressed in our costumes, laughing and kidding around. If it could always be like this, I'd move back to America. Dad's wearing a fitted, light blue velvet waistcoat with silver buttons and gray flannel trousers. The shirt is a pale blue with a silver thread running through it. He's wrapped a deep blue foulard under the collar and Mom ties it lightly in a soft knot. With his dark beard, he looks like one of the three Musketeers.

Mom has on a pale yellow silk pajama suit. She's wearing a golden necklace and pendant. On her head she has a chestnut-blonde wig with side curls. It fits her perfectly. We get all her hair tucked in and the wig nicely combed out. Dad's helping comb out the wig; it reminds me of when he used to cut our hair in the cellar when we were kids. He walks around in front of Mom.

"My goodness, Bette, you're beautiful!"

Mother's sitting in front of the dresser mirror, smiling at herself, directing the combing. The problem is her eyebrows are black, actually black streaked with gray. Mom solves this by rubbing in foundation cream, turning them brown.

I'm wearing a bright red blazer jacket I got for three dollars, along with red-and-white striped pants. We make quite an ensemble. I go buy some ice cream at the Lucky Market. Mother's scandalized because I wear my tea-with-the-queen costume to the market.

"You'll get arrested for sure, Jacky!"

Nobody notices me. After all, this is California, land of the kook. I get the ice cream, some pretzels and sugar cones. I'm on the watch for a dormouse and a Mad Hatter so I can invite them home with me.

Finally, after we've waited impatiently, checking every car within earshot, Joan arrives. We meet her at the door, bowing and scraping. We circle around her, curtseying. Joan laughs hysterically and is very unqueenlike, but finally settles into her role and is properly haughty as we escort her to her throne at the head of the table and crown her. Then she spots the new couch and is satisfyingly enthusiastic, sitting on it, spreading her hands while we hover over her. She graciously admires our costumes, smothering giggles, and bows or smiles sweetly to all our "Your Highness"'s. It's as if we've made a tea party with mud cakes and invited our parents.

I decide things are going well enough so I can leave Dad and Mom alone. I want to spend some time with Marty.

Marty lives near the Los Angeles County Museum, so we go there. It's wonderful seeing paintings again; it's so easy to forget the big life when one gets bogged down with the up-front part of things. I find myself spaced out in the Impressionist room.

When Gary comes home, we go to a Korean restaurant and talk about names for the baby. At that point it's Will for a boy, Nicole for a girl. I give them a quick blow-by-blow of what's been happening with Dad and Mom. They're anxious to find a new place to live. Their apartment specifies no children or pets. It's a very quiet, old-people's neighborhood.

I tell about Venice; how great it would be for a baby near the beach. They get enthusiastic. They're tired of the heavy smog where they're living and there's practically no smog near the ocean. We agree Marty and I will spend the next afternoon looking down there. I phone home and everything's OK. I tell them I'm staying over with Marty and Gary. I sleep on a couch in the living room, hoping everything's all right.

In the morning I take a quick buzz over to see Mom and Dad. It's almost like visiting another house. Dad comes out, gives me a weak hug and pushes his beard against mine. Mom puckers up for a kiss. She's still scared-looking but there's excitement in her eyes; she whispers she wants to talk with me. Dad goes out to water and work in his greenhouse; Mom and I go into the main back bedroom: her bedroom now, while Dad still has those bedsores. She sits on the bed.

"Jacky, you've got to do something. Somebody sensible like Dr. Ethridge needs to talk with him. He's crazy. I tell you, he's crazy. He's worse than you are. Do you know what he was doing this morning when I woke up?"

She waits, almost as if she wants me to guess.

"You know, he gets up at seven every morning now, humming and singing his crazy songs. This used to be the best time of day, but now I stay in bed.

"He sneaks his own clothes from the closet and drawers, then goes into the bathroom and takes a shower. Can you imagine, a seventy-three-year-old man taking a shower every morning at seven o'clock? He'll slip and kill himself."

Her face is so extremely mobile, going from complaint, to curiosity, to desire, to an escaped smile. I watch and wait.

"Well, this morning, Jacky, I don't hear anything for a while after his shower so I peek out to see what he's doing; you never know, believe me. No man ever changed so much, so fast.

"I look all around the house first and then out the window to see if he's in the greenhouse. He's on the patio and he's shuffling in a circle along the outside edge of the brick part. He has on that crazy running suit and those blue sneakers with the stripes. I think his Indian blood is finally coming out and he's doing a war dance, going to put his hand over his mouth and go 'Ohoo wahhh wahhaaa!'"

She's definitely smiling, fighting it all the way. She puts her hand over mine on the bed.

"Honest, Jacky; I'm scared to death. Maybe next he'll scalp me.

"I didn't know whether to call you or not. Instead, I opened the door and ask as nicely as possible, 'What're you doing out there, Jack?' He smiles with sweat running down his face and he's puffing. 'Jake, remember, Bette? Jake.' He swings his arms over his head. 'Just doing a little jogging, getting in shape; thought I'd do it in here so I wouldn't disturb the neighborhood. Tomorrow I'll do it back on the grass; this hard cement isn't good for the knees.'

"Jacky, you've got to admit, that's ridiculous; and he never stops while he's talking, just keeps shuffling round and round. He's hardly lifting his feet but he's convinced he's jogging. And this is *after* his shower. Now, you know, Jacky; nobody in his right mind jogs *after* they shower."

I'm trying not to smile. I promise I'll talk to Dr. Chad.

"And, Jacky."

Mother looks around to check if we're being observed by the CIA or the KGB.

"He keeps coming into my bed at night. He won't leave me alone! He pesters me all night long. Your father has always been a highly sexed man but this is insane! He wants to make love all the time, even yesterday, in the afternoon, right out there on the patio—me with two heart attacks!"

At this she ripples into a giggle.

"Nobody'd believe he's a seventy-three-year-old man who almost died a few weeks ago. Maybe his hormones got all mixed up, Jacky. You've got to talk with somebody. It's going to kill me!"

We hear Dad singing as he comes across the patio.

> "Oh, it ain't a-gonna rain no more, no more,
>   It ain't a-gonna rain no more!
>   How in the heck can I wash my neck
>   If it ain't a-gonna rain no more?"

That's one of his favorites. Another song that's driving poor Mom absolutely up the wall goes:

> Close the doors, they're coming through
> The windows.
> Close the windows, they're coming through
> The doors.

This is repeated over and over, with different voices, different intonation, different accents; without thought, sometimes rising, sometimes only the sound of whistling in. Dad walks through the side door into the hallway. He goes into the bathroom and takes another shower.

Mother and I wait for him in the living room, not saying much. When he comes out, he's quite debonaire in his "retired painter's" costume.

"Look, John, why don't you give me a driving lesson while you're here? I'm sure I'll pick up the knack of it fast."

Mother looks over at me.

"Don't you do it, Jacky! I'm not going to drive with him. He drove too fast *before* he turned in his license, I hate to think what he'd be like now."

Dad goes across to Mother.

"Don't you worry your little head, Bette; when old Jake Tremont gets behind that wheel, you're safe as if you were in your own bed. We'll only drive along slowly looking at scenery.

John here showed me a way to the beach where we won't have one red light the whole way. It's like country driving and you come out right there at the beach with plenty of parking."

He gives her a kiss on the neck, then another on the lips.

I'm only glad he didn't mention the motorcycle.

"Well, Mom, Dad's right. You should go to the beach more often. When you and Dad get to feeling better, and I'm gone, you can call a cab, go down to the beach."

Dad's lowering himself onto the floor in front of the TV. He stretches out on his stomach.

"Jack, what on earth are you looking for?"

"Jake, Bette. I only want to see if I can still do a pushup."

He tries pushing himself up with his frail arms but can't budge. Then he bends at the waist to push his shoulder and head up from the floor till his arms are extended. He lets himself down again.

"I'll call these old-man pushups."

He pushes himself up and down a few times. Mother goes to the bathroom.

"Johnny."

He grunts it out between pushups.

"I don't want to go in a cab; we'll probably wind up in Santa Monica. That town's an outside old-people's home. Everybody's moving along slowly, shopping for nothing, or waiting for the next meal. Every corner in that town's a bank or a doctor's office.

"I want to drive to Venice where we were, or walk down to Washington Pier. To be honest, I'd like to do it on that motorcycle of yours but I'm too old, I'd be. scared. I'd also like to get in some fishing off the pier. I used to like fishing. I can't figure when it was I stopped doing the things I like."

He struggles himself up off the floor and falls back into his rocking chair; cocks his leg under him.

"Mother and I should have some fun while we can. If we get feeling good enough, we should take a trip back to Philadelphia; visit all the old places, our family and friends. We had some good times there in Philly."

When Mother comes out of the bathroom, she's made herself up but she's weepy. She isn't crying, but the hollows under her eyes are dampish. I talk them into taking a car ride with me.

We tour slowly through Cheviot Hills where there are handsome, big houses and lovely gardens. This is something Mom loves. These houses represent her idea of what the good life should be and she likes to think she lives near it. She also enjoys making fun of any architectural idiosyncrasies. She constantly reiterates how glad she is to have just a little place in a quiet neighborhood, something she can take care of herself. It's painful listening to her vacillate between self-righteousness and resentment. But I know she enjoys it.

Dad's sitting in front again, imitating my feet and hand movements. He's pushing on his brake and steering an imaginary steering wheel. Mom giggles, snorts and tells him to stop it. But now he's enjoying clowning for her. With automatic drive there's nothing to driving this car. He probably could do it. And why the hell should he go through the business of a driving test? What'll they do if they catch him, throw him in prison?

I drive them home and suggest a nap. Mother's upset. She whispers to me.

"Tell him to stay in his own room, Jacky, tell him I need a rest."

How can I tell Dad that? I gently suggest that Mother's tired, needs a good sleep.

"I'm not going to nap, Johnny. I'm going to dig a hole in the backyard, sink a tin can in it and do some putting.

"You know, John, I've always wanted to play golf. I've got an old putter in the garage and some golf balls. I'll make my hole and put a flag in it; then I can tell people I'm puttering in my garden."

I think of his grave.

He gaily snickers as he works his way down the steps to the patio, out the gate and into the garden. I hop in the car and drive back to Marty's. It's Saturday, she has the day off, so we can house-hunt.

. . .

Marty's beginning to show. She's still looking for a doctor who will deliver her baby the Leboyer method; that's the *Birth Without Violence* Frenchman. What would the world be like if people could all be born with a minimum of trauma; come into this world feeling wanted and holding on to some memory of the pre-birth state? Maybe people wouldn't be so afraid of dying if they remembered what it was not to be born yet. I'm convinced a good part of the world's troubles are built around death fears.

We use my folks' car; it's more comfortable than Marty's old Toyota. We roll down Wilshire to Santa Monica, then south toward Venice. We tour around looking for "FOR RENT" signs. We'd like to avoid an agent if possible. Marty's paying two hundred where she's living and they can go up to two fifty or even three hundred for the right kind of place.

After asking at a few houses where the renters are still living, then telephoning some other numbers which turn out to be agents, we're beginning to get discouraged. Everything is either too small, has no yard or won't take children.

About three o'clock, I suggest we have a glass of wine and some cheese at Suzanne's restaurant on the boardwalk; Marty's never been there. Suzanne comes to our table. Suzanne remembers me from painting and sits with us. She won't drink any wine but has a cup of herb tea. I tell her our problem. She's all turned on about Marty being pregnant.

Suzanne asks Pap, the transvestite dishwasher, if Gerry Lynn has rented her place yet. Pap doesn't know but has the phone number. Suzanne says she'll phone.

Marty turns to me.

"She's so nice, Dad. Why is she being so nice when she doesn't even know us?"

It brings back what Dad said; almost the same words.

I'm still in a daze. I can't put together the timid, shy man who came down here on the motorcycle, the life-defying vegetable in the hospital, and now Jake, out there building himself a one-man, one-hole miniature golf course.

Suzanne comes back. She has fine, brown, lithe arms and legs, softly covered by a thin cotton blouse, no bra, wrap-around skirt and sandals. She also has thin feet and long toes. Some of these natural children-people can be a reminder of how humans are meant to be.

"Gerry says she hasn't promised the place and knows the landlord wants to rent again soon. The rent's two thirty. The trouble is she won't be moving out for another month. She's there now if you want to go over. Here's the address."

She hands Marty a small card.

The house is five blocks in from the beach, and we can't believe it. This is an old-fashioned, wooden, one-story place with overhanging roofs and gables. Most houses around here are stucco.

Even more impressive, there's a sequoia redwood in the front yard. It completely dwarfs everything, so the house looks like something from a fairy tale.

We're trying to figure the unlocking mechanism on the gate when a woman comes to the door. She has a baby on her hip and a three-year-old hanging on to her jeans.

"Wait a minute; I'll get that."

She skips down the two steps on the porch and untangles the hook and chain.

"You must be the people Suzanne called about."

Marty's staring at the house.

"I love your place; it's like a house in Germany, not Californian at all."

"Well, come on in and look around."

She turns and walks back up the steps; nice firm ass tightly held in by jeans. Having women take up jeans must be one of the main events of the twentieth century.

The door opens directly into a living room with two big windows. There's a wide arch separating living and dining room. In back is a large kitchen leading onto a service porch and a backyard. The right side is two bedrooms in line going back, with a bathroom between. The backyard's small, enclosed by bushes and a wall. Marty's entranced.

"What a wonderful house you have here, Gerry."

"If you like it, it's yours. I'm leaving next month. The rent's paid up."

She shows us around outside. I do some checking for ter-
mites, foundation sag or roof leaks, the real problems a house
can have. Gerry serves us apple juice and honey cake. Marty
calls Gary at work; he's coming right over.

When Gary comes, he and Marty check everything again.
It's fun watching them. They seem like such babes compared
to Gerry. Gerry and I sit in the living room; she asks if I'm still
married. I tell about Vron, Billy, Jacky and living in Paris.
While we're talking, she puts the baby on her breast.

I'm torn between watching the baby nurse and embar-
rassing Gerry. I love seeing a baby's rosy face when it's sucking
on a warm, turgid tit.

"It's all right; you can look; I don't mind."

Marty and Gary come back. They've decided to take the
place. Gary calls the owner and makes an appointment. Gerry
takes the baby off her breast. A pearl of thin milk forms on top
her nipple before she drops her T-shirt over it.

"You can move your stuff into the garage whenever you
want. Let me know if I can help."

We say goodbye and walk to where we've parked. Gary
gets in his car and goes back to work.

Marty and I drive to my parents'.

They're on the patio sunning. Marty hasn't seen Dad since
his resurrection and I've tried to prepare her. The beard is the
part she can't believe but I keep telling her that's the least of
it. Marty kisses Mom and goes over to Dad. He puckers up and
kisses her on the lips.

"My goodness, Martha, you've certainly grown into a lovely
woman, a blonde version of your mother."

Marty leans back, pleased, confused by this kind of talk
from a normally quiet, timid man.

"Thanks, Grandpa. That's the way I'd like to be, like
Mom."

Mother pushes up on one elbow to turn her face out of the
sun.

"That's certainly a pretty dress you're wearing, Martha,
those colors are perfect for you."

Dad peers and smiles his pirate smile.

"But what are you hiding under that dress, Martha? A football?"

Mom giggles nervously.

"Don't mind him, Martha. He's awful these days."

Dad pushes himself to his feet, goes over and kisses Marty again. He puts his hand on her stomach.

"Just think what's in there, Bette, another member of our family, somebody we don't even know yet, a blend of you and me, Gary and his parents, Johnny and Vron, Vron's parents. We're all in there, another new layer being formed."

He kisses Marty again.

"Thank you, little granddaughter, it's the best present in the world."

Marty breaks out crying. She's a tender, emotional person and isn't accustomed to such open expression, such clear feelings; none of us are. Mom has tears in her eyes.

"Don't be afraid, Martha; it's the biggest experience a woman can ever have and I'm sure you'll make a wonderful mother."

Marty leans over Mom and shares a soft kiss and hug.

"OK, everybody, it's time to break out the champagne. Is there beer in the refrigerator?"

We all try getting the conversation running at a less charged level. We tell about the new house in Venice. Marty mentions how she wants to have the baby by natural birth, mentions *Birth Without Violence*. Mother's convinced it's all nonsense and dangerous.

"You'll see, Martha. When you start having hard labor pains, you'll want a shot. I can *tell* you."

Marty's taking it easily. She doesn't know, but she's mucking in one of Mom's favorite martyrdom areas. Nobody, but nobody, should have a baby without fear, pain and violence. It's what verifies a woman.

I take Marty home and have dinner with them. They're excited about the house. I stay over and we don't get to bed till after midnight. What an exciting time for them, new house, new baby; I enjoy basking in their joy.

.　.　.

The next day after breakfast we loll around while I'm pretending I've gone to mass. I'm just ready to call my folks to see how they are when the phone rings. It's Mother.

"Jacky, you've got to come! He's gone completely crazy for sure. Come right away; I'm scared to death! I've got to hang up now, hurry!"

She hangs up.

Damn! It's never going to end! Mother smells I'm leaving soon and she's working up something to keep me. I know this isn't true, only self-justification, but it occurs to me.

Soon as I arrive, Mom's giving me frantic signals. This time she's *really* trying to get my attention without Dad seeing it. This must be serious.

Dad is vaguely preoccupied, distressed; I'm wondering what could've happened. Mom ushers me into her back bedroom and closes the door. Dad's wandering around, aimless, restless, in the garden.

"Jacky, he's crazy!"

She starts crying. I take her in my arms.

"What happened, Mom?"

She can't talk for several minutes, just holds me tightly. Then she lets go and settles onto the bed. Her legs are so short they don't touch the floor. She still has on her nightgown, bathrobe and slippers. Her hair's up in curlers and her face is cold-creamed. It must be serious for Mother to let anybody see her this way.

"Jacky, he's talking about people I don't know or people I'm sure are dead. He insists we go to Cape May, New Jersey, to see how things are. Can you imagine?"

She's crying again.

"And he's back to calling me Bess!"

She peeks out the window. Dad's weeding along the patio wall.

"Jacky, he wanders around the house, opening and closing doors, looking into closets, into the cupboards, all the time shaking his head. It's as if he's looking for something he's lost."

She pushes the back of her hand into her mouth.

"I think he's lost his marbles, Jacky. He can stare at me

as if he doesn't quite know who I am. It scares me. He'll be sweet and kind; then he looks at me with those crazy eyes and I almost expect him to ask, 'Who the hell are you?'"

Through the window, I'm watching Dad in the garden. He's pacing like a tiger or a lion in a cage he knows too well but, like a caged animal, still looking for some little chink, some opening or corner he's never found.

"He's strong, Jacky. I know him. I'm afraid when he comes into my room nights. He comes so silently, sneaking, as if we aren't married, as if he feels guilty about coming in. Then he talks to me while we're making love and calls me Bess. He even talks about the things he's doing. He was *never* like that, Jacky; he never said anything about things like that. I tell you, he scares me!"

It's getting awfully thick. I need to talk with Dad. It could be nothing, only Mother's love of dramatizing, or there might be something wrong. Maybe he's starting to slip back again and these are the first signs.

Dad's in the greenhouse. He's working his cuttings and plants into shape again. Maybe there's nothing to talking with plants but I'm sure they know when somebody cares. There's some kind of telepathy going on. Just because they can't speak doesn't mean there isn't communication.

In the greenhouse, Dad turns to me immediately; he looks in my eyes. Mother's right; it's almost as if he's somebody else, as if he's trying to decide if he knows me, can trust me.

"What did she say, John?"

I lean over and pretend to inspect a green plant with thick cactus leaves and a small yellow flower growing on top of the leaf.

"She says she's scared, Dad. She thinks maybe you're crazy."

He looks down at his feet, then picks up an empty bag for one of his flowers.

"Take me for a ride, John. I need to talk in private and I don't want any interruptions."

I follow him out of the greenhouse. When I'm out, he reaches back and sets the timer for his automatic mist-waterer;

a thin fog of water sprays with a hissing sound. I wonder if he invented this watering system himself or it's standard for greenhouses. You never know with Dad; he's always developing some little gimmick to fit his convenience and might just not ever mention it. Until the past few weeks, I never truly realized what an extremely private man he's been.

I warm up the car. Dad gets a sweater and his hat. I don't know what he tells Mother. I have a feeling again things are getting out of control. Dad gets in the car.

"Could we drive to Venice, John? It's a sunny day, I'd like to see the ocean."

I've just turned onto Beethoven Street when he blasts me with it. He isn't looking at me; he's staring out the front windshield.

"Johnny, what chance is there I have a wife and four kids in Cape May, New Jersey?"

My first response is he *is* crazy, Mother's been right all the time. My second is fear, closely followed by confusion. I concentrate on driving. I want to get parked before we go into this.

"I don't think there's much chance, Dad."

I try keeping my voice neutral, concerned; I'm fighting down panic.

"So far as I know, you've been living here in California more than thirty years, after living in Philadelphia almost twenty-five years. You held a regular job at Douglas for twenty years, and have been sleeping in Mom's bed every night except when you were sick in the hospital."

I'm trying to be reasonable; play the psychologist; stay on top of things.

"Of course, I've personally been away most of these last years, so I'm not really the one to ask; maybe Joan or Mom."

I want to act as if this is a logical question. I've *no* idea what I'm dealing with. I have a bad habit of being flip when I'm scared.

But my insides have started to jiggle. It's a sure sign I'm shocked, even when my head doesn't know it yet. Right now, the worst part for me about getting older is I'm losing my nerve, my ability to keep on thinking, solving, planning when I'm upset, tired, worried.

Dad's crying. At first it's only tears, deep sighs; no sobbing. I don't know what to do. I head for a parking area where we can have some privacy. I pull in facing the ocean with a view over wide beach to the breakers. A group of surfers are slipping on wet suits and unloading boards about seventy yards to the right but they're the only people around. Dad turns to me.

"You mean there's no chance I have a house in Cape May next to Bill Sullivan and Ira Taylor, across from brother Ed and Gene Michaels; that I don't have a truck garden there and I don't have four kids, you, Joan, Hank and little Lizbet?"

There's such anguish on his face, such hope that I've made a mistake.

"Look, Dad. I don't really know. I know I'm here and I'm fifty-two years old. Joan's forty-nine. I don't know about Hank or Lizbet. But if you want, we can take a plane and fly to Cape May. We can visit this place."

I'm not sure if I'm being cruel or not. He's taking it in, shaking his head; he stares in my eyes.

"But, Johnny, it's the best part of my life; how can it not be true?"

He searches my eyes some more, then looks down.

"I know you're right. How can you and Joan be in two places at once? Sitting here, I can't even make *myself* believe it."

We sit beside each other, quiet.

"But I've got to tell you. My life there's as real to me as we are here, sitting in this car looking at that ocean."

He stares out the windshield.

"All this time and I never put it together. I think I've spent at least half the last thirty or so years there. But it was always separate. I *know* I was here all the time. I *know* you're right, but sometimes, lots of times, my mind wasn't here, and not just when I was sleeping either. I've been away a lot."

The resident psychologist is intrigued. The scared son is being displaced somewhat.

"Maybe you made all this up while you were sick, Dad;

you were out of your mind for a long time. Maybe you got this idea in your head then and it's coming back to you now."

I wait. Dad stares more at the ocean. There's nothing to do but wait, let him put it together. We sit quietly for almost five minutes. My mind's racing ten to the second, all the way from Mother's "crazy" theory to wondering if this reality might only be a dream and what Dad's talking about is the real reality. Maybe he's about to wake up and we'll all vanish, the sky, ocean, car, Dad, me; everything.

"John, it's something like the ocean out there. The top, the waves, the surf, the foam are us, here, right now. We call it real because we can see it. But my life in Cape May is the water, it's under the surface and holds everything up. If I loosen my hold on that, I feel everything else will fall in."

He's quiet again.

"Probably Mother's right, Johnny; I am crazy. It might even run in my family the way she says. Dad had very personal ideas for running his life that were definitely peculiar. Who else would put together three row houses in the middle of South Philadelphia so he could have a regular old-time farm kitchen? You've got to admit that's not normal. I don't think Dad ever really left Wisconsin in his mind. Do you remember the pictures of hunting dogs on the walls, and that gigantic bear head along with the elk and deer heads, hung in the same room where we used to eat? Then there was that huge table he built so we could all sit down at the same time, with twenty-four drawers built into it all around, each drawer with dishes, salt, pepper, knives, forks. Nobody does things like that unless they're a bit strange."

I nod. I don't like hearing him talking down Granddad. He doesn't mean it; he's only searching for answers. My grandfather was such a pleasure to me, a proof some few people are still real.

"Then there's Uncle Orin and Uncle Pete; they never did adjust to the city, stayed farm boys all their lives. Neither of them ever held a regular paying job. And look at the people they married, big fat women who couldn't keep a house; their places smelled so bad you kids wouldn't even go visit."

He's speaking without screening; he's not acting out the role he's cast for himself, neither the reclusive, shy, dominated man nor Jake the big-timer, free spender. This is almost like hearing myself, or one of my few closest friends, desperately trying to break the walls of aloneness, searching for some communication.

"Johnny, I don't think I ever truly left the East Coast. Some part of me stayed back there and another small part never even left Wisconsin. I hated those jobs at G.E. in Philadelphia and at Douglas here in California, so gradually I moved myself down to Cape May and set myself to farming the way we did in Wisconsin. Now, all that sounds crazy, doesn't it, but that's what I think might've happened."

I look at Dad. He's another man all right. Why is it I had to wait so long to know my dad is a man like myself, more like me than anybody I've ever met; genetically self-evident, since I have no brothers. His casting me as his brother Ed makes sense now. We have, in our deepest selves, beyond the masks of time and experience, a communal identity.

What is it that keeps fathers and sons so far apart?

"You're not crazy, Dad. We all do what you've been doing. We make up daydreams, and who knows what's going on in our deepest sleep? Not even the best psychiatrists really know. You're not crazy, you've just been doing what we all do, only better."

I want to see how he's taking it; how much he can talk about his fantasy world. I think it might help.

"Tell me, Dad. What do you do in this dreamworld in Cape May? What do you do for a living?"

When I say "dreamworld," he blinks. He keeps looking at me but he blinks down hard. He's not sure he should tell me any more. I can almost hear the scales balancing in his mind.

"I'm not sure it's a 'dream' yet, John. All I know is it isn't here in this world. Do you think it's possible I could be living half the time in heaven before I'm dead on this earth? Have you ever heard of a thing like that happening?"

He looks at me seriously. I shake my head. I want him to

go on. I don't want to make any more stupid mistakes. He stops and looks down at his hands. He twists his ring, the JHT ring on his finger.

"You know, John, I even wear this ring there in that other place."

It's the first time he calls it "that other place."

"There, Johnny, I built a house exactly like the one we have here; only I built it there first. I drew the plans for this place from my memory of the one there. But for some reason I made this one all backwards. The L goes the wrong way, all the rooms are on the opposite side, going the other way, like left-handed and right-handed. Everything here is backwards. The house there is on a little hill and we have bedrooms in the attic, too.

"We have seven acres there. I raise produce for the market in Philadelphia. I truck it up in an old '29 Ford I converted into a flatbed truck. I go up on Tuesdays and Fridays. Gosh, Johnny, it seems strange telling you all this, because you're there too, only you're much younger; you can't be more than fifteen."

He stops and shakes his head.

It sounds great to me. I wouldn't mind going back and being fifteen again, living on a small truck farm at Cape May near the sea. I wonder if there are any chickens—some beautiful Plymouth Rock, black-and-white-check, brown-egg-laying chickens, or Rhode Island Reds.

"Are there any chickens there, Dad?"

Now I'm playing Lennie in *Mice and Men*.

"Sure there are chickens, Johnny; interesting you should ask because they're your job. Bill Sullivan showed us how to build a coop and we have a hundred laying hens now. I take up twenty or thirty dozen eggs every time I go to Philly. Kay, Ira Taylor's wife, showed Joan and Mother how to sew up potholders and I sell those too. We make out all right."

It's so crazy but I find myself wanting to get into his world. We sit there two hours with the sea rolling in on itself while Dad tells me about it. He wants to talk. He's kept it to himself all these years and now he wants to share. When he knows I'm not going to laugh, that I'm enjoying it too, he can tell me everything.

He has concocted the most incredible, elaborate, complete fantasy anyone could possibly imagine. He can give the names of roads, of his neighbors on both sides, up and down the road. He's peopled his world with his best friends, the people he's loved. The life is somewhere between the best of country living and an idealized suburb. It also includes the quality of a two-week summer vacation at the shore. There is all the good, the best parts of his life, and none of the bad. Listening to him is like Laura Ingalls Wilder, as told by Lewis Carroll, produced by Walt Disney.

The sun is setting and I realize it's late. I don't want to stop him but I know Mom must be worried.

"Look, Dad. What can we do about this? Mom can't take it; she's terribly upset. What is it you actually said to her?"

"I got confused, John. And that never happened before; I've always kept it all separate. But you know since I've gotten out of the hospital I've had so much fun; I'm having a hard time keeping the two places apart. I think I said something to Mother about how the corn was growing. Then I could see she didn't know what I was talking about so I changed the subject. Then, later on, I wasn't paying enough attention and I started talking about going into Cape May. I just meant walking into town for the evening. When I realized what I was saying, I turned it into talking about moving from here in California to Cape May and that got her all upset. I couldn't think of anything else to say that didn't sound completely crazy."

Boy, I can imagine how Mother reacted to that. No wonder she called me. First he's talking about corn plants, the farm boy strikes; then he's moving back East. Part of Mother's whole personal validation is how she "broke away" from all that life in the East. Any going back would be admitting defeat.

"You've got to be careful, Dad. You'd better think about all this some more."

"That's right, John. I've got to do some thinking. I guess you're right and all that life there isn't real, but then I can't let it go either. I'm not sure I could let go even if I wanted to. I just have to figure some way to put it together or else get it separate again.

"Moving to Cape May might not be such a bad idea anyway, John. We could be near the beach the way we are here. Bess's two brothers, George and Will, are just up at Wildwood and our Gertrude lives in New Jersey too, in Haddonfield; we'd be near our family and friends. I wouldn't be growing corn or anything, I'm too old, but I'd have the feeling of putting myself back together."

I ease out and begin driving up Rose. I imagine Mom's already called the police. She doesn't trust me any more than she does Dad, and she definitely doesn't trust the two of us together.

"Look, Dad. Would you like some help working all this out? I can ask around and find somebody who specializes in this kind of thing."

Dad isn't fooled. He closes his eyes, folds his hands and sits quietly. I turn onto Palms.

"You're right, John. I probably need a psychiatrist or somebody like that. At least he can tell me if I'm crazy. I don't think I can figure this all out by myself; you just can't imagine how big it is. It's a whole world. It's as if I'm dying or I need to kill part of myself and don't want to. Yeah, John, get me somebody; I don't care what it costs."

"It won't cost much, Dad. You're covered under Medicare. I don't think any doctor can deny help. They have psychiatrists at Perpetual, too. I could get you an appointment with one of them if you want; then it won't cost anything."

"No. Get me a good psychiatrist, Johnny. Get somebody who knows about old people and old people's dreams. Part of all this has to do with getting old, I can feel it."

We roll into Colby and I park in the driveway.

"Dad, I'm just going to tell Mother you had a dream and it was so real you got confused. That's not exactly a lie and it's something I can tell her."

He turns to me and smiles. God, he has a nice smile; it goes directly through me.

"OK, John. You're the boss. And I'll try to be more careful from now on."

As I expect, Mother's in a dither. She's called Joan. But she's so glad to see us, she swallows the dream story without much fuss. In fact, she's very commiserating with Dad and gives him a hug. I think bad dreams are something she knows. You don't have two nervous breakdowns without night traumatization of some kind.

That evening I call several friends. The Marshalls give me the name of a young gerontologist in Santa Monica. They'd had trouble with Joe's dad before he died and they recommend this guy highly. I try getting a call in to him but it's an answering service. I leave a message that I'll call in the morning. I make these calls at a phone booth around the corner while Mom and Dad are watching TV. Dad doesn't wear any of his costumes and seems detached. He's worried all right.

When I'm in bed, I'm surprised to hear the door open, and Mom comes in. I look at my watch and it's one o'clock in the morning. She has a small flashlight but I turn on the lamp beside the bed. I sit up.

"Jacky, I have to talk with you; I think I'm going crazy."

She sits on the edge of the bed and starts crying. I reach over and take her hand. She has incredibly small hands, like Joan. It's amazing how the two of them get so much done with such tiny hands.

"You've got to do something, Jacky. He crept into my bed and then got to talking about moving to Cape May again. Now you know that doesn't make any sense. He's living in the past, Jacky. He's talking about his brother Ed and Ira Taylor and Gene Michaels and Ken Barlittle. None of those people want to see us, Jacky. We're all too old. It's too late to move back there, especially with my heart. I can't leave Perpetual and Dr. Coe; he's the only thing that's keeping me alive. You know that."

Boy, what a mess! I guess he couldn't keep it to himself. He's so full of his "world" he wants to share it. It's love but it hurts. I don't know what to say.

"Jacky, you've got to get him a psychiatrist. There's one at

Perpetual. Maybe a specialist like that can talk to him. I think he's completely off his rocker; honest I do, Jacky. He's so peculiar."

"I've already called a specialist, Mother. I have an appointment with him tomorrow morning. Dad asked me to do it. He said he didn't want to use the psychiatrists at Perpetual, so I'm having him see a doctor for mental problems of older people."

It's hard to deceive the old deceiver but I got her this time. She stops crying and stares at me. She's giving me her "you never know when wonders cease" look. This is one of her rarer "specials."

"So *that's* what you were doing during the Mary Tyler Moore show."

I nod.

"But it'll cost a fortune, Jacky. What's wrong with the Perpetual doctors?"

"This is what Dad wants, Mom. It's covered by Medicare so it'll only cost you twenty percent. Who deserves the best of care more than Dad?"

There's no answer to that one. Taking the wind out of her sails best describes it; she sits there, canvas flapping.

"Now you go back to bed, Mom; everything's going to be all right. We only have to be patient; it'll work out fine."

She leaves without another word. I lie in the dark not able to sleep.

19

At nine-thirty we go downstairs and pay our garage bill. We get a receipt for the stud in Philadelphia. The car's ready; those poor guys were working before we even got out of bed.

Dad's more relaxed; all that rapping in the dark must've helped.

We begin rolling, gliding, through beautiful Pennsylvania countryside. Dad tells how when he was in high school his dream was going to Penn State, a university not far off the road here.

Our idea is to beat it clear into Philadelphia on this last leg. We'll be staying with friends of my parents. Their name is Hill. The house is in a suburb, called Bala-Cynwyd.

Late afternoon we get there, that is, Philadelphia; but it's seven o'clock before we finally find our way to the Hills' place. And then nobody's home. It's getting dark and we've no place to go. These people were expecting us; we can't be more than a day late, at most. And tomorrow we've got to deliver this boat to the mob.

Dad pulls out the Hills' letter again. There are directions on what we're supposed to do if they're not home. It says there's a key hidden on a two-by-four to the left of the inside back screen door.

We go around and look. There's a screen door but it's locked from the inside with one of those old-fashioned hook-and-eye locks. We peer in but can't see far around enough to know if there's a key.

Now this is a fancy house in a damned fancy part of town. All these houses are in the hundred-fifty-thousand-dollar class, at least. I'm expecting a cruiser to come along any minute; we'll have a squad of mustachioed heroes charging with pistols and tear gas.

There are lightning bugs flying around; we don't have any in L.A. or Paris. Every time one of those bugs lights up in the corner of my eye, I think it's a searchlight and we've had it. Dad looks at me.

"Billy, we'll just have to break in. They're expecting us; they only forgot and locked the screen door."

You never know with Dad; now he's leading us into five to twenty for breaking and entering. He finds a cellar window with a cracked pane of glass. We wiggle it around till the putty falls out. We lift the two pieces, reach in, open the window and lower ourselves into the cellar. We go upstairs to the screen door. The key's there all right. Then Dad goes back down to the cellar and fits the pieces of glass in place. He's too much. He doesn't want the Hills to know they blew it and locked us out. I'll never understand that generation.

On the dining table is a note. It says there's beer and hoagies in the refrigerator. The Hills know Dad's an absolute fiend for these Italian sandwiches stuffed with cheese, spiced meats, tomatoes, lettuce and who knows what else. At least it's a step up from pizza. The note says they're visiting friends and will be back later.

We demolish those sandwiches. Probably they're the Philadelphia equivalent to tacos. We guzzle the beer. Then we go sit in the living room. Man, this is a beautiful home. Three of Dad's paintings are on the walls. We're sitting on low couches in a living room carpeted wall-to-wall with a ruby-red deep-pile rug. It's like being inside a heart. Dad starts telling me about the Hills.

Pat is a physicist and Rita, his wife, is a mathematician; they have four kids, two about my age. One daughter's at Harvard, the other at MIT. The young kids are geniuses, too. Come to think of it, Dad has practically *no* artist friends. All his buddies are scientists; biochemists, physicists, astronomers; or they're mathematicians, doctors, dentists. Maybe he's in the wrong business. There's for sure something of the scientist in him. He's always full of weird semiscientific ideas and questions. He continually reads crazy books about black holes or genetic engineering. Or he's trying to explain gravity or working up half-assed all-inclusive field theories for the universe.

But, in another way, he could never be a scientist. He'd never bugger himself with all the facts and memory part. He's not one-eyed enough to make it; he's always seeing too many sides, more sides than there are most times.

There's a mob of pets around the house. First, a dog named Natasha trotted downstairs when we came up from the cellar. She doesn't bark, just goes to Dad when he calls her name, and nuzzles him. She's some kind of giant, grayish poodle. Two or three cats slither out of the woodwork, too. They brush against us, purring, then go their way. Upstairs, we find a medium-sized boa constrictor, some gerbils, a guinea pig, two parakeets, three fish tanks, six or seven lizards, what looks like a baby squirrel and a litter of hamsters. This place is a private zoo.

In the living room there's a grand piano with a cello leaning in one corner, French horn beside the fireplace and piles of music on top of the piano. It's a TV setup for "This Is Your Life, Albert Einstein."

It's hotter than hell. The humidity followed us all the way. We settle in a dining nook attached to the kitchen. There's an electric fan there and we turn it on to push the air around some. There's also a small television. We switch on and watch one of the local stations; it's amazing how the Philadelphia accent comes through even on TV.

At about nine, a car pulls into the drive. The people fit the house. Pat is tall, thin and bald. If you can imagine a Midwestern Oppenheimer, you've got it: a quiet, deep-voiced, slow-spoken, deliberate man. Dad had told me about Pat's strange childhood but I didn't believe it. Pat was born to deaf parents on an isolated farm in South Dakota. He didn't hear anybody speak till he was five years old. His home language is sign, and he has a slight finger accent in English. When he talks, it sounds like a simultaneous translation at the U.N.

Later, I ask about all this. You never know what embroidery Dad's working up. But it's truth.

Pat feels he has an enormous advantage over other people because spoken language is something he can tune in or out as he wants.

Rita is small, smooth, quick-moving and good-looking. This is the first of my parents' friends who turns me on. I don't know what it is; her moves, her voice, her vitality; and she doesn't seem old. She has laugh lines down the sides of her face and wrinkles at the eyes. After you've seen lines like that on a woman's face, young-girl faces are empty maps, undeveloped country, waiting for something to happen. I spend a good part of the evening sneaking looks at Rita.

The two daughters aren't there. They're both off working summer jobs trying to help pay off those enormous tuition bills. One's working on a horse farm; she wants to be a vet. The other is waitressing at the shore in Atlantic City. They call the beach the shore here. The younger ones, Sandy and Kim, are quiet, bright-eyed, listening to everything happening. We have a great time.

Rita lights mental fires and Pat blows gently, keeping them burning. We talk about everything. Halfway through the evening Dad begins telling about what's been happening in California. For the first time, I get the unexpurgated version. If he's telling the truth, then I don't know how he stuck it out long as he did. I hope he doesn't expect me to put up with anything like that for him.

That evening I give the university thing another think. What's physics or mathematics got to do with whether a conversation is interesting or not? Nothing I can see. But these people are interesting no matter what they're talking about. They have a way of approaching any subject with curiosity, originality, a personal viewpoint. They know how to think. They've read a lot, they know about music and painting; but that's not it either.

It's hard putting a finger on it; they're in tune, have good antennae. They know the rhythms of listen and respond. It's three in the morning before we stop.

Rita shows us the upstairs bedrooms, the older girls' rooms. Everything on the walls is interesting. By letting your eyes wander around you're constantly learning. There's the periodic table pasted on the ceiling over each bed. There are star maps stuck on the walls. There are classification trees for animals, insects, plants, everything, all in color, beautiful. There are rock and shell collections on the window sills. Each desk has a professional-type microscope. Just lying in one of those beds, scanning the walls, you could almost educate yourself. These people are deep into knowledge. I'm not sure I could make it here.

I lie there under the periodic table. Maybe I made a mistake. Maybe it was because I felt they were babying me. Maybe if I'd gone to a big university like UCLA or Berkeley I'd've made it.

Dad's already out of bed and downstairs when I wake up. It's raining like crazy. At least the rain makes the humidity bearable. This whole East Coast is one gigantic hothouse.

Dad and Rita are in the kitchen drinking coffee and eating doughnuts. They're having a very heavy private conversation and hardly notice me come into the kitchen. Probably Dad's unloading on her about California again.

I sit down and dig in. I've never seen doughnuts like these. There are some with holes, both glazed and sugared.

There are solid ones with jelly filling, lots of jelly; and even fancy variations like maple-syrup fillings.

Rita asks how I want my eggs and pours orange juice. This is the best food we've eaten in weeks. Dad's quiet; I have the creepy feeling I've interrupted something. But I'm not giving up on those doughnuts, no matter how much he needs that broad, firm, smooth shoulder.

I'm into my fourth, seconds on the sugar-coated, solid, jelly-filled ones, when Pat comes down. He's dressed for the university. I can see him at a lectern all right, the perfect university professor: bald head gleaming in the light; trying to be gentle and clear but scaring the shit out of his students because he gives off an aura of accumulated knowledge and know-how tucked behind those eyes, under that bald head.

Pat takes a glass of orange juice and some coffee. He chooses one of the plain glazed ones with a hole. Rita gives me two fried eggs with some weird-tasting stuff called scrapple.

Dad gets out the papers on our car with the delivery address and Rita unfolds a map of Philadelphia. Neither Pat nor Rita will believe this car's going to the address we have. We're delivering to a swarming, seething, black slum, one of the most dangerous sections in Philly. They say they wouldn't even drive a tank into that neighborhood. Dad and I look at each other; this is something we hadn't counted on.

Rita also hands me a letter she forgot to give me yesterday. It's from Debby; I dash upstairs to read it in private.

She's coming to meet me in Paris on the point of the island the way we said. She'll be there July 10th, wants to be with me in Paris to celebrate Bastille Day. She says in the letter "celebrate breaking out of my own personal prisons, too." I read that letter over about ten times. Holy shit, all my dreams are coming true. We're really going to do it. I realize Dad and I missed the Fourth of July in there somewhere without noticing; it could explain the heavy traffic after St. Louis.

When we try starting the car, it looks as if we won't deliver at all. We turn the motor over until the battery runs down. Pat has a charger, so we take the battery into the garage for a quick charge.

It's got to be all the rain and humidity has fouled the electrical system. For some reason, Dad's convinced it's the carburetors. Pat stands on the porch and makes suggestions of things to check. I can almost hear the relays clicking in his brain. It's still raining like hell and we're soaking wet. The trouble is, if we don't deliver today, the fifty-dollar bond is forfeited, even with the extra two days.

I take out the sparks and clean them. Dad's blown all the jets on the carbs; he smells like a fire-eater. This car is not only gigantic, but all the parts are tucked in the most impossible places. With Pat's help, I find the points and clean them. We put the battery back in and give it another try. Nothing. We turn it over till it's obvious the sparks are flooded again.

Dad tries calling Scarlietti to tell him his car's in Philadelphia, but can't get anybody. Things are screwed up as usual.

Rita comes out on the porch with a blue-and-white striped umbrella. She looks under the hood with us. I'm wondering if it might be the timing. But how could the timing get off overnight? Rita says she read somewhere, when everything's wet and humid so a car won't start, you should take out the electrical parts and bake them dry in an oven at a slow heat.

We look at her as if she's crazy. There's something hard to handle about putting automobile parts in an oven where you bake cakes, or cook roast beef.

But it makes a kind of sense; besides, we've run out of things to do. We twist out all the sparks again, unhook the coil, the lines from the sparks to the distributor, the distributor, the condenser and the brushes for the generator. We take off the distributor cap and rotor. We spread all these parts on a piece of aluminum foil and stick the whole mess into her oven.

We bake them slowly for fifteen minutes; according to Rita, about the time it takes for a batch of cookies; then we take them out. They're not only dry, they're red hot. We have another cup of coffee while they cool. I'm enjoying myself. Pat's stayed on. He says this is more interesting than anything going on at the lab.

Dad's more relaxed than he's been in months. This is his hometown and probably geography, geology, everything works on the body so you're most comfortable where you've grown up.

Maybe Grandpa's Coriolis effect has something to do with it, too; the body's a sort of hydraulic system, when you think about it. We should ask Pat.

Pat's explaining some of the decisions they're making about what to engrave in gold on the next satellite as a message to beings in outer space. It's complicated but it make me think of all the bottles with messages in them I've thrown into oceans since I was a kid.

After everything's cooled off, we put the parts back in, take the charger off our battery and turn her over. She booms into life with the first try—as if nothing had ever been wrong. We all take turns dancing with Rita and congratulating her. Any excuse. She needs to go change because we get grease over the back of her dress. The rain's stopped, the sun's out and it's hot, humid again.

Dad and I wash up, put on clean shirts and take off. Rita says she'll throw our other clothes in the washer and they'll be clean when we get back.

We drive through Fairmount Park, heading north. The farther north we go, the grimmer it gets. As soon as we pass Broad Street and tour past Temple University, it turns totally black. There are people standing around staring blank at this monster of an automobile going by. I know if we don't keep up speed we'll be jumped. Almost simultaneously, Dad and I push down the locks. Dad smiles; I wonder if he's scared as I am. I'll tell you if I were one of those people living out there, seeing this car driving down my street, I'd sure as hell be throwing things.

There's an elevated train here over the street, just like the Paris Métro out by Bir-Hakeim and through Passy. Only this is nothing like that, this is desolation! It looks as if there's been a war. It's worse than just slummy and dirty. There are burnt cars in the streets. There's garbage, old furniture, refrigerators and broken, rusted washing machines on the sidewalks. There's trash over everything. The curbs are packed tight with debris so they're rounded off between street and pavement.

The farther along we go, the fewer and fewer women we

see, and the men begin looking meaner. They've started stepping off curbs toward us, and twice guys stoop down and pick
up bits of junk to throw. I'm wishing we didn't look quite so
much like Captain Haddock and a bearded Tin Tin.

All the houses here are row houses. The windows are
broken out and the railings on porches are splintered and
hanging. The tiny bits of lawn in front of each house are only
packed dirt, with holes dug into them and more garbage strewn
around.

There are kids and women hanging out of windows,
mostly broken-paned windows, but the houses look as if nobody
lives in them. There are no curtains or drapes. Junk wrecks
of cars are pulled up on lawns and in alleyways. Boy, I never
knew what a real black slum looked like. There's nothing like
this in California or Paris.

I've been to Watts, but at least there it's individual houses,
not these walls of broken windows. There it looks temporary;
here it's as if it's been this way forever and is going to stay
that way.

People are stretched out on the streets and on pavements,
like Paris clochards—only young people, some of them wearing
jeans, T-shirts; and nobody's paying any attention.

Now we're starting to run red lights because every time
we slow down or stop, the car's covered with people. They jump
on the hood, knock on the windows, thump on the sides of the
car with fists or open palms. If we stop two minutes, goodbye
car; goodbye hubcaps, aerial, anything that can be torn off. So
we're carefully running red lights and staying away from the
sides of the car. I'm working over our map trying to zero in
on the address. Dad's hunched around the wheel as usual.

The wild thing is most everybody's laughing. They think
it's the funniest thing in the world seeing these two whiteys
in blue driving this wet dream of an automobile straight
through their territory. I don't think they actually believe it.
Maybe they're only trying to be friendly and aren't being
threatening at all, but it *looks* threatening and we're both
scared shitless. The car's beginning to stink from our fear, even
with the air conditioning.

There's another thing that's weird. Out there, everybody's in undershirts or without shirts and the sun's beating down after the rain. Pavements and streets are steaming, steam is coming out of manhole covers; it's all filthy and disordered. But inside the car, we're sitting on smooth leather seats. We're surrounded by clean, canned car air; the radio's playing stereo with soft background classical music. It's hard putting it together. We're astronauts, tearing through a hostile environment, only able to exist because of our support systems. If one thing goes wrong, if we make one mistake, we're goners.

The kings of France must have had the same feeling. Poor old Henry IV, with some nut jumping into his carriage in the Place des Vosges and doing him in. No wonder Louis XIV built that château out in Versailles; he was probably one of the first people moving to the suburbs, escaping center-city madness.

Well, we finally come to the address on our papers. We've got the right street, the right number, everything tallies, but this *can't* be the right place. This is 2007 Montgomery, but it's the worst of all. This area is unbelievable. There are practically no houses which aren't completely boarded up. The people in the street are virtually naked. There's a broken fire hydrant across the street and kids are jumping around bare-ass in the water. This is pure jungle in the middle of Philadelphia.

We go around the block three times, not knowing what to do. By the second time around, they're waiting for us. Kids run up as we go by with mouthsful of water, spurt at the windows and laugh. The house with the right number looks to be completely abandoned.

We're finishing the third turn and we're about to crash on out of there. We stop for one more close look to see if there's any chance anybody could possibly live at that number. Two kids climb up over the hood and sit on top of the car with their bare wet feet hanging down across the windshield.

Amazingly, a door opens in the house and a white woman comes running down toward us. She's wearing a yellow dress with no sleeves; she has dark, almost blue hair. She runs to the side of the car and presses papers against the window. It's a copy of the delivery papers with Dad's picture stapled to the top. I unlock the door, she pulls it open and slides in beside me. She smells of whiskey and perfume. Opening the door is like opening the door to an oven. It's the first time we've had a door or window open since we left Bala-Cynwyd.

"Are you Mr. Tremont?"

Dad reaches over and takes his papers out of the glove compartment.

"It says here I'm supposed to deliver this car to a Mr. Scarlietti."

He shows her the papers with that name.

"I'm taking delivery for him; Mr. Scarlietti is out of town right now. I'll sign for it and give you the fifty dollars. That's right, isn't it?"

Dad looks at me and I shrug. What the hell else are we going to do, sit in this car forever? At least the kids have all scrambled off and are sitting or standing along the curb across the street. Dad pulls out the repair bills; they come to over three hundred bucks. She looks at them, then at us suspiciously. Dad tells her he called from Los Angeles and Mr. Scarlietti gave permission to have the voltage regulator replaced; the universal joint was done right here in Pennsylvania on the turnpike, but we couldn't get to him for permission.

"If you don't believe me, just call the garage, the phone number's there on the bill; it's in a place called New Stanton."

He points to the number and she stares some more at the bills, then smiles.

"Looks as if this is some car. I don't have that kind of money on me; one of you'll have to come inside and get it. Four hundred would cover everything, right?"

Dad nods. I'm having a hard time putting together that kind of money and this car with this neighborhood, if you could call it a neighborhood. Dad says he'll stay in the car while I go in.

I'm more than a little bit nervous. This woman is good-looking, too good-looking, maybe thirty-five, flashing eyes, smooth arms, good legs in high heels with platforms.

She runs up the cracked cement walk between the worn-down lawns and up some broken steps onto an unpainted porch. Outside the car, I catch not only the full push of heat but the smells. It's a mixture of a burning dump and rotten oranges.

When I follow her through the door, I can't believe my eyes, or skin, or anything. First of all, the place is air-conditioned, but that's the least of it. I've stepped into a *gigantic* room. They've knocked down the walls to about ten of those row houses and put them together. The walls are covered with red brocade and there are mirrors everywhere with soft pinkish-orange lights. The rugs are dark, burgundy-wine red. It's like those last thirty-nine pages in *Steppenwolf*! It makes Caesar's Palace look like Savon drugstore. I'm standing there with my mouth open and the lady's disappeared.

I'm expecting to be hit over the head with a velvet-covered blackjack. This is some kind of big-deal gambling joint or whorehouse, maybe both.

I'm thinking I'd better just run and tell Dad to drive like hell. We can drop this car in some white neighborhood with square curbs. We'll phone from there, tell them where the car is and jump on a plane. We're way over our heads. I'm actually beginning to feel cold under my jean jacket. Maybe I'm going into shock, my circulation isn't pushing the blood fast enough.

I look around. There are staircases up for each of the different houses they've put together, so I can look down the line and see one staircase after the other. With all the mirrors and the dim lights, it's hard to tell exactly what you're actually seeing anyway. There are small wooden bars built in under each of those stairs, and leather or red plush couches all around the walls. It's got to be a whorehouse all right. I've never been in one, but this is the way I'd've imagined one up.

Finally, just as I'm ready to scoot, the lady comes back. She isn't hurrying so much now, and in these dim pink lights the yellow dress is turned orange. She gives me a soft smile and counts out four one-hundred-dollar bills, snapping them with her fingers as she hands them to me, the way they do in a bank. I'm convinced they're most likely counterfeit, they're brand-new-looking, but how much use do hundred-dollar bills get anyway?

I'm not saying anything; I just want to get the hell out of there. I'm so confused I put out my hand to shake, French-style. She takes my hand and gives me a good shake back. I don't think anything could surprise this lady. She goes over to the door and before she can open it, I come a bit to my senses.

"Do you want us to bring the keys in here or leave them in the car?"

She smiles.

"You'd better lock it up and bring the keys in; we still have to sign the delivery papers."

I want Dad to see this place. He'd never believe it and I don't blame him. I stick my head out the door and holler. He can't hear me inside, so I motion him to come in. He opens the door and sticks his head up over the car.

"Lock it up and bring the keys, Dad. Bring the papers, too."

Those kids and all the neighbors are lined up across the street. Nobody's moving. Dad locks his door, then sprints across and up the steps. I stand back to let him in.

He stops dead in his tracks like he's been sandbagged. He looks at me and looks at the lady. His head turns slowly to take it in. He looks back at the door. The lady puts out her hand for the key. She's enjoying this almost as much as I am.

"Would you give me the key? I gave him the money."

She points to me and I nod. Dad drops the keys in her hand. She tucks them in a little pocket at the hip of her dress. She reaches for the papers.

"What're we supposed to sign?"

Dad gives her the papers. His hands are shaking. The lady leads us to the nearest bar where there's more light. Dad's in front of me and she's leading the way. I let off two minor-note farts; I fart when I'm nervous.

We do the signing. She keeps her pages and Dad pockets his. Dad tries to pay back the change, about fifty dollars, but she waves it off.

"What are you two; brothers, or father and son, or what? It's like seeing double."

She couldn't've said anything to make Dad happier; but personally I'm getting fed up with being seen as some kind of carbon copy thrown off by a biological time machine.

"Yeah, this is my son Bill.

"Wow, you sure have a beautiful place here; it's the last thing you'd expect."

"You like it, huh?"

She smiles that same smile, more in the eyes than in the mouth.

"It's incredible."

"And you're curious about it, huh?"

She isn't being nasty, just leading him on.

"Yeah, to be honest, I am. For instance, how are you going to use a car like that one out there? What do you do with a fancy place like this in a neighborhood like this one?"

"This is just what you think it is, Mr. Tremont, a fancy place."

She smiles again.

That's straight enough. She offers us both a drink, and when we nod yes, she pulls ice from an ice-maker, puts it in shot glasses and pours Ballantine Scotch over top. The whole thing's so James Bond I can't get myself around it. I'm still expecting a quiet hit over the head, either here or when we get outside. I'm tasting the drink for knockout drops.

"If you two'd like to stay on and have a good time, there's not much going now; it'd cost just one of those soldiers you have in your pocket there."

Fucking A, the old man handles this as if he's been propositioned by beautiful whores in the afternoon all his life. He smiles and says we have friends waiting for us; he asks if there's a bus or streetcar back to Bala-Cynwyd.

"Lord almighty, I don't know anything about that. I never go outside. I don't even live in Philadelphia; I live in Newark. Sorry, I can't help you but I believe there's a bar around the corner to the left. Maybe they can help."

Since there's no more business with us, she gently slips past, smiling, talking all the way, leading us to the door we came in. All the other doors have been blocked out and covered with mirrors or brocade. This door has heavy drapes over it so you'd hardly know it was there.

So suddenly we're out in that blinding sunlight. There's the heat, the humidity, the smells and all those black people standing on the other side of the street staring. The fire hydrant's still spurting water. It's ten times worse than coming out of a movie in midafternoon; my eyes start hurting as if I'd just eaten a pint of ice cream in three minutes. And there's such a heavy feeling of hate, a chill would run up my spine if there were anything cool left in me. Now I'm dripping sweat inside my jean jacket.

We stroll, not run, down the street and around the corner. We find a place there you might call a bar. It has the word "BAR" written on what's left of a broken plate-glass window and there are black, mean-looking bucks hanging around in front of it. There's also one guy spread in the gutter, bleeding from his nose and mouth. Nobody's paying much attention to him. There's another sleek, thin type, with blood dripping down the front of his T-shirt, leaning in the doorway of what's supposed to be the bar.

Nobody's shouting or even looking excited. My crazy old man walks past the cat in the door to a fat guy behind the bar; there's broken glass all over everything. I stay outside. All those eyes follow Dad in as if he's Cleopatra stepping from her boat on the Nile. I almost expect them to twist shoulders and take the frontal position. Other groovy cats have started drifting onto the scene. I never really thought of myself as the kind of asshole who'd die a violent death in North Philadelphia.

One huge mother of a stud sidles up to me. He's wearing a black, leather, brimmed hat and a thin, yellow silk, tailored shirt. Dad's still in there talking with the fat bartender.

"Hey, man, what you doin' here?"

"We just delivered a car from California to a house around the corner and we're trying to find a bus out. That's my dad in there."

"Shit, man, you *are* in the *wrong* place. You got maybe *five* minutes to live if you stay around here. You all jes' come with me and right now. Get your old man and stick your ass *tight* to me."

This guy must be over six feet six and he's at least three feet across the shoulders. He looks like a muscular gone-to-pot basketball player or a linebacker for the Pittsburgh Steelers. He talks in a reedy, high-pitched quiet voice.

Dad comes out and I tell him this fellow's showing us where there's a bus. I can tell from Dad's face, things didn't go so hot in the bar. I suspect nothing ever goes well in that bar. He falls in behind me and we tail this tall dude with the black leather hat and the yellow shirt. He could be leading us up some alley for a real mugging and we wouldn't have a chance, even with the two of us, even if he were alone, which he wouldn't be. But we don't have that many choices. The giant keeps checking to see we don't fall too far behind. It takes two of our steps for every one of his, he's loping along like a Kodiak bear. There's a troop following in our wake, sharking along.

About three blocks later, he takes us into a place with the words "SETON HALL" scrawled across the doorway. It's another beat-up, run-down place from the outside, but on the inside it's a miniature Salvation Army. There are blankets on tables, and clothes, old clothes, hanging on hangers. The big guy walks over to somebody sitting behind a table in front by the door. There are flies buzzing all around the room.

"Look, Able, see these guys get on the bus away from here. Don't let them go out in the street."

He smiles, then walks through the door without looking back. Everybody working here is black, too. The one at the desk glances at us.

"You stay right there. I'll say when to get up. There's a public service bus comes past."

We sit and watch. In this heat they're spotting, repairing and ironing clothes. I don't know how they stand it. It's some kind of Catholic charity. On the wall there's one of those pictures of Jesus with his heart hanging out, brambles sticking into it and blood dripping.

Finally, this guy tells us to get ready. He goes out on the curb and flags down the bus. Shit, I wouldn't even have recognized it; all the windows have wire grille over them. It looks like an armored truck, only long. He hustles us out and we jump in. The driver's locked in a cage. We put fifty cents each through a small opening in the wiring; into a metal spinning counter meter. He pushes a button and we go through a turnstile into the bus. We're the only pale faces; even though we've just come from California, we really look pale. Maybe we're supposed to go to the back of the bus but the only empty seats are just inside the turnstile.

We have no idea where this bus is going. Dad says we'll stay on so long as it heads south and we'll get off when we see some faces that aren't purplish brown, bluish brown or brownish black.

The bus goes into Central Philadelphia and leaves us off by the City Hall. Dad says he knows a train from here that'll take us out to Bala-Cynwyd. He suggests we go get something to eat and celebrate.

It's almost three o'clock. It's taken more than four hours to deliver that car. It seems like three years on Devil's Island. I know I'm feeling like an escaped criminal. For old time's sake, we head toward the nearest pizza place. But this is a true Italian restaurant and these are genuine pizzas, not American dough with catsup and American soap cheese melted over top; it tastes like Europe. When I close my eyes, I can almost taste France.

This whole day has definitely put the icing on the cake. I'm ready to go home. I'm ready for some old-world civilization; I'm not up to coping with the great American democratic experiment.

A commuter train leaves us off about three blocks from the Hills'. What a difference walking in these streets. There are large, spreading trees shading everything, touching each other over the streets like umbrellas. The roots are so huge they lift the pavements up into little hills. But these pavements aren't cracked; they're cemented in gentle curves over these hills. The houses are natural or cut stone, three stories with graceful porches. There's the sound of power lawnmowers keeping grounds in order and the slamming of screen doors.

Ladies, alone, in big station wagons, cruise around at about twenty miles an hour, out shopping.

It's hard to believe we're only five or six miles from the jungle. What's going to happen when those people over there come charging into these places? I hate to think about it; I sure as hell don't want to be here.

20

In the morning, I call the psychiatrist; his name is Delibro. Over the phone I try getting across something of the situation. He asks if I can come in and talk.

We make an appointment at two o'clock for Dad, but I'm to come right away. I don't know whether he's picked up on the urgency in my voice or just doesn't have much business, but I appreciate getting straight in. He asks if I'll call Perpetual and have Dad's records forwarded. Perpetual says I can pick them up at noon.

Privately, I tell Dad I've made the appointment and I'm going in first to check it out.

I get to Delibro's office on Santa Monica Boulevard before ten. The office is comfortable, easy-California-life style. The walls are done in what looks like shipping-crate wood with stenciled black signs, "FRAGILE HANDLE WITH CARE ⬆ THIS

SIDE UP"; somewhat bizarre for a psychiatrist's waiting room.

Delibro himself is young, perhaps thirty-five, short, with bushy sideburns and a full-lip mustache. He looks like a French cop. He has a nice smile and perfectly neutral handshake.

In his consultation room there's no couch. It could be an office for selling insurance. He doesn't sit behind his desk but in a comfortable black leather chair at a forty-five-degree angle to the chair I sit in. We're semi-facing each other so I'm looking at him off my left shoulder and he's peering at me over his right. It's comfortable enough. I get a strong feeling nothing here is accidental.

He leads me on and I go through it all the best I can. He's asking cautious questions, but it's clear he's as interested in my anxiety as he is in Dad. Then he gets caught up in what I'm trying to tell him.

He asks why I'm so particularly concerned. It's a question I've been asking myself. I tell him this might only be ordinary senile experience, not worth wasting his time with; but I'd like an expert opinion. I also tell him Dad asked me to arrange for help.

The rest of the hour goes well. He's obviously listening, not pretending. He asks pertinent questions. I hope Dad won't be put off by the vaguely "hippy" atmosphere. I was half afraid Delibro'd be one of those displaced-priest or rabbi types with shiny gold-rimmed glasses and a permanent smile. Delibro seems like somebody Dad can relate to. He also doesn't give off "boss man" vibrations, doesn't project *any* threatening signals. Dad will feel more as if he's talking to one of his nephews or grandchildren.

I drive home. I tell Mom how Dad and I are going to go see a gerontologist that afternoon in Santa Monica. She thinks I said gynecologist and gets upset. I explain how a gerontologist is a doctor who specializes in problems of old age. I don't call him a psychiatrist; no sense giving more ammunition for the "crazy" theory.

I tell Dad what I feel about Delibro. He listens and nods his head.

"Johnny, I've been doing some thinking on this. The way

I see it, the biggest problem is keeping things apart. Sometimes I have to stop and make myself think about where I really am. I'll be working out there in the greenhouse, but in my mind I'll be back in Cape May. Working out there in the greenhouse is one place where I do most of my daytime visiting. It's another world, cut off, I'm out there alone with my plants and my mind goes. But don't you worry, John, I'm working on it. I'll lick this thing yet."

Just before two, we get to Santa Monica. It's easy getting Dad to the office because there's parking in the building and an elevator up from the garage. Inside, I give the secretary Dad's records I picked up at Perpetual. Dad's taking the place in.

"Gosh, this guy must be awful poor for a psychiatrist; he's paneled his walls with broken shipping crates. Maybe he'll have an orange crate for a desk."

Just then, Delibro comes out. He's wearing a calming smile and concentrates on Dad. Dad's looking straight back into his eyes and I'm hoping it'll be all right. Dad's trying to decide if this fellow is a boss or not. He has an office, and he *is* a doctor, but he's wearing a soft, dark blue turtleneck sweater.

We go into his consultation room together. Delibro told me in our meeting I could come in but he'd give a signal when I should leave. He's arranged the room so there's one chair relatively near the door; I figure that's mine and sit there. Dad sits in the chair where I sat before.

Very gently, Delibro speaks with Dad while he goes over the medical records.

He asks Dad about Mother, her heart attacks; Dad's operation. He's full of sympathy and brings it off as real. He's easing into the situation, establishing rapport, but in such a way it isn't obnoxious. Dad's nodding, smiling, listening. It's not the "boss man" nod. This is different; he's enjoying being the center of attention.

It seems like tremendously casual conversation at a hundred bucks an hour but he couldn't bulldoze into it; Dad would be put off. Then, finally, Delibro comes on.

"Mr. Tremont, your son's told me you feel you have another life. Could you tell me something about this?"

He smiles and waits. Dad looks at me.

"Sure, Dad. Tell Dr. Delibro. Tell him about Cape May; tell him what you told me."

He starts off slowly but as he senses the intense, positive interest of the doctor, he warms up. He intersperses his tale with "I know this sounds crazy but . . ." or, "This might be hard to believe but . . ." But he's bringing it out.

I'm hoping Delibro won't shoo me. Dad's telling things he hasn't mentioned before. More than when he talked to me, Dad's convinced he's been in two places at the same time. This bothers his sense of rightness. It violates his perfectionist, logical, engineering instincts.

At first, Delibro starts out using the standard psychiatrist come-ons: "Yesss". . . "That's right". . . "Go on". . . "Hmmm," and so forth; but after five minutes it's coming without help. This is a whole world wanting to be born; no need for forceps. I'm torn between watching, listening to Dad; watching Delibro; and letting my own head spin. Delibro's so fascinated his mouth is partly open.

It's the completeness of details, the description of making shoes, the box he designed for fitting the last, the leather sewing; there's the planting of potatoes, watching for the flowering and the harvesting; the tying of onions in a knot so they'll develop good bulbs. It keeps coming on. It's clear Dad wants to reveal all this. The combination of his pleasure in it and his guilt about it has been tearing him apart.

It's as if a painter spent thirty years painting a masterpiece of a mural in an empty room but hasn't been able to show it because he painted it with stolen paints on borrowed time in somebody else's house without their permission.

And Dad can tell it even more fully to Delibro than he could to me. Just then, I catch Delibro give me a blink of his eye; it's time for me to go. I try to slip out quietly but Dad picks it up.

"Where're you going, Johnny? Is it time to leave?"

"I'm only going for a drink of water, Dad; I'll be outside in the waiting room. You stay here and talk to the doctor some more."

He accepts this easily and I leave. I sit and wait. I read

all the magazines but they're in there almost two hours. Thank God, this guy doesn't have much business. I talk to the secretary; she's a Japanese girl, studying psychology at UCLA. She has some of the same professors I worked with twenty years ago. A university is a place where time seems to stand still.

I have an enormous temptation to get up and pace back and forth like an expectant father. I can't help wondering about the lack of patients. Maybe this time of day is slow for "crazies."

This office alone, in this building, must cost a fortune; then a secretary; some overhead. I'd worry myself into a loony bin in a week.

Finally, they come out. They're chatting and laughing.

"Well, Mr. Tremont, I must say your father's story is one of the most interesting things I've ever heard. I honestly don't think most people have as much reality in their daily world as he has in his Cape May existence."

I'm shocked. Here the secretary's sitting there listening. I've been conditioned to the idea of psychiatrists as mysterious super people delving secretly into the inner workings of the subconscious. Delibro's talking about Dad's delusion as if they've just come out of a good movie. It takes me three think-arounds to realize he couldn't take a better approach with Dad. The main thing is getting this all in the open so it can be defused. The way he's treating Dad as just another case, maybe an interesting, original one, but nothing to wet your pants about, is probably right.

Delibro gently puts his hand across Dad's shoulder. He does it nicely, nothing patronizing. He's the same height as Dad.

"We've talked about this, and your Dad understands it's all a dream; he has no confusion in this area at all. It's an ongoing, long dream he's made up for himself."

He takes his hand off Dad's shoulder and looks at me carefully.

"I'd like to see your father again, soon as possible. We need to work on putting together what's real and what's the dream; what's possible and what isn't. The important thing is to find ways he can bring into his daily life the best parts of his dream."

Dad leans toward me; he's watching carefully to see how I'm taking it. He's proud of himself; it shows in his stance, his smile: the artist revealed. Delibro is grinning at both of us.

"There's no reason why Mr. Tremont shouldn't put this all together. Over the years he hasn't been getting enough pleasure from his daily life and he's isolated his greatest joys into a dream. Since his recovery, all that's changed. In the past weeks he's been a happy person; the walls broke down and he's bringing into this everyday life the joy in living he's kept separate for so long."

Delibro asks Dad to stay in the waiting room for a few minutes while he talks to me. Dad smiles and backs himself into a chair. The secretary is smiling and I know he'll be talking to her soon as we leave. I ask Dad if he'll be OK.

"Oh, I'm fine. Maybe the doctor can explain things better to you than he can to me. It's all so complicated I still don't quite understand what's going on. You listen to what he's saying, then tell me."

We sit and Delibro interlaces his fingers across his chest. He asks if I have any experience with the analytic approach, if I've ever consulted a psychiatrist or done much reading on the subject. I figure now there's no backing out. He seems so reasonable I'm sure it won't matter.

"I'm a sort of fall-away psychologist, Doctor. I haven't practiced in over twenty years, but I did my Ph.D. in educational psychology. I've done some reading in analysis but I've never been analyzed."

"Then I can speak in relatively straight terms. I think your father is a successful schizophrenic. Do you know the work of R. D. Laing?"

I nod. It's someone I've read, at least his *Politics of Experience*.

"Well, I subscribe to his idea of schizophrenia as a potential alternate coping system. It's rare to find such an overt example as your father. Either people can't keep it together, thereby becoming nonfunctional, or they keep their delusion intact till death, inviolate, unknown. The trauma of your father's hospital experience apparently surfaced his whole schema.

"Your dad's typical of the people who do this successfully. There are several examples in literature where it's been converted into a shared event; Jonathan Swift or William Faulkner or, more recently, Tolkien. It takes an extremely intelligent, strong-willed and imaginative person.

"Your father's used all his tremendous capacities on his dream, totally independent of his daily life. Apparently he could find no use for them there. He's constructed, created, a personal existence more to his liking. His is a private, complete and apparently satisfying world."

He leans back farther in his chair and runs his fingers along the arms. A sneak-up smile begins to creep across his face.

"Sometimes already, I've had a difficult time keeping distance listening to your father. His fantasy is so compact, so texturally rich and at the same time idyllic. He's like a medieval spellbinder explaining the nature of paradise. And he's constructed this fantasy like a novel; one that fulfills his deepest desires. Most people participate in others' fantasies through films, books or TV, but he has his own and it's totally personal; more than that, it's built into his life. I'm not sure he can ever let go, or even should, totally."

I don't know whether to ask or not. But this guy's a psychiatrist, this is what he's paid for.

"Dr. Delibro, I know this sounds off the wall, but what's the chance Dad's on some other time continuum or slipped gears somehow and is really experiencing all this?"

Delibro looks at me carefully. I'm already wishing I'd kept my mouth shut. In one sentence I've blown whatever credibility I had.

"I know; it's hard to believe he's made it all up. I've had the eerie feeling he's only drawing back a curtain, letting me see something visible to him, something real."

He stops, stares at his fingertips.

"But we can't work on that hypothesis, Mr. Tremont. We must work within what we know if we're going to help. It doesn't matter much in terms of his immediate problem whether this is a dream construct or some time-warp phenomenon. Let's not turn your Dad into another Bridey Murphy, OK?"

He looks up at me and smiles. He's right.

"As I see it, the first thing we want to discover is what's wrong with his daily life so he feels the need to build this other world."

He's getting to the core of things fast. I try not to show much.

"At first, I wasn't sure if this mightn't be only a short-duration delusion resulting from the trauma of his hospital experience, his coma and his fear of cancer.

"Has he ever told you about his abnormal fear of cancer? He actually has images of this disease, feelings verging on the psychotic. My background is Catholic and I recognize some of his projections as evil, the devil. He personalizes cancer as an enemy intent on removing him, devouring all he loves."

Wow, Dad didn't hold back much. This Delibro's good if he got him to talk about cancer.

"But I'm convinced now his 'dream' has been going on a long time, perhaps thirty years or more. It's become the mainspring of his inner life. And his inner life has been totally isolated from his outer life. That's dangerous business, Mr. Tremont; it's amazing he's been able to function at all. It's no wonder his wife's illness, the shock of the operation, being removed from a stable environment, the news of his cancer caused him to retreat into his available 'other' world."

I'm beginning to worry about Dad out there alone. I'm still carrying in my mind all those disappearances.

"Your father's a charming man. It's rare finding anyone over seventy with such a boylike quality, an interest and curiosity in things. I see many old people, and a good part of being old is increased rigidity, loss of vitality and a general decline in curiosity and humor. But with your father this isn't true. What concerns me most is what forced him to develop his fantasy? What could be so wrong in his life?"

"Doctor, I wish you'd talk to my mother. I think it will help you understand Dad better."

"I was going to ask if that could be possible. In listening to your father, I sensed theirs has been a close union and she might be able to give me some insights."

Should I tell him? Would he rather find out for himself? I should at least warn him.

"Dr. Delibro, my mother's a very difficult woman. I'm not sure I can get her to come."

He leans forward in the chair. Sherlock Holmes hearing the dog that didn't bark.

"Please tell me anything about her you think I should know."

What a great way to put it. That must be a straight text-book phrase. It's so encouraging and yet so ambiguous. What the hell, anything to help.

"Dr. Delibro, Mom's already had two severe nervous break-downs. When she's threatened she strikes out; and she's easily threatened.

"She's convinced that marrying my father was the biggest mistake of her life; still, emotionally, she's absolutely dependent on him.

"I know this sounds like one more middle-aged man complaining about his mother, but it's what I feel. To put it succinctly, Mother is hard to live with: intelligent, sensitive, demanding, insatiable and ruthless."

So it's out. He brings his two thumbnails up and sticks them between his front teeth. Maybe he's feeling left out because his teeth aren't separated. I wait. It's quiet enough so I can hear the clock tick. Jesus, we've been consulting for over three hours; we'll have to sell the house just to pay the psychiatrist bills.

"Dr. Delibro, another thing. My parents aren't rich, neither am I. I'm not sure how much psychiatric help they can afford. I hate to be mercenary about this, but what are your estimates in time and money to do some good? If we get Mom involved in this, you've got your life's work cut out."

He leans his chair back, pushes his palms down on the

arms, fingers point out, slightly up. He looks at one set of fingers then the other, he reminds me of a pianist before he attacks the keyboard.

"Both your parents will be covered by Medicare, I'm sure. Perhaps we can get the rest from Perpetual or MediCal. Don't worry about it. If they can't come up with the twenty percent, we'll make it some way. I don't agree with the Freudian idea you need to make it expensive so the treatment will be appreciated. That's only a bit of Viennese sadomasochistic nonsense. Don't worry about the money; I'm not going to sop up their life savings. To be honest, it's one of the reasons I chose gerontology as a specialty. With Medicare I can choose my patients on a need basis, not just on ability to pay. Eighty percent of my fees keeps me fine."

We both smile. He couldn't be franker than that. Dad and Mom are going to get the full upper-middle-class treatment. Coming to see Delibro will be the high point of the week for years; it'll upstage the "soaps." I'm beginning to think I might actually get home.

He looks at the clock and stands up. Maybe there *are* other patients. I stand and we walk out to the waiting room. Dad isn't there! I almost panic; then I see him in the little alcove with the secretary. He's sitting at the typewriter. She's leaning over him. He has his hands on the keys. He looks up when we come over and smiles sheepishly.

"You know, Johnny, I've always wanted to learn typing. This girl's being wasted as a secretary; she should be a teacher. Look, I can already type 'he is it' without looking."

To demonstrate, he stares up at the ceiling and laboriously taps slowly at the keys. He has his fingers awkwardly hovering over the home keys. He looks down.

"See that, I did it again!"

We both lean forward and look. Spread over a page of f's, d's, g's, j's, k's and l's are three copies of his magic sentence. Dad stands up, holding his hands over the keys till he's standing. The girl helps and gives him his hat. They shake hands; Dad puts his hand over hers.

"Thank you so much, Junko; someday I'll type out a book and put you in it."

He comes around the counter. Delibro and I make two appointments for next week: one on Wednesday, the other Friday. If I can get Mother to come on any pretext, I will; if not, Dad'll take both.

So we drive home. I park and go into the house. Dad goes back to his greenhouse; I think he's staying away from Mom. He doesn't want to talk about what's happening. Maybe he goes back there and trips to Cape May.

I try telling Mother what the doctor said. I tell about the dreams of Cape May, about how Dad still calls her Bess there and that's why he makes mistakes now. I try giving her some picture of it all, how they're younger, have two other children; how Dad raises tomatoes and corn to sell in Philadelphia. As I go on, I can see it's not coming off.

Mom has both hands over her mouth again. She shakes her head slowly back and forth in disbelief. There are tears on the bottom rims of her eyes. Maybe it's too much, but I can't think of another way. I should have asked Delibro.

"I knew all the time he was crazy, Jacky. I told you. You can't tell me somebody who thinks he lives in Cape May when he hasn't ever even visited the place isn't crazy! How can I live alone with somebody who thinks things like that?"

Then, after the first shock, she seems to relax. Having a professional work on the case appeals to her idea of the way it should be; she doesn't feel quite so helpless. The movie and TV stars have psychiatrists; she's a part of the big world now; her husband's going to a psychiatrist. I review everything again, emphasizing how it's all only a dream and will go away. I feel more relaxed, too. I'm glad I told her.

Billy comes back from a visit up the coast to some of his friends at Santa Cruz. He drove all the way up and back on my motorcycle.

I ask Billy if he'll stay around some so I can get down to Venice and paint. I'm feeling a need to let my own id spread around some, bolster up my sagging ego.

While I'm painting, Gerry, the girl in Marty's new house, comes by a couple of times. She has her little ones with her.

We sit on the beach and I play with her kids. I roll and play bear with them in the sand. Something in me still isn't ready to be cut out from the parenting role. Maybe I'm only aching to be a grandfather. I'm caught up, beached, between two tides, the old one of fathering-husbanding and the new one of aging-dying.

My whole being is lifted by having those kids rolling, laughing, jumping on me. It could also be a contrast to the sadness and end-of-the-road feeling with my folks. It could be because of Gerry.

She flirts with me in the nicest way, somewhere between a grown girl teasing her father and a woman treating me as an available male. I enjoy responding. My life has been such that this no-holds-barred, minimum-expectation relationship with a woman is tremendously appealing. I feel I don't have to bring an orchid, take her to the senior prom; I don't have to buy her an engagement ring, find a cedar chest for the trousseau, hunt living-room furniture, demonstrate I have a job, a car, money in the bank; don't need a bunch of professional fools from state and church standing around, testifying to our seriousness. It's only the two of us, on a beach, casually enjoying each other. It makes the head of an older man spin.

But I'm not psychologically ready. I'm turned on, but I'm scared. Also, there's no room in my life. Still we have some good conversation. The father thing comes up. Maybe it's part of all her conversations with males but probably it's my age.

Gerry has a successful father; in her view, very authoritarian. She feels her relationship with men has always been in his shadow, a strike at him or a searching for him. She's been part of several therapy groups and knows all the jargon. I listen, play with her children and feel sorry for her father. He's been cornered into thinking he's done the right thing. He's tried to give her the illusion he's effectively, easily, coped with the world; that he isn't scared, worried, suffering daily fear and doubt like the rest of us.

It's an easy mistake, faking this illusion of invulnerability. Some people never penetrate the façade; never see their parents as ordinary people; all other humans seem second class, including themselves. I listen to her and wonder how well Vron and I have handled this part of our lives.

I finish two paintings in Suzanne's restaurant. One's from out front through the restaurant and into the kitchen. The other I'm in the kitchen, stove and pots in the foreground, tables in the middle ground and the ocean out the front window.

Suzanne serves only breakfast and dinner, so there's a four-to-five-hour period in midday when I can work. She lives over the restaurant and invites me up a few times. There's usually six or seven people smoking.

I take a few drags one afternoon when I'm finished. I don't know why but grass doesn't lift me; it makes everything very clear and far away. It's not an unpleasant sensation, only it gets in the way of whatever it is keeps me painting.

Wednesday I take Dad back to the psychiatrist. At home a storm's brewing with Mom. It's partly the way she's acting but she's also complaining. She's complaining about Billy, about Dad; and I'm sure she's complaining to them about me.

According to her, I don't know what Dad's really like; he's dangerous and twice in the past few days he's tried to hurt her. She says once he hit her with his cane and another time he bumped into her and almost knocked her down.

Dad still doesn't have total control of his body. There are certain almost spastic movements. I listen and try to reassure her; she must be mistaken. He'd never hurt her on purpose.

He's in with Delibro two hours again.

On the way home in the car we talk. I ask Dad if he's had any more dreams and he says he has; he still goes there nights and it isn't like a dream at all.

"John, I remember everything afterwards, better than I can remember yesterday. It isn't only at night either.

"I'll be sitting there in the rocking chair, not thinking, just drifting, and I'll go. Some big part of me leaves and is in

Cape May. I don't even know how long I'm gone. It happens all the time, whenever I relax, especially out there in the greenhouse."

He shifts his cane between his legs. He looks down, then at me. I give him a quick glance from my driving. I'm working up onto the freeway entrance at Lincoln Boulevard.

"Something I told the doctor, John. It's strange but this world here has come into that one.

"I told Bess about us, there in my own world, and now she knows all about everything here. She believed me. Dr. Delibro says it's because I want her to believe but I'm not so sure. Bess wants to know everything about our life here. She only wonders where Hank and Lizbet are; she's convinced I'm seeing into the future somehow. She wants me to describe how she looks as an old lady and she can't believe you're bald and have a beard. I didn't tell her I have a beard, too."

Wow, I'm feeling transparent again! These days the physicists are saying the subatomic structure of any object, this car I'm driving, anything, can't be fitted into a framework of space and time. Words like "substance" or "matter" have become devoid of meaning. This seat I'm sitting on is coming out of nothing, traveling through a non-medium in a multi-dimensional non-space. What we've been calling reality is up for grabs; time is a mind projection.

It's even possible the future has as much effect on what we call event, present, as the past. Causality is losing its effectiveness. My decaying bald-topped mind is spinning; maybe I'll create a few new solar systems without knowing it.

"What did the doctor say about this, Dad?"

"He made me go through it about three different times and asked a peck of questions. He's taken to writing these things down; I think he believes me, John."

He pauses again.

"But I'm beginning to feel he suspects I might be crazy. He just could be right about that, too. Your mother'd sure be glad; she's been saying it for years; she's better than any psychiatrist; cheaper, too."

With this, he leans back and laughs in the most uncrazy

way imaginable. I start laughing with him. I'm glad there are no cops patrolling this section of the Santa Monica Freeway. If they saw two older men with beards driving along laughing their heads off, they'd stop us for sure.

"I told the whole family there about you, Mother and Joan; about my operation, and about me seeing a psychiatrist. They all laughed and Hank wanted to know what a psychiatrist is. To be honest, Johnny, they're pestering the devil out of me. What on earth can I say to little Hank and Lizbet; I can't tell them their daddy just made 'em up. That's terrible. What do you think I ought to do?"

God, what a question! If I start advising him on what to do in that world, it'll grow *more* real, somehow make this one less true. I want to go home to *my* family, to Vron and Jacky. I'm realizing how in my own mind Paris, France, is less be- lievable, less real than Dad's crazy dreamworld. It seems so far away, so long ago. I can't believe I do actually live in a houseboat on the Seine outside Paris; that I have an old water mill in central France; that I'm an artist. It sounds like one of the biggest pipe dreams anybody ever made up.

"You'd better ask the doctor, Dad. I don't know what to say. Did you tell them they're all a dream and you have a real life here? Did you tell them that?"

"Oh, no, Johnny, I couldn't do that. I'm not so sure about things myself. I just told them how this part here is like a dream. I wasn't lying, that's the way it is. When I'm here, like now, that part's a dream but when I'm there, this gets to be the dream and I have a hard time believing it.

"I'll be honest with you, John, it's better there. If I had my choice, I'd make that part the real life for us."

At home we sit around the living room. There are some times when I'm sure Dad has left us. I'm itching to ask but I'm embarrassed. It's like asking a woman if she's having her period because she's acting differently. There's no real justifi- cation except simple curiosity and it's an invasion.

Mom's tough to be with. Luckily, Billy's gone back up on the forty acres. Mother, wandering around, the Lady Macbeth of Colby Lane, bugs Billy beyond endurance. I can't blame him. Mom's impossible when she's scared; she's striking out in all directions, trying to give some substance to things. Nobody's safe near her.

We're sitting there in the living room and she starts off. Dad's in his rocking chair, Mom's on one of the dining chairs turned half around from the table and I'm sitting in an upholstered chair by the door. We're all within a few feet of each other.

She begins talking to me about how crazy Dad is. She's pulling out all her memorized litany of Tremont variations from the norm through four generations. She's tolling them off like a rosary, the five infamous mysteries; I listen and fume. Dad's between pretending it isn't happening, and listening. He's like a very genteel woman who's forced by circumstances to hear barroom language.

It goes on and on; nothing's enough. I know she's wanting me to argue and I don't want to. But then I can't help myself. You only kid yourself into thinking you've grown out of it, that you can respond as an adult logically, sensibly, to parents. I turn to Dad.

"Dad, why do you let her talk like this? Why do you put up with it? It's not good for either of you to have her spout all this rot. *She's* the one who's acting crazy."

Mother keeps talking over my first sentence, but then shuts up. If I'd talked to her directly she'd have kept on, only louder. Using a carom shot, talking to Dad, has her buffaloed.

"We all know she does this because she's scared, but backbiting at everybody doesn't help. You've got to help her stop."

I turn toward Mom.

"And, Mom, you should know better. You don't really believe this nonsense; you're only saying it to make yourself feel like a big shot and three-star martyr. Dad's doing his best. We have an expert working with him. This doctor says Dad's *not* crazy. In fact, he's impressed with how Dad's survived the past thirty or so years *without* going crazy.

"If you're so convinced Dad's crazy, tell me in private and

we'll work things out. We can put Dad in a home, or you in a
home, or something. But for God's sake don't sit there talking
in front of him as if he's a dog who doesn't understand!"

Dad's turned white. He leans forward and lurches out of
his platform rocker. Instinctively I stand with him. I've no
idea what he's going to do. Maybe take a punch at me or maybe
Mom. It could be anything.

He leaves his cane and shuffles toward us. Mother's up,
too; looking even more scared than I feel. Dad spreads his
thin arms and we go toward him. He pulls us close to his breast
and holds us tight. His whole body is shaking. Nobody says
anything. It's as if we're in a two-hand-touch huddle, except
we're not leaning over, our faces are straight up, pushed next
to each other at different heights.

Dad kisses us both several times; it's the first time I can
remember his kissing me since the day I was sent off to first
grade. He begins talking and his voice is low, cracked.

"Don't do it, Johnny. Please don't say those things to your
mother; you're too clever, you know too much. We're family,
that's all that counts. Let's love each other and forget. Loving,
more than anything, means letting people do the things they
have to do. Johnny, you live in Paris because that's what you
have to do. Mother here has to do some things too; so do I.
It's the way it is. Please don't fight; it kills me hearing you
talk this way."

Then he starts crying hard and Mother breaks into sobs.
I'm crying, too. Now we're the Burghers of Calais standing in
our own rain. Maybe it's time to break the huddle, call the
signals and snap the ball. These kinds of stupid thoughts are
tramping through my mind. Real emotion is tough for me to
handle; I've got about twenty lines of defense to keep from
feeling.

Finally we sit again. Dad sighs and begins talking. I
can't get my mind around it; who the hell is this guy?

"There are some things maybe you don't know, Johnny.
When I met Bess she was only fifteen. She was just recovering
from a bad nervous breakdown. She could never even go back

to school again. I was eighteen and working at Hog Island as a carpenter. I wasn't happy; in fact, I was miserable. I didn't like living in the city and I was missing the farm. I felt everybody could see I was only a farm boy and was laughing at me.

"It was a big change, John. You know, winter and summer, none of us kids wore shoes regularly on the farm. We walked to school with shoes tied around our necks and put them on when we went inside. I never owned a pair of shoes till we got to Philadelphia. I'd get Orin's. Those shoes never wore out; we only put them on for school and church.

"You can't know what a change it was coming from Wisconsin where I knew maybe twenty people all together and half of them were my brothers and sisters. There I was in Philadelphia, talking funny with a farm-boy Wisconsin hick accent; I was afraid to open my mouth. I'd be jammed in trolley cars with people who didn't know anything about me and didn't care. Everybody seemed to know what to do and where they were going. People would bump into me because I couldn't even get out of the way. I didn't know how to flush a toilet, use a telephone or dance.

"I met Mother on a rainy day in a doorway near John Wanamaker's. She came into the doorway crying her eyes out. She was crying because she'd borrowed her older sister Maggie's fancy hat without asking and now it was getting ruined in the rain.

"I had a big old-time umbrella my mother made me carry and I opened it over her. Gosh, I guess if Mom hadn't made me carry that umbrella I'd never even've gotten to know you. Bess, think of that.

"Well, Bess was pretty, and scared. She was the scaredest person I'd ever met. It wasn't just the hat; she was scared about the thunder and lightning, she was scared the trolley wasn't going to come; she was scared about what time it was, and she was scared of me. Something inside me wanted to help her not be so scared.

"And, Johnny, Mother's always been that way. Sometimes she acts strong and likes to be bossy, but inside she's scared. It's something you've got to remember.

"That day she finally let me go along with her in the trolley, and when she got out I followed her, keeping my umbrella over the hat. She led me to a big stone house and said this was where she lived, and goodbye. I stood across the street waiting to see her safe inside but two big dogs came barking at the door. She ran away and down the street in the rain; it wasn't where she lived at all.

"That's the kind of thing she does, Johnny, because she's so scared. I chased her, laughing, but she was mad and I thought she might be crazy but I loved her already."

I look at Mom. Her eyes are blank, her face a mask; she's stunned.

"And you're not much different, Johnny. You were the scrawniest baby I've ever seen in my life. For the first three months you cried without stopping. It's a wonder that didn't drive your poor mother absolutely crazy. Then, you grew up to be the scaredy-cattest kid in the neighborhood. I used to think sometimes you caught it from your mother.

"You were afraid of the dark. You were afraid of loud noises; you used to hold your fingers in your ears at baseball games and you'd stuff cotton in them on the Fourth of July. You were afraid to ride a bike, to roller-skate, even to swim. I don't think you learned swimming till you were over thirteen years old.

"And you were afraid of all the other kids on the block. You'd come running home with some little kid half your size chasing you. That's how you learned to run, running away from everybody.

"I was sure you'd never learn to take care of yourself; that you'd live with us all your life. I remember being so embarrassed because you were one of the world's worst baseball players.

"And you grew so fast, early. For a while, when you were about ten or twelve, you were a head taller than anybody in your class. This made it worse. Little kids would take turns beating up on you so they could say they licked the big sissy down the block. Summers, you spent your time hiding in the cellar, on the porch reading or later fooling around with your birds. Sometimes I look at you now and I can't believe it's the same person.

"What I want to say is, you're a lot like your mother, John. You're fighting all the time but in your own way. Maybe that's why you live in France instead of America. You don't want to compete, you want to stay apart.

"But, in another way, you're different from Bess. You get that part from me. There's something in me that's wild, wild like a wild animal. It was in my father, it's in my brothers and two of my sisters; we aren't quite human, quite civilized. There's some animal quality and it can come out anytime. I'm surprised we've gotten as far as we have without having a murderer in the family.

"I don't know what brings it on; could be all those years living in the woods, or it could be the Indian blood.

"You know, Johnny, your great-grandfather was a trapper. He never lived in a house from the time he was thirteen; he married a full-blooded Oneida Indian. Your great-grand-mother, my father's mother, was over six feet tall. She was stronger than any man, and could talk only Indian and French.

"I never heard her speak one word. That grandfather and grandmother of mine lived practically like prehistoric people. They didn't homestead and settle till my dad was seven years old. They lived with the Indians and had no real religion; so far as I know they never got married—at least, not in a church.

"Dad used to tell stories about how they'd drift along, tending the traps, buying furs, caching, then packing them all out in canoes. They were animals, Johnny, and it's still there. It's in me, it's in you, too, and we always have to fight it."

Mother's nodding her head now; this is something she can live with. Jack the Ripper, North American version of Tarzan the apeman.

"One reason I married Bess was she liked beautiful things. She'd always lived in cities and all her family'd lived in cities as far back as anybody could remember. She likes nice furniture, she keeps a clean house and we live like decent human beings.

"You can see I'm not like my brothers or even my father; I'm civilized. I don't drink much and I don't run around. My brothers are all dangerous men, except Ed. Ed was lucky like me and married a good woman. Aunt Mary trained him just fine. You could never predict my father or my brothers; never tell what they were thinking or what they were going to do. None of them ever held full-time jobs in their lives. Pete and Orin and Caleb were always drinking or running back into the woods to hunt. Winters they'd curl up and hibernate like bears.

"Now, my mom did a good job with Dad. At least she got him into church and he took care of us kids. But he didn't dress like a normal person or do things like other people. You know, Johnny, he never paid a dime to Social Security or paid any income tax in his life? He lived on the outside of everything. He lived down there in southwest Philadelphia as if he was living on a farm or in the woods. All those buildings, cars and everything didn't mean a thing to him.

"I didn't want to live that way. Look, I'm a civilized man; look at these hands, they're clean, I've got all my fingers. Look at this house we've got here, with this beautiful furniture, rugs and all. We live like real city people and that's all your mother's doing. Don't forget that."

What can I say? I know he's serious; he wants me to understand. I'm wishing Delibro could hear this. Mother's sitting there, still crying. She's sniffing and peering at me, eye-talk, "See what I mean, Jacky, see what I mean?" And Dad's making such sense. I feel awful, like a child. He's been seeing through it all these years and saying nothing, letting it happen because he respected us.

"John, I know sometimes you must worry about Billy and little Jacky.

"It's hard for fathers to wait, but you have to give boys time, they're slow. Sons are what worry a man because most men are scared, so they're scared for their sons.

"Johnny, I'm not worrying about you anymore and I don't want you worrying about me or Mother. Let's enjoy our own lives. We're all fine.

"I'll keep going to that psychiatrist doctor till I get myself straightened out. Johnny, you go home to Veronica and Jacky. Mother and I will be OK; we all just have to stop worrying so much."

After this long speech, he leans back, rocking, smiling from one to the other of us, smiling as if all the rules of the family haven't been broken into a thousand pieces. The odd thing is Dad doesn't act as if all this talking is out of the ordinary. Here he's talked more in fifteen minutes, said more, than he has in the past fifteen years; and he's just rocking and smiling.

I begin to sympathize with Mother. It's not so much physical violence she's afraid of, it's mental. He's capable of saying anything, rolling through all the sacrosanct temples of thought and emotion built during more than fifty years of mutual hypocrisy. He's scuttled all the rules of their relationship.

Dad pushes out of his chair again and this time takes his cane. He moves off down the hall smiling back at us over his shoulder. He glances at the clock over the TV.

"Well, I'm going to put on my baseball-watching costume. It's almost time for the Dodger game."

He shuffles off down the hall to the back bedroom. Mom looks at me.

"Jacky, that's not normal the way he's talking. He never talked like that in his life. Something's happened; he's a different person."

She's stopped crying. This is my mother actually out there in front of me. She's scared enough so she's not putting it on or trying to pull anything over. It's the first time I have the feeling we can truly talk.

"Mom, I think this is the true John Tremont. He's been hiding for over fifty years. I think that's the way he really is inside; he's a smart man who didn't even know it himself. How was he ever going to find out he was smart? Everybody's been profiting by making him think he wasn't. I'll bet Douglas and G.E. has made ten million dollars off his ideas. They *wanted* to keep him down, get the most out of him for virtually nothing. Everybody's been leaning on him all his life, including us.

"The psychiatrist says Dad is one of the most intelligent, imaginative men he's ever had as a patient. He wants to give Dad some intelligence tests which don't depend on how much schooling he's had. Dad's probably a genius of some kind."

Mother leans back in her "don't kid me" lean and stares.

"Oh, come on, Jacky. He's smart maybe, but he's no genius. I've lived with him all my life. He's a perfectionist but he's never been able to think up anything except toys for you kids or different crazy gadgets. He's the original 'Jack-of-all-trades' and he's never earned more than six thousand dollars a year in his life. If that psychiatrist thinks he's a genius, he must be half crazy himself."

"Mom, you ought to go see Dr. Delibro. Maybe you can give him a new viewpoint on Dad. As you say, you know him better than anybody. Dr. Delibro is trying to help Dad get things together and you could help more than anybody."

I can actually *feel* her paranoia surfacing. Mother doesn't want any experts of *any* kind working on her. During the war, she didn't take a job in a defense plant because she was afraid they'd X-ray her chest and find out she had tuberculosis. Mom was a closet tubercular for over thirty-five years. When Perpetual gave her a chest X-ray as part of the entrance examination, she was shocked to find out she actually had lungs. I'm waiting to see how it will go.

"He'll probably decide *I'm* crazy, Jacky. If he thinks your father's a genius, he could easily think I'm insane. If he finds out about my two nervous breakdowns, he's liable to lock me up and throw away the key."

"You're not crazy, Mom; but it could certainly help him to understand Dad if you'd talk to him. He needs all the information he can get."

I'm starting to hope now. I have to be careful not to make any false moves. Just then, Dad comes up the hall. He's wearing his hat, his striped shirt and has a scorecard in his hand. He's begun keeping a line-score for the games he watches. He stops on the way up the hall and goes into the bathroom. Mother leans toward me and stage-whispers.

"All right, I'll go; anything if it'll help him come to his senses."

When the game gets under way, I sneak into the back room and call Delibro. I tell him Mother will keep the Friday appointment. Boy, we're deep into psychiatrists now; I can't help wondering how it will all turn out. I go into the living room and tell Mother it's set. There's no use trying to keep it from Dad, so I tell him Mom is going to visit his psychiatrist, too. He turns away from the game and gives me a quick look. But the ball game's on and we settle in to watch the Dodgers slip past the Phillies.

Later, out in the greenhouse, I tell Dad he doesn't have to worry about the psychiatrist telling Mother anything they talked about in private; I tell him a psychiatrist is something like a priest in confession. Dad's spraying liquid fertilizer on some plants. He looks up and smiles.

"Oh, I'm not worried about that, John, but I'm not sure it's such a good idea having her visit a psychiatrist."

I don't have time to answer because just then Billy arrives. He's almost as dirty as when he arrived the first time. He's been down in Ensenada camping on the beach.

After we get him showered, I ask if he'll stay around the house next day so I can visit Marty. I feel I'm not getting enough time with her. Billy can't really say no to that, and I think Mom's glad to have him there; she's that scared of Dad.

I call Marty and we agree to meet tomorrow down at the French sidewalk café on the beach and have breakfast together.

Billy will sleep out in the garden bedroom. I'm in the side bedroom, while Mom and Dad sleep in their own back bedroom. That evening, as she walks past in her nightgown, Mother gives off looks like a vestal virgin being sacrificed to the Minoan bull. I shut the door to my little side bedroom and pretend I don't notice.

21

Dad's awake and over to Marty's before I'm up. The bed in that back bedroom is like sleeping in a bowl of oatmeal.

I'm lying there awake, knowing I have to take a piss. I creep out quietly, bare-ass, sneak around back and pee against the wall. It's then I notice the car's already gone. I don't feel like going in the house so I streak back, jump into bed and start the slow, soft descent into feathers.

I'm not even asleep again when Grandma comes pushing her way in. I pretend I'm asleep. I want to watch what she's up to this time.

One thing, at least she's not being spooky. She stomps straight over and shakes my shoulder. I open my eyes slowly. She's white and shaking. I slide up so I'm sitting against the pillow.

"What's the matter, Grandma? Sit down here; you look awful!"

She collapses on the bed beside me and begins crying. She grabs hold of my hand. Isn't it just my luck, the day Dad decides to take off, somebody dies. Shit! I'm scared and I'm still bare-ass.

"Billy, you've got to help me! I don't know what to do! What can I do? He's acting completely crazy and I'm afraid to even talk with him!"

"What's he doing, Grandma, tell me! What's happened? What's the matter?"

"He's insane, Billy. That psychiatrist should see him now; then he'd know.

"Oh, God, I wish your father was here. I'm sure we'll have to lock him up this time; with my heart I can't stand it anymore!"

Jesus, if she'd only get to the point, or at least leave the room so I can dress and find out what's happening.

"Just tell me, Grandma; what is it? What's Grandpa doing? Tell me!"

"You won't believe this. He's there in the bathroom; he's been there all morning. I got worried and went in to see what could be the matter; you'll never guess what he's doing."

She pauses and gives me about two seconds. If I had two more seconds, I'd've said he was on the john trying to take a private morning shit. What else?

"Billy, he's floating tiny boats made out of matchsticks and pieces of paper in the sink. I almost died! He didn't seem to notice me so I stood there watching him.

"He fills the sink, puts his little boats in, pulls the plug and lets the water out. He even makes waves with his hand so the boats go around in circles, just like a kid. Nobody can tell me that's not crazy, Billy; he's completely insane."

"Yeah, Grandma, what happened then? Did you ask him what he was doing? He might only be trying to fix the sink."

She looks at me as if I'm crazy too. I'm stalling for time; what the hell could it be?

"Well! At last I got up my nerve and went further into the bathroom so he notices me. He turns around and smiles as if there's absolutely *nothing* wrong. I try to speak as normally

as possible; I don't want to get him excited. 'What're you doing there, Jack?' I'm scared to death. You never know what
he'll do next.

"He says something about a woman named Carol Alice,
then twists his fingers in the air muttering about the world
spinning; then, clear as day, looks me in the eye and says,
'Maybe you won't have to worry about earthquakes anymore,
Bess.'"

Jesus, if Grandma's got this even half right, Grandpa's
definitely flipped! He's been different lately but this is weird!

"And that's all?"

"Well, Billy, I was so scared I backed out of the bathroom
and came here to wake you up. Maybe we should call Martha
and tell your father. I don't know who this Carol Alice is, but
it sounds like a nigger name to me; probably one of those
nurses he was flirting with at the hospital. There's no fool like
an old fool, I always say."

"Look, Grandma. We can't get hold of Dad for awhile; he's
down at the beach with Marty and I don't know what they'll do
after that. You go outside while I dress. I'll go see what it is
with Grandpa. Then you can stay here and relax, just lie back
on this bed and pull yourself together."

I finally chase her into the garden, get dressed and settle
her in the bed.

I go in the house expecting anything. I've never had any
experience dealing with crazies except once when two girls
at UCK SUCK OD'd on acid. But that was only temporary and
there were mobs of other people around.

I sneak through the side door. The bathroom door's still
open and it's just as she said, he's leaning over the sink and
there are tiny matchstick boats floating in the water. He's
leaning back on the hamper with his cane beside him. He sees
me right away when I come in. I figure I'll go along with it till
I find out what's going on.

"Playing boats, Grandpa?"

He looks at me and smiles. He probably has one of the
nicest smiles in the world. Maybe that's part of being bonkers,
you have a nice smile.

"Billy, what do you know about the Coriolis effect?"

I'll tell you, he catches me with that one. I only vaguely remember it from an oceanography class. But Jesus, what a question in the early morning on an empty stomach.

"Not much, Grandpa, isn't it something about the water going down the sink twisting right in the northern hemisphere and the other way in the south?"

"That's part of it, Billy. But most experts insist the Coriolis effect isn't strong enough to make water in a little washbasin like this go any particular way at all."

He pulls the plug out again and I watch with him. Sure enough, the water twists around clockwise, as you'd expect. His little boats swing around, get caught in the whirlpool, and he fishes them out just before they go down the drain.

"Now, watch this time, Billy."

He fills the basin to the top and puts his boats back in. This time, before he pulls the plug, he starts the water spinning in the opposite direction, counterclockwise, with his hand. Then he pulls the plug. The boats are moving counterclockwise, but gradually the water reverses itself and they all go down clockwise.

"Did you see that, Billy? That's the twenty-sixth time I've done it here and it's been like that every time."

"But, Grandpa, that's what it's all about, isn't it? That's what the Coriolis effect is supposed to do."

He pushes himself farther back on the clothes hamper and picks up his cane. I can't say he looks particularly crazy. And where the hell did he find out about the Coriolis effect?

"Billy, here's the problem. This Coriolis acceleration effect is only point zero zero five, that's five thousandths of a centimeter per second per second, while normal gravity force is around nine hundred and eighty-five centimeters per second per second. In other words, the force of gravity is almost two hundred thousand times stronger than the Coriolis force. That's why scientists are so sure it won't happen in a basin of water; the gravity force should thoroughly beat out the Coriolis so it won't happen. By almost any computation, it just shouldn't show up in such a small basin of water. But right here now, with twenty-six trials, my coefficient of error is getting mighty small. Something's wrong."

He leans forward and starts filling the bowl again. I go up closer to him; it's almost like being back in a lab at school.

"Now, Billy, the reason water twirls with a cyclonic motion going out of the basin and down the drain is because friction from gravity is exerted on the water by the side of the basin. The water closest to the sides is subjected to the most friction; the water in the center, away from the sides, spins easier with whatever motion it has, so you get the water moving at different speeds, fast in the center and slow at the sides. This is sped up when the surface gets smaller as the water goes out the drain. So the whirlpool or water cyclone going out, down the drain, is what you'd expect. But it's the direction, its always being clockwise that gets me. I've been thinking maybe our basin here is designed with a warped bowl to make water twist out and go down faster; maybe that's it.

"Billy, would you mind phoning Standard Plumbing up on Sepulveda and ask if they design basins and tubs with some kind of twist? I'd do it myself but I hate using that phone."

I say sure I'll do it, anything to help him get his mind off this crazy business. Shit, where the hell did he learn about acceleration, gravity; coefficients of error? I thought he only went to eighth grade.

I find Standard in the phone book and, after about three tries, get somebody in the manufacturing division who assures me all their bowls, both stainless steel and porcelain, are regularly shaped. I'm sure he thinks I'm trying to work up a complaint about some crooked sink. I tell Granddad what he said. He shakes his head.

"Well, Billy, that eliminates one idea. Maybe we ought to try other sinks. Where can we go near here and find a lot of sinks?"

People keep asking me questions and then answering before I can say anything.

"I know, Billy. The bowling alley just over the hill. I went to visit there while I was doing the wash once and they have at least ten sinks all in a row."

Christ, he's pushing himself up off the hamper; he's ready to take off.

"But, Granddad, Dad has the car. We don't have any way to get there; it's too far to walk."

"The motorcycle's out there on the driveway, Billy. We can take that. I've ridden on back with your father and we won't have any parking problem."

He's serious! But if Grandma finds out I'm taking Granddad to the bowling alley on the motorcycle to float toy boats, she'll call the cops. Granddad gets out those crappy helmets we keep here; he's ready to ride. What the hell, if that's what he wants; besides, I'm beginning to get interested.

I push the bike to the end of the street before revving it up. Granddad walks along beside me; at least he didn't bring his cane. I'm hoping Grandma won't hear us. He clambers on back, kicks down the foot pegs and holds on tight. What the hell gave *my* old man the idea to tear around with *his* old man on back of this two-wheeled heap? You never know with Dad; in some ways, he's really flaky.

We roll up to the bowling alley, walk past the alleys and into the rest room. It must look like a very kinky pervert rendezvous. Thank God, it's early and there's practically nobody there; we have the place to ourselves. First, we make plugs with paper towels and fill all the bowls. This takes almost ten minutes. I don't know what the hell we'll say if the manager comes. I decide right then, if anybody does come, Granddad's doing the explaining.

Well, when we let the water out of those sinks, all ten go down clockwise. We fill them again, give the water a start counterclockwise before we pull the plugs; same thing, reverses and goes down clockwise. Granddad must be wrong about his mathematics and physics. I wonder where he got such an idea anyhow.

We tool back to the house. I let him off at the corner and push Dad's bike into their driveway. Granddad goes in the

front door and I walk around back to see if maybe Grandma's
dead on that soft bed. She isn't there.

I go inside and she's in the living room with Granddad.
He's finishing off a story about how we took a short walk
around the block. Lucky the helmets are out on the bike.
Grandma's looking at me to see what I have to say; she's still
scared. But I'm not saying anything unless Granddad wants
me to.

We sit like that, all separate, everybody waiting for somebody else to do something, or say something. I'm wishing Dad
would come home, it's getting very uncomfortable. Then
Granddad stands up.

"Come on out to the workshop, Billy; there's something I
want to show you there."

Grandma isn't liking this at all, but she isn't getting in
the way either. As I go out, I turn around and shrug my
shoulders, just to show I'm sort of with her; but I'm not.

In the workshop, Granddad picks up one of his little
specialty inventions he always made for us as kids. It's a stick
with notches cut down one side and a small propeller mounted
on the tip. We always called them "twirly sticks" and this one
is new made, a hand-carved propeller mounted with a straight
pin.

"Remember how this works, Billy?"

He hands it to me along with a short, smooth stick. I run
the smooth stick fast up and down along the notches till the
propeller begins spinning. It always mystified us as kids and
I still don't know what makes the propeller spin.

"Do you notice anything about that propeller spinning?"

He leans forward on his cane and stops the propeller
with his finger. I start rubbing the stick back and forth again.
He lets it get going fast, then reaches out and stops it.

"Now, watch carefully. If you notice, it always spins
counterclockwise."

This time he gives the propeller a good start clockwise
with his finger. But as I begin rubbing, the propeller stops,
reverses itself.

"I've been making these 'twirly sticks' for forty years and

I've never been able to make one go the other way. I've tried cutting the notches all angles, different spacing; I've made left-handed ones and right-handed ones; I've tried designing propellers every pitch I can think of, but they always go the same way."

He stops, looks at me and smiles again. He spins the propeller backwards with his finger and we watch as it reverses itself while I rub the stick.

"What's it all about, Grandpa? Why do you think it does that?"

"I don't know, Billy; maybe some scientist could explain it; I can't. What interests me is it's the opposite of the Coriolis effect in our sink. Come on, now I'll show you one more thing."

He leads me into his greenhouse. In there, he's rigged a little hose from his watering system so it runs into a funnel and the funnel is fitted into an old bucket. He has a small plug in the funnel with a string on it. First he turns on water till the funnel is full. Then he puts the tip of the notched stick on the edge of his funnel and begins rubbing back and forth till the water in the funnel is vibrating, quivering on the surface.

"Now, Billy, pull the plug and watch what happens."

I pull and watch the water pour out through his funnel into the bowl while he rubs away on his stick. The water goes down counterclockwise, anti-Coriolis!

"What do you think of that, Billy?"

"What made it go backwards, Grandpa? Vibrations?"

"That's another question for the scientists, Bill. But if they don't even believe water goes down the drain clockwise, how can they know about 'twirly sticks'?"

He leans his head back and laughs. Is that a maniac laugh?

We do the rubbing-pouring business five or ten times and every try it comes out the same. Then Granddad goes over and sits in an old wicker chair he keeps back there in the middle of the greenhouse. It's patched about six ways from the middle. Dad told me once Granddad actually made that chair himself over twenty years ago from switches he'd cut from trees in the Topanga streambed. I sit on a bench where he usually stores his empty flowerpots.

"OK, Billy, one more thing and this is more farfetched than the sink and the stick. But listen carefully."

He looks at me as if he's afraid I won't believe him; he crosses his legs. His legs are so thin they hang like sticks to the ground so you hardly know they're crossed. I'm ready to believe anything he'll tell me; I'm beginning to think I have a freaky hidden genius for a grandfather and never even guessed it.

"Billy, I got interested in the Coriolis acceleration effect thirty years ago when I was working for Douglas. We were trying to figure some way to build an automatic Coriolis correction into the navigation systems of bombers. It was all very secret, and I worked on it more than a year. Finally, we had to give up. The reason for the Coriolis effect is the earth's spinning, but it spins at different speeds according to how far from the equator you are. Right here in Los Angeles, we're spinning about seven hundred and fifty miles per hour, but in Boston they're only going about six hundred miles an hour; they don't have as far to go every day. The whole thing got so complicated it beat me and I was moved over to work on something else. The pilots would just have to keep making the compensation themselves. You know if you start in Seattle flying to New York City you'll wind up in Brazil if you don't compensate for Coriolis."

He's still peering at me as if he's afraid I won't believe him.

"But, Billy, that Coriolis thing stuck in my mind; I got to be a sink-drain watcher. I never let the water out without watching it go all the way down, always clockwise.

"Then, back in 1953, just before your sister Martha was born, it started going the wrong way. It went the wrong way for three days, just before we had that big earthquake up in Bakersfield. It kept going wrong for six days after that earthquake. I didn't say anything to anybody. What could these two things have to do with each other? It didn't make sense, especially since one thing wasn't supposed to be happening at all, anyway.

"Then, in 1971, we had that bad earthquake in Newhall, about twenty miles from here. I didn't notice anything before; I wasn't especially looking; but water went down the wrong way for five days afterwards. I told Joan this time because her house is even closer to Newhall; she checked and said the water went backwards there, too.

"Since then, both Joan and I've been keeping an eye on it. Two years ago, about this time, her water started going backward and she told me. We checked the sink here; sure enough, wrong way down. Two days later, there was an earthquake in the desert, one we didn't feel here, but it was five point three on the Richter scale."

He's telling me all this in the most calm, matter-of-fact voice. Here he's probably discovered something important and he's playing around with it in his mind.

"Gee, that's terrific, Granddad! Some scientists ought to know about this; maybe they can figure it out."

"I have a better idea, Billy. I know a way we can check it ourselves and maybe have some fun.

"You know your grandma loves California but she's always been scared to death of earthquakes. During that one in Newhall, we were sliding back and forth across the bedroom on our bed and I thought she'd die. Even a sonic boom can get her all worried. Now, with this heart attack of hers, it'd sure help if we could make some kind of earthquake predictor. What do you think?"

"Yeah, great, but how?"

"I think I know, Billy, but I'll need your help."

He holds his hand out in front of him.

"These hands aren't steady as they once were and they're definitely not so strong. Let's you and me make our earthquake predictor together. We'll keep it a secret till we're finished. It'll be a surprise for your grandmother."

"What'll we tell Grandma and Dad? They'll want to know what we're up to."

"We'll tell them it's a secret. We have the right to a little secret. After it's made and if it works, we'll surprise them."

"Yeah, but, Granddad, Grandma's already having fits about you floating toy boats around in the sink. What am I supposed to tell her? What's she going to think?"

"It'll be all right, Billy; I'll tell her we're doing a scientific project. I'll talk to her but there's not much we can really do. You see, Grandma's been convinced I'm crazy for a long time anyhow."

He smiles and shakes his head as if this is the funniest thing in the world.

"Here, Billy, take this pencil and a piece of paper; write down these things to buy. First, a big clear plastic funnel, the largest you can find, at least twice as large as this one here. Then, a fishbowl about ten inches in diameter at the mouth; we'll also need some plastic tubing with an inside diameter of five millimeters; a flashlight battery, a bulb, a door buzzer, and some of that new epoxy kind of glue. We'll also want a small electric pump, the kind they use to pump out goldfish bowls; not an air pump, a water pump. You can get the pump, the bowl and the tubing at a pet shop. Also, get some green Easter-egg dye. I've got an old inner tube here in the workshop and that's all I think we'll need."

He reaches into his back pocket and pulls out a wallet. He gives me a ten-dollar bill, then another five.

"If that's not enough, Billy, just let me know."

I go over what I've written down with him. It's such a weird assortment I'd hate like hell explaining to Grandma or even Dad what it is I'm off buying.

In the house, Grandma comes scuffling out from the back bedroom. Grandpa gives her a big hug and kiss. She's scared all right. She's giving me the high sign to follow her back into the bedroom. I wink at Granddad and go on back with her.

"What is it, Billy? Why's he acting so crazy? Did you see him kiss me, right there in front of you? He's never done anything like that before."

"Don't worry, Grandma; he's fine. He had a reason for all the business with the sink and the boats. He's making a surprise for you and I'm helping him. Don't you worry, he's not crazy."

"Jesus, Mary and Joseph! You're just as simple as your father and that psychiatrist. What's he doing, building me a toy boat? I wouldn't be surprised; I wouldn't be surprised at anything he'd do. If he's not crazy, then I must be; and if I'm not yet, then I will be soon enough. I can't stand it!"

Even if I tell her, it won't make any difference. I get on the bike and roll to Culver Center. I park behind a pet shop and in fifteen minutes I've got everything except the water pump. Nobody knows where I can even buy one.

When I get home, Granddad's in the workshop; he has something taken apart on his workbench. It's an old electric razor. I show him the stuff I bought and tell him about the pump.

"That's OK, Billy, I was afraid of that. We can make a small pump from this old motor here."

He points to the motor on the bench. How in hell can he make a pump from an electric-razor motor?

"You'll have to do most of the work, Billy. But you'll see, we'll have a dandy little pump in a jiffy."

We work all afternoon. He has me cut out tiny bellows from an inner tube; we glue these together with epoxy glue and glue this to some tubing. He shows me how to tie the bellows into the motor and, sure enough, when it's hooked into a tube going to water, it pumps like crazy.

Next, we drill a small hole about halfway up the side of our funnel. Here we epoxy a piece of the inner tube on the inside of the funnel as a flap valve. Long as the water flows one way, the flap doesn't open, but if it reverses, the flap lifts and water gets under.

Then we build a small T-junction with tubing where the water can come in. If water comes into the T, it completes the circuit through wires leading off to batteries. This sets off both a buzzer and a light.

We build a small box for the pump and he paints it black. Then we put the funnel in the mouth of the goldfish bowl. One end of the plastic tubing hangs over the funnel on a wired hook made from a coat hanger; the other goes through the pump, then back into the bowl. We fill our goldfish bowl with Easter-egg-green water. The water gets pumped up and flows into the funnel so there's a continuous draining of the funnel with Coriolis whirlpool effect. Granddad rigs a waterproof light inside the fishbowl so it stays lit all the time.

It works perfectly. The water's continually splashing in on top, spinning round, draining into the bowl, then being pumped up again. It's absolutely hypnotic, like watching a washing machine or one of those volcanic lamps. It's so beautiful it doesn't matter if it predicts earthquakes or not. We'll probably never know if it does, anyway.

In the meantime, Dad's come home and Grandma's all over him. Dad talks to me and I tell him how we've been building an invention. I tell him it's a surprise for Grandma. Dad's worried about how she's taking it more than anything. I tell him we'll be finished before bedtime and it'll be OK. He says Marty's really beginning to look pregnant and I should go over and visit. It's weird thinking of Marty being pregnant, makes me feel old, makes her like more than a sister.

Dinner's a drag, with Grandma all in a dither. Dad's either quiet or trying to keep conversation going. Granddad and I are itching to get back out working.

It's about eight when we're finished. The paint on the boxes is still a bit sticky. I put the whole machine in a cardboard box and carry it into the living room. Granddad comes along behind me smiling his head off. It's been one terrific day working with him.

Dad and Grandma are watching *Little House on the Prairie;* probably only Grandma's watching, Dad's keeping her company. I put our box on the floor beside the coffee table and hunt for an outlet. We set it up and I clap my hands.

"Folks, we are now going to have a demonstration of the greatest invention in our century, the one and only Earthquake Predictor. We are lucky tonight having with us the inventor himself, Herr Doktor John Tremont."

Granddad sits on the couch smiling. I can tell Grandma's nose is out of joint about a dirty cardboard box in the living room.

"Jacky, I'm telling you, those two are almost as simple as you are. What have you got in that box anyway, Billy? I won't have any pets around my house; they only make a mess and I'm the one who does all the wiping up."

"Don't worry, Mom. They said it was an invention; it's not a pet. Tell me, Tom Swift, what's the chance this thing will blow up on us?"

"It's safe, Johnny. Bess, I mean Bette, you know how you've always been worried about earthquakes? Well, we've solved the problem. This here invention tells when there's going to be an earthquake; it's an earthquake predictor. So long as it keeps running without giving any signals, you don't have a worry in the world. If there's going to be an earthquake, it starts a buzzer buzzing and a light comes on. You've got a couple days to get under a bed or wherever you think it's safe."

Granddad stands carefully and walks over to kiss Grandma again. She's looking past him at me while he's kissing her and I'm adjusting the predictor. I put the pump under the couch so it's out of sight. The rest of it we've worked on so it looks professional. I'm ready to plug in. Granddad throws out his arms like a symphony orchestra conductor.

"Hold your hats, ladies and gents, here she goes!"

He points at me and I plug in. The light comes on, the motor starts and she's pumping, pouring and spinning away, just like downtown. Grandma and Dad stare. Granddad's explaining.

"See, it keeps going like that. If there's going to be an earthquake, the water spins the other way and sets off our warning system. Now what do you think of that?"

I can't keep my mouth shut.

"It's an absolutely incredible invention and a work of art, that's what I think. It's a work of genius!"

Grandma's pushing her finger into her cheek; she's giggling, but looking worried.

"You two are out of your minds; it's in the blood. Nobody with any sense would ever make up a crazy contraption like that."

Dad's interested in how it's supposed to work. He's leaning over and Granddad's explaining the whole business about Coriolis and twirly sticks. I turn off the TV. The predictor spins along; it's like having a tiny fountain or waterfall on your coffee table. It's worth having a thing like this inside any house, earthquakes or not. I could sell this just to potheads. Grandma's still bug-eyed and beetle-assed.

"Billy, I don't know about earthquakes, but I'll tell you one thing; you can't keep that machine on the coffee table here in the living room. Just the bubbling would drive me crazy; it's like something from Buck Rogers. Jack, maybe you can put it up out in the greenhouse, then just tell me if it starts buzzing."

So that's the end of it. Granddad looks at me and smiles. I don't think any of us could expect her to take it any other way. To be honest, I'm sort of glad. I move the predictor into the back bedroom with me and put it on the chest beside my bed. I go to sleep that night watching it. I slowly close my eyes and pretend I'm listening to a waterfall. I'd sure be surprised if the damned thing started buzzing in the middle of the night.

22

I'm glad when Friday comes so I can take Mom to see Delibro. After the earthquake predictor, Mom's convinced Dad's dangerously insane.

She dolls herself up and, except for stops to get her breath, you'd never guess her age or know she's been so sick.

Delibro told me he only wants to explore her relationship with Dad; I imagine he's feeling something.

In the waiting room, Mom's wary as a fox. Her eyes comb everything; a special sniff for the Japanese secretary.

Delibro comes out and goes into his loving-son act again. Mom's flattered; I hadn't noticed before but, for a short type, he's a good-looking guy. Maybe he really isn't and he's only pulled some hypnotic job on us.

Mom drives right into the heart of things.

"Did you really call my husband a genius, or is Jacky making that up? You never know."

Talk about frontal attack, she's come on with machine guns and howitzers blazing. I jump in.

"Mother's concerned because yesterday Dad made an invention he's calling an earthquake predictor. Maybe he'll tell you about it when he comes."

There's no way to signal. Mother's cornered us so we're both covered by her field of fire. I hope I've blunted her first thrust but it's not that easy.

"Can you imagine, he has green water running through a funnel into a lit goldfish bowl and he insists it's going to predict earthquakes. Scientists all over the world with millions of dollars haven't been able to manage this, but he thinks he's done it with ten dollars' worth of dime-store junk. Call that genius if you want, but I call it plain crazy."

Well, it's out. Let's see Delibro earn his money.

"That's very interesting, Mrs. Tremont. Would you come in and tell just how this happened? I'm sure it's been an awful strain on your nerves, especially now when you must be so concerned with your heart."

He's smiling like a Fifth Avenue apartment-house doorman. He almost puts his arm around her, but without touching, and leads her into his office.

He's good all right; how the hell did he know about Mom's nerves? I didn't tell him, and Mom's been talking about her nerves since I was six months old.

I was twelve before I realized nerves weren't something like fingers, separate, that you could wiggle. I was sure Mom had a special pair dangling on her somewhere, hidden.

Delibro manages to squeeze off a quick blink at me to stay in the waiting room. I settle down with a book I brought along; one of those Rex Stout–Nero Wolfe things.

An hour later they come out. Mom's still blabbing away as if she'd never stopped. She probably didn't. Delibro doesn't look quite so debonaire; a bit shopworn, or maybe the hypnotic trance is worn off. He's flashing signals madly. He wants me to stay on but there's no way I can get loose without ruining the whole thing. He's trying to carry on his sign-language conversation under Mom's vigilance but it's hopeless.

I steer Mom outside. In the elevator, she looks around to make sure it isn't bugged, then leans against me and giggles.

"You know, Jacky"—giggle, giggle—"I think he's crazy, too. He was asking the most personal questions; questions nobody's ever asked me, questions about our sex life even. What in heaven's name has that got to do with Daddy being crazy? I'll tell you, if he wants to talk about your father and sex, he doesn't know the half! When I first told Fanny Hogan the things we were doing, she said I ought to notify the police and leave him, that he's perverted and it comes from all the so-called Indian blood. I told the priest in confession and he said he'd pray for me. Fat lot of good that did; when your father gets excited, police, priest, prayers or nothing is going to stop him."

I keep my mouth shut. I'm waiting till I talk with Delibro. I smile, nod my head and act as if she's talking about the color of her new shoes.

"This one's just another hippy, too, Jacky. Did you see that mustache? No sensible woman would ever have anything to do with a man in a mustache like that; he looks like a walrus. I'll bet he isn't even married."

Her walrus image, or maybe some spring-off from his not being married, or maybe only nervousness, starts her giggling again. I don't remember Mom giggling much before; it's the dirtiest, most intimate damned giggle I've ever heard. But I keep cool, hustle her into the car and home.

After I get her settled, I scoot around the corner to a pay phone and call Delibro. I get right through and he asks if I can come to his office. I tell him that'd be hard right now but I can come later. We make an appointment for five. I'll just say I'm going painting; Mother has this marked off as one of the nutty things I do. But Delibro can't wait; he has to get it off his chest.

"Mr. Tremont, has your mother always been like this? Has she always been so defensive?"

"Long as I've known her she's been that way, Doctor."

There's a pause. I can tell he's not happy talking over a phone; he'd like to read my face.

"She's certainly a suspicious woman; she's suspicious of me, she's suspicious of your father, of you, of your sister. There doesn't seem to be anyone she trusts; she's completely alone, a deeply frightened woman."

I don't have to say anything, it keeps coming.

"Do you know she's convinced your father is trying to hurt or even kill her, Mr. Tremont?"

"Yes, I know. These days it's one of her main themes. It makes it hard for my father. She'll also tell him he's crazy straight to his face and she's totally intolerant of his dream fantasies."

I want to say more but I'm not sure myself what's happening. Dad changes so fast, revealing new facets, I'm not sure from one moment to the next who, what or where he is. We decide I'll see Delibro after his last patient so we won't be rushed. We could be in for an all-night session.

I buy myself a beer at the liquor store next to the phone booth. I lean against the booth and drink it slowly.

At home, Mom's worried about where I've been. I tell her I went out and had a beer in a bar. I know this will shock the bejesus out of her, and I don't know why I do those things. She comes close and smells my breath.

"You *do* smell of beer! Did you really go in a bar? What would Veronica think of that? We have beer right here in the refrigerator; it's a waste of money. You don't have to drink in secret."

"Mom, I'm a grown man. If I want to stop in a bar for a glass of beer and relax a few minutes, it's my business. You've got a nice cozy bar around the corner, you ought to try it."

I completely fooled her. I chummed her with the bar and the beer so she forgets about my going off alone. Handily, just then, Dad comes out in his jogging costume.

"Hello, all you beautiful people! It's a lovely day; let's go down to the ocean."

He jogs in a set of small circles between us around the living room. He loosens his shoulders like a boxer coming into the ring.

"Maybe I can do a little jogging along the bike path. We

ought to take advantage of Johnny while he's still here, Bette."

He tries a few high knees, which means he lifts his feet about as far off the floor as most people do when they're walking. He's wearing his light blue Adidas shoes with the hole in the toe. He's *got* to know he's getting Mom's goat, but it could be he's having such a good time he doesn't notice. I look over at Mom.

"Not me! I wouldn't be seen in public with the two of you wearing those simple beards and him in that crazy costume. Why don't you take him to his psychiatrist in this costume one time, Jacky; then he'd know what it's all about."

I'm not responding. I'm learning, but slowly. Dad's pretending not to notice, too; he's still jogging his tight little circles, concentrating, his arms bent and held close to his sides.

"Sounds fine to me, Dad. It's a beautiful day, seems shameful to waste it indoors; let's go down to Venice. Mom, you're sure you don't want to come?"

She stares at me, sniffs.

"You two'd drive anybody into an insane asylum.

"Why don't you take him back to Paris with you? You can both live under one of those bridges with all the other bums and hippies. You two go, I'm sick of looking at you."

I back the car out and drive slowly toward Venice. It's one of those clear California days. On top of the Palms hill we can see the mountains in Topanga Canyon. I try picking out our forty acres by the patterns of firebreaks. I check my watch and it's only a little after two.

"Dad, how'd you like to drive up into Topanga and visit our forty acres? Billy's been camping there on and off with a friend but I haven't been up at all myself."

"Sounds like a good idea to me, Johnny. I can jog along the fire trail. Heavens, I haven't been in Topanga for over ten years. I always wanted to build a little cabin up there, sort of a hideout."

I cut over, switch onto the Santa Monica Freeway, then cruise along the Pacific Coast Highway. There are mobs at the beach, there isn't even a beach fog or mist. We're through the crowds when we pass Sunset; by the time we get to the Topanga turnoff, there's practically no traffic.

Soon as we get a mile into the canyon, things change. It's like a different country. It's drier, the air is lighter, it's warmer and there are new smells, sagebrush, chaparral, raw dirt and rock exposed to hot sun.

The road is steep and twisting, boulders hanging over one side, deep ravines on the other. I take it slowly around curves not to scare Dad, but he's hanging out his window like a kid. He drags one hand in the wind, gliding it up and down with the pressure of the wind, tilting it like a wing. He has his eyes pressed shut.

We drive through the Topanga community and turn up toward the Topanga school. Our property is on a ridge road heading out from behind the school.

It's about a mile and a quarter in. As we go up, the ocean becomes visible on one side and an expanse of the San Fernando Valley on the other. Between, and close around, are views up and down various small canyons leading into the main one. It's incredibly clear; even the Valley isn't too smudged.

"Boy, John, I'd forgotten how beautiful it is up on this hill. You ought to build yourself a house here, raise avocados and oranges."

He's leaning so far out the window now I'm afraid he'll fall out. He's up on his knees on the seat. I check the lock.

On top, it's a three-hundred-and-sixty-degree view.

I park the car. We climb slowly up onto the brow of our hill, where we find Billy's tent. I reach in and pull out blankets for us to sit on.

We settle and let our eyes drift off into the air. There's a slight mist hanging in the bottom of our canyon and the sun's glittering hard bright on the ocean in the distance. We can see the entire sweep of the bay all the way to Redondo Beach.

I wonder to myself why I don't live up here. I've never seen anyplace more beautiful. We could watch Marty's new baby grow. I probably could put in fruit trees and make a fair living. Jacky would go to school just down the hill, a real old-fashioned walk-to school and we know it's a good one.

I've already found out there are things here to paint. I've lived away long enough now I begin to see it. I could most likely paint here happily for years: the canyons, the beaches, maybe even the insides of those garages. When I get into painting something, it keeps expanding.

Dad might be right. Perhaps I am hiding in Paris to stay away from competition.

It sounds so logical, up here on the mountain surrounded by nature, but something shrivels inside me when I consider actually doing it, coming back.

Part, I know, is too many people looking over my shoulder. It's hard to believe in my own inside personal life when I'm forced to see myself as just another subject-object in the great outside delusion, always comparing and being compared. The closest thing to reality becomes a muddled consensus statistic.

Slowly it dawns on me I'm having a covert conversation with Dad. Without saying anything, I'm trying to explain why I live away, why I can't come back and live here. We've been sitting quiet for almost fifteen minutes. I've been meandering mentally, but somehow he's been there with me, inside me.

Dad's staring out, in some kind of meditation, nodding his head slightly once in a while.

"Yep. You could sink a well right over there and I'll bet dollars to doughnuts you'd hit water within five hundred feet. You could grow anything up here with water and all that sun."

He looks at me and smiles.

"But I suspect you and Vron are happier in Gay Paree."

Before I think, I give him a good punch on the arm so he almost falls over. He ducks, laughing, giggling, and catches himself with his hand. I've *never* touched my father like that, the kind of punch you give a man when you're feeling close. And he's laughing, no hiding, no hand over mouth; laughing out, a horse laughing at the sun.

We sit up there for half an hour. Then Dad starts jogging around the edge of the hump, windmilling his arms. He's beginning to lift his feet into something of a jog and not so much a shuffle.

At four o'clock we start down. We're facing into the ocean all the way and the sun's on our right. I feel like a mewing hawk slowly soaring to earth after a trip to the clouds.

I leave Dad at the door and let him handle the brunt of explaining. He says he'd tell Mom I'm going over to Marty's. He's turning into a splendid liar. Maybe that's what psychiatric therapy can do, give you the freedom to lie happily; how else can you fool yourself? I arrive at Delibro's just before five o'clock.

He wants to know my feelings toward Mom. I try telling him. I say it's hard to know what you actually feel and what you've made yourself feel to protect yourself. Somehow, I begin to talk about Joan.

"My sister and I are very close, Doctor. From as far back as I can remember it's been this way, an intense closeness. I'm quite sure I've modeled women on my sister, first in a feeling of protection to her, which has never really stopped, then a tremendous admiration.

"In a certain way, I think we blocked Mom out of our lives. Probably we didn't, couldn't, but that's the way it seemed."

I stop.

"Please go on. This is exactly the kind of thing I need to know. Your mother is a sensitive, intelligent woman. She must have felt this and resented it; this could explain much of her defensiveness, resistance to love."

"Now she's so ill, I feel guilty. I can't love her the way she wants to be loved. I have deep feelings she's obliterated Dad to her advantage. Probably, my fear is what keeps me away from her.

"Dad's become such a shadow in Mom's glaring light, I'd lost all feeling for him, too. It's as if he's been dead for over thirty years. In some ways he became invisible.

"It's only when we lived together while Mom was in the hospital, we got to know each other as adults. It's another whole resentment. For her own reasons, I feel Mom kept us apart."

"Seriously, Mr. Tremont, you must realize she didn't do

this alone. There's something in your father and in yourself which allowed it to happen. After all, your mother is only another human being, perhaps more scared, more motivated to dominate, than most; probably with a very weak ego; but what's happened to your father is exceptional."

"Maybe, but Dad retreated into his dreamworld, I retreated to Paris and Joan married a man Mom could never dent, a human barrier. Then again maybe I'm only rationalizing."

There's a long silence. I've committed the unforgivable error, doing the analyzing. I'm sure he's convinced I've definitely reverted to type, the half-baked educational psychologist who's read too many novels and do-it-yourself psychology books. He may be right but I *am* trying to tell him how I see it. He catches me with the next one.

"Has your mother ever threatened or tried suicide?"

This is hard to answer.

"She's been threatening and hinting at it all her life, Doctor. Her favorite expression is 'Nobody cares if I live or die'; still, overall, I wouldn't say she's suicidal. Her self-image doesn't include it."

He looks at me. It's not a stare; more an expectant, waiting look. It can be damned uncomfortable sitting in front of somebody with wide-open, listening eyes. Finally, he looks down at the papers on his desk.

"I'll be perfectly honest with you, Mr. Tremont. Your father is functioning. He's confused concerning his fantasy, but he's making it. I'm more worried about your mother. She's such a deeply unhappy person. As a psychiatrist, a professional, I feel a strong obligation to help her."

I sit, watch him and wonder how he'll react to what I'm going to say.

"Dr. Delibro, this might sound cruel, but I don't think it's worth the effort. I'm not sure you can help Mom in this life, even if you devote full time to it.

"Mom has a way of going on. I'm sure she's never going to commit suicide; the tracks she runs on are too deep, too much a part of her.

"I really wish you'd concentrate on helping Dad come to

terms with himself. I don't want him to reject his fantasy, but at least help him live without these terrible guilt feelings."

"But, Mr. Tremont, let's face it; I can't help your father so long as the original situation persists. I don't think he can resist your mother's pressures."

So here we are at the double bind, or maybe it's a triple bind. It's what I've been skirting around, refusing to look at, knowing the tremendous emotional energies involved.

"Is there any possibility your parents could live separately for a time? If your father had some time in a protected environment to strengthen his ego, it could help."

There it is, face on. I tell him the way I see it, the impossibilities. I explain how I don't want to come here and live, how I can't take either Dad or Mom with me, they're dependent on Perpetual medical care.

"We can't leave Mom alone and she raises hell at Joan's. We've been looking for nursing-in help but it's impossible to please Mother. It's like the old riddle of the chicken, the fox and the grain; there's no place for *Dad*."

We talk around it some more but don't get anywhere. I tell how she's convinced he isn't a real doctor and is probably a hippy. He takes it well. I'm tempted to ask if he's married but resist.

When I get home, everything is very uncomfortable. The tension is definitely building. The idea that Dad and I drove into Topanga and sat on top of the mountain does not help; it verifies our hippy status.

I don't know where Mother gets her ideas but the new one is a lulu. She's now convinced the psychiatrist wants to put Dad in an institution. Of course, she announces this in front of Dad. It *has* to be malicious; she's too smart to do a thing like that by accident. I try laughing it off but she digs deeper and deeper. Now she's pretending this would be the best thing. She goes on about how she can't take care of him herself, with her heart, and nobody else gives a damn.

Then we're into the routine about what a wonderful father Dad's been to all of us and we won't take care of him when he needs it.

I sit and listen, smiling at Dad whenever I get the chance. About three-quarters through, Dad finds a break and goes out to the greenhouse. I know he's off for a quick trip to Cape May. I begin to see how it's been like the alcoholic who takes a sneak to the closet where he has a bottle hidden.

I listen to her. But as I'm listening, I realize this might be the chance to separate them for a while. I plan and wait. It's going to take some careful timing. There's no sense interrupting. I know now she does run down, finally. It's almost like an actor stopping in the middle of a play and peering out over the footlights to see if there really is an audience when there's been no reaction to his best lines.

The secret is to sit absolutely quiet, give off no waves, not even look her in the eye. I concentrate on the little mole she has on the left side of her chin. It grows hairs and she plucks them. She keeps shifting her head to catch me and I know I've got her; sooner or later she'll stop. She does.

"Mother, you're right!"

How's that for an opener?

"You can't stick it any longer here with Dad. There's no sense going for a divorce; you've been married too long, it doesn't make much sense and besides it's against the church."

Let her hang on that one. It's almost as devilish as the lecture in the hospital about despair.

"Mom, why don't you take a little vacation? Don't do anything too strenuous and don't go too far from the hospital, but give yourself a rest. Maybe go to Gilman's Hot Springs, or take a hotel room down at the Miramar in Santa Monica with a nice view over the ocean. You could walk on the Mall in Santa Monica and have a good vacation, a vacation from marriage."

I throw in that last bit; it fits with her soap-opera view of the world. I wait to see how she'll react.

"You must be crazy, Jacky; I can't do anything like that. He'd kill me!"

"Oh, come on, Mom. He'd stay here with me. I know he's worried about you and it'll be the best thing in the world. It'd give him some time to put himself together, too. By the time you come back, he'll be a new man."

I shouldn't've said that. What she wants is the *old* man;

but I leave it. I know she isn't going to go anywhere anyway.

"Jacky, are you trying to break up our marriage, the marriage of your own mother and father? You've definitely been living in Paris too long. I'm not leaving your father for anything!"

"All right, then, Mom; at least take a little rest at Joan's. You've been saying all along you're afraid of Dad, that he's going to kill you or something, so you go there and I'll stay here with him."

I've mousetrapped her. She knows if she doesn't go I'll throw it up to her every time she starts on the Dad being crazy business. I *will*, too. She sits there, quiet; her mind's running so fast her eyes almost turn in circles. She shifts from crossing her legs one way to crossing them the other. I remind her not to cross them. She pushes one finger into the side of her cheek beside her mouth; dimple-making, I used to call it.

"I could never live with that wop. He wouldn't have me in the house anyway. I watched him the last time I tried staying there; why, he treats her like a servant!"

Now's the time to go into my lying routine. I know I can back it up so it's hardly lying, just a-priori declaration.

"I've already talked to Joan, Mom. Mario works till six o'clock every day with the playground. You'd have the boys' room all to yourself, with your own bathroom, your own entrance like a private apartment. You don't even have to eat with them if you don't want to. There are three restaurants and a McDonald's, all within a block. Joan could take you anyplace you want. You could be alone as much as you want. There's even a TV set back there; you wouldn't have to watch any baseball games or anything you didn't like. It'd be a real vacation."

I settle back to watch her wiggle.

"I could never stand that Valley heat and the smog. I'd be dead in a week out there. It's getting to be summer, Jacky; don't forget that."

"You can stay inside when it's hot and they have the whole house air-conditioned. Their car is air-conditioned, too. And remember how nice it is evenings."

"I'd miss having my own garden. You know how the big chief is; nobody can touch *his* garden."

"Think, Mom, you can enjoy a garden and not have to do any weeding or watering, just luxuriate like a queen with a private gardener, a nice Italian gardener."

That was a sneaky one; she likes the idea of Mario, her Italian gardener. She hems and haws, looking for an opening, but finally gives in. I tell her I'll drive her out tomorrow.

I call Joan to set things up. She agrees it'll take some doing, but is enthusiastic. I'm hanging up the phone when Dad comes back from his plants in the greenhouse or Cape May; who knows.

Mother really *is* afraid of what Dad will say. I tell him Mom needs a complete rest and is going to visit Joan's for a while. He nods his head, listening. His beard looks as if he's had it all his life. It's amazing how it gives so much life to his eyes. I'd never noticed how blue, cerulean blue, they are. I wonder how different *I'd* be if he'd had that beard all his life; little things like that make a difference. I tell Dad I'll stay here with him to cook and take care of things. He nods, looks at me, then over at Mother. She's tensed there in her chair, ready to spring or duck.

"That'll be just fine. Don't you worry about us, Bette; we'll be OK. Johnny's a fine cook and housekeeper; I'll help him and boss him around some. I'm getting stronger all the time; I might even be a boss one of these days, finish off right. You just rest up, get your heart in good shape and try not to worry about things. It'll all come out fine."

He's smiling and nodding. Mom's beginning to smell the rat but is too far into it now. Maybe she'd expected Dad to go through the ceiling, screaming and hollering.

We sit and watch Lawrence Welk again. In the middle, Dad gets up, pulls Mom from her chair and insists she waltz with him to the music. She's giving me horror and danger signals over his shoulders. I sit back and smile. He's staggering a little on the long steps but is keeping good time. Mom gets up on her toes and I can't help wondering again what the foot-dragging and shuffling is all about. I know Dad couldn't've thought up a better move to get Mother packing.

Monday morning I drive Mom out there. Billy's with Dad. Joan has fixed up the back bedroom so it's like a private motel room. She's barricaded the door to the rest of the house and the key is on the inside. She winks at me while she shows Mother how nobody can get in to bother her at all. She has direct access to the garden, with a comfortable chair there and a redwood table. She can come into the main room where the color TV is, if she wants. It couldn't be better.

Joan gives me the high sign and I leave quietly. I drive back over Topanga. It's the long way home but I want to go once more for those smells and to see the clear sky. I come along the coast down to Venice, then up Palms to Dad.

He's fine. He looks behind me as if to check that Mom really isn't there. He and Billy have built a simple sundial out by the birdbath in the garden. They've used an old burning set and burned out a message on a piece of driftwood. It says:

BE LIKE THE BEES AND FLOWERS
COUNT ONLY THE SUNNY HOURS

Billy's excited showing how it works. He's even more convinced Dad's a genius. I'd never have guessed you could make a sundial as easily as they did. It's only a plank of wood stuck in the ground at an angle with a length of dowling set at another angle. The hours are burned into the plank in Roman numerals.

We make ourselves toasted cheese sandwiches and drink two beers each, wiping out a six-pack as we lie out there on the patio watching the sun move across that sundial. I explain how great Joan has things fixed up, how Mother will be comfortable and have a good chance to get a rest. Dad asks if we know what a gnomon is. We both look blank. He gets up, walks over, points to the dowling stick on the sundial and smiles back at us.

Four o'clock, Dad has another appointment with Delibro. Billy wants to sleep up on the mountain again and borrows my bike. After Dad's finished with Delibro, we'll go down to Venice and I'll paint.

While he's with the doctor, I drive over to Aaron Brothers and buy three new canvases, some replacement colors and two sable brushes. Dad's in the waiting room when I get back. He says everything went fine. It's almost all beginning to get routine; it doesn't exactly hurt my feelings.

As we come out of Delibro's office, Dad takes a paper from his wallet; he looks at it, then at me.

"John, that nice one-green-eyed nigger woman, who visited me in the hospital, the one who gave me the African violets, wrote down her phone number here and said if I phoned maybe you could take me to see her greenhouse."

He peers up at me, innocence and timidity combined. God, he's always got some new surprise up his sleeve.

"OK, Dad, I can call her at the phone booth here or we can call after we get home from painting."

"Call now, Johnny, before I forget again. I keep thinking about it, then forgetting. I promised her."

I stop at a phone in the garage, dial the number he gave me. I'm pretty sure she'll be on duty or not home. Maybe I'm only hoping that. Somebody answers.

"Hello, is this Alicia?"

"That's right. Is this you, Jack? How's your daddy doing?"

Holy cow, she recognized my voice.

"He's fine, Alicia. He asked me to call you. He's wonderful; you wouldn't believe how strong and happy he is."

"I sure would like to see him and show him my plants. I'd like to see you, too, Jack."

It hangs there, a perfectly natural thing to say, it numbs me for two counts.

"When's a good time, Alicia? And where do you live?"

"I'm on evenings, so anytime in the mornings after ten o'clock or so; how about tomorrow?"

Dad's leaning toward me trying to hear. I hand him the receiver so I can get out a pen and pencil; also pull myself together. Hearing her voice, the strength and timbre of it has unnerved me.

Dad's listening, nodding his head, smiling, happy to talk with her but not saying much. He sees my pen and paper, hands the phone back. Alicia gives me an address off Cloverfield in Santa Monica. We agree to meet her there at ten.

I hang up and we go on to the car as if we made dates together every day.

I have painting clothes and paints in the trunk, so I change at the parking lot. We lock up and walk along the boardwalk.

I've made arrangements with Tony and Shelly to paint their place. I'll do it looking out across the tables spread with fruit and vegetables, then out the window onto the beach with a sky in sunset colors.

I set up the easel and get right into the drawing. Tony finds a chair for Dad; Dad's watching, enjoying the people, the painting, the fruit, the sunset. I'm not paying too much attention.

A little later, I look up and Dad's gone! I stand and scan the store. Tony's over in the herb section.

"Have you seen Dad, Tony?"

"Yeah, he went with Suzanne. Don't worry. Dad's OK."

I stand there with brush in hand. I'm tempted to dash off after him. I decide to finish the underpainting first. Suzanne will take care. Half an hour later, he's still not back. I wash the brushes in turp.

I head for Suzanne's; it's after six. Venice is beautiful but it's tough too; there are enough mean guys, drunks and addicts so you're never safe, especially an old man like Dad.

I walk down to Suzanne's. Pap's leaning out a window. He's dressed in his favorite drag costume, a purple spangled evening dress with a ragged boa draped across his neck. It looks wild with his sandy white Ho Chi Minh beard. He nods and beckons for me to come up.

I go around back and up the fire-escape stairs; it's the only way in except through the restaurant. The room reeks of pot, and there's Dad spread out on three silk pillows.

Suzanne folds down on the pillow beside him and rubs her face against his beard.

"Don't you worry about Dad here, Johnny. He's just fine. He must be one of the nicest men in the whole world."

What the hell do I do? Christ, I'm jumpy about pot myself and here's my father, ex-hippy hater, spaced out and smiling up at me. I step into the room and sink into a lotus position; all that Yoga comes in handy once in a while.

"How're you doing, Dad?"

"Just fine, Johnny. Do you think smoking them little joints will get me started smoking cigarettes again? You know, for years I was a regular smokestack; I'd hate to get started again."

"I don't think so; it's not the same as smoking cigarettes; how are you feeling?"

"They ought to give this to all old folks, Johnny. It's a shame wasting it on young people. I've been telling them here how they're squandering their lives away sitting inside smoking, doing nothing, with the whole world out there. But it certainly is nice for an old geezer like me."

He reaches for the roach from Pap, takes a drag and lets it out slowly.

"Yep, Johnny, this marijuana takes away those scared feelings. Also, I'm noticing things I've never seen before. Do you know there's a blue shimmering line between sunny places and shadowy places?"

I look at Suzanne. She takes the joint from Dad and passes it back to Pap. She gives Dad a kiss on the cheek, comes over, squats bare-flat-footed beside me in her free-flowing, practically transparent skirt.

"Don't worry, Johnny, he's OK. You go back to your painting and don't worry; he's having a fine time."

What the hell. There's no sense making a scene. He can't hurt himself. I go back to The Fruits and Nuts.

About seven o'clock, here comes Dad, feeling groovy. He waves at me from the front door, goes over, sits on his chair and stares at the sun setting; my father, the human sundial. I finish most of the impasto by seven-thirty and pack the box. We start home.

On the way, we decide we'll go to a ball game. The Dodgers are playing the Phillies in Chavez Ravine. We just have time to make it if we go directly; I cut straight onto the Santa Monica Freeway. We'll have hot dogs at the park for dinner.

I drive Dad to the ticket booth and park the car. When I get back, he's already bought tickets, good ones on the third-base line. I still can't get accustomed to Dad; he'd never have bought tickets on his own like that, not in the last thirty years, anyway.

Between the second and third innings, I buy us two hot dogs each and a couple beers. Dad's rooting for both teams simultaneously. Actually, he's rooting for whichever team's at bat. He stands, cheers and shakes his fist whenever there's a hit. He's having a good time hollering with nobody to say no; he's sure got plenty of hollering time to make up.

The Dodgers win on a homer by Steve Garvey and Dad decides he'll be a Dodger fan after all.

I suggest he might enjoy coming down with Mario; it's more fun going with somebody who really knows the game, and Mario's an ex-ballplayer.

"That's right, Johnny. You know, I've never gotten to know Mario the way I'd like to. He comes with Joan and sits there or sleeps or goes in the back room. It's hard for him not to let Mother get his goat."

We're just getting ready for bed when the phone rings. My first thought is it's Joan; Mom's had a heart attack and died while we were out carousing around. But it's Mother. She's wondering where we've been. I tell her we went to the ball game.

"Well, I've been trying to call since one o'clock this afternoon. You couldn't have been at the ball park all day. Let me talk to your father."

I'm about to tell her he's asleep, but then realize she's probably been phoning every half hour, and there's no time for him to have gotten asleep.

Dad comes up beside me. I put my hand over the mouthpiece, tell him it's Mom. He takes the receiver from me with a smile like a twenty-year executive taking the phone from his secretary. I figure here we go, the grounds for divorce are about to be ground, or maybe that's grounded. This is the ultimate test; is he going to collapse under pressure again?

D A D

Dad sits back in his platform rocker holding the phone in his usual uncomfortable way, not touching the receiver to the side of his head, holding it away like a snake. He's still not exactly an international executive, not to worry. I sit in the other chair.

"Yep, we went to the ball game, Bette. The Dodgers won with a home run in the ninth inning. We had hot dogs and beer, too."

Pause. Dad does everything but look into the phone.

"No. We ate at a pizza place around the corner here. We should go there ourselves, it's an easy walk."

Pause.

"We had a big salad with the pizza so don't worry about it."

He gives me a wink. I know we're in. I go into the back bedroom to get undressed. I'm beat. It's been a long day. Then I hear Dad calling me.

"Mother wants to talk with you, John."

He's holding the phone at arm's length.

"Hello, Mother?"

"Jacky?"

She goes into her stage whisper.

"You've got to get me out of here. That Mario's driving me crazy!"

"What do you mean, Mom; wasn't he officiating today?"

"Well, he came home for dinner."

"But, Mom, you don't have to eat with him. Remember, we talked about that. You just get yourself all upset."

"If that wop thinks he can keep me from eating with my own daughter and my grandchildren, then he has another think coming. I'll tell you that!"

Damn, here we go! I listen while she goes on with every imagined slight she can think of, including that Mario went to the bathroom after dinner before she did. I guess he's supposed to read the state of her bladder. She even has her *own* bathroom! I listen. I try not to really listen, just wait till she's finished. Dad's putting on his pajamas. He comes out and goes into the bathroom. I hear him brushing his teeth. At last there's a pause.

"What is it you want, Mom? You can't live with Mario, you can't live with Dad. Who can you live with? Just tell me and we'll try to set it up."

It's not a very nice thing to say; I know. But it's late, I'm tired and it's all so unreasonable. There's a long empty pause and she hangs up. I'm not really hurt, more sort of relieved. I go back to see how Dad's doing. He's in bed. He looks at me through the dark without his glasses.

"Don't worry, John; she'll get over it. She's always like this when she's upset."

"Good night, Dad, sleep well."

I'm just getting ready for bed when the phone rings again. I don't want to answer it, but I do. It's Joan.

"Hello, you miserable, lousy, bearded, hippy SOB. How are things?"

"I assume that's a direct quote."

"Well, it's more or less an expurgated version. My virginal ears and sensibilities won't let me repeat it verbatim. What in heaven's name did you say? She's in the back room stomping around with the door locked."

"Not much, Joan; all I did was ask her where she wants to live. This was after she charged through Mario as the black hole of the universe."

"Jack, I'm at my wit's end. It's as if she wants everything to stop, everyone to be miserable, just because she is. I don't know what we can do and I don't know how much longer I can stand it."

"If it'll make you feel better, Joan, you should know Dad had a great time today. You wouldn't believe the kinds of things we did. I'm beginning to think we have to get him away from Mom somehow, anyhow."

"Yeah, and how; you tell me. Do we kill her? What can we do so she'll be satisfied? I'm not kidding; I'm at the end of my rope. You should've been with her today. If you think she lit into Mario, you should've heard her about you and Dad. She has you two pegged as Black Bart the pirate and his first mate.

"Sometimes I almost had to laugh, that is when I didn't

feel like giving her a good swift kick. And if she'd just go through it once, but it's over and over, as if she's practicing for a play and is trying to get her lines right."

"I found Dad spread out on pillows surrounded by a bevy of lovely girls smoking pot down in Venice this afternoon. Also, I made a date for him with a beautiful black girl tomorrow morning."

"Stop it, Johnny! Stop this nonsense. That's the kind of stuff sets her off."

She giggles. Should I leave it at that? I *did* tell her. I can always claim I told her. But I can't leave it.

"I'm not kidding, Joan. I was painting down on the beach front, he wandered off and that's where I found him. He says all old people should smoke pot and it's too good to waste on kids. The black girl's the one who came and gave him the African violets; we're going to go see her greenhouse."

"You're making that up, Jack. No, you're *not;* not even a nut like you could make up a thing like that. Mother's right; you two can't be trusted."

Then she breaks out laughing and the laughing over the phone sounds as if it might turn into crying. I hadn't realized how close to hysteria she is.

"It's OK, Joan. He won't tell. He lied to her beautifully over the phone this evening. He told her we had pizza and a salad when all we ate was hot dogs and beer at the ball park. He's getting good at it; soon he'll be able to join the Peter Pan brigade with us; he can be Tinker Bell."

We finally decide we'll keep Mother at Joan's long as possible. Joan says she'll push Mario off to a movie and keep him out of the way. If we can only give Dad some time.

"But I'm telling you, Jack, if she insists on running around behind me, redoing everything I do and muttering about dirt and disgrace, I might just kill her myself."

"OK, Joan, you do that. I promise to put up bail, hire the best lawyer and stand behind any alibi."

We laugh privately around that idea for a few minutes, then she hangs up.

. . .

In the morning after breakfast, we drive over to Alicia's. Both of us are trying to act as if this is the most natural thing in the world; after all, we're just going to see a lady about some plants.

The house is set behind a duplex; we go through a gate and walk along a narrow alleyway which opens onto a well-kept garden and a small, low-lying, white, wood-frame house. The paint is cracking and peeling so there's almost as much natural wood showing as there is paint. We go up two steps onto a rickety porch and knock on the door. We still don't look at each other. We're fifteen-year-olds calling on some girls for a movie date, but it's only one girl, and she's one-green-eyed, golden-baked-brown and more than fifteen.

There are white trimmed curtains on the windows and window boxes filled with flowers. I look around, but I don't see any greenhouse. There *is* a birdbath filled with water and a bird feeder beside it. Linnets, blackbirds, pigeons, doves, starlings and sparrows flock around, pecking at the seed in it or on the ground underneath.

The door opens and there she is. She's wearing a blue denim halter and Levi's.

"I was afraid you wouldn't come. Come on right in."

She looks past me at Dad. The room is small but beautiful; light, filled with air and comfortable. She's somehow bridged the gap between hippy natural and decorator design— the room is wonderfully personal.

"Mr. Tremont. Oh my Gawd! You *are* a *sight* for sore eyes!"

While saying this, she walks up to Dad, takes him first by the arms with her powerful slim hands. He smiles into her eyes. Then, impulsively, she cups his bearded cheeks in her hands and gives him a strong kiss on the mouth. Dad doesn't even have time to pucker. This is a real kiss, not quite so real as the kiss we shared that night, but damned close. Dad stands there dazed, still smiling; he shakes his head and leans both hands on his cane.

"Good thing I've got this stick with me or I'm just liable to fall over, Alicia; you take the breath right out of an old man."

"Come on, Mr. Tremont, you're not so old; you're just the

right age, you're a man a woman can have some confidence in, ain't he, Jack?"

I nod my head; Dad looks at me then back to Alicia.

"Then maybe you can start calling me Jack, Alicia. Call him Johnny; that's what I call him. His mother calls him Jacky but I don't think he likes it. Come to think of it, I don't think he likes me calling him Johnny either; try John."

Alicia puts her hands on her hips, looks at both of us appraisingly, lips pursed.

"OK, then you're Jack."

She points to Dad.

"And you're Jack Junior. OK?"

"Sure, OK with me."

She links her arms in ours, pulls us toward her. That halter's loose and when she does this her firm, medium-sized breasts are beautifully visible.

"Come on, you two. I'm going to show you my plants."

She pulls us through the house, the kitchen and out the back door; this door opens directly onto a private jungle. It's almost the same size as Dad's but more lush, more tropical; there are more flowers and deep, overpowering smells.

Dad and I stand there, astounded, entranced. Alicia lets go our arms, takes two steps forward and turns to face us, hands on her hips. The sun filters through ferns and leaves, spraying her with patterns of light and shade. I think of Gauguin, some of the Renoirs, of the great garden paintings by Monet, and know what they were trying for.

"I made it all myself. This used to be nothin' but a broken-down back porch and I built it all up. I got these windows from a house they tore down on Twenty-third Street. I got thirty-five windows for only twenty dollars but I had to carry them all here myself. It's times like that when a woman can almost wish she had a man around the house."

We're still stunned. She's put crushed crystal white rock on the floor. The shelves are set back in tiers for flowers. This place makes Dad's look almost sloppy. There are orchids and cymbidium hanging in wooden holders around. There are exotic flowers, all colors from almost black through burning red, brilliant yellows, incandescent blues. These colors are spotted and striped; the petals long, smooth or twisted and curled like topological dreams.

"Well, how do you like it?"

She still stands there. Dad steps forward slowly, almost as if he might fall. She reaches out and catches him in her arms; Dad puts his arms around her. Neither of them says anything. I'm feeling embarrassed; maybe I should leave. Dad puckers up and gives Alicia a kiss on the lips.

"Alicia, it's the most beautiful place I've ever seen. It's more beautiful than Hawaii even. Now I know why you've got that green eye."

"And what about you, Jack Junior, Paris artist; what do you think?"

"It's almost as beautiful as you, Alicia. It's a perfect world for you to be in. It must be hard leaving every day."

"I call it Paradise; no matter how bad things go out there, I know I can always come in here by myself and be happy."

"You know, Alicia, at my place in Cape May, I built a greenhouse with some old windows, too, but all I grow is early tomatoes to be set out in the spring."

"I didn't know you lived in Cape May, Jack."

Oh boy, here we go. The cat's out of the bag. All this greenhouse business must've gotten him confused. I'm ready to head him off at the pass but Dad shakes his head and chuckles.

"Probably, I never did, Alicia; but I like to dream I do sometimes and I make up all kinds of stories for myself; places like this are great for things like that. I might just be a bit crazy, you know."

"Then I'm crazy too. I come out here and sometimes I'm an African queen and I talk to my flowers; other times I can make myself believe I'm a plant. I drink the sun, soak in moisture and feel myself grow into the earth. I bloom and open."

Holy Lord, these are two of a kind. Alicia's looking deep into Dad's eyes and they're off in another place.

"Would you show me what you have, Alicia? There are plants here I've never seen anywhere. And if I could have some cuttings I'd sure appreciate it. I never seen anybody make things grow the way you have."

And so they're off. Jack Junior is the invisible man again. I follow behind while they talk grafting, leaf mold and rhizomes. I'm not interested enough, so I go back inside and sit in the living room. They won't miss me, they're alone together. I find a stack of *Scientific American*s and work my way through three of them before they come out of the greenhouse. Dad has a soaked burlap sack filled with wrapped roots, stems, leaves and, I guess, seeds, tubers and spores. They're still talking, giggling and laughing.

"Jack Junior, we're sorry to take so long but we hardly got started. This is the first man I've been able to really talk with. Nobody else seems to care enough."

Dad's standing there holding his dripping burlap sack, looking shyly at me, glowing but timid.

"Alicia here knows an awful lot, John. She can make plants so real and live talking about them, I almost see them move, hear them listening."

"Jack Junior, you sure Jack's just an ordinary full-blooded white man. Look at that skin, look at those lips."

Dad giggles now, shifts his sack of plants.

"I'll tell you, Alicia, my wife's been convinced for more than fifty years I'm part nigger; she's also sure I'm crazy so you could be 'right on' there."

Right on? God, I'd better get him out before he takes up bongo drums.

At the door, we both get a big kiss. Alicia whispers in my ear.

"You was sure right that night when you said your daddy was easy to love. I remember the second part too. Why don't you come visit; maybe you can paint me out in my Paradise? I'd make a good model for you."

We say goodbye. I walk weak-kneed out the alleyway and drive somewhat erratically home; but not on the freeway. Dad's all excited about his cuttings, seeds and spores.

Next afternoon, Dad and I are straightening up his workshop. In the process, Dad volunteers to leave his tools to me when he dies.

"But don't hold your breath, Johnny. I intend to work a lot more with those tools during the next few years; nothing big, only some repairs and making toys for my new little great-grandchild."

The phone rings; I can just about hear it out there. I don't know how long it's been ringing so I dash across the lawn and patio, through the side door and into the bedroom. I pick up the receiver, sit on the edge of the bed and try getting my breath.

I wait to hear who it is, figuring it's Mother, but there's no sound, only sniffling and breathing. It probably isn't an obscene phone call so I'm sure it's Mom. I lie back and wait. The voice that comes is weak, choked with sobs.

"I can't take it anymore, Johnny. I give up; I've had it."

It's Joan! I sit up. She's broken into convulsive sobs.

"What is it, Joan? What's the matter?"

There's more quiet sobbing and deep breathing as if she's trying to get her breath.

"Come on, Joan. Tell me what's happened. It can't be that bad."

"She's all yours, Johnny, and I'm *not* kidding. I told her I'd never speak to her again and I mean it. Nobody can even *like* her, let alone love her. I told her that, too."

"If you want, I'll come get her right now. I'll be over in half an hour."

"No, she can stay. I'll cook for her, I'll clean up after her, I'll do whatever it takes to give Dad a chance. I'll do my part, Jack, but I'll be wearing earplugs. I refuse to listen all day long while she tears down everything and everybody I love. And I'll *never* speak to her again so long as I live. I mean it!"

That second "I mean it" is the only thing I have to build on. Since we were kids, Joan's always said "I mean it" just before she's ready to give in. Even her own kids know this now.

"Look, Joan, you've got the script all turned around. These are *my* lines. You're the calm, reasonable one. You're on the wrong page or something; you're ruining the whole play. If you're not careful, they'll take us off prime time."

I wait. She's back to crying again. When she talks, there's almost a giggle built into the sobs.

"Jack, you won't believe what she did. I *still* can't believe it myself."

"Listen, Joan, don't test me out on that. I'll believe she did anything. I'll believe she's excommunicated the Pope, shot the President, turned out the sun, cut off her toes so her feet fit in smaller shoes. I'll believe anything. Come on, tell me, what did she do?"

"I can hardly talk about it, Jack; it's so sad and it makes me so mad.

"I was out back raking leaves and trimming the lawn edges because Mom's been complaining what a mess it is out there. She insists none of us really care about our own home! So I admit we're slobs but to please her, trying to make her happy— I should know better by now—I'm out there working.

"When I come in, I can't find her. I peek in our bedroom and she's there. She's going through *our* family photo albums. There are torn photographs all over the floor. I lean down to pick them up; there are more than thirty pictures, torn, not just torn in half, Jack, torn in pieces!

"Honest, I'm convinced right then she's finally, totally insane!

"She tells me she's going through these old photo albums and tearing up some of the pictures we have of her.

"'That Mario always manages to catch me in the worst poses. I want you to remember me the way I *really* am, not like some monkey, or with my eyes all squinted up, or my mouth open and my tongue showing.'

"She demonstrates all this with her face, putting fingers in her mouth, pulling her ears, crossing her eyes, the way she does when she wants to look funny.

"Jack, I could've killed her right there! I gather up all those pieces of pictures. It's not just pictures of her alone; it's her with the kids when they're babies, or pictures with you or with Dad, or me. Just because she doesn't look like Elizabeth Taylor in every one, she's tearing them up. I take that photo album away; then I really let her have it.

"When I think of the things I said, I'll never be able to talk to her again, even if I wanted to. And I tell you I don't. I mean it; I never want to hear or talk to her again. If she has anything to tell me, she can send the message through you. Right now, every time she comes near, I put my fingers in my ears and walk away."

"Thanks a lot, buddy. This means I get to listen twice as much. How about if I come out there and get her now; it'll cut down on phone calls, maybe keep some of us out of the poor-house and a few of us out of a lunatic asylum."

She's started crying again.

"I feel like such a rat, Jack. How could anybody talk to a seventy-year-old woman the way I did, my own mother? I must be going crazy."

"We're all crazy, kiddo. Somebody's been trying to tell us that for years. And, personally, I think it might be easy to talk to this particular seventy-year-old woman any way you want; it's probably the first sane thing that's happened around her in years. By the way, what's she doing now, whitewashing the ceiling, maybe stripping off her clothes and sterilizing them in the oven? What's the latest?"

"She's locked in her room, the boys' room. Do you think she might hurt herself, Jack? I'm beginning to worry."

" 'Nobody cares whether I live or die!' Right? I think those were the last quoted rates; are you backing out now? I think I can live with it."

"Well, I can't; I'm going back, knock on the door and apologize. A few torn-up photographs aren't all that important; she needs us most now. I sure wish I could put back in my mouth some of the things I said; I was terrible."

"It's the Indian blood coming out in you, Joan; at heart, you're a bloody savage. But seriously, don't give in. I'm with you all the way. I only wish I had the guts to let her have it myself. If I did, I could probably throw away my blood-pressure machine, stop taking medication, give up Yoga; maybe even stop wearing glasses. Who knows? I'm saying, don't do anything you don't want to."

"No, I'm fine now. You don't need to come. I'll be all right. I'm going in to talk with her, or try anyway."

"You're sure?"

"I'm not sure of anything, Johnny; except I can sure be a bitch, sometimes. I hope I remember that. I hope too, I'm dead and rotted before I make myself such a pain in the ass to everybody."

Joan saying "bitch" and "ass" out like that, more than anything else, lets *me* know how bad it must have been.

Joan pulls it off somehow and we keep Mom there three more days. She refuses to go back to the "hippy" psychiatrist, and when he phones her, she hangs up.

But there's no keeping her there any longer. Her position now is it's going to kill her staying where she isn't wanted and isn't loved; she'd rather die in her own home. She's also come up with the idea she's run out of tears and her eyes are drying up. Joan takes her to an oculist because Mom swears she's going blind from dry eyeballs. He gives her drops and tells Joan there's nothing the matter but the drops won't hurt. Now Mother's continually interrupting her monologues to put tears in her eyes.

The next day I do get her. Dad's bedsores are fairly well healed and he doesn't want to sleep in the hospital bed in the side room; so he sleeps in back with Mom. Mom says if he isn't going to leave her alone anyway, they might as well sleep together. I figure the poor guy deserves some comfort.

As much as possible, I want to give them the feeling of being on their own again. I'm sleeping out in the garden bedroom. I've got to work my way out of all this somehow and get home.

During the next week, Mom's definitely on her good behavior, at least when I'm around. Dad is having fun getting himself in shape. He's started doing exercises with Mom in the morning. Even after her heart attacks, Mom has kept on with her sit-ups, flopovers and the other exercises she's been doing the past forty years.

It bugs the hell out of her having Dad horning in, wearing his jogging suit, imitating every move she makes. He can hardly do even two sit-ups and he's still working on his "old-man pushups." He thinks it's the funniest thing in the world how he can't push his chest off the floor.

I make breakfast these mornings during the workout sessions. Dad wants me to join them but I'm afraid this would be just *too* much. The living room from nine to nine-thirty looks like a Vic Tanny's gym for the geriatric. Mom resists Dad's insistence that she come out and jog with him. Now he's not only jogging in the patio, but around the back garden. Mom says if he goes out and jogs in the street she'll leave him.

On the seventh day she's home, Mom pulls me into the back bedroom. She starts crying and tells me she can't go on.

"I've tried so hard, Jacky. I don't want to make any trouble but I know I'll have another heart attack if it keeps on like this."

Dad's driving her crazy and she's afraid being alone with him. She's upset by his crazy songs, the flowers, the exercise, the jogging, the cooking, the miniature golf course, the sundial, even the new bird feeder.

"And now, you've seen him, he's started dancing around the living room to the music on the radio. He's not right in his head, Jacky!"

I've got to admit that when he dances in one of his wild costumes, and the beard, he looks like a satyr straight from a Rubens. Every time it happens, Mom panics. She leans back with her hands across her mouth and peers over them with scared eyes. He thinks she likes it, that she's wowed by his dancing. He reminds me of how some people dance when they're drunk, with an awkward grace they normally don't have. Dad's drunk all right, drunk on life.

Mother insists this is proof, another proof, he's insane.

"No man his age dances around by himself; it isn't natural."

I keep my mouth shut about how she always seemed to admire old Lawrence Welk doing the same thing. I listen to her until she's finished. Her nerves are definitely shattered; I don't know what to say.

"What can we do, Mom? Do you want to live in separate houses? We could probably rent this place and get enough so you could each have a small apartment. I don't know what else to suggest.

"Dad's perfectly fine; he's only enjoying himself, that doesn't mean he's crazy. We have the best expert in the area working on it. Dad's only trying to make the most of the little time he has left."

I should've stopped there.

"Honestly, Mom, sometimes I think you're the one who's acting crazy, making such a big fuss over nothing at all."

This sets her off.

"Me, *crazy*? You're the one with the beard, living in Europe and keeping my grandchildren away from me. I know you love your father more than you love me, and I don't blame you; I was never cut out to be a mother, I've always done everything wrong no matter how hard I try."

She's crying now. I can't get close; she keeps pushing me away.

"Even the grandchildren hate me. They never call or come to see me. And I know why, too. You and Joan talk against me to them behind my back; you poison their minds!"

Even she realizes she's gone over the edge with that one. I wait till I'm sure she's finished.

"Mom, why don't you stay here with me and we'll let Dad go live with Joan? That way Joan can watch and see if there really is something seriously wrong. You might be right; those psychiatrists don't know everything, and you've lived with him a long time. This way you'll get a chance to rest up your heart and you won't have any trouble with Mario. I promise to stay out of your way. I'll be your chief cook and bottle washer."

She stares to see if I'm serious. She's not crying anymore.

"I think I'd rather stay in a hotel."

"That sounds like a good idea, too, Mom. You go live in a hotel and Dad can stay here with me."

She expected me to be upset with that idea.

"No, Jacky, that'd cost a fortune. The kind of place I'd want to stay would cost forty dollars a day, at least."

"But, Mom, that's the way you should spend your money. That's what money's for, to do things you want. You're not going to live forever and you have a right to enjoy yourself. Go, get a nice comfortable room with a view over the ocean. You could have room service and really relax."

"Oh, no, I'm not going to waste the little money we have that way! You never know when you're going to need it, Jacky. I know damned well nobody's ever going to take care of me. Nobody loves me and nobody cares if I live or die, so I'd better have some money to take care of myself."

This little repetition of the old speech does her worlds of good; she begins to be more herself. We gab on some more, me trying to stay out of the familiar mousetraps.

Mom finally agrees to Dad's living with Joan while she stays on at the house. We're just going to sun on the patio and pretend we're on an ocean cruise. She acts as if she's doing me a big favor; some favor! I'll probably need a prefrontal lobotomy and a triple-strength straitjacket at the end of one week. A week or two with Mom in this state could be just what it would take to push me over the line. We artist types are notoriously unstable folk anyway.

I go around the block to a public phone booth and call Joan. I tell her Mom's ready for Dad to live with her and she'll stay with me.

"Are you sure?"

I rough out our conversation. Joan wants to know what Dad thinks about it. I realize I haven't even consulted him. I know he'll enjoy the chance being with Joan, Maryellen and John; talking with Mario. The other kids are away at school or married. Joan still isn't convinced.

"You're positive about this?"

"I think so, Joan. I can't say she's completely happy with the idea, but then she doesn't seem happy with anything. She wouldn't be happy at the Miramar Hotel even if it were free."

There's a long silence.

"Jack, you'll be absolutely insane at the end of three days, four days. I'll come over and find you hanging by a clothesline from that lemon tree out back. Maybe Mom's right, you are crazy."

"Look, just tell me something else; get me off the end of that clothesline."

Joan lowers her voice on the phone.

"Listen carefully. You go out into the back room, pack your clothes quietly, sneak over the fence and hop the next plane to Paris. Never write again and have Vron send a telegram saying you were killed in a plane crash.

"I'll take out a post-office box here and you can write to me once in a while under another name. I promise I won't tell a soul, not even Mario. Goodbye!"

With that, she hangs up. I dial her back.

"Hello?"

"Look, Joan."

"Who is this, please?"

"It's me. Cut it out, Joan. It's me, big brother, Jack, Johnny, Jacky, John Tremont."

"Sorry, you have the wrong number; my brother died in a plane crash five minutes ago."

She hangs up again.

I'm out of quarters. I go in the liquor store, buy a beer to back up my "bar" alibi and call again with a quarter from the change.

"Damn it, Joan, don't hang up again; I'm squandering the family fortune in quarters!"

"OK, Johnny. But don't ever say I didn't give you a chance to bail out. While I'm cutting you out of that lemon tree, don't give me any evil eye or anything."

"OK, nut, I promise."

"So Dad's going to live with me and you're going to— yeachk—live with Mother. Oh boy!"

So it's decided.

Joan and Mario will come over in the van to pick him up. I'll explain to Dad. The whole thing sounds sensible enough.

When I get home, I go in the garden bedroom and stretch out for a few minutes going over everything, looking for the loopholes. Then I go in and tell Mom I'm going to call Joan and work things out with her. I should've known from her answer it was never going to work.

"Sure, she'll say it's OK; she's been trying to steal your father away from me ever since she was a little girl."

I pretend she didn't say it; she's nervous, excited. I go into the living room and explain what's happening to Dad. Mom's followed me. Dad's willing to go along with whatever we want.

I call Joan and go through a replay. We're turning into a pair of fine international spies.

Back in the bedroom, I pull a suitcase from the closet for Dad; Mom's followed me again. Cripes, every time I pack something she takes it out. Finally, I give in. All that really counts is getting Dad away from this madhouse. Mom's throwing things into and out of the suitcase; she's going on about how it's hotter in the Valley in the daytime and colder at night. Dad's going to need light socks for the day and warm pajamas for nights. She insists he should bring an electric blanket. I know Joan has electric blankets. I say this but it's ignored. She pulls some wool blankets from the cedar chest and wants them packed too. By the time she's finished, it looks as if Dad's climbing Everest without Sherpas.

In the living room I explain it again to Dad. He's so calm about things I'm not convinced he understands. He only wants to make sure Mom is going along with all this. I tell him Mom's back there packing for him now. He smiles and says how nice it will be playing with John and Maryellen.

So we sit and watch some stupid TV program. Mom doesn't come out from the bedroom.

When you're living around a heart patient, there's always a fear, a deep anxiety. I get up casually and go back.

Mother's on her knees beside the bed. The suitcase is still open, half packed, overflowing. Clothes, blankets are spread on the bed.

"Whats the matter, Mom; are you all right?"

She gives me a sideways look as if I'm the stranger-intruder.

"I'm appealing to the only friend I have left, the only one who cares about me at all, God."

Piously she leans her face on the edge of her bed and mumbles into the bedspread.

"And now, even my husband of more than fifty years is leaving me."

Honest to God, the temptation to give her a swift kick in her pious, protruding rump is almost overwhelming.

"Mom, you know that's not true. This is your idea. You're the one who can't live with Dad and needs a vacation. Don't forget that. We're all making special arrangements for you, hoping to make you happy. Dad isn't leaving; you're sending him away for a while so you can rest."

But she's not hearing. She's maybe getting messages directly from God, but she's not hearing me.

"He doesn't love me, none of you do. He only wants to leave me. You saw it. He jumped at the chance; all he wants to do is get away from me, anywhere."

"That's nonsense, Mom, and you know it. Dad will do whatever you say. He wants you to be happy. It'll be good for everybody if he goes there. You and I can rest up here."

"That's what *you* say. It'll be good for him but it won't be good for me. I'll be here alone and he'll be over there with Joan's family laughing and living it up, having a good time. He'll forget all about me in a week. You'll see!"

"Come on, Mom; that's ridiculous. I'll be here with you and we'll have fine times together."

I help her up off her knees and she sits on the side of the bed. I try putting some of the things into the suitcase. I'm going to need at least three suitcases to get all the crap in.

"Leave it, Jacky. You can get his stuff later; he's never coming back here. You can take everything he owns later, another time."

This is my chance; I close the suitcase before she changes her mind again. I carry it to the front room and wait for Joan. Now Mom won't come out of the bedroom; she's mad at Dad.

Dad catches on fast and goes back. From in front, I can hear her crying and making a scene. After a few minutes, Dad comes and stands in the doorway beside the TV.

"I'm not going, Johnny. You were wrong. Mother doesn't want me to go. I'll stay here. You call Joan and tell her."

OK, I'm ready to unpack the clothes, put them in the

closet and call Joan. Dad settles into his rocker and stares at the TV set; I don't think he's seeing much. He might even be in Cape May again.

I carry the suitcase back to the bedroom. I'm beginning to feel like the fall guy in a Marx brothers' movie. I meet Mom on the way up the hall. She's pointing and pressing me back into the living room with her finger. Her head is tilted back and there's fire and tears in her eyes. I stop, back up as she advances.

"Don't you dare bring those things into *my* bedroom; he's not going to stay in this house one minute more than he has to. If he doesn't want to live with me, he doesn't have to. And if he doesn't want to stay married to me, just because I'm sick and have a bad heart, that's all right, too."

I retreat in front of her, suitcase in hand, all the way into the living room. Dad's face is white; he's stunned. He's sitting in the platform rocker with his foot tucked under him. Mom's raging away.

"Stop it, Mom! What're you talking about? What in heaven's name are you trying to tell us?"

Then she starts crying hard; puts her face in her hands, standing in the doorway, leaning against the jamb. I stare at her, not knowing what to say. Then she turns around and two-step shuffles down the hall, back into the bedroom and slams the door. I put down the suitcase and go over to Dad. I'm mixed up. Some deep part of me is beginning to see it all as hilariously funny. This could be hysteria or maybe I really am a cold-hearted bastard.

"Well, Dad, it looks as if she really wants you at Joan's after all. Come on, now, relax, it'll all work itself out; you know how Mom is."

Dad stares; there are tears in his eyes behind his glasses. He lifts the glasses carefully and wipes his eyes with his knuckles but doesn't say anything.

For something, anything, to do, I flip the TV channels until I find a Western with John Wayne. If anything can settle us down, John Wayne with his manly, crooning voice should do it.

We sit pretending to watch; neither of us really there. Perhaps that's one of the big appeals of TV; you can do something with someone else after you've run out of things to do; caromed togetherness.

About fifteen minutes later, Joan and Mario roll into our driveway with the camper.

I explain all that's happened since I last talked to her. Joan pulls over one of the dining-room chairs and sits close to Dad.

"What do you want, Dad? What can we do to help most?"

He starts shaking his head and tries to say something but can't. Then he bows his head and cries. His hands stay still on his lap and he cries. Joan looks over at me, then leans closer to Dad and takes him in her arms. She pulls him closer and the rocker rocks forward. He pushes his forehead into her shoulder next to her neck.

We three sit there like that with Dad crying. Mario's standing in front of the shut door with his arms folded. After a long time, Dad gets so he can talk. He says all he wants is for Mom to be happy. He'll do anything. It bothers him terribly she won't come out of the bedroom and now he's afraid to go back. He's totally immobilized by her fury. His eyes are like those of a mouse between a cat's paws, going back and forth from Joan to me, to Mario, to the bedroom door down the hall. I don't know how long he can take stress like this. He's still not all that strong. I'm fading myself.

Joan goes down the hall to talk with Mom. She no sooner gets the door open than Mom comes roaring out.

"Get him the hell out of here. I don't want to see his face again. He doesn't love me, he's always loved you kids more than he loved me. Get him out of here! I don't ever want to see him again! Here we're married more than fifty years, and now, when I'm sick, he wants to leave me."

Dad stands up in front of his rocker. He stands there, still slightly crouched over, leaning the backs of his legs against the chair, his arms spread.

"But, Bess, I mean Bette, that's not true. I don't want to go anywhere. I'll stay. I want to stay right here with you."

"Get out! I'm sick of looking at you. You're driving me crazy; what good are you to me or anybody?"

Jesus, if he leaves he's wrong and if he stays he's wrong. Talk about the old double bind; Mom is a past master. She's still got double binds on me dug deep into my soul, like wires wrapped around a tree when it's young. They've given me an unresolvable case of perpetual guilt. It's hard to feel guilty about anything real when you've got deep untouchable guilts like those.

Joan and I look at each other. We're paralyzed. It's the old black magic again. Mario takes two steps into the room. He leans over Dad.

"Come on, Dad; let's get in the car."

He turns to me.

"Jack, you get the suitcase. Joan, you try talking to Mom."

Joan walks down the hall.

"Now calm yourself, Mother. You're making a big deal over nothing. It was your idea for Dad to come visit at our house so you could have a little peace and quiet. Dad will be right back, soon as you feel better and Dad is more himself."

But Mom isn't hearing anymore. Her communications are strictly one-way.

"You too! I thought at least my daughter loved me. Now you're stealing my husband. I know you; you'll take him to your house and talk to him till he'll never come back."

By this time, Mario has gotten Dad up and through the door onto the porch. With Mom's last speech Dad starts back through the door. Mom breaks past Joan and blocks him.

"Don't you come in here, John Tremont! When you walked out that door, you walked out of my life. I don't want you in this house!"

She has the imperious finger out. Dad looks around for help, for some direction.

Then he looks straight into Mom's eyes. He stares for what seems forever but it can't be more than ten seconds. He shakes his head, turns away and starts out the door. Mario helps him across the short porch and down the three steps.

They're going across the lawn when Mom comes charging out the door and down the steps with Joan rushing after her. Mom grabs Dad by the arm and starts pulling. Dad's offering no resistance either way. Mario's holding on to Dad; as much holding him up as anything. Dad is definitely walking wounded; he's lost all volition. He seems to have stopped paying attention to what's happening. Mom's screaming.

"Don't leave me, Jack! Jesus, Mary and Joseph, help me; my own children are kidnapping my husband! Somebody call the police! Mother of God, help me! They're taking my husband away from me!"

Holy cow! I'm afraid some of the neighbors are going to come out and join in the fray, or at least call the cops. But this is California; they're probably all looking through the venetian blinds enjoying our little drama; better than Channel 9.

"Don't let them take him away! He's my husband! I love him! I want him here with me!"

Now she's dropped to her knees on the grass. Dad's staring at her not saying anything. I take his other arm.

"Come on, Dad, it's all right. Mom's overexcited; you know how she is."

Mario and I push Dad up into the back of the camper. They've got the bed all fixed for him. I go to Mom and take her arm to help her up. She gives me a strong elbow punch in the stomach. I step back. She's a strong woman all right. Those years of pushups, sit-ups and flopovers have given her a good elbow punch.

"Come on, Mom. You're making a spectacle of yourself. What will the neighbors think anyway?"

This registers. She lets me help her up, then shakes my arm loose. Mario gets backed out, turned, and they start down the street. Joan looks back and waves.

"Now, look, Mom; just let Dad go for today until you've had a chance to calm down. It's all for the best, you'll see. Let's have a quiet night without Dad, then if you want him here tomorrow I'll drive over to Joan's and bring him back."

Mom breaks away from me and does her quick shuffle up the steps and back into the house. At a time like this, the way she moves, you'd never believe she ever had a heart attack. I stand on the lawn to peek around cautiously and check if anybody's been watching; also to catch my breath. I don't see anybody. When I walk in the door, Mom's sitting in her chair.

"Stop right there. You can get out of here, too. If you're not packed and out of here in ten minutes, I'm calling the cops. This is private property and I don't want you here."

The temptation is enormous to take her up on it but instead I flop into Dad's chair. I spread my arms and legs to give myself the illusion of relaxation. I'm trying to figure whether I'm being a sadist or a masochist, or both simultaneously.

"All right, Mom, go ahead and call the cops. I'd really like trying to explain to some flatfoot what this is all about. Maybe in explaining it, I can figure it out for myself. Go ahead, use either phone, call the police, call the fire department, call a priest—whoever you like—let's have a party. Maybe one of them can tell me what in heaven's name's going on in your head. I sure as hell can't figure it. You know, we ought to go see that psychiatrist tomorrow. You need help!"

There's a whole minute of quiet. I don't even look at her. I don't want to. She starts crying.

"Now you're calling me crazy. You steal my husband and now I'm crazy. You'd all like to see me dead. If only I could have died when I had that first heart attack, we'd all be happier. If it weren't for my religion, I'd kill myself!"

I think about Delibro and his question. I wonder how often she's made threats like this when she's wanted her own way. Mom gets up and goes into the back bedroom. I'm too drained to chase after her. I idly wonder if she would kill herself. What's she got back there she could use to do it with? Who knows? She could have two liters of cyanide, a box of TNT and a Sten gun, the way she's so secretive and always hiding things. Then I think, "Oh, the hell with it. She's right; she's better off dead than alive; we'd all be better off, especially Dad. I'm going to sit here and try to forget."

I turn on the ball game and get out a bottle of beer. I'm wishing I had Dad's baseball-watching costume and a score-card. He knew what he was doing, anything to block the static. And, to be perfectly honest, after about fifteen minutes, I'm into the game. It's a good one, a pitcher's battle. I guess the truth of it is, the human nerves can only absorb so much. My mind wants to turn off Mom and her problems. It's an hour and a half later, in the top of the eleventh, score still tied, when she comes out. She goes to the bathroom first, then comes beside me.

"You don't really care, do you?"

I look up, take another sip of beer, my third bottle.

"Sure I do, Mom, but talking doesn't seem to help. I thought some quiet and a long think might do you more good than anything. Why don't you sit down and watch the game, settle your nerves."

She stands, looking down at me. I half expect she's going to fly into me with fingernails and teeth, but slowly she sits down in her chair.

"Mom, how about a glass of beer or some wine?"

There's a three-beat pause.

"You're drunk. I can tell. You're just like your father's brothers. You're beginning already. It's about your age when they start drinking seriously. I've been watching you. I counted one day and you had three bottles of beer and two glasses of wine. And that's only what I *knew* about, what you actually drank in the house; God only knows how much you drank out in bars. You're practically an alcoholic already."

I scrunch down a little lower and try to concentrate on the game. This is a new one. It's the first time anyone's called me an alcoholic; and it has to be my mother. If you have a mother for a friend you don't need any enemies. Maybe it won't be the last time, but this is the first; sort of a milestone in my life.

"Well, Mom, I don't think I'm an alcoholic but this *is* my third beer if you want to start counting. If you don't want anything to drink, then say so; but no song and dance, please."

Another significant long pause. While I wasn't paying attention, somebody drove in a run and I missed it; I even missed the replay.

"Well, if you're eating my food and drinking my beer, I might as well have some wine before you've eaten and drunk me out of house and home."

That's where we are, so I go into the kitchen and pour

some of the crappy cold, sweet wine for her. I'm acting out
All in the Family in my mother's house. I'm more like Archie
Bunker every day. I'll be calling black people "jigs" before I
even know it.

I ask from the kitchen if she'd like a cheese sandwich.
There's no answer, so I figure I'll make one for myself and one
for her. If she doesn't eat hers, I'll eat them both. So I make
two toasted cheese sandwiches. I come out and hand one to
her. There's no response but she bites into it and takes a sip of
the wine.

"Tonight I'll sleep in my bed all alone. Here I am a married woman with all I've had to go through, and I'm forced to
sleep alone."

What does she want, that I should *sleep* with her? I hold
back a minute before I answer; I try to remind myself she's
just out of her mind with frustration and worry.

"But, Mom, you said Dad was bothering you in bed, that he
was waking you up and you couldn't get any rest. Here's your
chance to have a good night's sleep."

The only response I get is a sniff.

The whole evening goes like that. We watch some TV and
she doesn't say anything except make nasty comments about
every show and everybody in them. I keep my mouth shut. I'd
like to go in the bedroom and read a book but that would be the
worst of insults, so I try to concentrate on the shows.

Before we go to bed, Mom's settled down some. One good
thing is she can't keep a consistent pose; she has to be changing all the time.

I'm beginning to feel it'll be all right; she's made her
scene, her point, now she's going to settle in and enjoy her
gains. Even so, I decide to sleep in the house, in the side room,
in the crib with the inflatable mattress, the oxygen and everything. I'm still a bit worried about her; she can make herself
so miserable.

After the eleven-o'clock news I say I'm going to bed; still
no response. I go back to that room, undress, climb into the
bed and pull up the sides. I experiment with the oxygen thing
in my nose with the tank on to see how it feels. I stare some
more at Mary and Jesus. I breathe through my nose, sucking

in oxygen and running over my mantra. I've a few frayed nerves to cool down. I must've passed out, because I don't even remember hearing Mother go down the hall to her bedroom. I sleep, plugged in, floating on air, like Jules Verne going to the moon.

I wake, I look at my watch and it's two in the morning. What woke me is the phone dinging as Mom picks up to dial the living-room phone.

I'm still half groggy; that oxygen really does it. I take out the plugs and turn off the tank. Who the hell can Mom be phoning at this time? Maybe she's phoning back East, thinking of going back there to live with one of her brothers. But hell, it's only five in the morning on the East Coast. I carefully pick up the phone.

The phone rings more than ten times, then it's Joan who answers. I'm sure she's scared out of her mind, being wakened from a dead sleep.

"Jack, is that you? Is everything all right?"

Mom pauses a second; I don't think she expected that. I almost interrupt but I want to hear what she has to say.

"No, it's *only* your mother. I want to speak to *my* husband and right now."

There's another pause.

"But, Mom, wait a minute, it's two o'clock in the morning; Dad's asleep. I can't wake him up. He had an awful time getting to sleep as it was."

"You heard me, I want to speak to *my* husband."

"Mom, please; why not call again in the daytime? Whatever it is can't be that important. Are you all right? Where's Jack?"

There's a sniff you can hear over the phone.

"Are you trying to keep my husband from talking to me? I'm his wife, just *you* remember that. I've been married to him for over fifty years and I want to talk with him right *now*."

There's quiet. I'm wondering if I should interrupt. This is insane. Then Mario comes on the line.

"Look, Mom."

Mario has called Mother "Mom" even before he and Joan were married.

"Let's be reasonable, huh? Dad's asleep. You know how hard it is for him getting to sleep when he's upset; give the guy a break."

On, and out she comes.

"Get off the line, you filthy wop! Let me talk to *my* daughter!"

I'd love to see Mario's face. Joan comes on again.

"All right, Mom; Mario's going in to wake Dad; I hope you know what you're doing."

There's a long pause. I hear Mom working herself up into a cry. It's easier listening over the phone than sticking my head out the bedroom door and really hearing her cry; it's like watching on TV, not quite real. Then there's some fumbling with the phone. I can almost see Dad in his pajamas standing there barefooted, without his glasses, looking into the hole of the phone.

"Hello, Bess?"

It's a faraway voice. It sounds as if the receiver is two feet from his mouth. Mom shouts through her crying, close to the phone, loud.

"It's Bette, Bette, remember, your *wife*?"

He's slow responding and they must've pushed the phone closer to his mouth.

"Oh, hello, Bess, I mean Bette. How are you? Where are you?"

"I'm not in Cape May! I'm right here at home, our home, that's where I am, in our house, where you should be; that's where I am."

There's another long pause. Then his voice is so low I almost can't hear it and it isn't because he's holding the receiver away either.

"Do you want me to come home, Bess? I'll get dressed and come home right now if you want. Joan or Mario will drive me, I'm sure. I'll be right there."

If Mom told him to commit hara-kiri, he'd spend the rest of the night looking for a proper knife.

I'm tempted again to break in and tell Mom to get the hell off the phone. I want to console Dad somehow.

Good old "Jake" is gone; this is John called Jack, Jack-of-all-trades, the guy who worked more than fifty years for nothing, who gave in on everything. Something terrible is happening.

I'm almost crying as I listen to Mom telling him how she's the only one who's ever really loved him. He keeps saying he'll come home right away and not to worry, that he's on his way; but she goes on and on. Then, after she's totally wiped him out, she tells him to go back to bed, he can come in the morning. Abruptly she hangs up.

I wait till she shuffles past my room and into her bedroom. Then I phone back. Joan answers. I tell her I was on the line. Joan's in tears.

"You should've seen him, Jack. He winced with every word; cowering like a dog that's been beaten too often. Mario's back there now trying to help him get to sleep again. He keeps jumping up, wanting to pack his bags."

Neither of us can make anything funny out of this. Joan says she'll pack Dad's things and bring him over tomorrow. She's worried she'll blow up at Mom again, so she'll leave right away. She asks me to please try talking some sense into Mom, try to find out what she really wants.

I hang up and climb back into the crib. I put the oxygen plugs in my nostrils again and turn on the tank. What the hell, maybe I'll get to be an oxygen freak, walk around with oxygen tanks on my back. It's a long time before I sleep; I can hear Mom shuffling around, mumbling to herself in the back room.

The next morning, I pretend not to know anything about the phone call. I get up refreshed; maybe sleeping with oxygen is the answer to senility, oxygenate the brain during the night.

Mom must have been up until at least three in the morning, so she doesn't wake till after ten. I fix us two good breakfasts and serve them on the patio.

I have the music going, the table is set and the sun is shining. It's a beautiful day. Mother's put her hair up for the big reunion scene and she's wearing her fancy housecoat; the vamp's ready to vamp.

She's having a hard time knowing how to react to all the service. She's still got the old iron will up, acting out her fantasy. I'm ignoring all that; talking about the beautiful flowers, the lovely day; sitting there on the poop deck pouring tea for the one and only first-class passenger. I don't respond to anything she says if it's along lines I don't want to hear.

After breakfast, we lie out on the chaise longues and the sun is wrapped around us. I've cleared the dishes, washed up, changed the records and come out again. I've got on the Hawaiian music; I have my shirt off and I'm spread out in the sun letting it soak into me. I feel deeply poisoned, polluted to my innermost being.

"This is the life, all right, Jacky. I don't know why you live in a dark, dirty place like Paris with all those foreigners."

I keep quiet. This is an old theme; at least the second part.

"You're right, Jacky. What I need is time to relax in the sun, calm my nerves. I can never get a minute's rest when he's around."

I wait, holding my breath. What's coming now?

"I phoned last night and asked Joan to bring your father home today but now I'm not so sure. I need a rest, Jacky; nobody should force me to play nurse to a man sick as he is. How can I do a thing like that after two serious heart attacks?"

Last night? Two o'clock in the morning is hardly last night. I keep quiet. I'll wait.

"Jacky, maybe you ought to call Joan and tell her not to bring him. Tell her to wait a few days. I'm not ready yet. I'll only strain my heart and kill myself, then what would he do? He'll just have to live without his free nurse for a few days. It won't hurt Joan to take care of him, she doesn't do much else."

"All right, Mom."

I get up slowly, trying not to break the mood and still move quickly, hoping to catch Joan before she's taken off over the hill with Dad. I go in and get her on the phone.

"It's all off, Joan. Stay there. We're out on the patio sunning and now she doesn't want to be a nurse; so keep Dad there."

Joan doesn't answer for almost half a minute. Then she's laughing, almost crying, the edge of hysteria again.

"Come on, Jack; are you kidding? If you're making this up, I'll kill you."

"Honest, Joan, that's where we are now. She's the Queen of Sheba taking her morning dose of the old sun king Ra. I don't know how long it'll last but let's take advantage. I'm sure you can explain to Dad. Maybe tell him last night was only a nightmare. If you want, I'll talk to him."

"No, it'll be all right. He's so confused he doesn't know what's going on. I'll spend the day with him sitting and talking, settling him down. He's in an absolute state, wandering around the house, looking into things, asking me all the time when we go home. I have his bags packed but he keeps going in and touching them. I can take care of Dad but would you mind asking the Queen not to phone at two in the morning again? My nerves are completely shattered."

I hang up and go out to tell Mom it's all arranged. She takes the news with her eyes closed; I go along with the game. I spread out, wishing I could get down to Venice and do some more painting. It's a damned shame wasting good light like this. I don't know where the hell Billy is but I hope he doesn't show up right now; it wouldn't help.

The next few days go fine. Mom doesn't make any effort to contact Dad, in fact, doesn't ask about him; he's off the drawing board for some reason. We even have some almost rational conversations once in a while. I take her down to the Oar House one night, not a good idea. Next afternoon I take her to the Williamsburg Inn, semi-catastrophic. The morning of the third day we have breakfast at the French sidewalk café on the beach in Venice. She becomes convinced an older hippy type is flirting with her and wants me to shoo him away.

Later in the afternoon, while she's taking a nap in the back bedroom, I call Delibro. He asks why Dad hasn't come back. I explain the situation. I try to tell what's been happening, how Mom's been behaving irrationally; he listens.

"Well, that all sounds bad, Mr. Tremont. I really should

see your father again, soon. This kind of trauma must be a terrible setback for him. His enjoyment and participation in this life is so tied up with your mother's approval."

He pauses.

"Frankly, Mr. Tremont, I don't know what we should do. I'm concerned for your mother and she's definitely dangerous to your father's stability. Still, I don't think we can put her in a hospital. She's so logical in her irrationality. She's a difficult woman, Mr. Tremont."

A hundred bucks an hour to find *that* out! I realize, after the fact, when he talks about putting Mother in a hospital he means some kind of loony bin. God, it's not that serious, is it? But at least, Mom isn't fooling him much.

Delibro asks if we can keep it the way it is for a while, give Dad peace and quiet in a loving environment and Mom a chance to simmer down. He wants to know if Joan can bring Dad in for an appointment at least once a week. He asks me to try my best to get Mother in to him again.

So that's the way we leave it. I sit down and write home one more postponing letter. I promise in the letter, and, more important, I promise myself, I'm getting out of all this within the next week or two at the most. For Christ's sake, how long can it go on? It's so basically hopeless.

Two days later, friends of ours, Bud and Cam Wilkes, phone. They want to know if I can join them for some talk and a barbecue dinner. Boy, am I tempted. I'm so tempted I bring it up with Mom. At first she's resentful but then reluctantly agrees to my going.

"I'm just a burden to everybody anyway; you might's well have a good time with your friends while you can; soon enough you'll be old and alone like me."

I promise I'll be back by eleven to watch the last shows with her. I write out the Wilkeses' phone number and put it beside the phone. Then I call Joan and tell her where I'm going. It's almost like wheedling an overnight pass.

The Wilkeses have a handsome home on a hill looking over Los Angeles. They also have a small heated pool. One time I swam nude in that pool at night all alone with a full moon reflected in the water; it was almost like night swimming at the mill.

Bud greets me with a gin-and-tonic and we begin catching up. They've phoned before, so they know something of what's going on but I tell them I'd rather not talk about it tonight.

We sit on the patio looking across the pool; behind me, Bud is turning small chickens on a barbecue; I feel I'm in the real California, whatever that is. When the phone rings, I can feel the hair rise along my neck; I'm getting paranoid about phones. This is the Wilkeses house, their phone, their phone call; I should relax.

Cam says it's for me. So much for relaxing. I walk into the living room and take the phone from Cam. It's Joan. I'm expecting the worst and I don't even know what the worst is.

"Jack, you've got to come right away! Something's happened to Dad! We need you now!"

"What is it, Joan?"

"*Please*, just hurry! Hurry! I can't talk about it."

She starts to cry. She doesn't hang up but is crying on the phone.

"All right, Joan; I'm on my way! I'll be there in half an hour."

She's still on the line crying. I wait a minute to see if she's going to say anything else, then hang up carefully. I'm feeling myself coming on with the shakes. It must be serious for Joan to cry like that. I wonder if Mario's there. I wonder if Dad's dead, if he killed or hurt himself. I want to phone back and ask these questions but I have a hard time making myself move and I know I need to get there fast.

Cam comes to me. She has my drink in her hand and puts it on the table beside me.

"What's the matter, Jack? You're white as a sheet. What's happened, is it your mother?"

"No, it's Dad. I don't know what's happened but my sister Joan needs me out in the Valley. I'm awfully sorry, Cam, but I can't stay; I've got to go right now."

I'm working my way to the door. Cam kisses me.

"Now, you be careful, Jack; take care!"

Bud comes out to the car, insisting all the way he'll drive me. But I back out the driveway. I don't think I'm rude but my mind is miles away. I'm churning, trying to think of all the things it could be.

There isn't much traffic. The sun is hanging over the mountains and the light is a weird combination of blue and red. It takes all my concentration to make the right turnoffs, get in the best lanes.

Twenty-five minutes after I leave the Wilkeses, I pull into Joan's driveway. Maryellen has been waiting for me on the porch. She comes running across the lawn, crying. She's hysterical and sobbing. I don't think she's touched me since she was ten years old, but she throws herself in my arms on the lawn under the birch trees.

"Oh, Uncle Jack; it's awful! I can't look. It's so awful!"

I keep moving, towing her across the lawn. The door opens and it's Joan.

"Thank God you're here, Jack. I never prayed so hard in my life; I was sure you'd be killed on that freeway."

Maryellen steps aside and Joan holds me. She's shaking. Her face is spotted, red spots on white, and her eyes are swollen from crying but she's not crying now.

"What's happened, Joan? What's the matter?"

I follow her through the door into the living room. Maryellen tags along behind.

"Sit down, Jack. Mario's back there with him. It's all right for now. Just sit down here."

I sit beside her on the couch. She takes both my hands in hers. She cries some, then starts.

"I'll try to begin at the beginning.

"All during dinner he was peculiar. You know how he was before. He'd seem to forget what things are for. Once he tried scooping up his peas with his cup and spilled coffee all over everything; then he'd pick up his fork or spoon and stare at it or turn it round and round in his hands. Once he put his face in the plate and tried to eat his meat with his mouth, like a dog. I told the kids to take their plates into the living room; poor Maryellen was almost fainting and John couldn't eat either. I moved beside him to try helping, and I put a napkin around his neck.

"Jack, he had that *same* look in his eyes, wild, empty. A part of him is looking at me like a stranger, an enemy; it's frightening. At the same time, I know he isn't really there, this isn't Dad anymore. Some lowest part of his mind is carrying on things with his body.

"Mario moved to the other side of him and we both talked, trying to reassure him, get him back on track again. But he'd only watch our mouths and listen to the sounds. When I helped him get his cup to his mouth with some coffee, he'd let me, but his eyes were staring into mine, empty.

"And I was crying, Jack. I couldn't help myself. It seemed such a shame after he'd been doing so well to see him slipping back.

"Then, every once in a while, he'd come around, almost be himself for a minute or a few seconds. He'd see himself doing something silly, pushing the spoon into the table or twisting the tablecloth, and he'd give that sly grin of his and stop, smooth out the tablecloth, look to see if we've been noticing. Except for his eyes, you couldn't really be sure if he might not have been putting on the whole thing to be funny.

"Mario and I decided to give him some Valium and put him to bed soon as possible. He's terribly upset about Mom. We hoped maybe with a little time, he'd be OK again. I didn't want to call you right then and I definitely didn't want Mom to know what was happening."

She takes a long staggering breath and I think she's going to cry again. I squeeze her hands and she squeezes back.

Joan's half listening all the time, listening for Mario, listening for Dad. We're both listening.

"I started dishes after dinner and Mario put Dad in the chair Dad likes, where he can see everything and watch TV; it's Mario's chair. Mario goes out in the garage to work on something with the car. We're trying to ignore the whole thing, wish it away. About five minutes later, I look up and Dad's gone. I figure he's gone to the bathroom so I duck out into the hall for a look. The door's open and I look in but he isn't there. I go down the hall to the end, into the boys' room. Maryellen and John are there, watching TV; he isn't there either. I'd quickly peeked into Maryellen's room on the way down the hall but didn't see anything.

"I'm beginning to get scared now, Jack. On the way back along the hall, I hear something in Maryellen's room. I go in slowly, the closet door is partly open. I look in and Dad's crouched on the floor of the closet with his back to me. He's violently tearing up Maryellen's clothes! He's putting the hems of the dresses in his teeth and ripping them apart with his hands!

"Honest to God, Jack; I almost fainted! I walked in slowly and squatted beside him. Dad turns his head and looks around at me just like a baby who's dirtied his pants, or a dog who's ripped up a slipper. He has a piece of Maryellen's prom dress in his mouth and pieces of the satin lining and tulle in his hands. I know he doesn't know who I am; I don't think he knows anything."

Now Joan's crying hard and puts her head down on our hands.

"Jack, I tried getting close to him so I could help him get up and he swung his arm! He hit me with his fist. He hit me hard. I fell back and banged my head against Maryellen's bed!"

God! I don't know what to do. I know I should go back there and help Mario but I can't face it yet. I sit there while Joan cries on our hands, her warm tears running over our fingers.

First I need to call Delibro; we need help. I have his home address in my wallet; he gave it to me in case there might be an emergency. I get up and leave Joan on the couch; there's a wall phone in the kitchen.

I dial and get an answering service. I tell them it's an emergency and I'm put right through. He's at a dinner party, too. I explain the situation as best I can. He asks if I can get

Dad to Perpetual; he'll meet us there. I hang up and go back to Joan.

"Please, Jack, you and Mario will have to do it. He acts so crazy wild if he sees Maryellen or me. I'm scared."

I motion Maryellen to sit with Joan, and go back. Mario's kneeling on the floor in front of the closet; he peers over his shoulder at me. I look past him and Dad's squatting with his face pushed into a corner at the back of the closet.

I get down beside Mario.

"Boy, Jack, he's something else. He's totally gone. I can't move him out of there. He doesn't fight me the way he does Joan, but when I tried to push this Valium in his mouth, he almost bit me. He's certainly strong for such a little old guy."

Mario must weigh one ninety or two hundred and most of that's muscle. I squeeze in front of him and he stands up. I look back up at Mario.

"I've called the psychiatrist. He'll meet us at Perpetual; we've got to get him there somehow."

"That'll be a good trick, Jack, I'll tell you."

I turn my head back to Dad.

"Hi, Dad, it's Johnny here. What're you doing in there? It's me, Johnny."

No response. Somehow he's gotten one of his shoes off and the sock is half pulled off his foot. He's wet his pants and there's urine all over the bottom of the closet, soaking into Maryellen's shoes and on the clothes he's pulled off the hangers.

"Come on, Dad. What are you doing in here, looking for something?"

Nothing.

"Mario, can the two of us pull him out? I can't think of anything else. We've got to get him into Perpetual somehow."

"OK, Jack, let's try. You take one side, I'll take the other. Watch he doesn't bite, and he packs a terrific wallop. Joan's got a black-and-blue mark the size of a cantaloupe."

We squeeze in on both sides and edge our way into the closet for some leverage. Dad forces himself deeper into the corner but we work him out. He doesn't fight but closes in on himself like a hedgehog or a tumblebug. We carry him curled up tight down the hall to the boys' bedroom. We ask Joan to leave and we sit Dad in a chair. Maybe "sit" isn't the word; we prop him in the chair.

"Mario, would you smash those Valium, and mix them with water?"

I stay with Dad. He stays wrapped into himself. He won't open his eyes or take his hands from his face. He has his thumbs in his ears, his index fingers over his eyes, his middle fingers up his nose, and he's holding his lips closed with his ring and little fingers overlapped. He looks like one of those bronze things with three monkeys they used to put on desks: see no evil, hear no evil, speak no evil, only he's all three monkeys rolled in one.

I hear Bess moving around upstairs. I can tell from the floor squeaking she's making the bed. I can even tell she's only taken the covers off, aired them, then spread them back on the bed again. There's a bit of quiet while she slips into her clothes. She comes down the steps so silently I don't know she's down till I see her.

"Well, look who's found a hiding place in her daddy's lap!"

Bess comes close, runs her hands over Lizbet's head and gently pulls her fingers out of her mouth. Lizbet turns her face into my chest and Bess leans forward to plant a soft kiss on my cheek.

"There's nothing like a fresh-shaved man on an early morning."

"Bess, maybe you could wash this one's hair. It smells as if she's been rolling in the hayloft again."

Lizbet sits up fast. The little imp hasn't been asleep at all, only pretending, getting in some extra snuggling.

"Gee, Daddy, I just had my hair washed yesterday."

"OK, little one; I was only joshing. I wanted to see if I could get you awake enough so I can squeeze out from under to do the milking."

I stand slowly and she slips between my legs. Bess takes her by the hand.

"All right, Lizbet, some washing up won't hurt even if we don't do your hair. Come on."

Bess is pouring hot water into the bowl. I pick up the milking cans at the door and head off to the barn. It's not cold; soft, damp, spring morning air. The chickens are clucking to be let out, so I go by that way. Johnny can get in a few more licks of sleep before school.

I turn the wooden door latch for the chicken coop. The chickens stare out at me, clucking and pecking. I go in behind to chase them out. I look around and there are eggs in most of the nests, all colors of light brown. I'll let Johnny gather them, he's so proud of his daily count. There are several hens setting and I leave them alone. I go outside and turn the latch shut again. When I made that little turn latch, it seemed so raw, crude, but now after thousands of turns, it's worn smooth, so the grain is working its way up.

Johnny sure has a beautiful flock. He could get more laying if he'd put in some white leghorns instead of all those Plymouth Rocks and Rhode Island Reds but he says he doesn't like white eggs, says they look all the same.

I throw out a few handfuls of grain, just to keep them interested till he comes out and feeds them. I pick up the milk cans and move off toward the barn.

Milly's waiting for me there. I'm a little later than usual, it's a lazy day. I pull down the milking stool, get the clean rag and wipe off her udder. She looks back at me. This is one cow who likes to be milked. I could probably leave her out in the field nights with the calf, but you never know about wild dogs. Besides, it's easier in the mornings milking her at the stanchion.

I lean in close and get my shoulder buttressed against her side. Most people like to stay back and milk, but I enjoy feeling Milly, big, warm, against me and listening to the rum-

blings in her stomach. I think I can hear the milk being made. I lean close to the smell of hay, manure and milk; all warm; all live. I can almost fall asleep milking a cow.

I finish and pour off some for Kitty the calf. I give it to her in the next stall. She's going to be a beauty all right, half Guernsey, half Jersey. That Guernsey bull I took Milly to for freshening this time was almost the size of a house and he got right at it. I had to walk Milly almost twenty miles each way, most of it on hard surfaced streets, but it was worth it.

I muck out the stalls and wash them down with buckets of salt water. Milly and Kitty lick the water; you don't need salt licks in New Jersey. I lead Milly out to pasture, Kitty follows along behind. Kitty's a silly name for a calf, but it was Lizbet's turn and Kitty it must be.

When I come out, Johnny's cleaning the chicken coop and feeding. He's already gotten his mash mixed and cooked up. I wave as I go by.

"Hey, Dad, two new hens setting, that makes eight all together; and fifty-seven eggs this morning."

"That's fine, Johnny. Before we know it, we'll have more chicks than eggs."

I give Milly a soft switch with my stick to stop her eating Bess's hollyhocks where they lean out from the garden. Every morning she goes for a mouthful and every morning I give her a switch.

I open the gate to the pasture and shoo them in. It doesn't take much, they're ready and hungry. I certainly wish I owned this pasture. It costs me twenty-five dollars a year, but Mrs. Praline won't sell it for under eight hundred dollars. There's no use complaining; I'm never going to get that kind of money and I do have the use of the space; at least I can keep a couple cows and a horse for plowing.

Just then I hear Bess calling out to Johnny for breakfast and I know she'll be calling me next.

DAD

"I'm coming, Bess; be right up."

I look at the house as I walk up and onto the dirt road leading to it. It's the kind of house I've wanted all my life, big enough and not too big. It's different from most houses around here since I built it L-shape like that. Ed thought I was crazy; it's not like a farmhouse at all. It was extra work and extra cost but it's fine having an enclosed courtyard on the sunny side. Bess can sit out there in good weather and string beans or peel potatoes and shell peas, or just relax.

Everybody's at the table when I come in. Johnny, Joan and Hank have their schoolbooks on the floor beside them. It's a mile walk to school and school starts at nine so they've got to hurry it up. Bess's made an omelet with bacon and milk for the kids and two steaming hot mugs of coffee for us. Coffee out of a mug tastes twice's good as cup coffee.

The kids scamper off after Joan puts the plates and glasses on the drainboard. Bess does the morning dishes and Joan or Johnny do the ones after supper. Right now is one of the nicest times of day. Bess and I sit and enjoy ourselves chatting, before we get into the day's work. I tell her I think it might be a good idea to do some berry-picking, she has the same thing in mind. Lizbet is out back looking for the kitten to give her some milk. We laze away ten minutes or so over two mugs of coffee.

Soon as the dishes are done and the kitchen cleaned up, I roust out the berrying pails. Bess and Lizbet are ready to go. We don't actually have any berries growing on our place, but there are plenty between us and the ocean in the salt flats. We can drive there in less than ten minutes. We'll stop and honk at Ira's and at the Michaelses' to see if they want to come.

The sun's burning through as I roll along the east-west road. I slow down and honk at Ira's place. I yell up to Kay we're going picking if they want to come. They're with us in less than five minutes. Kay brings her little one, Mary; Ira's at the ocean gathering seaweed for fertilizer. Kay and Mary jump up on the flatbed. We do the same thing at the Michaelses' picking up Gene and Peg. We're having a real picking party; there's plenty for everybody that's for sure, it's just hard picking. The land's boggy so the picking's barefoot.

I get to the best place, stop and everybody jumps out. Over the years, each person's found a favorite spot to pick. Bess and Liz head out to the skimpy elder where they always find theirs. I like to pick along the road, they get ripe first and have the most sugar. I always eat the first ten myself, after that take every twentieth one. For some reason, I count berries while picking. Every once in a while, somebody will find a particularly good patch and we'll all go over to join in the luck.

We pick till the sun's just past overhead. That rain last night was what we needed, enough to sink in but not enough to slow down growing. It probably set up enough little fresh water puddles and ponds to grow us up a whole new batch of mosquitoes, too. I've got to mend those screens before the real mosquito season comes on us.

When we get home, Johnny, Joan and Hank are already there. Joan's set the table and Johnny's on the back porch churning butter. Hank's upstairs, probably fooling with his butterflies.

Bess's had a pot roast with cabbage, onions and carrots on back of the stove while we've been picking, so it goes straight onto the table. Joan bought bread at the baker in town on the way home from school. We wipe out the loaf and the roast in fifteen minutes of concentrated eating. The pot juices soaked in that bread are delicious.

For dessert Johnny fetches a pint of cold fresh cream from the spring. We sprinkle our wild berries on top of that. The berries are still warm from the sun and sink into the cream. I think we eat up almost a quarter of the berries we picked all morning; but that's what they're for.

After Johnny, Hank and Joan head back to school, Bess puts Lizbet down in the back room for her nap and the two of us go upstairs and take about an hour in bed ourselves. It sounds downright lazy to get in bed in the middle of the day like that but we've been doing it for years, whenever we get the chance. It's the nicest time when you're not too tired, and you only have one life. After all, that's one of the reasons people get married.

It's almost three o'clock when I get out to the tomatoes. That rain drove some of them right back down to the ground. I must say I've sure got some beautiful tomatoes this year. Some of them are big as tennis balls already. I know I'm at least a month ahead of everybody. Don Ambrogi in the central market tells me if I bring in sun-ripened tomatoes before the middle of June he'll get me top dollar.

I greenhouse-started these tomatoes back in early March. That's the greenhouse I made from windows salvaged when they tore down the old Seaside Hotel in Cape May. There were big windows along the porch facing the ocean and they tore it all down. I've got over five hundred square feet under glass from those windows. I keep my plants warm in cold nights, or days without sun, with a little fire in a hut beside the greenhouse. By the end of April I had eight-inch-high leggy sprouts all ready to transplant.

I moved them into the fields on the first of May and prayed. Thank God there was no late freeze. Now I have beautiful, hearty bushes loaded with these new kind of almost seedless Beefsteak tomatoes. I'll bet I get a couple hundred bushels this year and I'll be out of that work in time for my big job with the corn. I'll have two good cash crops, one after the other.

I carry out some string and two bundles of straight cut sticks. There isn't much damage but there will be if I don't tie them now. The weight of the fruit, plus the extra weight from the rain, is too much. Ground-spotted tomatoes are worthless except for the canning factory.

The green smell of tomato surrounds me as I wrestle those devils up. It's easy to break off a branch because they're stiff with water and the fruit's so heavy. My hands are turning green from rubbing across stalks and leaves. I wonder why *they have the light white-green hairs; maybe it's to protect from insects. Tomatoes have always been sexy plants to me, even as a kid back in Wisconsin. Tomatoes look almost too good for ordinary people, like something from the Garden of Eden.*

I keep my legs straight and bend over from the waist. This is something Dad taught Ed and me when we were picking our cucumber patch. If you have to get down further, then squat, really squat, with your heels flat in the dirt. That way you never get a stiff back. Dad has a straight posture to this day and he's almost seventy years old. When he carpenters, he bends or squats the same way he used to in those fields up in Wisconsin.

The sun's well down when I tie up the last bush. I'm practically drunk with the green smell of tomatoes. When I put the cutters and the last of my sticks back in the shed, I can smell the dry wood and sawdust in there. There's definitely something in tomato smell which sharpens other smells. I know I'll smell all kinds of things as I walk up to the house, even the dirt path and rocks.

I go down to the settling pool and scoop water to wash up. I drink ice cold water straight from my hands. I dry them in my hair. Hair's getting long; tonight's probably haircutting night; the whole family's needing it. Nobody minds since I built us a barber chair from an old automobile seat and a broken swivel chair I found in the dump outside town. I cut everybody else's, including Bess's, and she cuts mine while I hold a mirror and help her along.

In our house we eat French-style, the way we did at home. That means a big meal at lunch, then soup and bread in the evening. Bess makes some of the best soups in the world and it's never the same.

I look around for Hank. He's probably butterfly-collecting again. He has all his drawers filled and the walls covered with mounted butterflies in the boys' room. Johnny says it looks spooky at night, especially when there's a moon, but he hasn't actually complained. John's good with his brother and Hank is a strange one. He's been collecting things since he was old enough to walk around. But this butterfly business goes on and on; it's been more than three years now. Bess tells me he's hatching cocoons in boxes in the clothes closet. All he wanted for Christmas this year was more butterfly identification books plus more of the little pins, tools, chemicals and pieces of glass he mounts the things with. He can talk your ear off on moths alone if you give him half a chance. You never know with kids, but Hank is something I'd never've expected.

Lizbet sees me and comes dashing down. I catch her as she throws herself with arms out. Either I'm getting older or she's getting bigger, probably both, but I'm going to miss her one of these times. I boost her on my shoulder and walk the last part up to the porch. I ease her down on the porch step.

Bess gives the call to supper. Hank comes down from upstairs and Johnny from around back. There isn't much talking, everybody's hungry. I wait till they're all settled in and Bess comes from the stove with the bowl steaming hot. I bow my head and say grace. I'm a bit Protestant here. I don't say the usual "Bless us, O Lord." Tonight I just say, "Thank God for tomatoes, Amen."

Mario comes back with the mashed pills in a paste. He holds Dad's head and I use a spoon to open Dad's lips enough so I can force the mash through the space in his teeth. It's like feeding a baby bird when it's almost dead, when the neck is bent and the food won't go down. I hold Dad's nose so he has to swallow. I'm fairly sure I get most of it in.

"Mario, I'll stay here; you fix up the camper with the bed and we'll take him in that."

Mario goes and I sit beside Dad. I watch as he gradually relaxes. He uncurls, takes his hands from his eyes, sinks into a normal sitting position. But his eyes are empty, his face a blank. He stares at nothing. His lips work once in a while, his fingers twist and twiddle with the fly on his pants.

When Mario comes back, I ask him to get fresh under-pants and trousers. We change him; there's no trouble, he goes along with us, not fighting. But then Joan peeks in the door. When he sees her, Dad puts his hands back over his face and pulls his knees up. I wave Joan away. I gently pet him on his bald head till he opens one eye, then the other, looking slowly toward the direction where Joan'd been standing. He takes his hands carefully from his face and lowers his knees.

I leave Dad with Mario and ask Joan, John and Maryellen to stay in the kitchen while we put Dad in the camper. I go back. Together Mario and I stand him up but he doesn't take any of his weight. As we go down the hall, his feet drag so we're hauling him along, dead weight. Each of us has one of his arms over a shoulder. When we get him to the camper, we lift him into the bed. Dad's eyes stare at the top of the camper; I cover him with a blanket. John hands me a paper bag with Dad's pajamas. Mario gets in front and we take off. I've asked Joan to call the hospital and tell them we've left. I sit beside Dad all the way over the pass. He doesn't mope. He's gone, totally, completely gone.

As we get closer to the hospital, the Valium begins wear-ing off. First his lips quiver, then he starts swinging his arms and struggling to get off the bed.

By the time we get on the San Diego Freeway, I'm lying across him, hugging him, trying to hold him down.

Mario keeps looking back and his face is blue-white again with fear and shock. He has a heavy beard, one of those guys who gets his five-o'clock shadow at about one-thirty in the afternoon. Right now, he looks like a hit man. I'd hate trying to explain what we're doing if some cop stops us.

We roll up to the emergency door. When the attendants look in and see me struggling with Dad, they run for a stretcher with restrainers. The four of us maneuver Dad onto the stretcher and get him strapped down.

Delibro is there and he's staring, not believing what he's seeing. Chad's there too. It's after ten o'clock by now and it's damned nice of Chad; or maybe he was on duty. Maybe Joan called him directly; I know she has his number.

They roll Dad into one of the emergency rooms; Chad starts all the tests, blood, urine, saliva, the works. They put an IV on him. Dad's settled down some; at least he's not fighting. Delibro motions me aside.

"Holy hell! What happened? He seemed so fine when I last saw him. What could've happened?"

I try to tell Delibro about the past week, with Mom at Joan's, the "kidnapping," then Dad at Joan's, the 2 a.m. phone call, everything. He listens. Some of it he already knows, some not. It's like bringing somebody up to date on a soap opera; it seems just about that real to me now.

He's looking at me carefully to see if I'm telling the truth. Maybe that's only in my own mind. I'm feeling guilty at least ten different ways. I'm feeling guilty mostly about what I know I'm going to do. My feet are wanting to run. They're tugging at my heart, my mind; the rest of my body. I don't want to be here with all this anymore.

"He's apparently had a severe reaction to the pressures your mother's been putting on him. He seems to have reverted, regressed to his earlier state. He's probably involving the greater part of his neocortex in his fantasy now."

"But what can be done, Doctor? How can we stop this from happening?"

"With more metabolic support he might come back, then rest and calm. But it's hard to tell with someone his age. He's too old for radical treatment. I can't recommend any of the stronger chemical or electrical approaches. Mr. Tremont, I think we need to wait and be patient."

Chad comes out just then. He looks as discouraged as I feel.

"He's asleep now. His BUN is up again. His blood count is down, too. But there's no sign of heart failure or stroke; it must be a combination of psychological factors and metabolism; it's hard to know which one triggers the other."

Basically, they don't know what's wrong with him and they're not sure what to do.

They're going to keep him in the hospital for observation and further testing. I walk into his room quietly and kiss Dad on the forehead. He's sleeping deeply, snoring; there's a thin scum of perspiration across his face and head.

Inside myself, I know he's gone. We had him with us for a short while but it wasn't good enough. He's gone back to his better life, away from all the problems of trying to live here. Also, I know if he leaves here again the way he did last time, he'll die.

What happens to his other life then?

Mario and I drive back to their place so I can pick up the car. It's after midnight. Joan and Mario fix some coffee to keep me awake for my drive back. We decide I'll only tell Mom how Dad began to feel sick and is in the hospital for tests. We definitely won't tell her what's been happening; it's going to be bad enough.

I get home a bit past one. She's still dozing in her chair in front of the TV set; colored splashes from the screen are playing across her face like Christmas-tree lights. I sneak in quietly, turn down the sound and manage not to waken her. God, she looks so alone, so vulnerable, so much like an expensive, unwanted Christmas present you're supposed to pretend you like. I sit in the other chair and try thinking. My mind doesn't want to think, it wants to disappear. I fall asleep. I wake up with Mom shaking me.

"Jacky! Wake up! Jacky, are you drunk? Do you know what time it is?"

I open my eyes and look at her. The television set is still running, soundless. I peer across at the clock, it's 3 a.m., the most dangerous hour for human beings. I take hold of Mother's hands.

"Sit down, Mom, I have something to tell you."

She backs three steps and sits in the rocker. Just then, I feel enormous sorrow, pity, love for her; for Dad, for all of us, for all human beings who need to go through the business of being born, staying alive, getting dead; the whole wrestle with life, a contest with one inevitable fall.

That's all Mom's been doing, struggling with life as she sees it, on her terms. I must be one of the world's biggest horse's asses not to know this. I get up and go over; I take her in my arms; she leans into me.

"He's dead. He died, didn't he? That's where you've been. Oh, Mother of heaven, what'll I do?"

"No, Mom, Dad's not dead, but he's in the hospital. Something happened, not even the doctors know what it is yet, and he's the same as he was before. They're keeping him in the hospital for observation and testing."

I hold her. She squeezes tight and her whole body is twisting with sobs. It must be terrible to love deeply and have no way to show it. Mom is a diesel engine built into a canoe.

We stay like that, not talking, holding tight. It's astounding how soft her body is compared to how she seems.

"I knew it would happen! Nobody knows him the way I do. Nobody can take care of him the way I can."

It's what she has to think. God, what do you do if you aren't cut out to be a wife, a mother, and you're stuck with the job for life? What do you do? She deserves a hell of a lot of credit for staying with it; some people don't; they cut out. Christ, it isn't her fault; it's a simple matter of miscasting.

I hold close and let her go through the whole thing. For the first time in my life, I can listen without blocking; I can listen as someone who loves her, I can listen the way Dad always listened. Her scenario makes sense if you take her part. She's got plenty to back it up. In a certain way, Dad is an incompetent; he doesn't know how to cope with this world, with the people of this world; he *couldn't* get along without her. Joan and I, all the grandchildren, *don't* show enough respect or love for her. That's one of Mom's problems, she doesn't know how to gain people's love, just as she can't show her own love easily. She really *has* nothing to live for; only Dad *does* care if she lives or dies.

It's awful; there's no arguing these things. I listen and she talks. We stay like that until she runs down. I'm watching the TV as color patterns, movement, not seeing what I'm supposed to be seeing, trying to hear what I should have heard a long time ago.

It's after four o'clock when I tuck Mom in bed and dose

her with ten milligrams. I sit beside the bed holding her hand until she goes to sleep. Then I go to the middle room, climb into the crib.

The next weeks are hellish. The hospital says Dad is custodial after he's in there four days. I know they're right; I'm not fighting it anymore. I've played custodian to him and I can't do it again. Joan and I agree we'll put him in a good nursing home. Neither of us wants to, but there's no other solution. He can't stay in the hospital and he can't stay with Mother.

Mom is relatively passive. She makes some noises about the "poorhouse," how we're abandoning our own father—all the old story—but I don't think she even believes it herself.

I'm feeling deeply guilty. *I* know I *am* abandoning him. Maybe with another tremendous effort he could be brought back. But I'm not sure what we'd do with him if, or when, he would come back. He's become superfluous to everyone's life. There's no room in this world for him anymore.

We try Cottage Villa again, but they can't keep him fed and he's back in the hospital after five days. Even Alicia can't help.

When he comes out the second time, we have the good luck to find a room in the convalescent home just down the street from Mom's house. It's a small place with only thirty beds and more direct supervision than Cottage Villa. Mom feels better having him close. She can visit by walking there when she feels up to it.

Dr. Chad agrees to look in once a week and regulate Dad's metabolism. It's as good an arrangement as we're ever going to make. Joan is pressing me to go home, get out while the getting's good; go back to Paris, Vron, Jacky. I'm not fighting anymore. Joan also finds a nurse to visit Mom twice a week, and Joan will come over twice. It's the best we can arrange.

Dad shows no signs of recovering. He's a total blank, not recognizing any of us since the trauma at Joan's house. He's erratically continent with his bowels and bladder both; he needs to be hand-fed. He has the same animal look in his eyes. He's gone, probably for good. I'm only hoping he's happy there in Cape May, or wherever.

Billy's a big help over this part. He spends a lot of time with Mom and tries to do all he can; but visiting Dad is too much for him.

He's definitely coming back to France with me. I agree to pay his way. We'll take a drive-away cross-country and try for a charter cancellation or standby in New York. I don't really want to take up Joan's offer to pay the fare. They don't have any more money than we do.

I call AAA CON. The guy there says they have four cars going out the next day and we can have our pick. I've driven cars for them before so they have me on their records.

I drive Mom's car to Marty's and say goodbye. I ask Marty to phone Mom once or twice a week and not to visit Dad. It's just too depressing and she's so vulnerable.

That night, Billy sleeps in the garden bedroom and I sleep in the crib. I have a tough time getting Mom down. She keeps sniffling and shuffling around the house.

She still feels I'm wrong to leave her and she's scared to be alone. On the other hand, when she's rational, she knows I can't stay. I don't know if she wanders around anymore after two o'clock because I'm asleep.

23

When we turn up the Hills' walk, Rita's standing at the door. She has a telegram in her hand. I think of Jacky racing out to me in the cold of the Morvan. I'm as vulnerable this time as I was then. My temptation is to run; run up and take the telegram or turn and run away.

I stop. Billy, who's close behind, almost bumps into me. I continue slowly, walking.

"This arrived just after you left; it's from California."

I don't know why I open it there on the steps. Rita moves back inside the door; Billy stands beside me. It's easy to read: yellow, not blue; A.T.&T. printout, not handwriting.

JULY 7

DAD DIED TODAY STOP FUNERAL FRIDAY STOP WIRE
FLIGHT STOP   LOVE JOAN

I hand the telegram to Billy.

"Your grandfather died, Bill. We have to go back."

It's as much as I can get out.

I walk past Rita, through the Hills' house, out the back door and into their yard. I cry. I don't think I've ever cried so hard in my life. Men don't usually cry well and I'm as bad or worse than most. I'm crying without thinking. I stand in the back of their yard against the wall and cry till I vomit.

I'm crying for many reasons, mostly various forms of self-pity. I'm crying the way the boy in that Hemingway story "Bimini" cried. His big fish got away after he came so close. My Dad got away. I didn't have the guts, the courage, the persistence, the generosity to make those last few hard tugs and pull him in.

I'm crying, too, because I'm going to miss him personally, not be able to hear his voice, see his distinctive moves, smell him, touch him again. He's gone.

I'm crying because I'm scared. I'm scared of death. I'm afraid to be alone; in the logical sequence of time and events, I'm the next one to die.

These are some of the things I know I'm crying about; there are others; they're not all so selfish. I'm crying for Mom, Joan, for Jacky, who will never know him, will remember him only as a name, not as a person. I'm crying for Vron, who loved Dad deeply. But more than anything else, I'm crying because a big part of me, my identity, will be gone.

I hear a sound and Rita's behind me. I turn and we go into each other's arms. She's so tiny, smaller than Joan, smaller than Mom, but strong, so strong she holds me harder than I hold her. I'm going catatonic. I don't want to leave this haven, this vaguely sexual source of strength and comfort. It's a reverse union, her vital forces flowing into me, a dying tree gaining sustenance from mistletoe.

At last, I cry myself out. Rita leads me to the house, into the kitchen. We sit, embarrassed, exhausted. Pat's still at school. Billy's upstairs. But I can't talk to her. When I try, I cry. She asks if she should make reservations for Los Angeles. I nod. It makes our car trip seem so futile.

The plane leaves at seven. Rita says she'll drive us to the airport. She also wires Joan our flight number. Billy and I pack; we're not talking much. He knows I'm not up to it and he seems withdrawn. He's my nearest male relative now and I can't touch him.

Rita gets us to the TWA terminal with half an hour to spare. The parking's impossible, so she leaves us there. Billy and I hurriedly unload, wave and turn in to the airport; I'm feeling detached, unhooked, moving without thinking much.

We're in line at the ticket counter before I realize Billy is distinctly dragging, is very upset about something. I pull myself together enough to ask what's the trouble. He shakes his head, says it's nothing. But as the line moves forward, he gets more restless. Finally he blurts it out.

"What do you think, Dad? Debby's expecting me to meet her in Paris three days from now. Should I wait till we're in California and send a telegram to American Express or call her parents from here; they might have an address. I was supposed to meet her on the point of the Ile de la Cité, where the weeping willow tree is. I hate to think of her waiting and me not coming."

There are three people in front of us now.

"Do you really want to go to this funeral, Bill?"

He looks me in the eye, the first time since the telegram.

"Gosh, Dad! He's your father; of course I'm coming! Nobody'd ever understand if I didn't go to the funeral of my own grandfather."

"I'd understand, Bill; so would your mother. My dad's funeral is not your problem. I can cover for you in California."

We're down to two people.

"I'd hate letting you down like that, Dad."

"That's not the point. I wouldn't want to go if I were in your place; I'd want to meet my girl under that tree. We're next in line; make up your mind."

"You're sure about this?"

I nod. He smiles and puts out his hand. We shake. It's the first time we've ever shaken hands. His hands are so much like mine, it's like shaking hands with myself. I turn to the woman behind the desk and buy one ticket. There's no trouble canceling Bill's reservation. The plane is boarding in fifteen minutes; we go over to check in my baggage.

"Look, Bill, here's four hundred bucks. It would cost that much flying you to California and back. See if you can find a charter cancellation or standby; I'll bet you'll land something for under a hundred bucks if you look around, especially as a student; that way you'll have some money."

I give him the four one-hundred-dollar bills we got from the lady at the whorehouse. Bill sees me to the flight gate and we shake again. We're both hurrying things, trying to get apart before it hits too hard.

I walk through miles of red-carpeted narrow halls with low ceilings. I feel better inside. For once, I've let go in time.

Bill's childhood is finished. Maybe, as a privileged spectator, I can project forward into the life he'll lead. My time with Dad is over; our relationship is made, inside, wrapped up for good.

I go through the whole astronaut-like, artificial, controlled movements of getting into an airplane: stowing hand luggage, squeezing into a seat beside the window, hooking up the seat belt. They pass out earphones and I adjust myself into them. I want to destroy the next five or six hours, let them happen. I want to become an object, human freight, being carried at high cost over a large distance. I'm in the non-smoking section at a window in front of the wing. It's my favorite place and the plane is only half full. There's nobody sitting near me.

We take off. It's a good feeling just to separate from the earth. After the original acceleration, I feel detached, gravity-less, dying in slow motion. There's something special, releasing, about leaving the earth.

I look down. The Pennsylvania Turnpike is twisting through mountains. So recently, Billy and I fought each mile, crawling along, putting our lives in danger every minute, absorbed by the constant concentration, insecurity, responsibility. Now flying, gliding, thrusting, soaring over it is like death compared to life. I'm feeling removed, drifting effortlessly, without control.

I put my head against the plastic double window. My earphones are playing Mahler's First Symphony. I'm hearing it now, but he wrote that music before Dad was born.

When they give me drinks, I drink; when they put down the food tray, I eat; but I'm out there in the clouds, part of Gustav Mahler's convoluted elaborations on a French nursery song. When the film comes on, I succumb to the wishes of the flight attendant and close my shade, but leave a tiny crack I can still peek through. I watch the patterns of land as we fly across, long shadows pointing back, back to from where we've come, back to where, in the end, I hope to return.

The East Coast alluvial tidelands turn into the Appalachians; the Appalachians slide off into the Middle West, the flatness, the endless rows, the patterns of irrigation, the rectangular planted fields. Little of this was visible as we were furiously rushing through, surrounded on all sides by eye-level corn, wheat or grazing animals.

We come to the immense lifting of the Rocky Mountains: high, pink rock pushing up at us out of the earth. On the other side, we go through turbulence and thick clouds. It's raining below.

I try putting some of it together, try to make some plan. I'm not ready to cope with what's on the other side of the Los Angeles International Airport; LAX, in air terminology. It's always seemed somehow descriptive of the Los Angeles style.

Here I am now, fifty-two years old and in good health. I have an intelligent, sane, loving wife, three fine children. I work at something I like and I'm good at it. Why is it I'm not running around smiling and laughing all the time?

I'm lucky, my reality closely resembles my dream in the probabilities available to me. Dad built his dream privately, split his life. Perhaps the probability Mom chose isn't even possible. That could be her tragedy.

I'm still agonizing over Dad, the path of his life. I'm thankful for that brief, bright period, something none of us could have expected. I'm glad I was there; I hope I profited from it.

Maybe it's time for me to start learning how to be old. If I'm lucky, I have about twenty years to do it.

Somehow, I've got to get myself ready to accept being weak, in pain, mentally debilitated, forgetful, less sensitive, less aware, inflexible, intolerant—a whole lot of things I definitely don't want to be.

I need to prepare myself for the inevitable muffling walls slowly rising between myself and others; accept the decline in love by my children until, at best, there's only tolerance. I need to absorb, without resentment, the hurt when my grown grandchildren feel violated by my most cherished values, while their ideas, in turn, will violate me.

I must get ready for the deaths of lifelong friends, relatives, the frequency increasing with time. I must also live with those who survive who will be boring, uninteresting. I shall watch Vron, Joan, Mario—my generation—degenerate.

And it will all be happening to me. I'll become a bore to others, a drag in conversation, repeat myself, be slow at comprehension, quick at misunderstanding, have lapses in conceptual sequence. All this will probably be invisible to me. I won't even be aware of my own decline. Like a snake's belly, it will insinuate without any distinct, discernible steps.

Each morning, I'll wake older. My measuring systems will be caught in the quantum squeeze. I'll think the world has changed, is changing faster, that it's becoming less enjoyable, less stimulating, less reasonable, and altogether less acceptable. Easy things will get hard and hard things impossible.

On the other hand, I must learn to take advantage of being old. Dad was a good example. I probably won't have to work, do much of anything I don't want to do. I can drop out of the chase for dominance, women, work, power, status. Practically no one will be dependent on me. For the first time since childhood, I can know something of freedom, freedom to be myself. I'll probably sleep less, have more time for passive pleasures, daydreaming, thinking and, if my eyes and mind hold out, reading.

I'll have time to meander over my life, relive good moments, restructure and try to integrate bad ones. And I hope I can consider something of death, have some insights into its seeming abruptness, irrevocability, see it as the source, the reason for life as we know it.

Knowing me, though, I'll be doing my damnedest to put off all this. I don't let go, give up, easily. This could make my getting old, dying, difficult. My desperation, "finger in the dike" mentality will get in the way. I'm already involved with meditation and Yoga. When I get back to France, I'm going to start jogging and running. I definitely should watch my diet.

I know the alternative to getting old is dying young, and I'm not ready for that either. Still, somehow I've got to learn to grow old before I'm too old to learn.

The deserts are pink and violet, long shadows making blue holes in the blankness. I have an image of Egypt, the land of the pharaohs, the tombs of kings. Thoughts I've never had about death come easily, looking down at this quiet desolation and passive landscape.

Now the massive Sierra Nevada Mountains reach up and we start falling, are pulled down; the motors change pitch and we enter the long gliding descent. I see housing developments laid out in simple patterns with turnabouts. There are azure and turquoise glimmers of swimming pools set in necklaces of houses.

Off in the distance is the ocean. A numbing calm envelops me. Somehow, I feel ready for it all.

Well, maybe some of it anyway.

A NOTE ON THE TYPE

The text of this book was set on the Linotype in a face called
Primer, designed by Rudolph Ruzicka, earlier responsible for
the design of Fairfield and Fairfield Medium, Linotype faces
whose virtues have for some time now been accorded wide
recognition.

The complete range of sizes of Primer was first made available in 1954, although the pilot size of 12 point was ready as
early as 1951. The design of the face makes general reference
to Linotype Century (long a serviceable type, totally lacking in
manner or frills of any kind) but brilliantly corrects the char-
acterless quality of that face.

Book design by Judith Henry